SPELLCASTERS

Like a panther the woman leaped into the arena and, as she did so, Garth reeled from the impact of a psionic blast that flayed the strength out of his body. He staggered forward, knowing that the spell was so powerful that it would in fact harm her as well, though the damage he would receive was far worse.

An approving crying of awed respect rose up from the spectators at the audacity of her move.

Garth finally waved his hands, erecting a barrier of protection to block the attack, thus conceding the offensive to her. Within seconds she drew upon yet more *mana* and wolves appeared to either side of her and a small host of goblins materialized in the middle of the arena. All rushed toward him.

An icy shadow filled the middle of the arena and there was a great rushing of air and a loud trumpeting.

A great mammoth stood in the middle of the fray, its feet trampling down the goblins. The wolves paused in their headlong rush toward Garth, recoiling and cringing against the side walls of the arena as the mammoth thundered, its heavy trunk flaying about to snatch up the last of the goblins . . .

MAGIC™
The Gathering

ARENA

William R. Forstchen

HarperPrism
An Imprint of HarperPaperbacks

HarperPaperbacks *A Division of* HarperCollins*Publishers*
10 East 53rd Street, New York, N.Y. 10022

Cover illustration by Kevin Murphy

First printing: November 1994

Printed in the United States of America

HarperPaperbacks, HarperPrism, and colophon are trademarks of HarperCollins*Publishers*

❖ 10 9 8 7 6 5 4 3 2 1

For Kevin Malady and John Mina—
because I know they'll enjoy it.

CHAPTER
1

"STEP BACK, GIVE THEM ROOM!"

Garth One-eye, a thin smile of amusement creasing his face, followed the orders of the raggedy man who had appointed himself as circle master. Stretching lazily, Garth moved to the back of the gathering crowd. The owner of a fruit stand set up in the shade of the building was preoccupied, eagerly watching the excitement, and Garth helped himself to a Varnalca orange. Drifting away from the stand, he pulled out his dagger and sliced the treat open, tilting his head up to drain out the juice, which washed away the dust of the road. He adjusted the patch which covered where his left eye used to be and then moved around the back of the crowd, looking for other such opportunities. Seeing none, he moved in closer to watch the excitement.

In the middle of the street the two fighters, moving warily, paced back and forth, eyeing each other as they pulled off their robes in the chilly evening air. The crowd around them was swelling, pouring out of the alleyways, hovels, and swill houses, shouting and laughing. After all, it wasn't every day that one could watch a fight for free, even if there was a minor risk of getting hurt when the spells started to fly. Overhead, shutters were pulled open, people leaning out of the windows to watch the fun.

The raggedy man, chest puffed out, strutted about, his spindly, dirty legs kicking high as if he was a true Grand Master of the Arena. With a broken stick in place of a golden staff he drew a circle in the mud.

"Names and Houses?"

"Webin of Kestha," the stouter of the two fighters snarled, puffing his chest out and thumping it.

"Okmark of House Fentesk."

"Type of fight?"

"One spell cast which is also the wager," Okmark said.

Webin nodded angrily in agreement.

The crowd excitedly shouted the names back to those who were too far back in the press to see. Old men, women, and even young boys started to recite the wins and losses of the two fighters and arguments instantly broke out as to which one would win.

The Fentesk fighter, standing a good head taller than his rival, snorted disdainfully at his opponent as he calmly took his robe off and passed it to a street urchin who had sidled up to the edge of the circle. The boy looked at the finely embroidered robe and started to back away. The Fentesk fighter turned, fixing him with his gaze, and the boy stopped.

Okmark looked back at his opponent.

"This fight isn't really necessary," Okmark said quietly.

A hooting roar thundered from the mob but Okmark ignored them. He looked straight at the fighter in gray livery and slowly extended his arms, palms turned slightly downward, the gesture of reconciliation with the subtle distinction, however, of not submitting.

Webin spit angrily on the ground and the crowd cheered. Okmark shrugged his shoulders, resigned to what was coming.

The raggedy man continued to strut around the circle, waiting while the two fighters went through the ritual, their heads lowered, arms extended outward, gathering their strength.

"Four to one on Gray. I'll cover your bets if you think Gray will win," a voice shouted from the back of the crowd, and instantly there was a frenzied move toward him as the mob started to place their bets.

Garth stood silent, watching the two prepare. It was so obvious. Reaching into the satchel that hung under his right arm, he fingered the few coppers that were still there. It'd make enough for a meal and lodging.

He moved over to the gambler, taking the coins out, waiting quietly. Finally he extended his hand and the gambler looked disdainfully at the bet.

"On Orange," Garth said, referring to the bright livery of House Fentesk.

The gambler looked Garth up and down and started to laugh, and then fell silent as Garth stared at him coldly.

"I suggest you take it," Garth said. There were snickers from the bettors gathered around, as if Garth was a fool, but Garth kept his attention fixed.

"I'll only cover bets in Gray's favor. Don't bother me, One-eye."

Garth ignored the insult.

"Do you work for him? Is this fight a setup?" Garth replied smoothly, still holding the gambler with his gaze.

The man looked about furtively at the crowd, which had grown silent, even though they thought Garth a yokel from the outback for wasting his money on what would obviously be a certain win on Webin's part.

"One to two," the gambler replied sarcastically.

"One to four," Garth replied softly, and his hand drifted down to the hilt of his dagger.

The gambler looked around furtively and saw that there was no support from the mob.

"One to four," the gambler snarled, as he made his mark on a smooth chip of wood and shoved it into Garth's hand.

Garth turned back to watch the show, arms folded, pulling his robe in tight to keep the chill out.

The crowd quieted down as the last of the bets were placed, all now waiting for the ritual of preparation to end.

Gray finished first. Raising his head, he fully extended his arms and took a step out of the neutral square drawn just outside the circle. Even though Orange was not yet finished with his ritual, Gray raised his hands and the crowd fell silent. Garth shook his head disdainfully. It was a breaking of the rules, but then again this was a street fight, and any who believed in rules in such an encounter was simply too stupid to live.

A mist started to form in the center of the circle, coiling, swirling, and yet still Orange did not move, or even acknowledge that Gray had started his attack. The mist started to twist in upon itself, growing brighter, glowing, the light reflecting on the pale faces of the eager mob. The light suddenly darkened, a cool chill sweeping out.

"An undead," someone gasped.

In the middle of the circle a decaying form appeared and started to move toward the Orange fighter, who finally stirred, raising his head. Orange stepped into the circle and reached into the satchel dangling from his right hip. Instantly a small cloud appeared over the undead, a sheet of fire flashed out, blinding the crowd, who recoiled backward at the thunderclap roar. A swirl of smoke roiled outward and Garth pulled his cloak up tight around his face to block out the stench of decaying flesh that had just been burned to cinders.

An awed gasp swept the street. Okmark, his gaze still fixed on his opponent, finally allowed a thin flicker of a smile to show.

"I believe, sir, that since I have won, your spell is now mine to claim."

The Gray fighter looked around at the crowd and Garth could only shake his head with amusement. Only seconds before Gray had been their champion and hero, but their champion had just cost most of them their money. Garth looked over quickly at the gambler and the picture was now clear as the gambler started to drift back to the edge of an alleyway. It had been a wonderful setup, a classic con job on a bunch of yokels in town for the festival and eager for a bet.

Webin looked around anxiously at the mob.

"To the death, to the death!" a shout came from the back of the crowd and the cry was instantly picked up by the mob, which pushed to the edge of the circle, chanting and laughing for blood. Webin, who had strutted so haughtily only moments before, looked back and forth and then toward Okmark.

"Do you want it?" Okmark said softly and, as he spoke, he stepped back into the neutral square at the edge of the circle, indicating his willingness to fight again. Gray hesitated and then, with an angry curse, he reached into his satchel, pulled out an amulet, and threw it to the ground at Orange's feet.

Turning, he fled the circle, pummeled by the crowd, who showered him with curses, mud, offal, and kicks.

Okmark, with a disdainful gesture, reached down and picked up the amulet that had controlled the spell of the undead. He looked over at the boy holding his cloak and took it back. The boy stood waiting, expecting a reward, but Orange ignored him.

The crowd was silent and Garth looked around. The gambler had moved to one side of the Orange fighter and Garth saw the flicker of recognition between the two.

Garth moved to the edge of the circle.

"Pay the boy for his services," Garth said, his voice carrying through arguments breaking out around the circle as the mob hotly discussed the fight they had just witnessed.

Orange looked over at Garth and instantly there was silence.

"You pay him if you care so much about it," Orange replied.

"If you don't feel like paying him," Garth said, a smile creasing his features, "perhaps your friend over there might spare some of the money you won." As he spoke Garth pointed at the gambler.

All eyes turned on the gambler, who stood silent for a moment. The man finally reached into his purse, pulled out a silver coin, and threw it into the circle.

"Your winnings, One-eye," the gambler announced. "Take it and pay him with that."

Without hesitating, Garth stepped into the circle and a low gasp echoed through the crowd. The raggedy man started to dance excitedly.

"He stepped into the circle; a challenge, a challenge!"

The crowd started to pick up the chant and the gambler smiled.

Garth leaned down, picked the coin up, and, wiping the mud off, pocketed it.

"I still believe you owe the boy a reward," Garth said.

Okmark looked at him with a cool, superior disdain.

"Spoken in the circle, that's a challenge," Okmark replied. "I think, One-eye, that it'd be safer for you to leave now before you get hurt."

Garth slowly took his cloak off and, as he did so, he stepped backward into the square at the edge of the circle. He held his cloak out and saw that the boy he had been arguing about was there to take it.

"I expect to see it when this is done," Garth said quietly, and the boy, grinning, nodded.

"If he kills you, can I keep it?"

Garth smiled.

"It's yours."

Okmark shrugged his shoulders as if bored with the whole process. The gambler moved to the edge of the circle and stared at Garth for a moment. The raggedy man stepped up to Garth.

"Name and what House?"

"Garth and no House. I am my own."

The raggedy man started to laugh.

"One-eyed Garth of no House, no House," and he danced around the edge of the circle, singsonging the words.

"Type of fight?" the raggedy man asked, looking at Garth since he was the one who had made the challenge.

"Single spell and spell as prize, the same as the last fight."

The raggedy man looked over at the Orange fighter, who nodded in agreement.

The gambler, laughing, held his hand up.

"Two to one in favor of Orange, taking only bets in favor of One-eye."

The crowd did not react.

"All right, four to one then."

Still there were no takers.

"Ten to one! Ten to one in favor of Orange. I'll take only bets that this no House, a *hanin*, will win."

A shout rose up and the crowd surged around the gambler, placing yet more bets, gambling a copper on the forlorn hope that Garth would win. Garth waited for the frenzy to die down. Reaching into his pocket, he pulled out the silver coin.

"On myself," Garth announced, and he tossed the coin over to the gambler. The crowd started to laugh.

"A real fighter," the raggedy man chortled, dancing around Garth. "So poor he bets on himself. A real fighter!"

The crowd laughed and there was another frenzy of betting, for who ever heard of a fighter who was so poor that he would disgrace himself by betting on the outcome of a fight he was in.

Garth lowered his head, extending his arms, gathering in

his thoughts, calming them, focusing, remembering and not remembering, clearing away all. He reached outward, probing, looking toward the other's heart, sensing and knowing until all things dropped away and the land and waters within him were as clear as crystalline snow. The *mana*, the source of all power of spells, was ready.

He stepped into the circle and looked up.

Orange stepped forward as well. Garth did nothing, waiting.

He did not need to look up to know that a cloud was forming over the circle again, darkening the street, and though he heard the gasp of the crowd, he heard it not. He could feel the tension, the strength drawing out of the Orange fighter, focusing on the power he was drawing upon from distant lands and places—the *mana* which he controlled—bringing that power into the circle to serve his will. The fireball that Orange was creating started to build with a terrible intensity, bathing the street corner in a hellish light.

Garth looked up and extended his hand.

Instantly another cloud formed above the one created by Orange. A cold gust swept outward. The street was as dark as night. Flickers of light flashed and then there was a swirling of white. Snow, a blizzard of snow, coiled and twisted, devouring the cloud created by Orange. There was a howling of wind and then, in an instant, all disappeared and the evening sunlight again filled the narrow street, reflecting off the sheets of ice that now caked the sides of the buildings. Instantly they started to melt, the cold ice breaking off, showering down on the mob, who covered their heads with their arms.

As the tinkling of broken ice drifted away the street was silent. A scattering of applause and cheers broke out, especially from those who had wagered a mere copper and now would have a silver in their pockets. They had found a new hero and cheered lustily, while those who had thought even that bet to be a waste silently cursed themselves for not having the foresight to play. Those who had lost everything in the first duel were ecstatic as well, since the source of their losing had been defeated.

Garth fixed the stunned Orange fighter with his gaze.

"I believe your spell of fireball is now mine," Garth said quietly.

Okmark looked at him, gape mouthed.

Garth stood silent, waiting.

Okmark looked over at the gambler, whose expression was one of seething fury as the mob started to close in on him to claim their winnings. Okmark looked back at Garth.

Reaching to the dagger hanging from his belt, Okmark pulled it out and flung it so that it plunged into the ground in the center of the circle.

"To the death," Okmark hissed.

Garth looked at him and said nothing.

"To the death, damn you!"

The raggedy man looked around nervously, his enthusiasm gone.

"It's against the law, except in the arena," the raggedy man hissed. "We could all be arrested if the Grand Master finds out."

"Gutter sweep, who are you to quote law to me? I demand death!"

"The fight is not over yet!" the gambler shouted. "If he withdraws, Orange still wins!"

"That's not true!" the raggedy man whined in reply. "The fight was finished. Those are the rules of the circle."

The Orange fighter turned and looked at the raggedy man. He fell to the ground, eyes rolling in his head, hands clutching at his throat, a sickening gurgling sound gasping out of him.

The crowd fell silent, watching the agonized struggle as the raggedy man rolled in the mud.

Garth took his dagger out and tossed it so that it stuck in the ground next to Okmark's.

"To the death then."

Orange looked back at him. The raggedy man gasped out a rattling cough and he crawled out of the circle.

Orange nodded grimly and, ignoring all ritual, he leaped into the circle. Staggered by a blast of fire, Garth stepped back, holding up his arms to protect his face. A small circle appeared in the mud around him and the fire was diverted. Around him he could hear the cries of the mob as they fell back, some of them writhing in agony, their clothes afire. The side of the building behind Garth burst into flames.

Garth raised one of his hands up and a skeletal form appeared in the fire, stepping forward through the flames, toward Okmark. Okmark's eyes grew wide with fear as the skeleton continued to advance, impervious to the flames, and Okmark stepped back, the fire abating. There was a crackling roar and the ground beneath the skeleton opened up and, with a clattering of bones, the skeleton fell into the fissure which now split the circle in half. Garth nodded and the skeleton rose into the air, hovering, and continued its relentless advance.

Cursing, Okmark now raised his hand, pointing at the skeleton. An explosion rocked the streets and a spray of powdery dust swirled outward. Garth seemed to blanch from the savage counterstrike. Okmark, grinning now, raised his hand and pointed at Garth. A coiling shaft of light came straight at him. An instant later a shimmering mirror appeared before Garth. The blast of light reflected back.

Orange barely had time to scream.

The flame engulfed him. Writhing in agony, Okmark spun around and around, trying to extinguish the fire that would not die. Garth stood impassive, watching, his arms folded. The shrieking died away as Okmark curled up into a blackened ball of smoking flesh and died. The fire winked out of existence, the one who had conjured it having expired by his own spell.

A gasp of astonishment rose up from the crowd, which stood silent, ignoring the fact that the building behind them was crackling, fire racing up its side, while on the street behind where Garth had stood, half a dozen were dead and more than a score injured and crying out their lamentations.

Garth leaped across the fissure, stepped up to the twisted body, and reached down to take the satchel which hung from his belt and, strangely, did not seem to have been touched by the fire.

"You have no claim to that," the gambler snapped, stepping into the ring. "You are *hanin*, without House, and have murdered one of the House of Fentesk; his property now belongs to the House."

"Then try and stop me," Garth said quietly, fixing the gambler with his gaze. The man stood silent, hesitating, and then drew back.

"I'll tell them, One-eye. They'll be looking for you," the gambler cried.

"Before running off, perhaps you owe these people some money and you owe me some as well."

The crowd, which had been watching the confrontation in silence, suddenly sprang to life and swarmed around the gambler. As they rushed across the circle some of them fell into the fissure, their wails of anguish cut short as they hit the bottom. Garth reached down and pulled the satchel free. Turning, he looked around and saw the boy still holding his cloak.

Garth leaped back across the fissure, took the cloak, and then reached into his own satchel to find a coin. There was nothing.

From out of the press around the gambler the raggedy man appeared and he slipped up to Garth's side.

"I got your money for you," he said and extended a grimy hand, opening it to reveal nine silvers.

"Minus your commission as circle master, of course," Garth said, taking the coins and then tossing one of them to the boy, who bowed excitedly and ran off.

"But of course. You were stuck with the bill. Gray disappeared and as for the Orange"—the raggedy man looked over at the corpse—"unless his commission is in your prize."

Garth reached into Okmark's satchel and felt around, surprised by the touch of some of the amulets contained within. The man was indeed powerful, more powerful than Garth had assumed. Okmark, however, had been a fool, not to anticipate that an opponent might hold a reversal of spells for something as dangerous as the fire that does not die. The man most likely thought he was dealing with nothing more than a first- or second-rank fighter out to make a reputation and thus did not want to reveal the spells he would use later in the Festival.

Garth touched a coin and pulled it out. It was gold, and the raggedy man's eyes glistened with greed.

Garth flipped the coin to the raggedy man.

"Your commission from Orange. Now see that he is disposed of with respect."

"Not my responsibility now," the raggedy man chortled, and he grabbed hold of Garth's arm. "His friends are coming even now; perhaps it's time we moved on to safer parts."

Garth looked up the street to where the raggedy man was pointing. A phalanx of men was coming down the street, obviously not in a friendly mood. They were all dressed as fighters, with heavily embroidered shirts, loose-fitting trousers of silk that billowed out over the tops of their polished, calf-high boots, their leather capes trimmed with orange fluttering as they advanced with a purposeful stride, their golden satchels, which contained their spells, bouncing on their hips. Behind them came the warriors of the Watch, the men of the city guard who could not use spells but were nevertheless quite efficient at killing.

Garth stepped back into an alleyway, careful not to stride on the injured from the fight, and followed the raggedy man. In the background he could hear what sounded like a riot brewing and then the clattering of a bell as the fire watch finally started to arrive.

The raggedy man looked back over his shoulder just before they ducked down a side alleyway.

"Ah, how I love the Festival," he announced, while down at the end of the street the front of the burning building collapsed into the watching crowd. A shower of sparks soared into the evening sky, and as the crowd swayed back from the collapsing building, yet more fell into the fissure and disappeared.

They weaved their way down a slime-choked lane, Garth fighting back a retch from the stench of moldering garbage, human refuse, now-unidentifiable dead animals, and, in one case, what looked like part of a person sticking out of a refuse heap. The raggedy man stopped at the sight of the corpse and pondered it for a moment.

"I was wondering what happened to her," he whispered, and then, with a shrug of his shoulder, he continued to lead the way, finally ducking into the back of a broken-down building of sagging logs, gray with age, and apparently soon ready to go to dust.

As the raggedy man opened the door, Garth looked in cautiously and the old man smiled a toothless grin.

"Don't trust me, after I fetched you your money and led you out of that mess?"

"I don't trust anyone," Garth said quietly, narrowing his eye to look into the gloom.

"Ah, brothers, we have company," the raggedy man announced, and he stepped through the door. In the darkness Garth saw movement and his nose wrinkled at the smell of unwashed bodies. He heard hoarse laughter inside. An old man and then another started to laugh.

"I suggest, One-eyed Garth with no House, that you either come in or move along," the raggedy man announced. "The Orange are undoubtedly looking for you and are in a less than friendly mood. Besides, the Grand Master's watch is on the prowl as well."

As he stepped up to the door his eye started to adjust to the gloom. A small fire burned in an open fireplace to one side, a hunched-over form stirring a pot hanging in the flame. Garth cocked his head slightly, listening intently. With no vision to his left side he had learned to rely on other things. He finally stepped through the doorway and then, just as quickly, leaped back and to one side.

The blow missed him, the wooden staff striking down through empty air. With a catlike move, Garth snatched the man by the wrist and yanked him out from behind the open door, while with the other hand he pulled out his dagger and brought it up under the man's chin, barely nicking his throat.

"You breathe too loudly," Garth whispered, "and besides, you stink bad enough to gag a maggot."

The raggedy man watched the exchange with open amusement, nodding his head with approval.

"You'll do, you'll do just fine," the old man laughed. "Now please let my brother go."

Garth looked into his assailant's eyes, seeing the fear, smelling his fetid breath. He flicked his dagger, making a small cut under the man's chin, then released him, the old man howling with pain, while the others in the room roared with delight.

"You'll do just fine," the raggedy man said, motioning for Garth to come over and sit by the fire.

"No more tricks now, I swear it by the honor of my brotherhood."

The other old men in the room laughed and Garth looked around at them. Most of them looked like scarecrows, several were missing fingers, a few their right hands; one of them sitting by the fire was missing both.

"Pickpockets and cutpurses?" Garth asked. "I'm to take the word of the brotherhood of pickpockets?"

The raggedy man laughed.

"Believe me, No House, it's as good as the word of any of the fighting Houses."

There was a murmured chorus of agreement, as if Garth had just offered the most grievous of insults for doubting his host.

The old man motioned Garth to sit down and a moment later a fine goblet was placed before him, the raggedy man lifting a heavy jug from under the table and filling his guest's goblet with wine and then filling his own. Garth took the drink and tasted it.

"Borleian," Garth said, obviously surprised.

"Ah, you know your grapes."

"How did you get such a good vintage?"

"How does a No House, a *hanin*, know such a vintage?"

"I've been around a bit."

The raggedy man put his own goblet down and looked appraisingly at Garth.

"How old are you?"

Garth smiled and said nothing.

"Hard to tell with one who can control the *mana*; you could be twenty-five as you look, or you could be near to a hundred. I'm willing to bet twenty-five."

"Am I supposed to answer you?"

The raggedy man shook his head.

"As a *hanin* you know it's suicide to be in this city during Festival. You have no colors and the Grand Master forbids any *mana* user without colors to be in his city on pain of death."

"The Grand Master," Garth said softly and the raggedy man could sense a sudden hardness. "First the bastard will have to find me."

"He has his ways," the raggedy man replied, and he looked around at his friends, who nodded their agreement, the one without hands holding his arms up and cackling, his voice twisted with insanity.

As Garth sipped his wine, the raggedy man regaled his comrades with a description of the fight and Garth's victory. At the end of his tale he reached into his tunic and pulled out half a dozen purses and tossed them on the table.

"You seem to have made a profit from the spectators as well while you played the circle master," Garth observed quietly.

"Merely a business proposition."

"Festival must be a good time for business propositions."

The room was filled with laughter.

"We're too well known to most folk of this city," the raggedy man said. "Now for all those fools coming into the city, we're more than happy to relieve them of some excess baggage. Call it a poor tax if you will. There's enough to be made in the next seven days to feed us through the winter."

The raggedy man refilled his cup and then Garth's.

"So are you here for Festival?"

Garth said nothing, his attention focused on the cup, as if studying the intricate gold inlay.

The raggedy man leaned down low and looked up into Garth's face.

"How'd you lose the eye?"

"A childhood prank that got serious," Garth said quietly.

The raggedy man nodded slowly, peering up into his face.

"Looks like it got cut out, from the scar on your cheek."

"Something like that."

The raggedy man sat down, silently looking at Garth.

Garth leaned back, drained the rest of his cup, and set it back down. The raggedy man quickly refilled it.

"You know, we could put a patch on the other eye, a loose weave you could see through, and take the patch off the bad one. You'd make a hell of a pickpocket."

The raggedy man chuckled at his joke and watched Garth closely.

Garth snorted disdainfully and took another sip of his drink.

"But you're a fighter, not a pickpocket. The way you killed Okmark of Fentesk, a masterful reversal, a rare spell, only a true adept controls such power. He had fourteen wins in the arena and was at least a third-rank. How did a No House like you obtain such a spell?" And as he spoke the raggedy man looked down at Garth's spell satchel with open curiosity as if he was struggling with the temptation to tear it away and look inside.

Garth looked up from his drink and fixed the raggedy man with his gaze.

The raggedy man extended his hands in mock horror and recoiled backward.

"Never ask a fighter where his victories and powers are won," the raggedy man said. "I know, I know the customs."

One of the old men came over to the table and dropped a silver plate down in front of Garth while another brought over a roasted duck from the fire. Garth cut away a leg and munched on it meditatively.

"You're hungry, that's obvious," the raggedy man chortled, watching as Garth sliced meat away from the bird and hurriedly popped the hot slices into his mouth, washing them down with another goblet of wine.

"Are you master of this brotherhood?" Garth asked between bites.

The raggedy man laughed and extended his arms wide as if beckoning Garth to view his domain.

"My brothers here and others hiding in other hovels. The loyal order of pickpockets, with a lineage as august as any of the fighting Houses and just as ancient. And, might I add, with far more honesty."

"How's that?"

"The fighting Houses, Fentesk, Kestha, Bolk, and Ingkara, they claim to be the upholders of honor. They are nothing but harlots." The others in the room grunted their agreement. "Since the night Zarel became Grand Master of all the colors they think of but one thing, the profits to be won by their powers, the *mana* to be drawn from the lands to support their spells, and the common people pay the price. At least we are honest about it all; we steal and we admit we steal; thus we are honorable men in comparison. At least we do not hide behind the mouthing of platitudes that have lost all meaning."

The others in the room fell into a solid round of cursing, the insane man without hands cackling out an obscene song about the Grand Master while hugging a goblet that had been fashioned so that he could pick it up with the stumps of his arms.

Garth ate the rest of his meal in silence, listening to the old men pour out their hatred and anger. Finishing the duck, he meditatively picked his teeth with a bit of bone, slid his stool back, and stood up.

"Thank you for the meal, old man. I think it's time I moved along."

"You have a place here for the night."

"Why?"

"I find you amusing and a bit of a mystery."

"How so?"

"Amusing that you so easily set up Okmark for the kill and fleeced his gambling manager. At first I thought you were the yokel from the countryside, some boy puffed up with a couple of spells in his satchel thinking to prove something and usually losing his life before Festival has ended."

"It's been a long time since I was called a boy," Garth said coldly.

"Son, to me you're still a boy. Killing Okmark might have given you his powers, but you now have nearly a hundred sworn enemies of his House looking for you. Beyond that, the Grand Master must have word by now that a one-eyed *hanin* did the killing. Every warrior and fighter in his command will be looking for you."

"I'll get by."

"Ah, and that's the mystery. Just what is it that you want here? If you want my advice, I think that you should point yourself south before dawn and put some distance between you, this damned city, and the Festival."

The raggedy man smiled and held up his hand before Garth could reply.

"I know. You don't want my advice and you plan to stay and you'll be damned if you'll tell me why you're here."

"Something like that."

"Then stay the night. It's free and I've given you the promise of the brotherhood. You won't be bothered."

"The Watch!"

Garth turned and saw a legless beggar come in through the door, hopping on the stumps of his legs. The excuse for a guard that Garth had cut under the chin bounded to the door and slipped a beam across it and the room fell silent. In the alleyway all could hear heavy footsteps approaching. After a moment's pause they moved on.

"We pay the bastards enough to leave us alone," the raggedy man chuckled, "but you never know who might have paid them more."

He looked back at Garth.

"I daresay that you are the object of their concern. You're a criminal, No House. Orange might even have kicked in some money to have your throat cut without any fanfare and the spells they lost returned. If you're some village idiot who came here thinking about honor and rules, forget about it."

Garth shook his head disdainfully.

"Typical."

He looked back around the room.

"Which corner has the fewest fleas and lice?"

Varnel Buckara, Master of the House of Fentesk, set down his inlaid cup of gold and looked over coldly at his host.

"I really don't like the implication of what you've just said."

"It was your man who started the incident by dueling illegally, first with Webin of Kestha. Distasteful, my good man, distasteful for two fighters to brawl in the gutter for the amusement of the mob."

"My fighters have high spirits; otherwise, they wouldn't be fighters. You know that doesn't bother you in and of itself. It's the fact that they did it as a public display and your agents could not control the betting that bothers you."

Grand Master Zarel Ewine laughed, his bulging stomach shaking like jelly. He set his own goblet back down, motioning for the servant to refill it and that of his guest and then to leave.

"As if I need to be concerned about a bit of silver," Zarel finally replied, leaning forward and fixing Varnel with his gaze. "I got past such concerns a long time ago."

Varnel said nothing, looking around at the room, the imported tapestries from Kish, the fine wood carvings of the legendary La, the gems that were ringed to Zarel's beefy hands.

"I serve the Walker in administering the Western Lands, and with it the games," Zarel continued. "That is honor enough."

Varnel wanted to burst out laughing with the hypocrisy of that line. But fear stayed him, not of Zarel but of what might be standing behind him now, invisible in the shadows, lurking, waiting.

He looked around anxiously and then realized that Zarel had undoubtedly sensed the moment of fear.

"No, he is not here. Not until the last day of Festival will he come for the winner and for the yearly report."

"And will this incident be part of the report?" Varnel asked, finally getting to the heart of the matter.

"Ah, old friend, you've been generous in the past. There is no need tonight for the distasteful ritual of a bribe to have this forgotten. Consider it a gift. If I tried to stop every fight outside the arena, I would have gone mad long ago. During the rest of the year, what you and the other House Masters do in your own territories is your concern, not mine. During the rest of the year you can kill each other in your own lands as you please, and hire out to whomever you wish. But now you and the other three Houses are gathered in my city for the testing of skills and that is indeed my concern. I can expect an occasional wager fight, but to the death in front of the mobs is for the arena only. Otherwise, there'd be chaos, and that I will not tolerate. I fully expect you and the other Houses to go around brawling, but please do it inside your own compounds. It's tradition. But public displays are out—that is for the Arena—and if the peasants and finer folk want to watch, they can pay. That's tradition too."

And besides, the mob pays to see the fights in the arena but they won't pay if they can see all they want on the streets for free, Varnel wanted to reply.

"Do we understand each other?" Zarel finally asked.

"We understand each other," Varnel replied softly.

"Now, on to the other concern. This fighter of no House, this *hanin*, do you have a description?"

"None of my people were there."

"Come now, what about your fighter's gaming master?"

Varnel shifted uncomfortably.

Zarel laughed and took another drink.

"Either your man was an idiot fighting for no reason other than to gain a spell or he had a gaming master there to fleece the crowd. I'd hate to think that all your fighters are idiots."

"The gaming master was thrown into the fissure by the mob when he ran out of money to pay them back when my man lost."

"A logical response. And speaking of that, I now have a crack in the middle of one my main streets that's a good twenty fathoms deep. Do you know how much that will cost to fix? Also, half a block of slums burned to the ground and nearly fifty people dead."

"Well, they are only peasants."

"My peasants; that's fifty fewer peasants to pay taxes. That's fifty fewer peasants who, through their mere existence, contribute to the pool of *mana*. My, my, Varnel, the bill just keeps adding up. I'm not talking bribes here; I'm talking damages. I don't know how many cartloads of dirt it's going to take to fill that hole your man created. The funeral costs, rebuilding the block of slums, it'll be quite a bill."

"As if you're going to pay it yourself," Varnel shot back.

"Damn it, no. You're going to pay it," Zarel roared, "and that's not a bribe. That's coming out of the bond you and the other Houses set against damages to my city during festival."

"What about the House of Kestha? He's the one who started the fight," Varnel snapped.

"Oh, Tulan and his House will pay too," Zarel said smoothly.

I bet they will, Varnel thought angrily as he snatched the decanter of wine and poured himself another drink, figuring that at least Zarel was footing the bill for the refreshments and he might as well get the most out of it.

"You should take it out of the hide of this no House warrior."

"Oh, I will. He'll help pay for the damages before I have him quartered for fighting in my city without sanction of House. The problem is no one knows who he is or where he went."

Varnel smiled at that one.

"Surely your loyal subjects should be eager to help the law."

"Scum. They think the whole thing was vastly amusing. He's quite their hero, now, for winning them money. Lousy scum. They're out there laughing in the streets and your House helped to start this. Oh, I got the usual descriptions. He was black, he was white, he was yellow. He was tall, short, fat, skinny, pox-marked, fair-skinned, two eyes, one eye. The only thing they agreed upon was that he had no House."

Varnel sat back and looked away.

"What is it?"

Startled, Varnel looked back.

"Nothing. No, it's nothing."

Zarel stared closely at his guest.

"Something I said bothered you."

"No, just wondering, that's all."

"About what?"

"Who is this man? He killed a third-rank fighter. That's a bit unusual for a *hanin*. Usually they manage to gain a House or are dead by the time they reach such a level of skill. That means he's good, as good as a master of the third-rank. And yet he has no color, no House. It's strange."

Zarel looked away for a moment.

Varnel was right, it was unusual. Not only that but the fact that the man had vanished without a trace. There was something else as well. A sensing more than a knowing, an innate feeling that something was not quite right, that this was not just another incident, a stupid brawl, that would be forgotten by tomorrow. He couldn't quite touch what it was, but the uneasiness was a warning that had to be heeded.

"We'll find him," Zarel finally said coldly.

Varnel looked up over the edge of his goblet and smiled in reply.

CHAPTER
2

"SO WHAT ARE YOUR PLANS FOR TODAY?"

Garth, scratching the fleabites he had picked up during the night, looked around at the room full of old men, who were stirring as the first light of dawn peeked in through the cracks in the shutters and roof.

"Leave here for starters."

The raggedy man chortled.

"Here to do whatever it is you came for. Ah, your great mysterious quest."

"Something like that," Garth said dryly.

"I'm coming."

Garth looked down at the toothless old man.

"I had a feeling you would," Garth said softly and the raggedy man looked at him in surprise.

"Why?"

"'Cause you can't stand a mystery. You want to find out what will happen next."

The raggedy man rocked back and forth on his stool next to the fire, laughing with delight.

"I want to watch the fun. I think someone's going to get killed out of this and I want to be there. Always a business opportunity in such ventures."

The old man leaned over the fire and cut off two thick

slices of meat from a roast that had been slowly cooking over the glowing embers. He tossed one over to Garth, who snatched it and gingerly tossed it back and forth in his hands until the meat cooled enough to eat. The old man, finishing his breakfast, unbolted the door and peeked out cautiously.

The legless beggar was sitting across the street and waved his hand as if swatting away a fly.

"It's clear," the raggedy man announced. "Let's go."

Taking a staff from beside the door, he stepped out into the street and then, turning, relieved himself against the building. Garth looked at him disdainfully and then realized that he had to follow suit and stepped up beside the old man.

"You know, this is as good a moment as any for introductions. I'm Hammen of Jor."

The old man, finishing, buttoned his greasy trousers and then extended his hand.

Garth, finishing as well, buttoned up and looked down at Hammen, who grinned at him, his yellowing teeth looking like jagged, rotting posts in a dark cavern.

Garth tentatively took Hammen's hand and then did not bother to hide his actions as he wiped his palm on the side of his pants.

Hammen laughed.

"A cleaner handshake than what you'll get from any House Master."

Garth could not help but smile.

"Where can I find the Gray House?"

"Why do you want to go there?"

"Just curious to see, that's all."

Hammen, raising his staff with a flourish, pointed down the refuse-choked alleyway and they were off.

Garth followed behind his self-appointed guide, cautiously looking up side streets as they passed. It was well past dawn and yet the city was still barely stirring, the revelry in celebration of the approaching festival having obviously consumed the energy of the citizens. Hammen stopped for a moment to poke at several prostrate forms lying next to an overturned rain barrel. One of them stirred slightly, the other two remained still.

Garth looked down at them. He could see all three were

alive but would soon regret that state of affairs when they woke up.

"They've already been picked over," Hammen announced, and continued on out into a main boulevard that was nearly a dozen fathoms across.

Garth turned and looked back up the street, where wisps of smoke were still rising from yesterday's fun. Around him shopkeepers were just beginning to unshutter their stalls, placing their wares out on tables in front of their doors. A few early risers were already out purchasing food and Garth strode along slowly, unable to hide his amazement at the multitude of goods for sale.

Hammen looked back at him.

"I don't think you've had much experience with cities."

Garth nodded.

"I could see that; no one but a fool would have followed me down a back alley the way you did. Such trust is only found in yokels from the countryside. No citizen of this city would be so stupid."

"Either a fool or someone who could take care of himself," Garth replied coolly.

Hammen looked up at Garth and nodded in agreement.

"I think you can take care of yourself. But survive here? That will be interesting to see."

Hammen slowed and pointed to a fruit stand.

"Ah, my favorite, pomegranates from Esturin." Hammen strode up to the fruit monger, who was setting out bundles of pomegranates, oranges, exotic fillagrits from across the flowing sea, exquisite and delicate lollins, and other glistening delectables of red, green, orange, and deepest blue which Garth had never seen before.

The merchant looked up at Hammen, shook her head with an exasperated smile, and tossed him a pomegranate. Hammen motioned for her to favor Garth as well.

Garth took the fruit and bit into it, smiling as the juice trickled down his throat.

"It's good."

"Never had one before, have you?"

Garth said nothing as he finished off the treat, half-listening as Hammen and the merchant, who were obviously old acquaintances, talked about the news of the city.

"The guards of the Grand Master swarmed through here last night like flies on the scent of offal," the merchant announced, while all the time staring straight at Garth. "Looking for the fighter."

"So did they find him?"

"Oh, they arrested the usual suspects."

Hammen laughed and turned away. The merchant, smiling, tossed Garth three more pomegranates and winked. Garth tucked them inside his open tunic.

"You won a lot of money for these people yesterday, plus you bearded an Orange," Hammen announced. "You can eat free for awhile."

Hammen nodded to the dirty brown pennants that fluttered over many of the stalls lining the street.

"You can see, most folks in this quarter are Brown supporters."

"Why? The fighting Houses mean nothing to them and I'm certain the Houses don't give a good damn what commoners think anyhow."

"How do you know that?"

"I think it's fair to assume such," Garth replied.

"You don't seem to understand much about the human soul, One-eye," Hammen replied. "For most of these folk the Festival is the one thing to look forward to in their lives, that and the hope of a winning lottery ticket. The games are everything.

"You can go to most any stall or swill dive"—and he pointed vaguely over to a tavern which was already full—"and the meanest beggar can recite for you the wins, the spells possessed by his favorite fighter, especially if that man or woman won him a few coppers in the wagers. Win money for the mob and you're a hero."

"Some hero," Garth sniffed. "A fighter now would burn a peasant alive just to test a new spell and feel less remorse than if he squashed a roach."

"What do you mean *now?*" Hammen asked quietly.

"Oh, I hear the story of the old days, when things were different, when fighters were required to go on pilgrimage, to serve others who needed them."

Hammen spit on the ground.

"The old days are dead, *hanin.* If you came here thinking different, I think I'll simply leave you right now. I've taken a

bit of a liking to you and would hate to see you dead before
the day is out. Only a fool would believe that fighters care
about the rest of us."

"So why should the people care?"

"That's what I mean," Hammen replied. "You don't understand the human soul. They know the truth, but they'll still
cheer their hero on and by doing so feel that somehow they're
part of his glory and power. Once Festival starts they're trans-
ported to heaven for three days. They can forget the squalor,
the sickness, the short brutal lives that consume them.
They're out there in the arena, listening to the chanting roar,
dueling for power, for prestige, for their lives and for the
approval of the Walker, who takes the final winner with him
so that he can serve in other worlds. For three days out of the
entire year the mob can live the dream."

Garth looked over quizzically at Hammen, whose voice had
grown soft, his tone serious, and surprisingly the touch of an
accent of high breeding creeping into his words.

"You speak like you've been out there," Garth said, fixing
Hammen with his gaze.

Hammen looked back at him and, for a brief instant, Garth
felt as if someone other than a raggedy pickpocket and gutter
dweller walked beside him. He sensed a distant power as if the
man could control the *mana*, the foundations of power for all
fighters, which was derived from the lands and all creatures
who lived upon them. Hammen slowed in his walk and Garth
sensed an infinite sadness and then like a frost melting away
in the light of dawn Hammen became the raggedy man again,
cackling, hawking, and spitting on the ground, pointing out
the sights of the city to an outsider.

They continued up the street, which was now starting to
fill. Garth pulled out the two pomegranates tucked into his
tunic and tossed one over to Hammen. Garth bit into the fruit
and ate it slowly as they strolled along. They passed by the
street of steel and Garth stopped for a moment to watch as the
merchants hung out their cheap blades in front of the store.
Stopping in front of one, he looked into the gloomy interior
and saw the finest weapons hanging inside, the merchant's
guards sitting in the shadows. Scimitars, broadswords, and
light rapiers caught and reflected the pulsing glow of the

forges working deeper within the shop, the smiths hammering out their creations in showers of sparks.

"Good blades in the back, blades with long histories and names for connoisseurs of refined weapons capable even of piercing through fields of spells to draw a fighter's blood," Hammen whispered as if filled with a distant longing.

Next came the street of brass workers, and then the silver-smiths and workers of gold, each stall guarded by armed men and even an occasional spell caster of the first-rank, who could conjure a single creature of the beyond to kill thieves. Garth looked at the first-rank men and shook his head. Most of them were old men, who had never gone beyond the first-rank since they lacked the skills and the innately given power to harness the *mana*, to manage and control anything beyond the simplest of powers. In a real duel with another fighter they would lose their single spell in seconds and most likely their lives, thus they were doomed to the back alleys, the guarding of miser hordes and fat merchants. Most of them, he sensed, were scared within their hearts that someday they might actually be challenged by something beyond a peasant with a dirk, and even that peasant was a source of fear.

After passing the streets of metal they came closer to the heart of the city and Hammen looked around warily, watching closely as a squad of the Grand Master's fighters marched by on patrol, their multihued jackets, capes, and trousers shim-mering in the morning light. Not one of them looked toward Garth and his companion chuckled.

"Overdressed popinjays. Out looking for you, most likely, and too stupid to sense such things."

Garth noticed that the color of the pennants lining the street had started to change. For several blocks there was a mix of browns, grays, and even an occasional orange or purple.

"We're getting near the center of the city, where the five quarters of the city converge. Directly ahead in the center of the Plaza is the palace of the Grand Master and the barracks of his fighters and warriors. The Houses of the four colors flank the main Plaza."

Garth looked up the street into the main Plaza, which was nearly three hundred fathoms across, and finally saw the tow-ering five-sided pyramid, which was the Grand Master's

home. The building stood at least thirty fathoms to a side and
soared nearly as high and was sheathed in polished limestone
that glowed like fire from the reflected sun. The main palace,
in turn, was flanked on all five sides by the dark, squat barracks of his warrior guards and fighters. The entire complex,
in turn, was surrounded by fountains, which danced and
splashed in the morning light, the columns of water soaring
nearly as high as the great palace, the water in the fountains
dyed every color of the rainbow.

As Garth reached the edge of the Great Plaza he slowed.
On four sides of the Plaza four more palaces were now plainly
in view. Each was different; each flew a color of the four great
Houses. Fentesk, on the far side of the Plaza, was a heavy,
squat structure with massive pillars lining its front, with four
great banners of solid orange fluttering at the four corners of
what Garth decided was positively an ugly building.

Next to it was the House of Ingkara, this one similar to the
Orange House except the tedium of pillars was at least relieved
by a great arched entryway from which a purple banner hung.
To the other side of Fentesk was the House of Bolk, this one
looking like a fortress, with crenellated towers and battlements, and finally, next to the Brown House, was that of
Kestha, its front decorated with massive squat statues repre-
senting fighters, with their hands raised upward as if about to
cast spells across the pavilion against the other buildings.

"Whoever designed the palaces should have been drowned
at birth for the benefit of all mankind," Hammen sniffed.

"They're Houses of fighters, not palaces for potentates,"
Garth replied. "The old Houses were different but things have
changed of late and these new ones went up."

"Still, there is such a thing as taste."

Garth started walking toward the House of Kestha, Hammen
hurrying to keep pace with him.

"You know, this is really rather foolish of you," Hammen
sniffed. "You're a wanted man around this city."

"So much the better."

As they walked toward the House of Kestha Garth slowed,
turned, and looked toward the fifth side of the Plaza. The
Plaza was lined with squat shops, eateries, and several small
palaces of what were most likely well-heeled merchants.

Garth turned and walked toward the buildings and then came to a stop at the edge of the Plaza and looked around.

"This is where the fifth House used to be," Hammen said quietly.

Garth turned and looked back at Hammen.

"The fifth House?"

"Turquoise. Twenty years ago there were five Houses."

"I know that."

"Then you know that the other Houses, led by the old Grand Master and his assistant, Zarel, massacred the House of Oor-tael on the evening of the last day of Festival. They fell upon them in the night, burned the House, and murdered nearly all the fighters."

"Nearly all you say."

"Some supposedly escaped," Hammen replied.

The raggedy man paused and looked up at Garth.

"You were most likely too young then even to care," Hammen snapped, an edge of anger to his voice.

Garth said nothing, looking at the corner of the Plaza, which looked so out of place with the grandeur of the other four sides.

"And the last Grand Master," Garth said, his tone more of a statement than a question.

"Kuthuman? That bastard," and he whispered the imprecation. "Who the hell do you think the Walker is? Where do you think he stole the *mana* that opened the portals to other worlds. Turquoise was the most powerful of the five and refused to help him in his quest."

Hammen nodded back over to where the House once stood.

"So they killed the Master of Oor-tael, his entire family, damn near everyone, and took their *mana*."

"What about Zarel?"

"Why are you interested?"

"He's interested in me, isn't he?"

Hammen shook his head.

"Some say that it was Zarel's hatred of the Master of Oor-tael that triggered it all and Zarel who suggested the idea and the Walker finally went along with it, even though Cullinarn, the Master of Oor-tael, was an old friend who had once saved Kuthuman's life."

"So why did he do it?"

"I said before I wasn't sure if you were damn good or simply a fool," Hammen replied. "Sometimes I think it's the latter of the two. When it comes to power, friendship is usually the first thing to die. Kuthuman wanted the power of a Walker; Zarel knew that if he helped him, he would then ascend to being the new Grand Master once Kuthuman left. So Zarel organized and led the assault, the *mana* of Turquoise was used to pierce the veil between worlds, Kuthuman left, and Zarel came to power. With him all things changed. The Masters of the other Houses had either helped or stood aside while their own was murdered and the bribes afterward flowed like crap out of a force-fed goose.

"The lost treasury of Turquoise paid for that monstrosity of a palace," and Hammen nodded toward the pyramid, and the new Houses. "Everyone profited from the deal."

Garth stood in silence for a moment and then turned away, pressing through the throng that now flooded the Plaza. Approaching the House of Kestha, he finally started to slow when the flagstones beneath his feet changed color from the limestone that paved most of the Plaza to a dark gray slate. Garth paused and looked up at the six towering statues of fighters that dominated the front entryway into the House.

Garth shook his head with disdain and started forward. A hand reached out and grabbed him.

"Just what is it that you want here?" Hammen pressed.

"If you don't have the stomach for it, go home, old man," Garth hissed, shaking Hammen's grip loose.

The crowds were no longer by his side, as if an invisible barrier marked the line in which they could press no closer to the Houses of fighters.

Garth strode across the semicircle of gray stone that denoted the boundaries of the Gray House, moving with a casual ease. He heard hurried footsteps behind him and looked back over his shoulder to see that Hammen was struggling to catch up, his staff clattering on the pavement.

From out of the shadows of the great statues half a dozen fighters emerged. They were dressed in gray tunics and trousers, their capes made of the finest leather and decorated with mystical signs and runes. Dangling from ornate sashes that went from their left shoulder to their right hip were golden satchels for their amulets, spells, and tiny silken packages of earth that contained the *mana* they controlled from distant lands. The bundles of earth aided the fighter in creating this psychic link back to the power of the land from which his magic grew. They moved toward Garth, walking with a casual, haughty ease and stepped in front of him to block his path.

"Go away, beggar. You walk on our property here," one of them hissed and, placing his hand on Garth's chest, gave him a shove.

Garth stepped back a foot and did not turn away.

"I said go away!"

"I've come to join this House," Garth said calmly.

The six looked back and forth at each other with exaggerated expressions of surprise.

"A one-eyed scarecrow followed by a beggar," the man who shoved him roared. "You insult our House by tracking your filth on our walkway. You'll scrub it with your tongue for your arrogance. But first I want to see your teeth on the ground."

The man stepped forward to punch Garth. Even as he moved in to hit him Garth stepped quickly to one side, grabbing the man by the wrist and flipping him to the ground, knocking the wind out of him. As if sensing another blow coming from behind, Garth rolled on the ground, kicking out, catching his second assailant on the side of his knee. There was the sound of snapping bone as the man fell over, howling with pain. Coming back up to his feet, Garth heard a cracking sound and saw from the corner of his eye a dagger skidding across the pavement, a third fighter staggering away, holding a broken wrist while, with a flourish, Hammen caught the man across the small of the back, knocking him over.

The other three started to back up, the one in the middle fumbling with his satchel, pulling something out and then extending his arms out wide. As if from a great distance Garth could hear the roar of the crowd, screaming that a fight was on.

Garth strode forward toward the fighter, preparing to cast, pointing at him.

"Don't! Don't try it. We have someone else to fight now."

The man looked at him, wide-eyed, his concentration obviously broken by the power of Garth's words. He suddenly let out a yelp of pain, for he had made the mistake of drawing upon his *mana* without immediately focusing it into a spell. Suffering now from *mana*-burn, he staggered around, clutching both hands to his brow, while Garth watched him with an expression of pity for one so amateurish.

"That man is ours!"

Garth looked back at the Gray fighter.

"Don't do it. I think we have other fish to fry." And he turned away from him as if he was no longer of concern.

A squad of fighters from the Orange House were advancing across the Plaza with purposeful strides. One of them, wearing a cloak heavily embroidered with gold and silver and obviously of higher rank, led the way.

Garth slowly extended his arms in preparation for a fight and the man slowed.

"A witness in the crowd says you were the one who murdered Okmark yesterday. You're ours."

"Then take me," Garth said quietly.

The fighter started to move forward as if deciding not even to bother with a spell.

Garth smiled and pointed at the man. His walk slowed as if he had stepped into an invisible barrier. Cursing, he stumbled backward.

Next Garth raised his hand, pointing to the heavens. A dark swirling cloud took form, buzzing, humming, and dived down. Hornets, as big as a man's thumb, swarmed over the Orange fighters, stinging with such viciousness that blood ran in rivulets down the faces of Garth's foes.

A roaring crowd now ringed the edge of the Kesthan pavement, howling with delight, laughing even louder when some of the hornets diverted away from the half dozen they were tormenting and slashed into the crowd, their victims screaming, waving their arms to ward off the stings. The antics of the peasants and common folk getting stung caused the crowd to roar even louder with delight.

The leader of the Fentesk, bellowing with rage, struggled to his feet and extended his arms, pointing them heavenward. The hornets plummeted to the ground, their wings trailing smoke and flame. But even as they writhed on the ground they still managed to cling to the ankles of their targets, stinging even through boots so that the leader's companions hopped about madly.

Garth waved his hand again and the hornets burst into flames, the fire spreading to the boots of the fighters and tormented peasants in the crowd. The peasants ran off screaming, heading to the fountains to douse their burning shoes, followed by the Orange fighters; only the leader remained.

The leader pulled his arms in tight around himself, his cloak fluttering, and a mist started to form around him. Garth reached into his satchel and then pointed even as the deadly mist started to move toward him. The Fentesk leader staggered, and for a moment it appeared as if a whirlpool was pulsing around him, sucking his powers away into a void. Garth moved his hands back and forth as if stirring the whirlpool, while the fighter twisted and writhed inside the power sink that was drawing his strength away.

He collapsed on the pavement.

Hammen scurried forward to the prostrate fighter and reached for his satchel.

"Only one," Garth commanded. "It is the rule; this was no death fight."

Hammen reached greedily into the man's satchel, pulled out a ringed amulet. "His bind against flying creatures, the one he used against your hornets."

Garth nodded and then looked back at the Gray fighters, who stood gape mouthed.

A loud trumpeting echoed across the Great Plaza and seconds later it seemed to be repeated from inside House Kestha. Already there was a knot of Grays standing around the doorway and seconds later dozens more poured out.

The crowd which had been watching the show pushed and shoved as if a force had struck it from behind. It finally parted as yet more Orange fighters came pouring into the open semicircle around Gray's House. Within seconds half a dozen of them were fighting with an equal number of Grays, several of them conjuring up spells while the others simply pulled daggers and set at each other.

"Master, isn't it a healthy time to leave?"

Garth looked down at Hammen, who was busily stuffing several cut purses into his tunic.

The crowd was roaring with delight, pointing, shouting, screaming with hysterical abandon when blood was finally spilled and a Gray fighter went down clutching his throat, which had been cut from ear to ear. A fireball struck his assailant, even as the man reached down to grab his victim's satchel, sending him sprawling, writhing in flames until one of his companions cast a spell of protection, dousing the flame. Two Gray fighters rushed to help their hemorrhaging lodge brother, applying hands and incantations to stem the bleeding.

Garth ducked low, when from atop the Kesthan palace sheets of lightning snapped down, striking into the plaza, bowling Fentesk fighters over like ninepins. Garth scrambled up against the building and sat down under the shadow of one of the great stone pillar fighters. He reached into his tunic, pulled out another pomegranate, and calmly started to eat.

"Master, please!" Hammen whined, sneaking up to Garth's side and squatting down beside him. "Let's just get out of here."

"Not yet. Why don't you go and arrange some bets for me on Gray."

More trumpets brayed and Hammen looked around furtively.

"The Grand Master of the Arena is coming. It's time to get out of here now."

"In a minute."

From the edge of the swirling mob, which was laughing and dancing about while watching the show, a heavy phalanx appeared. There were at least twenty magic wielders in the middle of the column, the fighters flanked by several hundred crossbow men. At the front of the column rode the Grand Master of the Arena himself, his multihued cape reflecting all the colors of the rainbow.

The crossbow men, with weapons cocked, fanned out around the edge of the gray semicircle, some facing toward the mob, which reluctantly gave back, while the others faced inward, raising their weapons and taking aim on the combatants.

More trumpets sounded and drums rolled. The fight started to break apart.

"Tulan of Kestha, come out!" a herald, standing next to the stirrup of the Grand Master, roared, his voice apparently magnified by some magical power so that it thundered even above the tumult of the crowd, several of whom were now screaming after being shot by crossbow quarrels at close range.

"I'm here!"

Garth slowly turned and looked up. Atop the head of one of the great stone fighters stood a man who he assumed was the Grand Master of the House of Kestha. Garth finished his pomegranate and tossed the ends of it aside.

"This fight must cease or you shall be placed under injunction," the herald shouted.

"Then tell those Orange bastards to stop soiling our pavement with their filth."

The Grand Master turned his mount and looked at the knot of Fentesk fighters, who stood in a circle around their wounded.

"You are engaged in trespass; you must pay damages for violation of the law and leave this place at once."

The leader, who had first fought with Garth and had regained some of his wits, was helped to his feet.

"We were here to seek arrest against a man who murdered one of our brothers."

"Who?"

The leader looked around the plaza.

"Master, please, nowwww!" Hammen whined.

Garth stood up and casually started to walk toward the Grand Master.

"I think he wants me," Garth announced loudly.

"That's him!" Orange shouted. "He's the one who killed one of our men yesterday."

The Grand Master wheeled his horse around, the herald motioning for several crossbow men to train their weapons on Garth.

Garth, ignoring them, turned his back to the Grand Master and looked up to the top of the statue where Tulan stood.

"I came to join the House of Kestha. I stand on land not owned by the Grand Master of this city but rather by the House of Kestha. Will you allow one who fought for you to be taken thus from your very doorstep?"

Tulan looked down over the edge of the statue and then nervously turned to look at a ring of fighters of the highest rank who stood around him.

"Surely you would not bear such an insult to your reputation and honor," Garth shouted, the slightest edge of sarcasm in his voice.

"He's my man and he is on my property!" Tulan finally shouted, though the nervousness in his voice was evident.

The Grand Master reined in his mount just behind Garth.

"This is my city and I am the Grand Master of the Arena."

"Without the four Houses to fight in your arena," Garth replied, looking straight back at the Grand Master, "you will be penniless."

Garth turned and looked back up at Tulan.

"Isn't that so, my lord Master of Kestha."

"That's so, that's so!" Tulan shouted. "Touch him and we'll go on strike for the first day of Festival and so will the other Houses. You have no right to arrest one of us on our own property."

At the mere mention of a possible strike the mob watching the drama started to howl in protest. Garth turned and looked back at the crowd, bowing low to them with a dramatic flourish, and wild applause broke out. He looked over at the Fentesk fighters and saw that even they were backing away from wanting him, out of a higher solidarity to protect their precious rights.

"That man is a Kestha fighter," Tulan roared. "He is on Kestha property and under my protection. There's nothing more to be said."

Garth turned and looked back at the Grand Master, who was gazing down at him coldly.

"I'm sorry to have caused you trouble, sire."

The Grand Master looked down at him with a curious expression, as if using his powers to somehow probe. Garth felt the power swirling around him like a cold breeze. The power pulled away.

"You won't survive Festival," the Grand Master hissed, his words barely audible and, yanking the reins of his mount, he turned and spurred his mount into a gallop, the mob parting before him.

Garth bowed low to the departing Grand Master and then, turning, strode toward the doorway into the House of Kestha. As he passed beneath the shadows of the great statues he looked closely and finally saw Hammen, crouched down low, peering out from behind the colossal feet of the statue nearest the door.

"Stand up like a man, Hammen," Garth said quietly. "The servant of a fighter of Kestha should show more dignity."

"Servant, is it?" Hammen said. "The demons take you. You're a plague. Anyone who comes near you will turn up dead."

·   Garth laughed softly.

"I need a servant now. The job is yours for a silver a week."

"I can make that in a morning in my regular profession."

"You'll find the change amusing. I just need you for Festival."

"The busy season for my profession."

"If you don't come, I think you'll always wonder what you missed out on."

Hammen lowered his head and mumbled to himself.

"Oh, the devil with it, damn you. All right. But I get sole gaming rights to you outside the arena."

"Fighting outside the arena is illegal."

Hammen threw back his head and laughed.

"Like yesterday and just now."

"Sole gaming rights then."

Grinning, Hammen swaggered out from his hiding place and fell in behind Garth.

Gray fighters were returning to their House, helping their wounded. They looked over at Garth with open curiosity but none approached him. The doors into the palace were wide open and Garth followed them in and then, out of the shadows, a heavy rotund form appeared. The man stood as tall as he did, at just over a fathom, but Garth estimated that he easily weighed twice as much. Grand Masters were no longer expected to fight in the arena and it was evident that this one had taken that security to heart, and to his stomach as well.

Heavy jowls jiggled as the man drew closer, his fat, sausage-like hands glistening with jewels on every finger. He had power; Garth could sense that. And though it was gone to dissipation, he was still someone who could beat nearly anyone who stood against him.

"Well done, lad, well done," Tulan roared, coming up to Garth, who went through the ceremony of bowing low.

Tulan grabbed him by the shoulders and raised him back up.

"You stood up to that damn Zarel, that pox-eaten Arena Master. Good show, lad, good show."

"In service to you, my lord."

Garth ignored the slight fit of coughing that beset Hammen.

"My servant, my lord. He was robbed of his clothes this morning, thus the rags, and he has been ill."

Tulan looked over at Hammen who grinned up at him, his yellow teeth showing in a jagged grin. Tulan wrinkled his nose with disdain

"Somebody give this man a change of clothes and a bath."

"A bath. Like . . ."

"Hammen, you heard our Master. Now obey."

Hammen was led away, looking over at Garth and making a sign against him as if to ward off the evil eye.

Tulan, his hand still on Garth's shoulder, led him down the main corridor of the House. The walls were of heavy oak, polished to a mirrorlike sheen, racks of weapons set against them, crossbows, lances, morning stars, battle-axes, and swords. Looking up, Garth could see that there were holes set at regular intervals overhead, undoubtedly for heavily weighted bolts which could be dropped down by the flick of a lever, crushing anyone who dared to try and take the palace through the main door. A fifty-pound razor-sharp bolt dropped from such a height would be a powerful argument, even against a spell caster of the tenth-rank if he was caught unprepared. Looking down, he could see that the parquet floor was not in fact solid. Sections of it could easily drop away if unwanted company was standing on it. Pits of snakes most likely down below, Garth thought, or maybe even a Gromashian spiderweb.

"I heard how you killed Okmark. Spell reflection, a powerful tool." As he spoke, Tulan looked down at Garth's satchel.

"He was foolish."

"He was a third-rank; my man Webin. A second-rank should have known better than to be tricked into a street fight like that."

"How is Webin?"

"Demoted in rank for causing such a humiliation," Tulan snapped, "his latest spell forfeit."

Garth said nothing, surprised that any fighter would allow himself to be stripped of a spell without the honor of a fight.

"Oh, I fought him for it," Tulan chuckled. "Maybe I'll regenerate his left hand if I have the time."

The fighters who were walking behind Garth and Tulan laughed coldly.

Tulan led Garth into a room and the most pleasant of smells wafted around him.

"You're in time for a late-morning repast."

Tulan motioned him to sit down at the long feasting table, which was cleared but for a serving for one. Tulan clapped his hands and motioned toward Garth. Servants came scurrying out from a side room and quickly set a plate to the right of Tulan.

Tulan motioned for his advisors to leave and, with a hearty sigh, he sat down in a high-back chair at the head of the table. More servants came out, bearing plates with stuffed pheasants, great rings of sausage, a small suckling pig stuffed with cloves and basted in honey, and smoked fish baked with lemons and ginger.

Heavy crystal glasses were set and filled with dark Tarmulian wine, another with pale honeyed mead, and another with a clear wine that sparkled and danced with bubbles.

Tulan took a loaf of bread, tearing off five pieces and tossing them to the great powers that upheld the five corners of the world and followed with five tosses of salt while Garth did the same.

Without wasting a word, Tulan reached across the table and picked up a pheasant. Sighing, he bit into it, and soon devoured the morsel. Next he reached over to the suckling pig and held it up, motioning toward Garth if he wanted part. Garth shook his head, devoting his attention instead to one of the remaining pheasants. Grabbing the pig by the haunches and forefeet, Tulan proceeded to devour the midsection, using a knife only to scoop out the stuffing, which was still steaming hot. Finished with that, he tossed the remains back on a platter and then dived into the thick blood sausages, downing half a dozen before finally turning his attention to the fish, chewing and spitting out the pieces of bone into a silver tray set by his left elbow.

Leaning back, he belched, with a loud sonorous rumble so that Garth thought the high stained glass windowpanes would shatter. As if moving down a line Tulan then drained the three heavy goblets, one after the other, barely pausing for a gulp. Sighing, he belched again and then picked up one of the fish bones to pick his teeth.

Garth, finished with his pheasant, took the glass of Tarmulian wine and sipped at it contentedly.

"If you beat Okmark so easily, you must be equal to at least a fourth-rank, maybe a fifth-rank."

He paused, looking over at Garth as if expecting a reply. Garth said nothing and Tulan laughed, but it was evident that he was annoyed over Garth's secrecy.

"The contents of one's satchel are, according to tradition, known only to the owner," Garth finally said.

"I need men like you," Tulan finally said, acting again as if they were old comrades. "Once this Festival is over there's contracts to be met, cities and merchants to be guarded, wars to be fought and, believe me, those of the House of Kestha get top pay for their services."

"Minus your commission and the House dues, of course," Garth replied.

Tulan paused for a moment, looking sharply at Garth.

"Why us, why not another House?" Tulan asked coolly.

"Why not? Do you want me to tell you that the fame of the House of Kestha is higher than all others, that only the best come to you? Is that what you want me to say as if I was a first-rank acolyte who one day had discovered that he was born with the talent to control the *mana* which creates spells?"

Tulan said nothing and Garth laughed cynically.

"I don't need the training of this House or any other House. I learned that on my own."

"Where? I've never seen you before. I've never heard of a one-eyed *hanin*, a fighter without colors. Where are you from?"

Garth smiled.

"That's my business, sire. You know my skill; you saw it out there on the Plaza."

"It's my business to know. To check your pedigree, your family lines, to see if you come from a line with strength to control the *mana*."

"It's not your business. Your business is to manage my business, to make both of us money."

"How dare you!" Tulan roared, standing up and kicking his chair back.

Garth stood up and bowed low.

"Since it is obvious we don't have a deal, I'll take my services elsewhere. I think Purple might want me."

"You won't step out of here alive," Tulan snarled, and he started to extend his hands.

Garth threw his head back and laughed.

"You might kill me, sire, but I can promise you there'll be a devil of a fire in here by the time we're done fighting and I'd hate to ruin your tapestries; they look like they're from the Naki weavers of Kish and are worth the fees of fifty fighters."

Tulan paused and looked over at the great tapestries woven of gold-and-silver thread that lined the wall opposite the stained glass windows so that they could catch and reflect the light. A slow smile crossed Tulan's features.

"You have an eye for art. That's good, that's very good. One eye and can see better than most of the brutes I have working for me with two." And Tulan chuckled as if he had made a great joke.

"Sit down, Garth One-eye, sit down. I think I might even like you." And he made a show of pouring Garth some more wine.

Garth smiled and nodded his thanks.

"Your commission?" Garth asked.

"The usual twenty percent for your services retained by outside contracts, plus ten percent of any purse you win in the arena during Festival. In return you'll receive your room, board, and the full legal protection of the House. And believe me, the outside contracts for your services will be in your favor.

"Gray fighters can count on higher fees than the other Houses," Tulan boasted, while patting his stomach. "Our reputation insures that and you'll be placed with lords and merchants who appreciate good value and will treat you with respect. You must already know that in the last twenty Festivals it has been a Kesthan fighter who won the championship nine times and was thus selected to be the new initiate to the most high power of the Walker."

Tulan paused for a moment as if fearful that the most powerful of all users of magic might suddenly appear at the mere mention of his name.

"Such a record insures that we are held in the highest esteem by those who contract us and gives us the right to expect certain advantages. There'll be the finest food, the best of quarters when you are out on contract, and the finest mates of your choosing, provided at no extra fee."

Garth smiled and said nothing.

"We'll place you according to your skills and you will answer to no law other than mine"—he paused for a moment—"and Zarel can sit and fume over you and not touch you, something which I think might be a concern right now."

"Not really."

Tulan looked over at Garth, not sure if his comment was simple bravado or the truth. Finally he laughed coolly.

"I like fighters with nerves like yours. But do not doubt the power of Zarel. Step out of this House without colors on and a score of his best fighters will swarm over you. You need a House, One-eye; without it you're dead."

Garth finally nodded slowly in reply.

"In return you must obey all orders of the House, which means my commands."

"Agreed."

Tulan smiled as if already holding the commissions he would receive for placing Garth.

"You are to fight only according to the rules, there are to be no personal grudge fights or fights for personal profit. I don't need you out there wasting your skills and wagering your spells to no profit for this House."

"That might be hard to obey."

"Why?"

"That's why I joined this House. Half of the Orange House wants me dead."

"Oh, because of that incident with Okmark?"

"No, other things."

"What other things?"

"I'm oath sworn not to reveal them," Garth said quietly. "Let's just say it has something to do with this," he added, pointing at the patch over his eye.

"A personal issue then?"

Garth leaned forward.

"Since you are my guild master, I think I can share it," he said with a conspiratorial whisper.

Tulan leaned forward eagerly to hear the secret.

"It happened several years back. Losing the eye was almost worth it but now that they know I'm here they'll come for me. That is part of the reason I decided to stop being *hanin* and join a House. I knew the less than friendly feelings between Fentesk and Kestha meant that at least here I would have some protection."

"What happened?"

"I seduced the first consort of the Master of Fentesk and also their twin daughters at the same time."

Tulan, who was in the middle of downing another draught of mead, sprayed most of the contents back out on the table and looked at Garth wide-eyed. His features turned bright red and, laughing, he started to pound the table.

"No wonder he cut her throat last year! How delightful, how absolutely delightful! Tell me, how good were they?"

Garth smiled.

"The honor of ladies, sire."

"Ladies; hell, all the women of Orange are harlots, especially their fighters. So you got caught and had an eye gouged out before you could make good your escape."

"Something like that," Garth said quietly, and as he spoke he looked away from Tulan as if a dark memory had suddenly come to haunt him.

"Fine then, fine. It'll be a delight to rub Varnel Buckara's face in this."

"I prefer not, my lord. For the daughters' sake. After all, they're still alive, and reminding him might cause a refreshing of his rage against them."

"All right then, all right, but still." And Tulan beamed at Garth with pride.

"You can take the oath in ceremony on the morning Festival starts. Till then you can wear the Gray mantle of an initiate."

Garth nodded and, looking over his glass, he smiled.

"I eagerly anticipate the honor," he said quietly.

CHAPTER
3

"THANK THE ETERNAL WE'RE OUT OF THERE."

Garth looked down at Hammen and suppressed an urge to laugh. The pickpocket no longer looked like the same man. His rags were gone, replaced by a clean tunic of white with a gray circle over his left breast. The filthy unkempt hair was gone as well, close-cropped as befitting the servant of a fighter. Hammen looked back angrily at the House.

"You can keep this, Garth One-eye. I have no desire to play this game any longer. Go find another servant. I'm for home," he announced, and tore his tight-fitting collar open.

"Then you'll miss the fun."

"Fun. You call this fun? Groveling as a damned servant—yes Master, no Master, let me wipe your backside with my right hand for you, Master." His voice took on a sarcastic, singsong whine. "You can shove that up where it belongs. I'm my own man."

"Fine then, leave."

Hammen slowed and looked up at Garth, barely visible now in the darkness.

"All right, I'm going."

Garth reached into his satchel and pulled out a coin, handing it to Hammen.

"Your pay for the week."

Hammen took the coin without comment and shoved it into a small purse dangling from his belt.

"So long then."

Garth turned and started to walk slowly on.

"One-eye."

Garth turned and looked back.

"Just how did you lose that eye?"

"You won't find out by leaving."

Hammen remained silent for a moment.

"Nor anything else."

Hammen stared at him closely, wondering, trying to sense, to reach back somehow into a thought long since deliberately buried. He felt for an instant that something in Garth was flickering around him, a magical flashing of light, reaching far into memories best left undisturbed. For an instant he felt a tightening in his throat as if a long-forgotten pain had come back. And then it was gone and there were only the sounds of the night, the mob walking about the Great Plaza, the drinkers singing, and the lovers whispering. All of it held for Hammen a deep mystery, a lingering memory of laughter, of another world and another time, and it seemed to come from this stranger who stood before him in the shadows.

"Who are you?" Hammen whispered.

"Stay with me and find out, Hammen of Jor, if that is really your name."

Hammen stiffened slightly, a chill of fear coursing through him, and then the chill was gone, replaced by a distant warmth that held for but a second and then was also gone.

Hammen finally moved, ever so slowly, and came up to Garth's side.

"Buy me a drink then, damn it."

Hammen walked in silence, watching the way Garth moved. He walked like most fighters, with a deliberate catlike ease, his head always turning, watching. There was the sense of the *mana* about him, what others might simply call charisma but was in fact raw power which to the trained eye was almost visible, like flashes of lightning on the distant horizon that are but half-seen and half-heard. It could be hidden when need be, but it was there in abundance and Hammen knew it.

Leaving the Plaza, Garth wandered up a side street, drawn by boisterous laughter and a crowd standing before the open door of a swill dive, several of them holding torches aloft. Edging up to the crowd, Hammen could see that a couple of fighters were brawling in the street, one Brown, the other a woman who he suspected was not even a fighter, merely a warrior proficient in weapons. The Brown fighter was not using his powers but was struggling with mere physical strength. A circle was drawn around them in the mud, the two fighting *oquorak,* the ritual fight of tying their right hands to each other by a length of short rope, while holding daggers in their left hands.

The Brown fighter was bleeding from a long cut which had slashed his tunic open across his chest and another across his forehead, the blood trickling into his eyes. Yet Brown was obviously the far more powerful of the two. He yanked his right arm down, pulling the woman in toward him. She spun around, ducking underneath his slashing blow, and came up, a cool smile of amusement on her face.

"Benalish woman," Garth whispered, noticing the seven-pointed star tattoo on her left forearm, which was the mark of her particular clan within the Benalish caste system.

Garth moved closer into the crowd to watch the fight.

The Benalish woman waited, poised on the balls of her feet, her short-cropped black hair matching the color of her leather jerkin and tight-fitting trousers. The Brown fighter tried the same maneuver again, nearly knocking her off-balance. This time she plunged forward, diving to the ground and then somersaulting head over heels. As she did so she pulled with her right arm, using her momentum to add weight to the pull. The Brown fighter was spun around and knocked down. The crowd roared its approval of the maneuver.

Brown slashed out, trying to kick her feet out as she started to stand back up. She easily leaped over the strike. Brown scrambled back up and came in low, going for a stab, a movement against the rules of *oquorak,* which allowed only slashing with the dagger.

The crowd went silent. This was no longer just a little sporting event, it was a blood match. Within seconds the bets started to fly and Hammen slipped into the confused mass. Garth, ignoring the betting frenzy, moved in closer to the circle. He watched Brown closely as the two circled each other warily. The man was still holding his dagger for a stab, the Benalish woman looking at him disdainfully, but still holding her blade backhanded for slashing.

Her left hand flashed out and Brown's right shoulder was laid open.

"Again blood," she announced. "Three times now. It's finished."

Her blade flashed again and she cut the one-fathom length of *oquorak* rope that bound their right hands together.

Brown stood before her, panting, features contorted with rage. She watched him disdainfully, her slim boyish figure silhouetted by the torchlight.

"The wager was three gold. Your payment," she said quietly.

"You cheated."

She laughed coldly.

"How the hell can I cheat in an *oquorak?* Your payment."

With a bellowing roar Brown came in low, his blade glinting in the torchlight. The Benalish woman leaped to one side, blade flashing. The Brown fighter howled with pain, staggering away. His left ear lay on the muddy ground.

Screaming, with one hand clasped to the side of his head, he turned and Garth saw the Brown fighter look aside for an instant to a heavily cloaked man standing to Garth's right.

Brown broke off from a close-in attack, circling back around so that the Benalish woman's back was now turned to Garth and the man standing beside him. Brown moved forward slowly, blade poised, and the Benalish woman shifted her knife to her left hand, changing her grip to a stab.

"There, you cheated," Brown roared. "You fought *oquorak* but you're left-handed to start with."

"You never asked. By ritual you could have, but you were too drunk with arrogance," the Benalish woman said quietly. "Now, your payment before someone gets hurt."

"I'll cut your liver out and jam it down your throat," Brown snarled, and he moved a step closer.

The Benalish woman backed up slightly, changing her stance, ready to receive his charge.

The cloaked man next to Garth stepped across the line into the circle and there was a flash of steel in his hand.

Garth caught the man across the neck with an open-handed blow just behind the ear, knocking him senseless. The Benalish woman spared a quick glance backward and, as she did so, Brown charged.

Garth started to shout a warning but there was no need to. She deftly sidestepped the strike, kicking Brown's feet out from under him. With a serpentlike strike she was on him, knocking the dagger from his hand, and in an instant was on his chest, dagger point up under his throat.

"Your payment," she said quietly.

Brown looked at her with a murderous rage in his eyes. She pushed the dagger ever so slightly, nicking the skin over his pulsing jugular.

"I can get it with you alive or with you dead."

"Kill me and my House will avenge me."

"Is that supposed to frighten me?"

Garth moved up to her side and, without waiting for her approval, he tore open Brown's satchel. Ignoring the paltry amulets in a side pouch within the satchel, he felt around for money.

"He's only got a couple of silvers," Garth announced, and pulled them out.

The crowd, which had been watching silently, roared their taunting disapproval of a fighter who would accept a simple wager without the ability to pay.

The Benalish woman pressed the blade in a bit more, a trickle of blood creasing down Brown's neck.

"I'll come by your House tomorrow morning at second bell for payment. Be there."

She flipped her dagger around and slammed the hilt against the side of Brown's head, knocking him senseless.

She stood up, the crowd cheering its approval.

Smiling, Garth handed the coins over.

"Thanks, One-eye," she said, and tilted her head in acknowledgment.

"Garth."

Garth turned as Hammen came up to his side. Hammen hesitated for a second.

"I mean *master*."

"Damn it, Hammen, just Garth, but skip the One-eye." And as he spoke he looked back at the Benalish woman.

"My apologies, Garth, and thank you."

"We didn't win that much. The money was in favor of this woman, one silver for four."

Hammen looked back at the prostrate fighters.

"Ah, the old days of honor are gone," he said, with a sad shake of his head. "The world is nothing but corruption now."

Garth looked over at Hammen with surprise and the old man shrugged his hunched-over shoulders as if embarrassed to have been caught saying such a thing.

The Benalish woman turned as if to leave.

"A drink on what we won on you?" Garth asked.

She turned, looked at him, and then smiled.

"On me. I appreciate your help, even though I really didn't need it. I knew he was moving behind me."

"Of course."

"Maybe someplace else," Hammen interjected, looking down at the downed fighter and his companion, both of whom were starting to stir.

The three set off, Hammen hawking and then placing a well-aimed shot on the Brown fighter. The mob now fell upon the two who, when they finally woke up, if they were lucky, would simply find themselves stripped naked, their precious spells for sale on the black market.

Hammen led the way down a narrow street, the shops lining the way shuttered up tight for the night. From overhead windows could be heard laughing, arguing, lovemaking, and all the other sounds that filled the city, while from underfoot wafted up the smells, most of which were less than pleasant. Hammen trudged through the muck and chuckled when the woman fought to suppress a gag.

"Some place for Festival," the Benalish woman sniffed.

"All cities are sewers which trap the worst," Hammen replied as if disgusted as well.

Garth looked down at him and said nothing. The old man looked up at him as if lost in depressing and disturbing thoughts.

"What is it?" Garth asked.

"Nothing, One-eye, nothing at all," Hammen said quietly.

Garth looked over at the Benalian and found that, in spite of himself, he rather liked the woman. She was a tough fighter, to be sure, yet there seemed, as well, a touch of near-childlike innocence to her in regard to the ways of the world.

He sensed that she had fought the *oquorak* out of a true need for money and had actually expected the Brown fighter to behave honorably. Though she tried to conceal it 'neath her leather armor, she moved with a soft feminine grace that somehow seemed out of place.

Hammen led the way through the warren of streets, finally stopping at a small tavern, and, leading the way, he ducked in through the low door. The tavern master looked at the three suspiciously.

"I'm closing."

"You mean you don't serve strangers here," Hammen replied, looking around the crowded room, which had fallen silent.

A number of the patrons were gathered around a table, watching as two of their compatriots played a card game which represented the fighting of magic users, the onlookers ignoring the new arrivals, so intent were they on the duel being fought out with the cards.

The tavern master pushed his way past the crowd watching the game and walked up to Hammen. He looked at him closely and then threw his head back, laughing.

"Hammen, have you gone mad? I'd sooner expect to see you dressed as a whore than as a fighter's servant, and damn me if, come to think of it, the two aren't the same."

"Then your mother would make an excellent servant, and so would your wife and daughters," Hammen snapped back, and the tavern master laughed even louder, pointing to an empty table in the corner of the room.

Hammen led the way to the table and the three sat down, the master coming up with a heavy earthenware pitcher and three mugs clasped in one hand and a red-hot poker in the other. He slammed the mugs down and then plunged the poker into the pitcher, the scent of boiling rum wafting up.

"Hot buttered rum, the best in the city," Hammen announced with a sigh as the woman reached into her satchel and pulled out three coppers and placed them on the table. The tavern master looked down at them, disappointed, and then back at the woman.

"Three coppers for a pitcher is the going rate where I come from," she said quietly.

"Well, not here."

"Yes it is," Hammen replied, waving the master away.

"I hate cities," she said quietly, pouring a full mug for herself and draining off half of it.

"Then why are you here?" Garth asked.

She looked over at him.

"I can see you're part of a House."

"For the moment."

She sniffed disdainfully.

"*Hanin* are not welcome in the Grand Master's city," Hammen replied, "and especially during Festival. The four Houses make sure of that as well."

"Well, you won't see a Benalian serving a color; we're our own."

"So why are you here then?" Garth asked, and then he paused, looking at her.

"Norreen, that's good enough for here."

"Norreen, then, so why are you here?"

"I was a shield carrier to my lord,"—she paused—"but he's dead."

"So you failed to protect your lord and now you're unemployed," Hammen interjected.

"Something like that," she said quietly.

"So go home then," Garth said.

"She can't," Hammen said. "It's a question of honor. The Benalia caste system is strange beyond imagining. At the start of every new lunar year the highest caste of the year before becomes the lowest and the next highest moves up and so on down. The only one who can break the caste cycle is a hero, a rank awarded to warriors who are shield carriers to a lord or win great honors and renown. I'm willing to bet her caste ranking is going to be the lowest and she wants nothing to do with it. Since she is not a hero, she would be a servant, which isn't to her liking."

Hammen looked over at her and she said nothing.

"Let me finish my conjecturing. There's a man in here someplace, there always is, most likely a loathsome fat toad. Women of the lowest caste cannot refuse the demands to mate from one of the highest class; this toad wants you, and I half suspect that you're a virgin and want to save your honor, plus you don't like warts."

She looked at him coldly but her face reddened slightly and Hammen snickered.

"Madness," Hammen said. "I never could understand you Benalians."

The Benalish woman stiffened.

"No worse than this damned Festival."

"Ah, there's at least logic there. The Houses get to test each other to see which has the best and thus gain prestige and contracts for the forthcoming year. Merchants and princes can evaluate fighters they might wish to hire, the mob is entertained, and the winner gets to go with the Walker, bringing prestige to his House. It's all so amusing." And he shook his head.

"And the Grand Master makes all the money," she replied coldly.

"So why do you care?" Garth asked.

"I don't."

"But you are looking for employment here since all the great princes will be arriving for Festival."

"Would you tell your servant to shut up," she snapped angrily.

"Hammen, shut up."

"Oh, please don't beat me, Master," Hammen whined sarcastically, before emitting a long belch. He looked over at the woman and grinned lasciviously.

"I think my master here is rather taken with you. If you're in agreement, we can take care of this virginity problem. I have a cousin who owns a rather nice place to lodge the night. I've heard Benalish women are rather exciting. All I ask is that I get to watch through a peephole. My cousin rents them out to old men like me."

She pulled her dagger out and slammed it into the table, a clear signal of challenge.

Hammen held his hands up with mock terror.

"I am not a fighter of magic or a warrior, so don't soil your blade, good lady." And he laughed again.

Garth looked over at Hammen and flicked his own blade out of its sheath as well.

Norreen finished the rest of her drink and slammed the mug down with such force that it shattered.

"I wouldn't sleep anyhow with a One-eye, especially one

with a servant who makes me want to vomit from the stink of his breath."

She stood up and stormed out of the tavern. Garth looked over coldly at Hammen.

"Thanks for your help."

"Oh, no bother, Master. Just saving you a lot of trouble. Benalish women who are warriors are notorious for crushing men's hearts. They make it a sport, especially if he's a different caste. It's one of their ways of gaining prestige. Besides, she's a virgin and they are an eternal bother, always falling in love with the man who relieves them of that concern, following him around and whining about love. I figured it best to protect you from it."

"I don't need your damn protection."

"Around here, Garth, you need my protection," Hammen said quietly. "Benalians are usually more trouble than they're worth, always picking fights, always trying to break out of their caste cycle, especially when they're women and thrown to the bottom of the heap. Ones like her are half-crazy from it, and the half-crazy are the sane ones compared to the rest.

"Now if you're interested, my cousin keeps a nice supply of exotic women in his lodging and for a small fee I can arrange some entertainment. With your money I bet we could even get two at once," and, as he spoke, Hammen leered hopefully. "Certainly you won't mind my renting a peephole while we're there."

"Let's go back to the House," Garth said coldly, and Hammen looked at him, crestfallen.

As he stepped out into the street Garth looked around, as if expecting to see someone, and then looked back at Hammen.

"Thanks a lot," he snapped angrily.

"My pleasure to serve you, Master," Hammen replied with a cackle, steering Garth away from the shadow of a woman who lingered on the other side of the street.

"I want a full check on him," Zarel Ewine, Grand Master of the Arena, snarled.

Uriah Aswark, captain of the fighters of the Grand Master,

bowed low in fear, for the Grand Master was known to lash out at whoever was nearby in moments of rage, and this was clearly a moment of rage since the august presence had been publicly humiliated.

"As you wish, sire," Uriah whispered.

"Go to our usual contacts in the city and the Houses, pay the usual sums, but I want a full accounting of every silver spent"—he paused—"and you know what happened to your predecessor on that score."

"I would never think of cheating you, sire."

Zarel looked down at his captain with contempt.

"No, of course you wouldn't. Because if you did, especially now, I think I'd throw you in with the others for the entertainment of the Walker. Now get out of here."

Uriah started to back out of the room, his head still kept down in the proper show of obeisance, eyes averted from the Grand Master's visage.

"Uriah."

He froze in place.

"Yes, sire."

"I am holding you personally responsible for this. I want him. I want to know who he is and what his game is. There is something there to him. I don't know what; I tried to probe but he had enough power to block me. I couldn't take him because he was a member of a House and is protected as long as he wears colors."

Uriah looked up cautiously at the Grand Master, surprised at the admission that a mere *hanin* had sufficient power to block his power. His features looked somehow distant, as if lost in a memory that was somehow clouded and unable to be clearly pierced.

"Who is he?"

Uriah was startled to see the Grand Master looking directly at him, his features filled with doubt.

"I will find out, Master."

"Do it. Arrange an expulsion so that he no longer has House protection and is mine. I don't care how it's done; I just want it done. And do it right, Uriah, for I really don't think you would enjoy providing entertainment for the Walker when he arrives. I have to provide the usual fare for him and there's always room for one more at the party. It's either this one-eye or it's you."

Uriah withdrew from the room, not ashamed of the fact that the guards outside the door could see the trembling of his knees. The Walker was always hungry for the power that could be drained from souls and those who were the enemies of the Grand Master usually provided the feast . . . along with those who had simply failed.

Zarel watched the dwarf who was his commander of fighters withdraw from the room.

Why should this fighter trouble me? he wondered. Something was alerted by his mere presence and Zarel knew that such a sensing almost always had a truth behind it.

Had he met him before?

Zarel cast through his memory. Since the man was a fighter who controlled *mana,* his mere physical appearance was not an accurate gauge of his age. He could be around twenty-five as he looked, or he could be a hundred, maybe even older.

To remember all who might be enemies across a hundred years was nearly impossible. Was it from before, when Kuthuman was still the Grand Master? There were many enemies, to be sure, from that time, when the climb for power as assistant to the Grand Master had resulted in more than one body being found floating in the harbor.

He tried to focus his thoughts, searching. A one-eye. But for how long? He might have lost it last year or scores of years ago. A one-eye. He had helped to gouge out the eyes of many men and women, for as assistant to the Grand Master it was his task to be the administrant of justice. Eyes, hands, feet, and heads, that was his trade.

Or was it afterward? After the downfall of Oor-tael, Kuthuman had ascended to the power of a demigod, becoming a Walker, and left Zarel in charge of this realm as a reward for helping it to be possible. Thousands had died in the first days, the settling of old scores that were impossible to settle while Kuthuman still walked the world. Deaths as well to insure power and to wipe out disloyalty. Could the one-eye be from that time?

Zarel sat in silence, disturbed that the answer could not be found.

It would have to be found, he realized; it would have to be found before Festival.

"There's been inquiries about you."

Garth nodded.

"The Grand Master of the Arena, I assume."

Tulan, Master of the House of Kestha, looked at him in surprise.

"My lord, isn't it obvious? I humiliated him in public and you had the courage to back me up. I know there is no love lost between the Grand Master and the House Masters and he is looking for a means of retrieving his honor. I must assume you were offered a bribe to discharge me."

Tulan stiffened slightly.

"House Masters do not accept bribes."

"Of course not, sire," Garth said calmly.

"To even imply such a motivation is a dishonor to me and to my House."

"No dishonor was ever intended," Garth replied smoothly. "I know that of course you would refuse since no House Master would ever want to be thought of as being in the pocket of Zarel."

Tulan paused for a moment to drain his goblet of mead and then to wipe his greasy fingers on his tunic. The clutter of half a dozen plates before him was filled with the remnants of his breakfast.

"Though the questions posed by the captain of his fighters were, in fact, most curious."

"Such as who am I?"

"Precisely," Tulan rumbled, pausing for a moment to emit a long rumbling belch that gurgled and rattled.

"You came to me unknown, a *hanin*. I took you in because you displayed remarkable skills, not only before the doorstep of my very House but in regaining the prestige of my House in defeating that Orange brawler who bested my man. Then to top it off you all but tell the Grand Master to go to the demons. I would have lost honor and prestige in turn if I had not taken you in while you stood upon the gray flagstones before my House."

Tulan paused and looked at him closely.

"On the one side I could call it innocent, the fact that you fought Fentesk the way you did, all over a minor point of honor, innocent as well that as a *hanin* you came to my House seeking employment and that the confrontation that ensued happened as it did."

"But then again you could call it something else," Garth replied calmly.

"Yes, damn you," Tulan snapped. "I won everything out there yesterday. I bearded the Grand Master and Fentesk; I won an edge in the games. But I've also won the increased enmity of the Grand Master for harboring you. So was this innocent?"

"But of course, my lord."

Tulan poured himself another drink and looked up coldly at Garth, while draining it off in a single gulp.

"Who are you?"

"I was a *hanin*, my lord, from the back country of Gish near the Endless Sea and the Green Lands."

"Who was your *yolin*, your master trainer? What was his House, the origin of his *mana*, the contracts he held?"

"I had none, my lord. I learned on my own that I had the power to draw on the *mana*. I practiced my skills alone; I acquired my spells and amulets in the challenging of other *hanin*. When I found myself ready I came here to join a House. The fight I picked with Orange was simply convenient to demonstrate my skills and also a touch of revenge for that past humiliation regarding the Orange Master's wife and daughters."

"You expect me to believe that?" Tulan roared.

Garth bowed low.

"The penalty of lying to my Master is expulsion," Garth replied smoothly. "And, given the current state of affairs, I would be a fool to lie since I suspect the agents of the Grand Master are even now waiting for me. And I daresay that if I walked out of this House without colors, they would be upon me and you would win a handsome sum in payment."

"How dare you even imply that I would accept such money?" Tulan snarled.

"Come, my lord. You can present such a front to initiates of the first-rank, who are all agoggle at such trivial idealisms. Anyone who is an idealist in this world is either a madman or an idiot. You have your needs and I have mine. They happen to coincide and you are the winner as a result. You have managed to humiliate someone you hate, your House gained prestige yesterday, and I think I shall earn you a win in the Festival."

Tulan paused, looked at Garth, and there was a momentary flickering of power—a probing.

"What do you have in your satchel?" Tulan asked quietly. "What artifacts, amulets, and spells do you control?"

Garth laughed softly.

"According to the law not even a House Master, not even a Grand Master, may ask that of a fighter."

He paused.

"There is only one way to find that out," Garth finally said, "but might I add that a House Master or, for that matter, any member of a House challenging another of the same color to a fight goes against all custom and tradition."

Tulan refilled his cup and looked into it sulkily.

"And if you should do so and kill me," Garth continued, "the other House Masters will think that you caved in to the demands of the Grand Master."

"So you have me," Tulan snarled.

"Rather the other way around," Garth replied smoothly. "Remember, I am now of your House. I am an unknown factor for the Festival. You should win handsomely on the betting and on my commissions from the purse. I think, my lord, that the potential winnings far exceed whatever bribes that tightfisted bastard of a Grand Master is willing to pay for my betrayal."

Tulan downed his cup and belched again, this time more softly.

"You give me a headache, One-eye. Either you are a master conniver or an innocent fool."

"Whatever you wish it to be, sire, but you will profit as you deserve."

Tulan finally nodded.

"Get out."

Garth bowed low and started for the door.

"If you should decide to go outside, I'd suggest you watch your back."

"I always do, sire."

CHAPTER

4

AS THE SECOND BELL OF MORNING SOUNDED Garth looked around expectantly. The Plaza was still something of a shambles from the previous night's festivities, littered with broken glass, shattered wine amphorae, torn clothing, and a scattering of bodies, some of which would have to be swept up and borne off to the paupers field for interment at city expense. The first of the morning crowd was already starting to wander about, most of them beggars looking for coins that might have been dropped during the night, some of them pawing over the bodies, which had already been picked clean before dawn had even begun to brighten the eastern sky.

Hammen yawned wearily.

"This is foolishness, Garth. I told you Benalish women are nothing but a royal pain."

"I'm curious, that's all." He paused. "And besides, it might fit my purpose."

"What purpose is that?" Hammen asked quietly.

"You'll see and, besides, here she comes."

Garth nodded to a lone figure coming across the Great Plaza, her cloak pulled in tightly to ward off the morning chill. She walked with a purposeful stride, the growing crowd in the Plaza backing out of her way as she passed. A small knot was already following her, for where a Benalish woman went, there was, more often than not, an interesting event about to unfold.

She walked straight toward the House of Bolk, and her rag-tag followers stopped at the edge of the dark paving stones that marked the territory of the House.

"Come on," Garth said quietly, and he moved out of the shadows of an alleyway to follow.

"All this skulking about over a woman," Hammen sniffed. "First you leave the warmth of your bed before dawn, then you drag me out through a secret entrance to throw off the Grand Master's watchers, and now you step out in public like this when obviously there's a fight brewing."

As Norreen approached the Bolk House guards appeared from the doorway, motioning for her to stop. She came to a halt and placed her fists on her hips in a defiant manner.

"I seek audience with the Master of Bolk House," she announced in a clear voice that carried across the Plaza.

"You are not a magic wielder, just a warrior," one of the guards sniffed. "Be off."

"I fought one of your men *oquorak* and he reneged on his wager. I'm here to seek satisfaction, either in payment or blood."

"Must have been Gilrash," one of the guards said, looking over at his companion and shaking his head. "He looked pretty cut up last night."

"Then get Gilrash out here."

The first guard who spoke looked back at Norreen and realized he'd been more than a bit foolish.

"Go away. Come back after Festival. We have things to worry about other than your so-called claim."

"I witnessed the fight," Garth announced, and he stepped forward onto the brown paving stones.

"Damn it, Master," Hammen sighed, and he stepped out behind him as Garth approached the trio.

"I witnessed the fight and searched your man after this woman had won. It's as she said—he was penniless. He violated the honor of an *oquorak* on three counts. First, the fighting without money to back the wager. Next, he attempted to stab when the fight went against him, and, finally, one of his accomplices tried to step into the circle to stab this woman from behind."

As Garth spoke he raised his voice so that the gathering crowd could hear. Immediately there was a rumbling chorus of comments, for the ritual of *oquorak* was held in high esteem, and to violate it on not just one, but three different points was, to the crowd's way of thinking, a despicable act lower than attempting to relieve oneself in the public fountains. *Oquorak* was supposed to be nothing more than a friendly little game, with at worst an occasional eye slashed out.

The two guards looked around uneasily and Norreen spared a quick glance back at Garth.

"I don't need your help," she hissed coldly.

"You heard her; let's beat it," Hammen urged.

"Gilrash is lower than a night soil collector and without honor," Garth pressed. "Bring your Master out here to make restitution and to punish your cur the way he deserves."

One of the guards spit on the ground.

"You're trespassing, Gray One-eye. Withdraw now before I teach you a lesson."

At the mention of his nickname a gasp went through the crowd as recognition finally dawned as to who was participating in the confrontation, since his back was turned to the crowd. Cries of bookmakers could now be heard, singing out the odds. Garth looked quickly over his shoulder and saw that Hammen was already backing up, reaching into his purse, and Garth nodded a quick approval. He looked back at the Brown guard.

"Anytime you're ready," he said easily, extending his hands out to either side.

"Stay out of this," Norreen snarled.

Garth, with a quick wave of his hand, motioned for her to step back and out of the way.

The Brown guard looked at Garth nervously and then made a quick gesture to his companion, who turned and ran back toward the House. Garth waited, concentrating his *mana* carefully, choosing his spell, and as he did so the guard he was confronting started to back up. A loud hooting roar came up from the crowd, which grew to a thunderous tumult when the Brown guard lowered his hands, acknowledging defeat without even having crossed spells. Garth turned his back on him in contempt and faced the crowd, bowing toward them as if they were the Grand Master and a duel had just been completed. The winners of the betting broke into a loud ovation. And then the mob went silent.

"Naru," someone hissed.

Garth turned and looked back. And even as he started to turn, the crowd broke into another frenzy of betting. He made a subtle hand gesture to Hammen and then moved to face what was approaching. The cry of his new opponent's name echoed behind him and he could hear the stampeding of the mob from the far ends of the Great Plaza, drawn by the prospect of seeing a champion fight.

He could feel the power of the man's *mana* wash over him even before he was visible in the doorway. The fighter was a giant, standing nearly a fathom and a half in height, powerfully built, his shoulders so wide that it appeared as if he would have to turn sideways to get through the door. He emerged through the doorway dressed in nothing more than a loincloth, his satchel dangling from a gold-encrusted strap. Steam from the sweat of his morning exercise wafted up from his body as he strode barefoot into the Plaza.

His shaven bullet-shaped head turned slowly back and forth, surveying the mob, some of whom broke into an ovation for their favorite. Behind him came a score of Bolk fighters, who fanned out behind him. Naru walked up to Garth, moving with a cold, steady purposefulness as if Garth was nothing more than an insect who would have to be stamped on.

"Get out of here, One-eye."

His voice was a low, rasping rumble that grated.

"This woman is owed a debt from an *oquorak* which one of your cowards skipped out on. Pay her and then we'll leave."

Naru looked over toward Norreen and snorted, his breath coming like a bellows.

His hand shot out like a falling tree, swinging to catch Garth with a crushing blow on his blind side, the fighter not even bothering to waste time conjuring a spell. And yet somehow Garth sensed it coming and ducked low. Even as he ducked he slashed out, his foot catching Naru in the groin.

The giant grunted like a bull, his eyes bulging out of his head so that he looked like a dying codfish. He went down on his knees.

Garth caught him again, kicking him under the chin, knocking Naru over backward. Blood and several teeth sprayed out as the giant toppled to the pavement and was still.

A hoarse gasp arose from the crowd, the few betting on Garth whooping with joy, for even though it had not been a fight of magics, Naru was now flat out on the pavement and the battle was an official win.

With an angry cry, one of the Brown fighters leaped forward, raising his hand at Garth.

A thundering howl seemed to emanate from the Brown's hand, a loud shrieking roar that struck with such intensity that Garth staggered backward even as he raised a protective shield about himself. The sound was blocked within his circle of protection but behind him he could hear the screaming of the mob as the demon howl bowled them over. With a wave of his hand Garth extended the wall of protection to the crowd, many of whom were writhing in agony, blood pouring from ruptured eardrums, so shattering was the scream summoned from the demon realms.

Garth nodded his head and the Brown fighter started to wave his hands around in agony as his *mana* was drained away. The demon howl subsided, Brown still shaking his hand, which now started to glow as if on fire.

Another Brown fighter raised his hands, and then another and behind Garth the crowd started to scatter in every direction.

"To Gray!"

Garth spared a quick glance over his shoulder and saw that Hammen was shouting at the top of his lungs, hobbling back toward Kestha House, from which some fighters were already coming on the run, drawn at first by the excitement of the crowd and now by Hammen's rally cry.

Garth clapped his hands together and then extended them, holding them aloft as if they were claws. Seconds later, even as skeletal forms started to appear around him, conjured by Brown, his own spell took form. Coils of light swirled around him and out of each coil a lumbering bear appeared, snuffling and snarling. Garth shouted a word of command and the four bears charged toward the line of Brown, pausing only briefly to bowl the skeletons over. Several of the Brown broke and ran while another diverted his spell, which he had been aiming toward Garth, and threw it toward a bear, which simply exploded and disappeared. Another bear died from a bolt of lightning from above but short seconds later two of the bears crossed the killing zone, both of them throwing themselves on the Brown fighter who had first attacked Garth and was still distracted by his burning hand.

The Brown fighters turned to help their comrade, throwing spells, but it was already too late as one bear grabbed the fighter by the legs, while the other closed his mouth over the man's head and shoulders, drowning out his shrieks. The two pulled in opposite directions and then ran off with the still-twitching halves of the dead fighter, shaking their heads back and forth so that blood and entrails were scattered across the Plaza.

A wild frenzy now seized the Brown fighters, who all turned their attention back to Garth. His circle of protection was stunned by volley after volley of spells so that he was forced to stagger backward. He saw through the haze of explosions that Norreen, moving as if she was nothing but a blur, had thrown herself into the fray with sword drawn, leaping upon a Brown fighter and dispatching him with a quick slice to the throat. Brown staggered off, both hands clasped to his throat, while the arterial blood sprayed out from between his fingers. With a single fluid motion she was past her first victim, still running, closing in on the next one, stabbing low, catching him in the stomach so that he howled and fell backward. He fumbled to raise an artifact and again her blade slashed out, severing his hand, the glowing artifact tumbling to the pavement. And then the others finally caught her, a black cloud swirling around her. Her eyes went wide with terror and she recoiled backward, flaying with her sword to strike at the invisible terror that engulfed her.

Garth moved to block the spell against her but the volleys from a dozen fighters, some of whom were obviously fifth-rank or better, were too much. Finally he broke his own protection for an instant to strike the terror down that held her and she scrambled away on hands and knees. But the move cost him and he was hit by a terror spell in turn that, for an instant, nearly blinded him with a heart-tearing fear. The Brown fighters, sensing they had the advantage, started to move closer, eager for the kill, several of them conjuring demons to render Garth into pieces.

A flash of light snapped across the square. Seconds later, more were launched, followed an instant later by what looked like an icy storm that extinguished the power of the demons closing in on Garth.

Garth reestablished his own circle of protection, using a healing spell on himself to wash away the fear, and looked to his left. A swarm of Gray fighters were closing in, hands raised, engaging the Bolk fighters, who now turned to face the new assault. From out of the door of the Bolk House more fighters were emerging. Behind him he could hear the familiar high clarion trumpet calls of the Grand Master, his own fighters racing across the Plaza to break up the melee.

Blood started to spill as fighters traded attacks at close range, several of them falling, the victors administering death-blows and then cutting off satchels to claim their prizes, all rules of the fight now lost in the confusion. Garth closed his eyes and raised both hands upward, the spell momentarily draining the power from him.

He opened his eyes again and smiled when atop the Bolk House a giant spider, its bloated body at least four fathoms across, appeared. The spider looked down at the mad melee and saw its opportunity for a feast. Leaning over from the top of the building, its hairy forelegs touched down to the ground and, even as it crawled down the side of the building, it turned its head back and forth, spraying out acidic poison. Fighters, both Brown and Gray, caught unaware, writhed on the paving stones, shrieking in agony, especially when the poison struck their eyes. Garth looked around and saw Norreen, still moving backward from the melee. He raced over to her side.

"Let's go!"

He reached under her shoulder to pull her up. Garth snapped his fingers and a cloud of green smoke concealed them.

He started to run and she struggled to keep up as they joined the edge of the mob, which was now running in every direction, shrieking in terror as dozens of uncontrolled spells swept across the square, the brawl now completely out of control, with fighters simply conjuring and tossing out their denizens to strike at whatever was nearest. Undead moved with shambling steps, several of them holding shrieking citizens of the town aloft in their gray-green hands as trophies. Great serpents, half a dozen fathoms in length and as thick as a man's waist, darted about, looking for someone to bite, several of them wrestling with their victims, one of them already swallowing a still-kicking form. The usual skeletons walked with clattering motions, looking for human flesh to sink their white bony fingers into. Off to one side the two bears were finished with their repast and started to run across the square, looking for another meal. Garth waved his hand, causing them to fall in by his side.

Cursing and shoving, fighters belonging to the Grand Master hit the edge of the fight, some of them turning to take care of the various creatures pursuing the fleeing crowd. One of the fighters turned toward Garth and he released the bears and continued on. Seconds later he heard the shrieks of the fighter who had tried to stop him.

"Master!"

Garth looked over his shoulder and stopped as Hammen shuffled toward him.

The Plaza was chaos, more than forty fighters from each House trading it out in front of Brown's House, the spider, now minus several legs, scrambling about crookedly, holding a writhing Kesthan fighter in its pincer fangs, another struggling form, cocooned in silk, strapped to its back. An explosion erupted atop Bolk's House, tearing off part of the facade, sending a shower of stones into a side street while fires licked from half a dozen buildings farther up the alleyway. The Great Plaza was a sea of confusion as thousands tried to flee while thousands more pushed eagerly forward to watch the fun.

Hammen reached Garth's side and pulled a satchel out from his tunic.

"Where'd you get that?" Garth asked.

"Oh, it belonged to that big chap whom you taught to sing soprano."

Garth spared a quick look inside at the amulets. It was a fabulous haul even if it wasn't quite legal.

"I think we should move out of here," Garth announced, watching as a phalanx of warriors came forward at the run, their crossbows raised. The first line of warriors spread out and started to lob shots at the spider, which merely seemed to enrage the creature even more, so that it turned and started to charge toward them, tossing the Gray fighter aside.

The warriors of the Grand Master who had fired hurriedly placed the front of their weapons on the ground, hooking their feet into the stirrup of the crossbow while they struggled with both hands to cock their weapons. The rest of the phalanx now fired as well, and yet the spider still staggered forward. The reloading crossbow men, to a man, abandoned their efforts and, turning, fled. The phalanx scattered in every direction, Garth, Hammen, and Norreen darting out of the enraged spider's path.

The spider slashed out with its clawed forelegs, knocking men down, crushing them underfoot, and continued to spread its poison, which bubbled and hissed as it struck pavement, metal, leather, and flesh.

Several horsemen came galloping through the crowd, knocking fleeing citizens and crossbow men aside. Directly behind them was a wagon, the driver lashing the team. The driver pulled in hard on his reins, causing the wagon to skid around to a stop. On the back of the wagon a heavy ballista was mounted, manned by a dwarf firing crew, the weapon already cocked. The head gunner peered down the length of the shaft, shouting at his two assistants to wedge the elevation up higher. The spider, seeing the wagon, started toward it. The team of horses shrieked with fright, the driver standing up and hauling in on the reins, struggling to keep the horses from bolting.

The ballista seemed almost to leap into the air as the gunner pulled the lanyard, the heavy bolt shrieking as it rocketed across the Plaza and slammed into the spider.

The stricken beast reared up, a loud cry of pain echoing from it, greenish blood pouring out of its wound as it tumbled over, its legs twitching spasmodically. The cocooned warrior who had been strapped to its back twisted and writhed beside his captor, looking like a great maggot.

"I think the fun's over," Garth said with a smile. "Let's get out of here."

He darted into the swirling mob, still holding Norreen up. She struggled to free herself and he finally let go.

"Just what in the name of all that's holy were you doing back there?" she snapped angrily.

"Helping," Garth said quietly, even as he continued to push her forward. Behind them the crowd roared as an explosion rocked the Great Plaza, followed by the crystalline tinkling of glass shattering from dozens of buildings.

"You weren't there to help me," she snarled. "You were out after something else and you got it."

Garth slowed and looked at her.

"I was there to help you," he said calmly, "and things got out of hand."

"Don't play the game with me; you wanted that fight."

Garth said nothing and continued on.

"I still don't have my honor back from them," she snapped.

Garth looked over at Hammen.

"How much did we make?"

"We've got thirteen gold now," he chortled gleefully. "It was fifteen to one with Naru."

"Let me see."

Hammen, struggling to keep pace with Garth, reluctantly pulled out the coins and handed them up.

Garth turned and offered them to Norreen.

She slapped his hand away, the coins spilling to the pavement. With a loud cry of dismay Hammen scurried about, picking them up, pulling out his dagger and screaming when an urchin snapped one of the rolling coins up and disappeared into the crowd that was swirling about them.

"Money is meaningless; it is honor I was after."

"You still have to eat," Garth snapped hotly, and snatching a coin from Hammen, he forced a gold coin into her palm.

"That will keep you till after Festival. You're now known throughout the city for having the courage to challenge Bolk. People will remember the whole thing started with a Benalish Hero. Just avoid the Grand Master's people; they'll be out after you."

She looked at him coldly and started to raise her fist as if to throw the coin back.

"You have to eat," he said quietly and then, turning, strode away.

"He's mad," Hammen said, shaking his head as he looked up at Norreen.

"He's a bastard," she said softly in reply, a look of confusion in her eyes and then, turning, she disappeared into the crowd.

Hammen scurried to keep up with Garth, ducking low when another explosion erupted, sending debris soaring a hundred or more feet up into the air. The Plaza echoed with explosions and the sharp call of trumpets. From out of the main gate of the Grand Master's palace another column of warriors emerged, running full out, swords and crossbows at the ready. Behind them came a dozen more fighters, the strength of their *mana* evident so that they appeared to glow, spreading spells of protection over themselves and the warriors. In the middle of the column rode the Grand Master. His face was a mask of fury and for a moment he turned his attention toward Garth, who froze in his steps.

Hammen watched him, sensed that somehow Garth, for an instant, did not really appear to be present, as if he had gone shadowy and opaque, like a drawing on smoked glass. The Grand Master stared straight at him for several seconds. Another explosion rocked the far end of the Plaza and the Grand Master stirred, as if awakening from a dream. He turned away, shaking his head as if confused, and rode on toward the widening brawl. Garth was present once more, still walking purposefully.

"A neat spell," Hammen gasped, struggling to keep up with Garth.

"It helps sometimes, especially if the searcher is not concentrating," Garth announced matter-of-factly.

"What now, Master?"

Garth looked back at Hammen.

"Master, is it?"

"After what you pulled off back there. It was beautiful."

"What do you mean?"

"Triggering that fight."

"I didn't do anything," Garth replied.

Hammen hawked and spit in reply.

Crossing the Great Plaza, Garth moved straight toward the

Ingkara House. The front of the House was packed with scores of fighters, who were watching the confusion at the other end of the plaza and roaring with appreciative delight.

Garth moved straight toward them and for a moment they barely noticed that he had crossed the line of paving stones and was now on the semicircle of purple that arced out around their House.

"Hey, a one-eyed Gray. Are you running away?"

Garth turned toward the speaker, who stood laughing.

"I want to join Ingkara," Garth said, his voice cool and even.

Several of the fighters started to laugh and taunt him.

"A little too hot over there, isn't it? Might get hurt. And now you can't go back since you ran."

Even as he turned and started to extend his hands a young Purple fighter, his tunic blackened and singed, came racing up to the crowd. He slowed and, turning, looked at Garth.

"That's him. He's the one that started it!" the new arrival shouted.

The fighter preparing to challenge Garth looked over at the scorched messenger with surprise.

"He started the whole thing. He took down Naru and then fought a dozen of them to a standstill," the young Purple gasped.

Garth's challenger looked around in confusion and Garth made the defiant and self-confident gesture of lowering his hands.

"Naru?" his challenger asked.

"He needs a new set of teeth," the messenger announced excitedly as if he had somehow performed the feat himself, "and he'll have to fish somewhere up under his ribs for what's left of his manhood the way this one-eye kicked him."

The Purple fighters looked first at the messenger and then back at Garth, several of them slowly breaking into grins of delight. The crowd started to part, the fighters lowering their heads in respect as a lean, angular form moved toward Garth, his purple robe made of the richest velvet and covered with heavy rope like coils of gold embroidery.

Garth lowered his head in a respectful manner.

"Jimak, Master of Ingkara," Garth said.

Jimak slowly looked Garth up and down as if examining some minor work of art that he might consider buying if the price was right.

"You bested Naru like Balzark over there said?"

"It is as he said," Garth replied.

"And fought a dozen Browns until help arrived."

"I had some help from a Benalish woman but, in general, yes."

Jimak nodded as if pondering a deep thought.

"Why come to us? I should send you back to Tulan for punishment for breaking the peace of Festival."

"Because if I beat Naru I can beat others and your House will profit. Besides, I am not fully initiated into Gray yet so technically I am free to leave when I please. Those are the rules as you know and frankly I'd prefer to skip the punishment coming out of the little incident over there." He nodded back across the Plaza, which was now wreathed in coiling smoke illuminated by bright flashes of flame.

"I daresay Ingkara now has a couple dozen less fighters to compete against come Festival thanks to my effort and I wish to profit from that. Beyond that you can profit as well, so this could be to our mutual benefit."

Jimak looked haughtily at Garth and then the thinnest of smiles broke his skull-like features.

CHAPTER
5

"BOTH OF YOU SHUT UP!"

Tulan and Kirlen, Master of Bolk, looked over angrily at the Grand Master.

"You might be Grand Master," Tulan said coolly, "but you have no right to address us as if we were your servants."

"I have the right to address you any way I might please," Zarel Ewine replied haughtily. "You are in my city, and both of you, in fact all four of you, should remember that I do know certain things about you that would best not be known by others."

Tulan shifted uneasily. Zarel smiled inwardly. Tulan was a coward who could always be intimidated.

"If you're referring to the massacre of Turquoise, you were the instigator of that," Kirlen replied smoothly, the rings on her bony fingers flashing in the lamplight.

She looked up at him with a cool disdain, leaning heavily on her staff for support. Her face was always disturbing to Zarel, for it was the face of death, the face of a fighter who had extended her life through the use of spells to the very edge, until flesh and bone were held together by the slenderest of threads. Her skin was yellowed, like old rotting parchment, and hung from her skull in loose, wrinkled folds as if it were about to peel away in corruption. There was always a faint smell to her, the smell of moldering graves, decay, and darkness.

Zarel looked at the Brown Master coldly.

"But I am the Grand Master and I did it at the behest of Kuthuman. As for the four of you, no one knows of your parts."

"So go on and tell the mob, I don't give a damn," Kirlen cackled. "Besides, it is ancient history now and those idiots on the street don't give a copper. All they care about is what will happen in the next Festival, so don't threaten us with that old line."

"Did your man break the rules of *oquorak?*" Zarel asked, deciding it was best to shift ground.

"Does it matter? She wasn't even a fighter, just a mere warrior, a Benalish woman at that."

"Duels of magic are supposedly forbidden here," the Grand Master snapped angrily, "but *oquorak* is legal and the mob expects the rules to be observed."

"Are you ruled by the mob?" Tulan sniffed.

"No, damn you. But I've got half a million people living in this city and at least another million pouring in for Festival. If they riot, it's my property that's damaged, my taxpayers who go and get themselves killed. *Oquorak*, at least, keeps them entertained until the Festival, but if it gets out of hand, next thing you know fighters are using magic spells on the street and things get ugly."

"I'll run an inquest into this if that will make you happy," Kirlen finally replied in a bored tone. "Witnesses have to be found and questioned. The Benalish woman has disappeared and so has your One-eye." The Brown Master looked over with a smirk at Tulan.

"Your people murdered him and I expect compensation," Tulan snarled back. "He was one of my best, easily eighth-rank, and a score of your fighters ganged up on him. We couldn't even find the fragments of his body."

Tulan looked back sharply at Zarel.

"You're worried about *oquorak* rules and ignore the fact that one of my best fighters was attacked viciously and murdered."

"He was on our property. He cheated one of my ninth-ranks and worse yet, that man's satchel was stolen."

"If he's still a man," Tulan chuckled.

"Damn you, I want compensation!" Kirlen roared. "My House is damaged, four men and a woman fighter are dead, damaged, or simply devoured so that no spell could revive them, and another score are injured. Nearly a dozen satchels are missing as well, including Naru's, one of my best fighters."

"You started it," Tulan cried angrily, slamming the table before him with his beefy fist. "I lost eight dead and thirty injured and satchels as well. Compensate or by the Eternal I'll burn your House to the ground!"

"Both of you are under injunction!" Zarel shouted.

The two House Masters looked over coldly at the Grand Master.

"No one is to step foot into the street until the beginning of Festival. Anyone leaving your Houses will be arrested, their spells stripped from them, and barred from Festival."

"Try to take my people's spells and you'll have a war," Kirlen snapped, and Tulan nodded in agreement as if the Brown Master was now his closest friend and under attack.

"We'll withdraw from Festival," Tulan announced, and Kirlen looked over at her enemy, who suddenly nodded in agreement.

"If we boycott, you won't have Festival and you won't earn a thin copper on the betting." With that, Tulan snapped his fingers at the Grand Master and laughed.

Zarel looked back and forth at the two, sputtering, unable to speak for a moment, the two moving closer to each other as if all past hatreds were now forgotten.

"Get out, both of you, get out, and so help me if there's another incident, my fighters are ordered to kill on sight! Now get out!"

The two walked out of the room together though as soon as they had cleared the doorway, they fell back into bitter recriminations against each other.

Zarel watched them go, his face purple with anger. Storming over to his desk, he picked up a small bell and rang it. Seconds later a diminutive hunched-over form appeared in the still-open doorway.

"Get in here, damn you."

Uriah walked slowly into the room, head bent low.

"You approached Tulan last night, didn't you."

"As you ordered, Master."

"And?"

"I offered him a hundred gold for the head of One-eye. He didn't even have to turn him over, simply send him out the front door after dark and we'd take care of the rest."

"And his response?"

"He laughed and told me to get out."

"But did he seem willing?"

Uriah nodded.

"I think he was seriously considering it."

"So what happened this morning?"

"Master, he must have slipped out of a secret entry. You know that as quickly as we find one they go and make another. Beneath the Houses there is a warren of tunnels and a watch could not be kept on all that we know, let alone all that we don't know."

"What else did you find?"

"I've sent out inquiries. The Baron of Gish arrives the night before Festival and I shall make sure he's asked if he knows of any fighter who claims to come from his land. All we know about One-eye is that he arrived in the city two nights ago, fought an Orange and killed him, disappeared with a pickpocket, and then appeared at the door of the House of Kestha the following morning."

Zarel sat silent for a moment.

"The pickpocket, do we know who he is?"

"Hammen is his street name. One of the heads of the brotherhoods that control the vice and crime in the city. He's well thought of and has connections."

"Obviously not so well thought of that you couldn't find a traitor."

"Money always talks with that sort."

"How did this Hammen fall in with One-eye?"

"The pickpocket was mastering the fight."

Zarel cursed softly, annoyed at what was an infringement upon his rights, even if it was by a lowly scum out to make a few coppers. Mastering the fights was the sole prerogative of the Grand Master. Even in the old days of Kuthuman and before him the role of the fight master was an honored position. And now pickpockets were presuming to the right.

"Where are they now?"

"They were last seen during the fight this morning and then

disappeared, the same as the Benalish woman. It's believed the three were killed in the fight and their remains devoured or blasted apart."

"Too much of a coincidence that all three would disappear into death like that," Zarel said quietly. "I want more inquiries run. Start with this pickpocket. Send some warriors and fighters to track down his lair. He must have accomplices. Use the usual methods."

"Yes, Master," Uriah whispered.

"Remember, Uriah, either the Gray or you will join the Walker for some entertainment, so do your job. Close and bolt the door on the way out."

Trembling, Uriah withdrew from the room.

Zarel sat in silence for a moment, looking down at his beefy hands, which were folded over his more than ample waist.

What to do?

Again this morning there was the sensing. It had hit him with a terrible urgency when he had first laid eyes upon the one-eye. Now this morning it had come again, when he had first ridden out into the Plaza to put down the fighting. There was a sensing that something terrible was lurking, and for a moment he thought he had found it. And then the sensing had drifted away.

On the eve of Festival far too much was going wrong. The tension had been building for years, he thought. Under Kuthuman, especially in the final years of his quest to pierce the veil between worlds, all had lived in fear of him and his power. After he had become a Walker all still feared him, even more so. And yet he was present but for one day of the year. The old balance of power, between the fighting Houses and the Grand Master, had been a finely tuned one. The Grand Master was not as powerful as the combined might of the Houses, but the Houses, by the very nature of their competitiveness, would never unite against him. In turn he had to keep a semblance of order in the lands so that the *mana* would grow, and to prevent chaos.

Now it was shifting. The Houses were becoming increasingly competitive with each other and against the Grand Master there was increasing defiance. Zarel sensed that by the very nature of the system he had created, the increasing bloodiness of the Festival to satiate the mob and generate even more betting had helped to create this. Yet the increasing number of death fights in the arena served as well to keep the power of the Houses down since each year they lost more and yet more fighters in the fights, thereby sapping their strength.

And there was the other dark dream as well. That ever so slowly he could hoard his own *mana* and in the process one day do as Kuthuman had done and become a Walker in his own right. That was the dark secret, for he knew with a grim certainty that if Kuthuman ever truly understood that part of the plan, he would kill him out of hand and replace him with a new Grand Master. It was a numbing game of plans within plans, the striking of a balance, the keeping of the House Masters off guard, the gathering of the *mana* tribute for the Grand Master, and, above all else, survival.

Somehow he could sense that this One-eye had become a wild card in the deck of the game. It would have to be addressed.

Though he dreaded the thought of it, Zarel now realized that Kuthuman would have to be summoned and told, if only as precaution, and with the hope that he might even know the answer.

Sighing, he finally stood up and walked across the room, stopping before what looked like nothing more than a paneled wall. He raised his hand and the wall slipped back, revealing a small room within. Zarel walked into the middle of the room, stepping into a circle traced in gold, which shone brightly against the jet black rock though there was no torch or lamp present. The hidden door closed behind Zarel and he lowered his head, his hand slipping into his satchel, clutching the bundles of *mana* of all the colors of the rainbow. Shafts of light began to swirl around him, coiling and twisting, rising up in a cone around him.

He waited long minutes in silence, his eyes closed against the brilliance of the unearthly light that bathed him. Finally he sensed the presence coming, as if it were an avalanche racing down the side of a mountain. Zarel Ewine, Grand Master of the Arena and High Baron of the City of Kush, fell to his knees.

The Walker was before him.

"Why summon me?" the voice whispered, filled with annoyance and what might be rage. "Festival is still three days away and I have other things to concern me now."

"It was necessary, my lord," Zarel whispered.

"You are but one of a hundred domains, a hundred planes of existence. I have better things to attend to other than your grovelings. This had better not be frivolous."

"I don't think it is."

"Speak and be quick."

Zarel, in a hurried tone, told him of Garth One-eye and the fighting that seemed to follow in his wake.

The Walker was silent except for the crackling of energy which reverberated like a bell through the room so that Zarel wanted to cover his eyes but dared not.

"The reports are that he is dead, but I think not. I think he is still alive."

"So search for him. Why bother me? Surely you don't expect me to track down this insect."

"No, my great lord. But I have a concern."

"Speak it then, damn you."

"There is something behind this man. I know not what, but it is there. For a brief instant I thought I saw him in the confusion of the riot, but then he wasn't there and I rode on. If that is so, he has powers. I thought long on this and then the connection came. It came to someone else from long ago who had mastery of such a spell and you know of whom I speak."

Zarel sensed a brief instant of hesitation on the part of the Walker.

"If that is so, then find him!"

"I thought, great lord, that . . ."

"Find him and kill him now. I have no time for this. I have other concerns beyond your miserable plane. I will be back for Festival and I expect this to be resolved."

"My great lord . . ."

But the presence was already gone and Zarel sensed that somehow there was a great urgency to his departure, as if a struggle was taking place even as they spoke and that the Walker could not spare a second longer for what to him was a trivial concern.

Exhausted, Zarel sat down in the middle of the circle and

opened his eyes, the only light in the room coming from the gold circle which circumscribed him. He had known but brief glimpses into the realms of his lord and master, the Walker, and knew it was, as were all places, a domain of wars and struggle against others of the highest powers. The glimpses were chilling in their terror and yet seductive in their power, for a fighter could, if he survived long enough, become, one day, a Walker. He could become capable of leaping beyond the myriad planes of existence. In such realms he could gather in *mana* undreamed of, the foundation of the power of all spells and artifacts. In such realms he could, in fact, become immortal and exist for countless aeons until he was at last cast down by another Walker who finally managed to steal his *mana*. There was only so much *mana* in the realm of planes, even though they were rumored to be uncountable. Therefore, a Walker did not care too much for emerging rivals.

Zarel sighed. It was the dream of immortality that was all so seductive. As a wielder of magics he had the ability to extend his own life span significantly, to a millennium or more. But each extension came with a price, and one did slowly age. Until finally the power to extend was nothing more than the insane act of senile old fools who were good for nothing more than sitting in dark shadows and drifting in a world of impotent dreams.

His most implacable foe, Kirlen of Brown, was already becoming such a person, terrified of death and equally terrified of the final lingering. He knew her dream was to destroy him, to become a Grand Master and thus gather enough power to try for immortality. The mere thought of her and her constant plotting aroused a desire yet again to find a means somehow to quietly kill her.

What might she do with this One-eye and what was his plan in all of this? For it was obvious that he must have a plan.

The One-eye was alive and had to be found. It was evident that his game was indeed dangerous to the existing order of things. And if the existing order of things was disturbed, then the Walker would be disturbed. If the Walker was sufficiently disturbed, a new Grand Master could always be found and Zarel realized with a cold certainty that he had to find One-eye before Kirlen got to him first.

*   *   *

"Enter."

Garth One-eye walked calmly into the inner office of the Master of the House of Ingkara, Jimak Ravelth. The House Master looked up, his waspish angular face chiseled by the glare of a single lamp that flickered on the table behind which he sat. The table was strewn with shimmering objects and as Garth drew closer he saw that they were stacks of gold coins, emeralds, blood red rubies, opals the size of cats' eyes, multifaceted diamonds that seemed to explode with light, and cunningly wrought artifacts of metals unknown to this plane of existence.

Jimak looked up at him and smiled, his bloodless lips pulling back so that his face looked like a skull.

"My toys," Jimak said softly, motioning for Garth to come forward and admire them.

The gesture seemed friendly and yet, as Garth approached, he could sense a barrier go up, Jimak leaning forward slightly as if to fling his body over his possessions in order to shield them from the lascivious looks of others.

Garth scanned them, pausing for a moment on the artifacts, and then he shrugged his shoulders as if he was looking at nothing more than pathetic trinkets that a beggar was trying to sell in exchange for a few coppers.

"They're of no concern to me," Garth said evenly.

"That's what some might say, even as they connive to rob me," Jimak replied sharply.

"I'm interested in other things."

"Such as?"

"Power and revenge."

"And both can bring you gold."

"No," Garth said coldly, "the payment is in here," and he pointed toward his heart with a clenched fist.

"Does it concern the eye, is that it?" Jimak asked, licking his bloodless lips with a bloodless tongue.

Garth lifted the black patch that covered his eye and, seized with a perverted curiosity, Jimak held the lamp up to look closely, his breath coming in short, shallow gasps.

"It looks like it was gouged out, not just cut in a fight. Messy, very messy." He licked his lips again.

Garth lowered the flap.

"Works well with women; they recoil at the sight of it," Garth said coldly.

"Women. Who needs them when one has this?" said Jimak, scooping up a ruby and rubbing it lovingly with his clawlike hands.

"The wound has ached for five years, five years I have gone to sleep with the memory of the pain. For five years I have awaked at dawn, the empty socket filled with agony."

"Who did it?"

Garth hesitated for a moment.

"Go on."

"The Grand Master and Leonovit, the cousin of Kirlen, Master of Bolk."

Jimak cackled softly.

"My, my, our vengeance does aim high."

"It was several moons after Festival five years ago. Leonovit and I fought. He had taken my sister against her will. When I started to best him several of his groveling fighters jumped me from behind. I was taken to the Grand Master and charged with breaking the peace and as punishment my eye was taken, my satchel stripped, and I was driven out."

"So now you've come back for revenge."

"Something like that."

"Why didn't anyone remember you today? Naru has served the House of Bolk for decades."

"Do you remember the number of first-rank fighters, who are *hanin* without House, whom you have destroyed or maimed in your time?"

Jimak chuckled softly.

"They are like noisome flies."

"I'm forgotten, but I have not forgotten."

"So why me?"

"Why not? I know you like these things." Garth pointed at the treasure strewn across the table. "I can earn you more. I can earn you more in the arena, I can earn you more in commissions once Festival is done. And I can bring damage to a rival House. I've already done that for you today."

"You betrayed Tulan and the House of Kestha."

"That fat pig?" Garth snorted with disdain.

Jimak looked up at Garth.

"He is a fellow House Master. I should cut your tongue out for that."

"And if you did and offered it to him, he'd devour it uncooked. He is a pig, a man without breeding, disgusting."

Jimak leaned back in his chair and a thin, reedy chuckle escaped him.

Garth reached into his tunic, pulled out a small leather bag, and tossed it on the table.

Jimak stared at it for a moment and then eagerly tore the pouch open. He drew out a single ruby and held it near the lamplight, studying it intently.

"As long as I have the shelter of this House and can wear its livery I have no need for such things. Consider it an offering of respect, a payment to the pension fund for aging fighters who refuse to get themselves killed and out of the way. I should add I do have more, but they are hidden away in a place I alone know. If things work out well, they can be added to the fund in due time."

Jimak, not even bothering to look at Garth, simply nodded his head, his attention still focused on the ruby.

"Exquisite, flawless."

"Are we agreed then?"

"Yes, yes," Jimak said absently. "For the pension fund. You can be initiated on the morning of Festival."

He quickly looked up.

"You said you have more?"

Garth nodded and Jimak, smiling, returned to his examination of the gem. Garth waited for a moment but Jimak said nothing more. Bowing low, Garth withdrew from the room, closing the door behind him. The last sight of the House Master was of him still bent over the lamp, studying the ruby as if it were a book of arcane knowledge containing spells yet unheard of.

"Master."

Garth turned and saw Hammen lingering in the shadows, motioning for him to come over. Hammen pulled Garth into the alcove where he had been waiting.

"While you were resting earlier I decided to take a little walk."

"Fleshpot hunting now that we have money."

"No, damn it. Back to my home. I felt the need to get a little information; after all, I do have a brotherhood to run, even
while I'm out getting in trouble with you. Also, I had this sudden feeling that something terrible had happened."

"What?"

Hammen looked away for a moment, his fists clenching and
unclenching, and then he looked back up, his rheumy eyes
clouded with tears.

"They were all dead. All of them dead."

"What happened?" This time his tone was flat, cold, and
distant.

"The Grand Master. I should have known better. Somehow
I sensed something was wrong when I hit the alley. It was too
quiet, as if even the rats had gone into hiding. The door was
ajar and I went in." He paused for a moment, breathing hard.
"They were all dead.

"Rico, Matu, Evanual, old legless Nahatkim, all of them
dead. My other brothers gone. I hope they escaped but somehow I know they didn't and were taken. Those they left
behind were tortured and their heads cut off and . . ." His
voice trailed off.

"You were chased?"

Hammen nodded.

"Someone came in the door behind me. I darted to the back
of our shack, going down our sewer hole."

"I can smell that."

"I made my way back here, but I think they followed me. I
tried to lose them in the sewers. I finally had to come back
here, coming out where I knew there was an entry into this
House. They were closing in."

Garth nodded slowly.

"Damn you, why did you come back?" Hammen snarled
angrily.

Garth looked around and then pulled Hammen deeper into
the alcove.

"I don't know what you mean," Garth whispered.

"You know damn well what I mean. My friends, all of them
dead because of you."

"You're mistaken. I don't know what you're talking about,"

Garth said quietly. "But let me ask this. You've lost friends before, haven't you?"

Hammen looked up at Garth, the tears streaking down his filthy cheeks, tracing twin lines of white.

"Yes, long ago, another life. I tried to forget and they went to the land of the dead, where I thought they all would stay."

He looked up angrily at Garth.

"None of us can forget."

"And now they're dead."

Garth reached out and put a gentle hand on Hammen's shoulder.

"Believe me, Hammen, if I had known your friends were in danger, I would have done something. I didn't think the arm of the Grand Master would reach that far. Something is pushing him and he is acting. I expected that, but not that he would reach toward you."

"Through me he reached you nevertheless."

"I think something needs to be done," Garth said coldly and, grabbing hold of Hammen, he started down the long corridor. "The pot needs to be stirred a bit more."

"What do you mean he's alive?"

Tulan spit out the half-chewed hunk of boiled squid that he had been working on and picked up a goblet of wine.

"Just that," Uriah said quietly. "He's alive."

"Impossible. Brown claims they killed him and several of my people saw him explode in a cloud of green smoke."

"Could the smoke not have been a masking spell?"

Tulan tossed down the wine and slammed the goblet on the table, the fine crystalline stem shattering.

"We spotted his servant, who was reported dead as well. If he is alive, then I think that until we find a body, we must assume that One-eye is alive."

Tulan tossed the broken goblet to the floor, cursing as he sucked on a cut to his grease-coated finger.

"Then if he's alive, where is he?"

"We think with Jimak."

"Purple! Those lowborn scum." Tulan roared with laughter and slapped his thigh.

"I'd sooner cut my own throat or, worse yet, starve to death before I'd go to those maggot-born scum."

"Nevertheless, we think he's there."

Tulan suddenly grew serious.

"Why?" he asked softly as if talking to himself.

"Precisely. I think it safe to assume you wouldn't have punished him for what happened today. Rather you'd reward him."

"Damn right. One against twelve, and on top of that rearranging Naru's jewels the way he did. Damn, he'll be a wonder in the arena."

"But he deserted you. You gave him shelter, removed from him the onus of being a *hanin*, and this is how he pays you back."

Tulan nodded meditatively.

"So what is his game?" Uriah asked.

Tulan looked across the table at the diminutive servant of the Grand Master.

"You figure it out," Tulan snapped. "Now get out."

"I think you know that there's a price of five hundred gold on his head if it is brought in not attached to his body. Bring him in alive and stripped of his powers and the price is doubled. That's far more than you'd make in an open wager on him in the arena."

"Is that a bribe offer?"

"No, just a straightforward business arrangement. He's no longer of your House, so he's fair game. If you should kill him, the money's yours."

"I thought there was an injunction against members of one House killing another in this city except in the Festival arena."

Uriah nodded as if presented with a serious dilemma.

"Rules, as always, can be bent."

"The Walker, I suspect, would not be amused to hear that."

"He is somewhere else," Uriah said, his voice suddenly nervous, "and we are here, and what is not said when he arrives is of no concern."

Uriah paused for a moment.

"And do remember, this One-eye has humiliated you. He wore your colors and then shucked them off for another.

Would you let it be said that one of your fighters could walk away thus without consequences?"

Uriah's words struck home and Tulan brought his fist down on the table, sending the bowl of boiled squid flying end over end, the squid splashing out onto the table and floor.

"Have your money ready. I expect to collect it. The question is, as long as I bring him in, will any questions be asked about my methods?"

"None."

"Then have the money ready by Festival morning."

CHAPTER
6

"WHAT ARE YOU DOING, MASTER?" HAMMEN hissed, his voice near to breaking with fear.

"Just shut up and do as I tell you to do."

"You mean go back there?" He pointed nervously down the alleyway.

"Precisely, now move."

"This is madness."

"Chances are they still have someone watching this place in the hope that you might be so stupid as to come back again."

"Only an idiot would do that, so don't insult me."

"You might have treasure hidden. They know you didn't have enough time to get it the first time, so maybe you'll venture it again."

"There is treasure hidden," Hammen said quietly.

"Good. So we'll get it back. Now get moving."

Hammen let out a slight yelp when Garth's dagger poked him in the backside, sending him out into the middle of the alleyway. Hammen turned as if to go back, but Garth's angry stare stopped him.

"So help me," Hammen whispered while rubbing his injured parts. "I quit."

"Is that official as of now?" Garth hissed. "Because if so, they've already seen you. Now get moving or I'll leave you."

Hammen, muttering a curse, started down the alleyway, moving furtively through the shadows, stepping lightly over the piles of offal, and hoping against hope that the Grand Master's people were not still there. But again there was that sense, the street far too quiet. And he knew.

He wanted simply to try and run on past what had once been his hiding place, hoping that they would not recognize him and thus let him pass. But that was madness. They knew. They had seen him once, and they knew.

He reached the door and quickly opened it as Garth had ordered. Cursing, he stepped in, darting to one side as he did so.

The blow barely missed him, the club brushing within inches of his face. Screaming, Hammen dived backward, ducking under the table. As he rolled under the table he bounced up against something cold and stiff. It was his old friend Nahatkim; he could tell by the missing legs. His hand fumbled over the place where a head should have been, sticking in the congealed slime of blood.

At least he had the advantage in the total darkness. He felt a hand reaching past him, and with a quick grab, took hold and bit down hard, nearly severing the man's finger. The hand jerked back, a loud howling filling the room. Hammen scurried out from under the table, moving toward the sewer bolt-hole in the back of the room. *The demons take Garth*, he thought. *I'm getting out*.

He reached the hole and dived into it headfirst . . . and straight into a hammerlike blow that sent his senses reeling.

Through a haze of pain and nausea he felt hands grabbing him from behind, pulling him out, while the man who had been waiting in the sewer laughed cruelly, striking him in the face yet again for the fun of it.

Pulled out of the hole, he was thrown down on the floor and a light was struck, a lamp flaring up.

His vision blurred, Hammen looked up at two leering faces. Though they were dressed in filth-stained leather, he knew these were not two simple thieves . . . they were warriors of the Grand Master, their well-fed faces looking down at him, laughing.

One of them leaned down and held a bleeding hand before him and then struck him again across the face.

"Don't kill him yet," the other hissed. "I want him when we're done."

"When we're done," another voice said. Through eyes that were starting to swell shut Hammen saw three more men come into the room, all of them obviously magic-wielding fighters, all three of them dressed in the multihued tunics of the Grand Master.

The three moved across the room, looking around disdainfully, one of them covering his nose with a scented handkerchief.

"Is it the same one?"

"I think so," the one in the center replied. "Get him to talk. Find out exactly where One-eye is."

The warrior with the bleeding hand snicked a dagger out of his belt and held it close to Hammen's face.

"Can I start with the eyes?" he hissed softly.

"I don't care. Just don't cut his tongue out or kill him."

For an instant Hammen wasn't sure if the flash of light was blindness descending upon him or not. Then he heard the high, keening scream and felt the heat. There were more screams and the heat started to build, followed an instant later by a cool blast of air.

Hammen looked around the room, which was blurred and hazy, and it took him a moment to realize that he was in fact wrapped in a circle of protection while the rest of the room blazed with a white-hot intensity. His five tormentors rolled back and forth, shrieking, trying to beat out the flames that engulfed them.

Though the shield protected him from the heat, the scent of burning flesh still wafted through and he suppressed a gag. The five started to become still, curling up into tight, charred balls so that they looked like blackened dolls. The fire winked out as if the room had been washed with a blast of rain. Through the smoke he saw Garth emerge, a cold look of fury still in his eye.

The circle of protection vanished.

"Are you all right?"

"Not really, damn it. I think I lost a tooth."

"I had to make sure they all came in. I knew they wouldn't hurt you too much until then. I'm sorry."

Garth laid his hands on Hammen's temples and the pain washed away. He felt for a moment as if he were floating. He closed his eyes and then reopened them. His vision was again clear.

"Were they the ones who attacked you before?"

"I think so."

Garth nodded, looking around the room.

"I'm sorry your friends' bodies had to be burned like that."

"I don't think they really cared one way or the other," Hammen replied coldly. "Besides, the pyre had some curs on it to be their servants in the land of the dead; it was fitting." He paused for a moment. "Thank you."

"It served my purpose."

"I think it was more than that," Hammen said, and Garth mumbled a soft curse and stood up.

"You want to collect your treasure? I think we better get moving. The fireball caught them by surprise, but it'll draw attention. There'll be others here in a moment, maybe more than I can handle."

Hammen stepped over a charred corpse and went up to the fireplace. Reaching up inside, he pushed a brick aside, pulled out a heavy bag, and tucked it into his tunic. He started back across the room and then paused. He pulled the bag out again, opened it, fished out four gold coins, and quickly tossed them on the four corpses of his friends.

"For the ferryman," he said to Garth almost as if apologizing.

"Let's go. Someone's coming," Garth replied, moving away from the door and toward the back of the room. Hammen followed him, pausing for a moment to spit on one of the corpses of fighters and then went down the bolt-hole, Garth following.

"Take us toward the Fentesk House."

"Why there?"

"Don't you think they'll cover the paths toward Ingkara?" Garth asked, and Hammen grunted in agreement.

Choking from the fumes, Garth followed Hammen through the stygian darkness, cursing as the sewage washed up over the top of his boots and poured down inside to squish between his toes.

"I can't see you," Garth whispered.

"Then strike a light."

Garth pulled his dagger out of its sheath and held it aloft. An instant later it started to glow softly. He looked around and a chill washed over him. The sewer walls were dripping with slime. They passed a narrow side channel and the sound of rats echoed from it as they scurried away from the light. Garth looked up the narrow pipe and saw cold eyes glowing. Hammen moved with a swift ease, turning one way and then the other, and Garth stumbled to keep up. And all the time the chill cut deeper into him. The walls seemed to crowd inward like nightmare memories in a dream from which he could not awaken. Hammen turned and looked back.

"Garth?"

Garth, startled, looked up but said nothing.

"What is it, boy?"

Surprised, Garth looked at him closely, struggling to control the shaking that racked his body. And as he looked at him there was somehow a sensing. It was in the old man's rheumy eyes.

The nightmare drew in closer, as if now to consume his very soul. Garth sagged against the sewer wall, the dagger lighting his way waning to a mere flicker.

"Garth. What is it?"

"I don't know. I don't know."

Hammen came up and, reaching out, grabbed him by the arm as if to hold him up.

"No, don't take me. I want to go back!" Garth cried, struggling as if to break away, but his movements were weak, feeble, as if all strength had been drained away.

"Garth!"

Garth looked at him, his eyes wide.

"I want to go back!"

Garth stiffened, a gasp escaping him, and he doubled over for a moment as if he was about to vomit. He finally looked back up, his features drawn as if he were emerging from a fevered dream.

"What did you say?"

Hammen was silent for a moment.

Garth pushed Hammen away and the dagger glowed brightly again.

"Let's go," Garth said huskily, even as he wiped his eyes as if to sweep away what he had just seen, his hand coming away wet with tears.

"Galin?" Hammen's voice was barely a whisper.

Garth looked back at him.

"What did you say?" His voice was quiet.

Hammen was silent and then he shook his head sadly.

"Nothing, Master, nothing. Anyhow, there's a sewer cover just ahead that comes out behind Fentesk House."

Hammen turned up into a narrow pipe that was so small Garth had to bend over and crawl on hands and knees. His breath was labored, coming in short, grunting bursts, the sweat beading down his face even though the sewer was chilled and damp like a tomb.

Hammen finally stopped and pointed up. Garth came up beside him, looked up, and saw the grating overhead. He stood up and slowly pushed the grating aside and peered out.

He pulled himself out and then, leaning over, reached down and hoisted Hammen up out of the darkness.

"Now where?"

"I don't think going back to Purple is a wise idea at the moment," Garth said quietly, even as he led Hammen over into the shadows opposite Fentesk House. He stopped at a small fountain and pulled off his boots, rinsing them out and then putting them back on, splashing water on his tunic and trousers to wipe off the filth. Hammen watched him and said nothing.

"They traced you back there," Garth finally continued. "A report must have been turned in. And now, after our bit of revenge, they'll swarm over it."

"Thank you, Master," Hammen whispered.

"For what?" Garth replied sadly. "If it hadn't been for me, your friends would still be alive."

"You couldn't have known it would happen."

"I should have."

"But anyhow, for the shadows of my friends I thank you."

"Shut up."

"What happened back there?" Hammen nodded back toward the sewer grating they had just crawled out from.

"A spell, I guess," Garth said hurriedly. "Now let's go."

"To where?"

"To Fentesk, where else?"

"Damn it, Master, not again."

Ignoring him, Garth stepped out of the shadows and strode toward the front of the building.

"I demand that you open up your door and submit to a search!"

Jimak peered out through the small hatch set in the middle of the heavily bolted doorway into the House of Ingkara.

"You have no authority."

Uriah peered up at the door, the dwarf fighter standing defiant and a flicker of light starting to swirl around him.

"I have eighty-nine fighters in here," Jimak said coldly. "If you try anything, I guarantee you that when they are finished parts of your body will be raining down on this city for the next three days."

Uriah hesitated for an instant and then looked over his shoulder.

"Open up, Jimak."

The Master of Ingkara could not conceal his surprise that the Grand Master himself was outside the door. He had ignored the midnight summons to the palace but the fact that the Grand Master would then lower himself to come to the House of Ingkara in the hour before first bell was simply astonishing.

"I'll not open up for you or anyone else," Jimak replied. "You are breaking all the covenants of the Houses by appearing here and demanding a search."

"Jimak, you know I have enough strength with my own fighters to take your House. They're waiting just around the corner for my orders to blast their way in."

Jimak turned his head away, spit, and then looked back.

"And three other Houses will storm your palace before daybreak. We might hate each other, but we'll always stand against you if you attempt to break us."

"The same as with the Turquoise House?" the Grand Master whispered.

Jimak looked over his shoulder and then back at the Grand Master.

"That was different. Besides, they wouldn't ally with you against me."

"And this is different as well. Now open up; I'll come in alone. I lose face standing out here like this and I intend to regain it one way or the other. Now open up."

Jimak hesitated for a moment and then stepped back, nodding to two of his fighters to remove the heavy beam that blocked the door. The Grand Master slipped through and the door slammed shut behind him.

"If I'm not back outside by first bell, this place will be a smoking ruin," the Grand Master said haughtily.

"Are you that afraid for yourself?"

"I just wanted you to know how things stand. As for fear, I think there's reason enough for all of us to be afraid right now."

Jimak motioned for the Grand Master to follow him down the corridor and into his office, closing the door behind them.

"Now what is it?"

"How come you ignored my summons to appear before me?" the Grand Master snapped angrily.

"At midnight? I don't give a damn if it was the Walker himself who commanded it. I am a House Master and I don't answer a summons like that from anyone."

"Well, please excuse me if I didn't send a sedan chair over along with a phalanx of scantily clad women to throw flowers in your path, but it was urgent."

"Those types of inducements are meaningless to me," Jimak replied coldly. "Try them on Varnel—it'd work with him."

The Grand Master settled into a chair without waiting for Jimak to offer the hospitality.

"Listen to me. We are a balance to each other. I rule this city and this land but my power is balanced not only by the princes of neighboring realms but also by the four Houses of magic fighters. No one of us is truly over the others. I am stronger than any two of you put together and you, if united, are stronger than I. We all know the game and we all play it. You are divided by your mutual rivalries and I insure that those rivalries continue. It is thus because the Eternal created it thus when the world was young and the power of the *mana* was fresh. But we must live here for our entire lives and the Walker comes but once a year to Festival."

"Why are you boring me with this lecture?" Jimak interrupted.

"Because I am leading up to something. I fear that there is some new factor at play here, the same as what happened twenty years ago."

"Oor-tael?" Jimak said quietly.

The Grand Master nodded.

"We destroyed them for their defiance of the wishes of the Walker."

"He was merely a Grand Master then," Jimak snapped, "so stop speaking of him in such reverent tones. He wanted to pierce the veil between worlds and frankly I didn't give a good damn whether he did or didn't. My tribute of *mana* was simply to get him out of my life and I'm glad he left. The only problem is that he chose you to be the new Grand Master."

"And it should have been you, is that it?"

Jimak smiled coldly.

"No one of you four House Masters would have tolerated such a rise for a rival. As for the power of my post, Tulan is too cowardly, Varnel too consumed with fleshly pleasures, and Kirlen, she simply desired it too much."

"And I am too hated by the others, is that it?" Jimak snapped.

"Something like that," Zarel said smoothly.

"So you won the honor instead. The toady gets the reward."

Zarel bristled.

"I did my job in his service and he rewarded it."

"And you call the way you run things now as being better. At least under Kuthuman he was so preoccupied with his quest that he did not rule us too heavily as long as we cooperated. But you, you've corrupted the Festival for the sake of the mob, which wants more blood and yet more. I lost four good fighters in the arena last year and two more crippled beyond repair so that all they're good for is keeping watch by some merchant's door. How many death matches will you have this year to increase the betting?"

"I need money. It is that simple, and the mob bets more when there is blood at stake. Besides, your fighters desire it such as well for revenge against a rival and the hope of winning an entire satchel in a fight rather than a single spell. With such a fight they can gain in a moment what would take years upon years of labor and study."

"And for what do you need this money? The buying of *mana*

on the black market? The bribing of princes for the *mana* of my fighters who ever increasingly die of mysterious causes while out on contract with a claim that their satchels were lost? You wish to be a Walker yourself, isn't that it?"

Zarel smiled.

"If that should ever happen, who would succeed me? Uriah, a hunchbacked dwarf? No one would follow him. Who would succeed?"

"So you imply that it could be me then."

"Why not?"

"And you have undoubtedly offered it to the others."

"I'm not so much of a fool as to encourage them to think thus."

Jimak snorted disdainfully.

"Of course you'd offer the same to them. Don't take me for an idiot. You'll play us off against each other."

Zarel laughed coldly.

"I might offer it to the others but would I be telling the truth to them? I already told you my reasons why the others aren't worthy of consideration, but you are."

He paused.

"If you cooperate."

Jimak laughed, shaking his head, but Zarel could see that his words had hit the mark. Jimak viewed the other three Masters with contempt and he would find it inconceivable that they might rise above him if Zarel should ever manage to pierce the veil. That is, if he could do it without the Walker finding out first.

Jimak nodded as if he had been granted information that was to be believed. *But suppose*, he thought, *suppose I could betray this man to the Walker just before he did try his move or somehow bring him down? Then it would be I who was the new Grand Master, for he was right in that Uriah was not even to be considered for the post. Then I, in turn, could make my final move.*

Zarel smiled as he watched Jimak's features, sensing all that he was now thinking.

"You came here for other reasons as well," Jimak finally said.

"Because there is something wrong here. This One-eye."

Jimak snorted and smiled.

"He's created problems for you, hasn't he?"

"It is more than that."

"I heard a rumor that three of your fighters now look like burned toast," Jimak chuckled. "Is that why you are here?"

The Grand Master bristled.

"You know the law. Your killing of each other on my streets outside of the arena is crime enough. The killing of my own fighters is a capital offense."

"And it happens every year anyhow. Our fighters are high-spirited. You really can't expect us to contain over three hundred fighters in the days before Festival. Killings are bound to happen. Old rivalries, old grudges can't be contained."

"This is different. Think of it. Wherever this man has walked chaos follows in his wake."

Jimak chuckled.

"And Brown and Gray are bleeding from it."

"And you were next."

Jimak paused, saying nothing.

"His trail led straight back here. At first I was tempted to storm this House to get him out, especially when you lied and said he was not here."

"It was not a lie," Jimak said coldly. "I searched for him after your summons, though admittedly to reward him. But he's gone."

The Grand Master nodded.

"That is what I finally realized. That is why this place is not engulfed in flames. Don't you see he is setting us against each other and playing our mutual hatreds to some advantage? What he did was the perfect setup for you and me to be at each other's throats, me thinking that you were lying about his whereabouts, and you defending your honor."

Jimak said nothing.

"He is not here then?" the Grand Master asked, his voice a hoarse whisper.

Jimak nodded as if he were barely paying attention, his thoughts someplace else.

"Fine then."

The Grand Master stood up again.

Jimak suddenly looked up at him.

"Why?"

"Why? I'm not sure. I have my suspicions but I'm not sure and I don't want to voice them till I know. According to the laws of the guilds if he is wearing a color, I cannot take him. Though I know he murdered three of my fighters tonight, I have no witnesses and thus no proof. Any of you Masters can resist me in taking him. But I want him and, I should add, the Walker wants him."

Jimak shifted uncomfortably.

"And what is the offer?"

"Five thousand gold and no one will ever know that you gave him to us."

"Are you that afraid of him?" Jimak asked, his voice edged with sarcasm.

The Grand Master paused and then finally nodded his head.

Jimak lowered his head and thought of the ruby that even now was in his lockbox, balancing the two against each other.

"Ten thousand," he finally whispered.

The Grand Master smiled.

"I must assume the topic of their conversation is me," Garth said quietly.

Varnel Buckara, Master of Fentesk, stretched languidly and nodded in agreement as he dismissed the messenger who had observed the Grand Master's nocturnal visit.

"I suspect that another messenger will come here with an offer," Varnel finally said.

"And?"

"It depends on the offer."

"It might be good enough for the moment—but for the future?" Garth replied.

"Explain, One-eye."

"The offer to Jimak is easy enough and that is why I left his service. Too consumed with his lust for gold. Such men are easily bribed. Perhaps even Tulan of Kestha can be bribed with an endless supply of some rare delicacy or wine. I've heard that for you it is women."

Varnel chuckled.

"According to some sources, you have fifty right here in this House."

"More, far more."

Garth smiled.

"So what can he offer you? Another woman."

"There's always the exotic. Each is different."

"And each is the same. Beyond that gold does not talk, nor does food. But a woman, especially one coming from the hands of the Grand Master . . ."

"Put that in the plural. It would take far more than one."

"All right then. How could you trust them?"

"I'm not interested in trust," Varnel laughed coldly. "I've never been that foolish and any man who is should be drowned as a mercy killing."

"Trust or not, you would have someone whom the Grand Master had first laid hands upon and I daresay to take his leavings would be rather distasteful."

"Virgins, my good man, virgins."

"And they can still be handled," Garth replied. "Beyond that, you would never know what enchantment they had been placed under. A hairpin into the base of your skull while you are lost in your ecstasy, a spy in your House to send information back to the Grand Master, perhaps even a gossip planted with the rest of your women to make them turn against you. More than fifty women are difficult enough to manage in the best of times."

Varnel grunted softly, a troubled look crossing his features, and Garth smiled.

"So do you have a better offer?"

"I do not traffic in women," Garth said coldly, a flash of indignation evident in his tone. "But I do traffic in winning."

"Which reminds me," Varnel rumbled. "You did kill one of my men."

"If he was stupid enough to be killed like that in a street fight, then he was worth little to you. Your honor would be more than restored by having me wear your colors. Though money is meaningless to you, what I will win for you in the arena can buy many pleasures, pleasures, I should add, that would be untainted by the hand of the Grand Master."

Varnel nodded slowly in agreement and then looked over at Garth.

"You did, however, betray both Tulan and Jimak. Am I next?"

"Tulan is a pig and Jimak sick with greed. Given the way things currently stand between me and the Grand Master, I felt here at least I would be protected by a color that would not sell me."

"You may wear Orange."

"Thank you, my lord."

"And if you betray me in turn, I promise you death will be a pleasurable release by the time I am done with you."

"But of course, my lord."

Bowing low, Garth retired and as the door closed he caught a quick glimpse of several naked forms coming into the room from a hidden doorway, a low grunt of expectation rumbling from Varnel as the door finally closed to guard his secret pleasures.

"I think, Master, that this move was foolish."

Garth said nothing as Hammen came up beside him.

"You changed your clothes but obviously you didn't wash," Garth replied.

"One bath a year, whether you need it or not, is good enough for any man."

As they walked down the corridor to the House barracks Garth looked around warily. Second bell had just sounded and the fighters were starting to awaken. As he passed he could hear the whispers behind him. Stopping to ask a guard for directions, the two went down a long flight of stairs, their noses soon guiding them to the feasting room.

Men and women fighters were already gathered around some of the tables. Garth went to a corner table, motioning for Hammen to follow.

"Master, I don't see any servants eating here."

"You're eating here; now go cut me some meat."

Garth settled down on a stool, leaning back so that his back was pressing against the cool stone wall. A moment later Hammen returned, bearing two plates weighed down with slices of roasted pork, and two heavy goblets of wine.

Garth pulled out his dagger and, cutting off a slice, he chewed on it slowly while watching the room.

More and yet more fighters were coming in and all were turning to look at him. A low buzz filled the room.

"I think there's going to be trouble," Hammen said softly.

"Are you worried?"

"After what you've put me through, yes, I'm worried. The entire House is in here."

"Eat your meat and be quiet."

Garth cut another piece of pork and chewed. The food was not as good as Kestha's. Tulan's culinary obsession was reflected in how his own fighters ate as well, but it was far better than what he had been used to over the years.

He ate in silence, watching the men and women who were now supposed to be his comrades. One of them finally stirred from his table, his stool falling over so that it clattered on the floor, and the room went silent. The fighter made a casual show of adjusting his satchel and walked toward Garth.

"Master."

"Shut up."

The fighter came up to the table, and several more rose from the same table and fell in behind him.

"Only fighters may eat here," the man grumbled. "Servants and scum eat in the cellar."

Hammen started to stand up as if to leave.

"Sit down, Hammen."

Hammen looked over at him.

"Not again," he whispered.

"I like his company," Garth said, cutting another piece of meat and then chewing on it as if the conversation was finished.

"Get out of here, cur!" the man snarled, and he grabbed hold of Hammen by his collar and started to pull him away.

Garth looked up and the man let go of Hammen with a howl of pain.

"No magics!" someone shouted, and a lean, angular woman with flowing red hair came up and the others stepped back slightly at her approach. Garth looked at her, sensing that here without doubt was a ninth- or tenth-rank fighter who commanded authority over the others.

"No magics within this House against those of your color," she snarled angrily.

Garth fixed her with his gaze.

"Then tell him to keep his hands off my man."

The woman stood silent, hands resting lightly on her hips.

"You think you're quite the fighter, don't you, One-eye?"

"I get by."

"If you want to get by in this House, then live by its rules. No magic is used against another of your color except in practice."

"And the rights of my satchel and my property are to be respected. That man is my property."

Hammen snorted disdainfully and fixed Garth with a malevolent gaze.

"He's the one who killed Okmark in that street fight," someone shouted from the back of the room.

"He was a fool to challenge a *hanin* that he didn't know anything about and the death challenge was his offering, not mine," Garth replied sharply. "Besides, he was an embarrassment to the House of Fentesk."

An angry murmur swept through the room.

"I think I need to take a walk," Hammen whispered, and he started to stand up.

"Stay where you are," Garth snapped, and Hammen froze in his place.

"I heard you beat Naru," the woman said.

"Yes."

"Think you can beat me?"

He looked up at her and grinned.

"Care to try?"

With a mock sincerity she bowed, holding both hands outward in the ritual display of a fighter accepting challenge.

Garth made a show of cutting another piece of meat and chewing on it before finally standing up, extending his hands and bowing as well.

The woman led the way out of the feasting hall, Garth following. There was a clatter of stools and excited shouts as the other fighters fell in behind them. Ascending the stairs out of the hall, the woman turned left, going down a corridor paneled with a dark rich wood, and lit by high stained glass windows set into the ceiling so that the hallway was awash with color. Reaching the end of the hallway, she flung open the doors to a circular room a dozen fathoms across, the walls lined with benches, which were quickly filled by the other fighters of the house. The arena was occupied by half a dozen fighters, who were going through their morning exercises of weapons practice with lance, dagger, and throwing spikes. At the far end of the room several other pairs of fighters were sparring with spells, one of them struggling to use a team of goblins against his opponent's dwarven warriors.

"Clear the arena," the woman snapped.

The sparring fighters looked up and an instant later their minions disappeared into smoke and they withdrew.

The woman stepped out into the circle.

"Rules of the House. No fire, no creature of disease, and no spell which can go out of control or damage the House."

"Is this match a mere testing, a wager of spell, or to the death?" Garth asked as if the answer really didn't matter one way or the other.

"You know the answer to that," she snapped. "Unless we have permission of the Master, it can only be a testing."

"Well, do you have the Master's permission?"

She smiled softly.

"Not yet."

"Then a testing."

Garth stepped into the neutral box at the far end of the arena while his opponent stepped into hers.

Garth waited until another fighter stepped forward as circle master and held his hands up.

The two bowed to him, then to each other, and then back to the circle master. He clapped his hands three times and on the third clap jumped back. Like a panther the woman leaped into the area and, as she did so, Garth reeled from the impact of a psionic blast that flayed the strength out of his body. He staggered forward, knowing that the spell was so powerful that it would in fact harm her as well, though the damage he would receive was far worse.

An approving crying of awed respect rose up from the spectators at the audacity of her move.

Garth finally waved his hands, erecting a barrier of protection to block the attack, thus conceding the offensive to her. Within seconds she drew upon yet more *mana* and wolves appeared to either side of her and a small host of goblins materialized in the middle of the arena. All rushed toward him.

An icy shadow filled the middle of the arena and there was a great rushing of air and a loud trumpeting.

A great mammoth stood in the middle of the fray, its feet trampling down the goblins. The wolves paused in their headlong rush toward Garth, recoiling and cringing against the side walls of the arena as the mammoth thundered, its heavy trunk flaying about to snatch up the last of the goblins.

There was another swirling cloud and out of it hundreds of rats emerged. Their hot red eyes gleaming with hunger, they swarmed toward the mammoth, leaping upon its legs, sinking their yellow razor teeth into it. More and yet more clawed their way up its sides, clinging to its heavy coat and burrowing in.

The great beast shrieked in pain, and Garth, mercifully, raised his hand and the creature disappeared. The rats that were clinging to it tumbled to the ground, dazed. And then they started to look around for something else. As if driven by a single hand they charged toward Garth and then as suddenly stopped. They turned and started back toward the woman and then paused, slowly turning back toward Garth.

The two wrestled, laying spell upon spell to control the rats, who weaved back and forth, while the wolves cowered and stayed out of the fight. First one way, and then the other, the rats were driven back and forth. Some of them started to collapse, twisting and kicking from the stress of the powers swirling around them.

The struggle continued for long minutes so that the arena pulsed and glowed from the power, neither fighter pulling in other spells, both attempting to control the rats as a singular demonstration of their ultimate power over the other. A hazy glow started to build up around the two, flickering with flashes of light, becoming so bright that those who sat nearest to them had to turn their heads away.

Suddenly there was an audible pop, not quite an explosion but rather a caving in. The rats turned and swarmed straight at Garth.

He lowered his head and stepped back into the neutral square. Still the rats came toward him and he stood with arms at his side. Even as the first of the rats started to leap toward his throat, the woman raised her hand and they disappeared. A loud cheer went up from the assembly.

Garth stepped back into the arena and bowed low at the waist. The circle master stepped back into the fighting area.

"Win to Varena of Fentesk."

Again there was loud cheering and Garth straightened as she approached him.

"Good fight," she said quietly.

"Good fight."

Garth started toward the exit, ignoring the crowd of Fentesk fighters that pushed around him, laughing, going up to Varena. Hammen stood to one side.

"So how much did we lose?"

Hammen smiled.

"Nothing?"

"If you beat her, I really don't think you would have gotten out of here alive and that would have included me. She was obviously a favorite and if she had not intervened, you would have had to fight them all over that man you killed the other night."

Garth looked over at Hammen and said nothing as they left the arena.

A hand came to rest on his shoulder and he turned back to look.

"Good fight, One-eye."

"You're an excellent challenge."

"We need to soak; come with me," she invited, pointing toward a narrow flight of stairs. He followed her down, the air becoming damp and hot. They stepped into a small, dimly lit room filled with steam. The room was lined with alcoves; inside of each of them was a hot bubbling pool. Varena looked over at Hammen and stared at him pointedly.

"Hammen, either it's in the pool or take a walk," Garth announced.

"I'll walk," Hammen said, a bit of a leer lighting his features and he disappeared back up the stairs.

"He really does stink, you know."

"It's his way."

"And you don't smell so good yourself."

"I had a little adventure last night and haven't had a chance to completely wash off."

Varena casually untied the cincher around her waist and

pulled her tunic off over her shoulders. Garth found it difficult to ignore what he was seeing. He had assumed her to be almost boyish in figure, but realized now that the tunic had been deceiving. Next she stepped out of her trousers and loincloth as if he wasn't even present and, folding her clothes up, she placed them on a stone bench, though she made a point of taking her satchel with her as she walked into one of the alcoves. Stepping down into the circular pool, she stretched out and floated, sighing with contentment, resting her satchel on the edge of the pool.

Garth hesitated for a moment, then undressed and, like her, took his satchel with him. He then walked through the swirling steam and into her alcove.

"Am I invited?"

She sat up and nodded.

"Just pull the curtain shut."

Doing as ordered, he stepped down into the pool and stretched out beside her. Hot bubbles swirled up around him, smelling slightly of sulfur, and he let them massage the tension out of his muscles.

"That fight was a sham," she finally said.

He looked over at her for the first time. She was sitting up on a bench in the water so that her body was fully exposed from the waist up.

He sat across from her.

"What makes you think that?"

"Every counter you placed upon the rats was just barely stronger than mine. You did no diversions. I could sense your *mana* out there in that first moment when I struck you with a psionic blast. You were as strong as me, that was evident."

Garth said nothing.

"We should still be fighting up there and I suspect I should be losing."

"You won."

"That's not good enough. Why did you throw it?"   .

"I didn't."

She smiled, the first time he had seen her do so, and he found himself smiling in return. Her light blue eyes seemed filled with amusement and curiosity.

"You won," he said softly, "and everyone now knows it."

"Did you think I was testing you for Varnel?"

"Of course you were! That's your job, to test new fighters. You also were supposed to kill me but only in a manner that was not obvious, say after a long fight and we were both exhausted and it could be claimed that it was an accident. I daresay having rats tear my throat out while I was in the neutral box would be too obvious."

She stared at him coldly.

"Your honor is intact, the others will accept me, the issue is laid to rest for the moment. You'll have your chance at me later."

"I think you could beat me," she said quietly.

Garth smiled again.

"We're inside a circle here, we have our satchels. Shall we try again or postpone such things for now?"

She looked at him, saying nothing.

Finally she stirred, slipping across the pool to where he was sitting, putting her arms around his shoulders and pulling herself in tight against him.

CHAPTER
7

DUCKING INTO A SIDE ALLEY, GARTH REMAINED
silent, wary as a company of the city Watch marched past,
their torches casting wavery shadows down the thoroughfare.

"So what is it this time?" Hammen whispered.

"Got a little too stuffy back in there, that's all."

"How was she?"

"How was who?"

"You know who."

"Rather not say."

"Rather not say," Hammen mumbled. "I'm too old for it, he
won't let me watch, and now he'd rather not say."

Garth stepped back out into the street, pulling the cowl of
his cape up close around his face. He slipped back into the
flow of the crowd, which was wandering aimlessly up and
down one of the five main thoroughfares of the city. It was
only two nights till Festival and the air was electric with
excitement as the city filled up to the bursting point with visitors pouring in from the countryside and town from as far as
Yulin and Equitar five hundred leagues away.

Besides being the final match of skill for all fighters of the
Western Lands, it was also a time of market. Merchants came
laden down with their wares and their order books. These
were not just the peddlers with a horse or mule load of goods

to sell but were the owners of the great trading consortiums which controlled vast caravans, warehouses, caravels, and galleys. They were here not only to place and fill orders, but also to pick the fighters they would need to protect their enterprises and harass those of their rivals.

Entertainers came so that the streets were filled with jugglers, singers, musicians, and actors. *Hanin* by the score slipped in as well, in spite of the Grand Master's injunction, hoping to be noticed and gain the precious right of color before they got themselves killed. And most important of all came the princes, barons, dukes, and lords to watch the fights and make bids upon the contracts for next year. The Peace of the Land had started as well upon the first day of the moon and would hold until the last day of the month so that they could prepare themselves for the season of wars that would follow in the time between Festival and the beginning of winter.

Garth drifted down the street, stopping to watch a troupe of jugglers, one of whom must have been a *hanin* who could control a single spell, for the balls they were juggling turned suddenly into snakes as they rose into the air, hissing and rattling, and then turned into balls again as they came back down. The crowd watched appreciatively and at a safe distance. Several of them kept taunting the juggler they suspected was the *hanin*, hoping it would break his concentration so that he'd wind up catching a poisonous serpent and thereby provide a good show.

Garth continued on and all around him the conversations were on the Festival. Gambling sheets were being printed by the tens of thousands and made available for a few coppers. Each scroll listed the lineup from each House and in an arcane code told of the fighter, his pedigree, trainer, spells believed to be carried, and, most importantly, the win and loss record in previous Festivals. There were even sheets for the illiterate, which far outsold the ones with writing, marked with coded symbols and slash marks along with betting guides that detailed the odds for the probable matches fought by the higher-rank fighters.

The street echoed with arguments, some of them heating up to the point of fists and drawn daggers as the milling mob argued their favorites.

"It never ceases to amaze me," Hammen said, as the two

stepped around two old women who were rolling in the street and trading punches, "how the mob follows Festival. Here they barely have enough to eat. Taxes from the Grand Master, and for that matter the princes of the surrounding lands, are ruinous in order to pay for fighters. Yet do they see that?"

Garth looked down at Hammen.

"You seemed to be enjoying yourself when I first met you."

"I was surviving and don't interrupt me. As I was saying, any thought much beyond where their next meal comes from and which hand to wipe themselves with is beyond them. They don't care about anything beyond that, and worse yet they don't want to think anything beyond that. And yet when it comes to the arena they can tell you the pedigree, the training master, the rank, wins, and spells of damn near every fighter of the four colors. It amazes me. Since you fighters live longer than us anyhow, we're talking about records that sometimes go back several hundred years. Those two old crones fighting back there in the gutter most likely already had their favorites while still in swaddling and have been following them their entire lives.

"Yet you fighters, do you care?"

"Are we supposed to?"

"Like I said, son, shut up and listen, I'm in the mood to lecture. Most of the fighters I've known would squash a peasant like a bug. Especially those who carry black or red *mana* in their satchels. Using those bundles of *mana* to focus their psychic links gives them dark and near-godlike powers when compared to a stinking peasant who can only fight with his hands."

"I have a few of those."

"I know, and that's disturbed me. But as I was saying, most fighters are nothing but leeches. They live like royalty in their Houses, they hire out to lords of quality or to merchants who can pay. And there they live like royalty as well. They fight and if it's against those without the power, they usually kill them out of hand. If it is against another fighter, usually you just surrender a spell and be done with it, then go back and tell your employer that your *mana* was not strong that day. You stage these elaborate fights and in an entire year not more than half a dozen of you get killed. It's only during Festival that things get a little bloody and even then most of it's a sham. Most of you don't give a good damn for anything other than yourselves, you're all so damn haughty just because, as an accident of birth, you came into this plane with the ability to control the magics. As for the rest of us, we live our lives out in filth and misery to support you."

"Am I being lumped into this?"

"I honestly don't know at times, Master."

"And the fighters of the Grand Master," Hammen continued, "they're even worse. They get recruited into his service and stay in his direct employ for the rest of their lives. They're there for one reason only, to offset the mob, the rival princes, and the other Houses. They're even worse than the leeches of the Houses. They're parasites that eat us alive from the inside out. At least the House fighters have only recently been corrupted; there was a time when they did do service to the people. But those serving the Grand Master, they're lower than snake crap in a wagon rut."

Garth, chuckling softly over Hammen's rage, stopped for a moment at a fruit merchant's stall and came back with two pomegranates, tossing one to Hammen, and he continued on. As he ate the delicacy with relish he made sure that his cowl still concealed his face so that he looked almost like a holy dervish of the Muronian order. The Muronians made their livelihood by passing out tracts promising that the entire universe was doomed and generally annoying the rest of the world so that some people wished it would end just to get rid of them.

Several city warriors slowed as they approached Garth, as if they recognized him. He reached into his pocket as if to pull out a tract and they quickly hurried on.

"I like this disguise," Garth said.

"I still think you're crazy to be out and about like this. Better to stay in the House. I'm willing to bet everything we've won so far that Varena would be happy to join you in bed tonight."

"I want to see some things," Garth said absently as he tossed aside the ends of the pomegranate.

Up the street a trumpet sounded and the crowd gave way as a line of horsemen came down the thoroughfare, swinging to either side with their riding crops to clear a path. Behind them came some petty princeling, who looked out from his carriage window with haughty disdain. As he drew past Hammen let fly with the remains of his pomegranate, catching the prince on the nose.

There was a howl of protest and the horsemen circled back. Hammen, laughing, pushed his way back to the side of the street. The princeling stuck his head out of the carriage, roaring obscenities in a high, cracking voice. Within seconds the carriage was pelted with offal and whatever else was handy and the guards lashed the horses of the carriage forward so that it continued up the street.

The incident left the crowd in a good mood as they soundly cursed all nobility.

"Talk about trying not to draw attention," Garth hissed.

"See, it's right there," Hammen laughed. "They hate the bastards but they don't even realize that by worshiping the fighters they in fact prop them up."

"I understand there was a time when the Houses weren't that bad," Garth said quietly.

"Ah, the legendary golden age, silver age, or whatever it is people want to call it. Memories of history are usually bunk— it was never better before, and it won't be better tomorrow."

"An optimist."

"All right. Yes, it might have been better. Before the last Grand Master. When there was still the fifth House, Oor-tael, which used more of the *mana* of the islands and the forest. Fighters of that House were obligated to give part of their time in service to those not of the merchant and noble classes. They had to go on pilgrimage, to wander as part of their journeyman and master's training, and help the poor with their skills. Even after obtaining the highest rank, every third year they were expected to do this. And the other Houses finally came to hate them for it."

"Is that the only reason?"

"I don't know, I was only a . . ." Hammen paused. "You know the old injunction still stands."

"And that is?"

"A death sentence on any who wore Turquoise, be they

fighter, warrior, mistress, and"—he paused—"even the lowest of servants. It also applies to any who even talk of it or suspect another of being of the order and do not report it."

"And you were about to say?"

Hammen looked up at Garth.

"I called you Galin last night. Do you remember?" Hammen whispered.

"Not really," Garth said quietly.

"Do you know why?"

"You must have confused me with someone else."

"Master. Any who wore Turquoise are now dead. There might have been a few who escaped the massacre but they are dead. Leave it that way. The dead cannot be brought back and Turquoise is gone forever."

Hammen paused and looked up warily at Garth.

"Every hand throughout the city, through the realms, was raised against them and the Grand Master paid." Hammen's voice grew faint. "He paid, he paid by the tens of thousands in gold to bring in the few who escaped the massacre when their House was stormed here in the city on the last night of Festival. If they were fighters, they were stripped of their satchels and impaled in the arena.

"And do you know what the mob did?"

"No." Garth's voice was barely a whisper.

"Oh, there might have been some who cared, but too many were there cheering, laughing, placing bets on how long it would take the impaled to die. That is the mob. They've been so fed on bloodlust, on Festival, on groveling before the Walker, that they don't even care, they don't even know.

"There was a time when Festival was a private ritual, when the fighters met alone to test their skills." He paused. "The previous Grand Master built the arena and started to change that and the mob loved it. And then this Grand Master turned it into spectacle and blood sport."

"Why didn't the Houses resist this?"

"I'm still not sure if you're simply a fool or not. Money, my boy, money and other bribes. The Grand Master kicked back to the House Masters, giving them more money than the dead fighters would have made on contracts for a dozen years. With the death matches, the betting went insane, going from a few paltry coppers per match to entire life savings wagered on a single fight. He's impoverished the mob with it and even some of the princes. Look around you at this city, it's falling down in squalor. Why?"

Garth tried to answer but Hammen interrupted him.

"Because he's using the money to secure *mana* and power for himself and also to get funds to obtain *mana* the Walker demands. That's his cover, of course, to blame the Walker, but believe me, he holds back enough for himself. The old role of the fighters has been long forgotten; they're nothing more than entertainers now."

"You haven't forgotten. How come?"

"I'm an old man," Hammen said quietly, looking away. "Just a disgusted old man."

"Yet you steal."

"And why not? The Grand Master has made it an honorable pastime. Besides, there is nothing else I could do to survive."

"Nothing?"

Hammen looked up at Garth and then shook his head.

"So what happened to those who survived?"

"Who?"

"Turquoise."

"Don't ever ask that," Hammen snapped. "Never. If someone should hear you, you are dead."

"I'm dead already if the Grand Master gets me."

"Dying as Garth One-eye is one thing, dying as a suspected Turquoise or even a supporter of that House is quite another. And the mob that favors you now would sell you in a second for the money it could bring.

"Out in the countryside, where Turquoise was strong, out there it wasn't so bad and I suspect it might still be that way. I heard that a number of men and women in the distant chapter houses managed to escape."

Hammen sighed.

"What can peasants do against warriors, against the other fighters? Even then there were enough willing to inform and help in the tracking down. A hundred for a servant or mistress or mate, five hundred for a warrior, a thousand for a fighter. That can seduce even the best of men."

"Not all," Garth said quietly.

Hammen snorted and spit.

"You know what they did when they took one prisoner? The very first thing after they felt they'd got all the information they could get? They cut his tongue out so he could not talk and tell the truth of what was happening. They cut the tongues out of anyone who gave the fugitives shelter or who were known to have conversed with them.

"And now they are gone, they are all dead, or best to be believed that they are dead," Hammen whispered.

"There are still rumors that they're alive."

Hammen looked up at Garth, suddenly wary.

"We both could be killed for what I've just said," Hammen hissed. "Even to mention they might still live is a death sentence. Even to be suspected of knowing such things, or worse, knowing of someone, is a death sentence now."

He paused for a moment.

"Just who are you?"

"I am Garth One-eye."

"Go back home, wherever that is," Hammen suddenly blurted out. "You ask too many questions. You won't live to see the end of Festival if you stay."

"I have things to do."

"They're not worth it. Whatever it is you are after is dead."

"You're free to leave my side at any time."

Hammen cursed loud and long for a minute.

"Thanks. And you know I won't. Not now. You know you have me. It's as if you planned it that way from the beginning, just like everything else. That your meeting me in the circle I drew in the mud was planned."

Garth laughed and shook his head.

They walked in silence for long minutes, the crowd around them boisterous, laughing, arguing, the now ever-present gambling sheets being waved in the air, dirty fingers pointing at them, arguing over favorites and odds. "Any reason we're passing here?" Hammen finally asked, nodding toward a tavern and the crowd milling about outside, watching an *oquorak* match between two warriors, one Brown, the other Gray.

"Just happened to be along the way."

"And it's where you met that Benalian."

Garth nodded and slowed to watch the fight, which ended seconds later as Gray made three quick slices, one after the other, flaying open the shoulder of Brown.

Brown staggered backward and grudgingly paid his wager as the cord which held the two together was cut, while copper and silver was passed back and forth by the crowd.

"Could you do me a favor?"

"Now what?"

"Track her down for me. I think it fair to assume you have contacts all over the city. She would be easy enough to find."

"I tell you she's nothing but a bother; all Benalish women are strange."

Garth smiled.

"I think I can take care of myself. Take a couple of the gold coins and spread the money around if need be."

Hammen looked up at him coldly.

"Don't worry, your commission won't be touched. And while you're at it, I'd like you to find a hovel someplace, preferably on or near the Plaza. It has to be secure."

"A hiding place or a place of rendezvous?"

"The former, and who knows, maybe the latter as well."

Hammen snickered.

"Fat chance. Like I said, she's Benalish."

"Anyhow, just do it. It might come in handy if we need a place to disappear to."

"What do you mean we? I can take off at any time and disappear."

Garth looked down at Hammen and smiled.

"Then just for me."

Hammen cursed and spit on the ground.

"All right, I'll see what I can find."

Garth turned to look back to where some of the mob was busy taunting the Brown fighter who had just lost the *oquorak*. A gust of wind swept down the street and Garth's cowl fluttered off his head for a moment and he quickly pulled it back up to hide his face.

"Hey, don't I know you?"

A beggar came up toward Garth, weaving drunkenly and pointing a stubby finger at him and then at Hammen.

Garth started to turn away.

"I knew it!" the beggar shouted triumphantly, scurrying over to Garth's side. "I never forget a man I win a copper on. You're One-eye."

An instant later the name echoed through the crowd, which swarmed after Garth.

"One-eye, One-eye!"

The mob swirled around him, hands reaching out, patting him on the back. Slobbering voices offered drinks, women, and other pleasures.

"Which color is it now? Will you fight in Festival? What's your favorite spell? My cousin saw you fight against Naru; he won five coppers on it!"

Fights broke out in the crowd's wake as a few partisans of other fighters argued against the mysterious One-eye.

"You're certainly popular," Hammen shouted, trying to be heard above the tumult, "but I think we better get out of here. That Brown warrior's heading off in the opposite direction. Most likely to get his friends."

Garth slowed to a stop, the mob swirling in around him, cheering, hands reaching out to grab at his tunic or just to touch him.

"Friends, you know the Grand Master wants me. If you continue to do this, his Watch will come."

"A fight! Let's have a fight!" someone shouted, and the cry was picked up, so that within seconds it echoed down the street, the meaning changing as it traveled so that those farther away thought a combat was actually in progress. As they swarmed toward the commotion some of them were already placing bets on One-eye, though they had no idea against whom he was fighting.

Garth extended his hand and a green swirl of smoke rose up around him. He grabbed hold of Hammen's hand and tried to push his way through the crush, most of them falling back, coughing and choking.

And yet as he ran down a side street, the mist still around him, the mob set off in pursuit.

"There he goes, follow the smoke, the smoke!"

The mob followed after him, shouting and laughing, as if he were playing a prank for their amusement.

"They're going to get us killed. Try that disappearing act of yours."

"You have to stand still and stay within the circle of protection," Garth replied. "It won't work now."

As they reached the edge of the Great Plaza Garth slowed to a stop, the crowd again swarming in around him.

Garth reached into his tunic and snapped off a small bundle tied around his throat and pressed it into Hammen's hand.

"Get away from me," Garth hissed, "get away now!"

"Master?"

"Now, move it. Now!"

Hammen looked up at him, confused, as the smoke drifted away. Out in the Plaza a line of warriors was drawn up, crossbows raised. Hammen looked back at the mob that was closing in around them and saw at the far edge another line, this one of fighters wearing the Grand Master's livery, pouring out of a side street.

"Run, damn it, run." And with that Garth pushed Hammen with such force that he knocked him over into the crowd. Garth darted through the crowd, disappearing from Hammen's view. The old man tried to regain his footing, people tripping over him, kicking, cursing. Finally he grabbed hold of an ankle and bit it, sending his victim to the ground, howling and cursing, and climbed up over him.

In the confusion Garth was gone from view.

Garth continued to run, dodging down a side street, his admirers still following in his wake, laughing and shouting, revealing to the Watch the direction he had taken. He dodged down a side alley, leaping over piles of refuse, cutting between buildings, and still the mob followed. He ducked into a dark alcove and the mob stormed past until finally one of them, wheezing for breath, stopped directly in front of Garth, coughing and hacking. He looked up and saw him.

"Here he is! One-eye!"

The mob turned, shouting, and Garth set off again, pausing to block his path with an invisible wall, which stopped those behind him. But as he reached another thoroughfare the hue and cry was raised yet again, fans swarming in around him.

Pushing his way through the press, he reached the side of the House of Fentesk. There was no hope of finding a secret entrance without Hammen leading the way and he darted for the front door. Out in the Plaza a crowd was already gathering, cheering, laughing, and he could hear them placing bets as to whether he would gain sanctuary or not. As he stepped into the Plaza a crowd rushed forward to engulf him, slowing him down yet again.

A blast of light exploded in the Plaza directly in front of Garth, knocking a dozen or more of the mob over, and they scattered in every direction. Garth bolted toward the main door and, reaching it, grabbed the handle.

It was locked shut.

He turned and stepped back. A circle of fighters was drawn up around him, fighters of the Grand Master.

The blasts came in rapid succession, forcing Garth to dodge about even as he created a circle of protection from the fire. Beyond the ring of fighters he could see crossbow men closing in, running in formation, and beyond them several ballistae on wagons coming toward him, their gunners swinging the weapons around to point forward.

He quickly flared off one spell after another, rolling and dodging. A mammoth appeared directly in front of him, physically blocking the strikes of fire. The great animal reared up on its hind legs, trumpeting, and then lumbered forward. Half a dozen fighters turned their attention to him, the others continuing to focus on Garth. Within seconds the space between Garth and his attackers was filled with goblins, dwarfs, serpents, and skeletons, all fighting each other, conjured into being to attack or defend.

Far out in the Plaza the mob shouted and howled with delight, cheering Garth on in his impossible fight.

The mammoth managed to grab and tear asunder one of the fighters before the others finally destroyed it by opening a fissure directly beneath it, the creature falling in, managing to snag one more fighter around the ankle and pulling him down as well.

A line of crossbow men rushed up and leveled their weapons. Garth flashed a wall of fire before them, their bolts passing through it and disappearing, leaving nothing but trails of smoke.

Three berserkers, shrieking in unknown tongues, appeared, charging straight at Garth, and he stopped them with a line of Llanowar Elves, who hewed into them with staves of oak that shattered helmets, shields, and bones.

Several of the fighters, working together, conjured forth a hill giant who stood nearly half as tall as the House of Fentesk and came forward with slow, lumbering steps, the mob gasping and shouting enthusiastically at the sight of such a rare wonder even though it was bent on crushing their hero.

The fighters opposing Garth paused in their attacks to watch the fun since Garth had no offensive strikes up, his elves trading themselves off against the berserkers so that all lay dead.

The giant, laughing with a low, rumbling roar, raised his foot up and slammed it down, trying to squash Garth. Garth dodged aside and moved behind a pillar. The giant tried to kick him and stubbed his toe so that he cursed with pain and the mob roared with delight.

Garth stepped out from behind the pillar and the giant raised his foot, bringing it down again. Garth rolled, picked up a sword from a fallen beserker and braced its hilt on the ground, the point aimed straight up.

The giant impaled his foot.

His howl of anguish was almost as loud as a demonic roar and he hopped about, the sword still stuck in the bottom of his foot. Garth extended his hands and the giant tottered off balance and then came crashing down, crushing several fighters beneath him, the impact of his fall rumbling across the Plaza like an earthquake. The giant, cursing and moaning, started to rise up again and the fighters who controlled him pointed with disgust at their bumbling creation. The giant fell into the fissure that had taken the mammoth, and his shrieks did not stop until he hit the bottom. In the brief seconds created by the confusion with the giant Garth again turned to the door and pulled on it. It was still locked.

He raised his hand to burst the door and felt an even stronger spell protecting it.

Cursing, he turned back to face his opponents, who were now nearly doubled in number to twenty by the arrival of more reinforcements. The crossbow men, having reloaded, were moving to either side of the fire which he had erected to burn their bolts.

The next seconds were a mad confusion, spell after spell striking back and forth. Several times he was staggered by psionic blasts which slammed into him, those throwing the spells collapsing from exhaustion. But it was not one on one and so it did not matter if a single opponent felled himself into unconsciousness, as long as he injured the lone man they were facing.

Another blast hit him and another and Garth fell to his knees. The mob continued to cheer, caught up in the sheer spectacle of such a fight.

He tried to erect a circle of protection and a crossbow bolt slammed into his shoulder, spinning him around, sending him facedown to the ground.

Gasping, Garth came back up to his knees. The fighters were closing in on him, gloating, hands raised. He threw one more spell, knocking a fighter down in flames, the man turning away, shrieking and running in circles, the crowd howling with delight at this final act of defiance.

Garth looked back at the door into the House of Fentesk. It was unbarred and filled now with spectators. Even as the next blast struck him, he tore his satchel off and threw it toward the door.

"Varena! Sanctuary!" Garth shouted as his satchel skidded to a stop before the Orange fighters gathered about the door.

His *mana* now no longer at his side, he was naked, and the next blast knocked him into oblivion.

CHAPTER
8

"HAMMEN."

The voice was a whisper, as if drifting on the wind. Frightened, he turned, expecting to see the fighters of the Grand Master.

The alleyway was deserted.

In the distance the clamor of the mob out in the great square could still be heard. Rioting had broken out after Garth fell. Some of it triggered by lost bets, because many had come to believe him almost invincible. Others, however, were enraged because a favorite had been taken and in some primal sort of way the mob felt it to be unfair. Their sense of honor had been offended both by the Grand Master and by Orange, which had barred the door to their hero. The adventure of the almost-legendary One-eye, which had grown in the telling to near-mythical proportions, was now finished, and they were disappointed.

Windows not broken in the brawl of the day before were being smashed, and chants of "One-eye, One-eye" could be heard swelling on the wind.

Disgusted, Hammen listened, knowing that if anything it was just an excuse for a little free shopping and that the actual rightness or wrongness of what had happened was secondary. Later they could say that they had protested the unfairness while gorging on the food and wine they had appropriated and parading about in the fine silks taken from some unfortunate merchant. Thus it had always been with urban mobs, who would riot on a whim, a mere pretext of an excuse, Hammen thought, and yet remain mute when real injustice occurred.

"Hammen."

He ducked back into the shadows and reached for his dagger as he saw a shadow drift through the alleyway, moving stealthily, the only sound the squealing of rats disrupted from their late-night repast.

The shadow stopped.

"It's Norreen; it's all right."

It was the Benalish woman and he breathed a sigh of relief. She came up to him.

"I saw you in the Plaza and followed you," she whispered.

"Some hero you were," Hammen snapped. "You could have made your name out there."

"Did you go up and stand by his side?" she growled in reply.

"No."

"Why not?"

"I'm not the hero, you are. Besides, it was useless; he was finished."

"That's why I held back. Never pick a fight that's suicide."

Hammen nodded sadly.

"So it's over. Now leave me alone."

"It's not over. He's still alive."

"So what? They have him. Either they'll torture him to death tonight, or keep him for the amusement of the Walker. Either way it would have been better if he had killed himself with his last spell."

"He threw his satchel away before the end."

"What?"

"Who's Varena?" she asked, her voice suddenly soft.

Hammen chuckled and shook his head.

"A final pleasure."

"Oh." She was silent for a moment.

"You say he threw his satchel away?" Hammen asked curiously.

"He called her name and then demanded sanctuary for his spells. I saw a woman snatch it up and then go back inside."

Hammen chuckled softly.

"Just like him. What did the Grand Master's men do then?"

"They took him and bound him up. Some of them went up to the door and demanded the satchel be turned over as a rightful prize and Orange barred the door shut. The mob loved it. They then loaded Garth into a cart and that's when the rioting started."

Hammen looked expectantly back up the alleyway, the sound of the riot still echoing over the city, and he started to step out of the shadows.

"There's nothing we can do now," Norreen sighed. "There's hundreds of warriors out there and nearly all the Grand Master's fighters. Besides, they're hunting for you and for me; go out there now and we'll be in a cell right beside him."

"What do you mean *we*, Benalish?"

"Just that, we."

For the first time since it had all started Hammen felt the small leather bag Garth had tossed him. He opened it up and peeked inside, the glinting within barely visible in the darkness.

If he was alive, there still might be a way.

"Come on, we've got work to do."

As he spoke he reached out and attempted to pat her on her backside and withdrew his hand with a yelp.

"I demand the satchel!"

Varena looked over coldly at Varnel, Master of the House of Fentesk, and shook her head defiantly.

"He declared me his heir out there by shouting my name. He also called for the sanctuary of his possessions. The fight waged against him was not a challenge fight and even if it was, those dogs don't deserve to divide up what was his."

"What right do you have to his possessions?"

"I made love to him this morning. That's my claim."

Varnel looked up at her hungrily and licked his lips. She looked back, cold, defiant, the faintest sneer of contempt lighting her features.

"If we could make that same arrangement, perhaps this incident might be forgotten," Varnel finally said.

"You are my House Master and according to the rules that is as far as it goes. I made that clear the day I joined."

"Damn you." He stood up as if to challenge her.

"Fight me and you might win," she said coldly. "But I'll be dead and this place will be a shambles. You'll also have a rebellion on your hands. You betrayed one of our House tonight. Do it twice and you'll have nothing come the start of Festival."

"Do you think they really care out there for One-eye? Most of them are glad he's dead. They don't give a good damn about honor, only their pay."

"True. And most of them are now wondering, even if it is just a faint tugging, wondering if you might not protect them as well if the offer from the Grand Master was great enough. Kill me over this and that suspicion will be firmly planted."

Varnel stood silent as if weighing the possibilities of trying to force both the satchel and more from her.

"Stick with weaker minds and bodies," she sneered, pointing to the back of the room where several naked women lounged on a silk divan, watching the confrontation with detached boredom. "It's safer."

Laughing coldly, she slammed the door shut behind her, almost feeling pity for his concubines, who would know the darker side of his passion tonight.

It was well past midnight, exhaustion was finally starting to take hold, and she headed for the hot baths to soak out the tension. She entered the steamy room, which was empty, and felt a momentary pang. It was, after all, only a passing encounter, if anything, even a bit of a game of power and control, but it had still been pleasant enough.

She undressed, keeping her satchel and his with her, placed them on a ledge next to the pool, slipped into the bubbling water, and stretched out.

It was time to leave this House, she realized. Varnel would not dare anything now, not on the eve of Festival. Beyond that he would have to make a show of defiance toward the Grand Master and refuse the return of the satchel. To do otherwise, after his miserable display of ordering the door bolted, would show a complete subservience. But once Festival was over, and most of the fighters had gone to their yearly assignments and chapter houses, that would be the time for him to get even for the humiliation before his harem and before the other fighters.

He, like the other House Masters, was not above arranging an "accident" for a recalcitrant fighter, such as a contract where a prince agreed to a hidden clause that if the fighter was killed, he'd receive a full refund. As she floated in the pool she felt a moment's regret for accepting the sanctuary call of Garth and grabbing up the satchel. *Why did I do it? Was it the powers the satchel contained or was it something else?*

Damn!

She reached over to the small ledge where she had placed the satchels and was tempted to look inside and see what powers he had controlled. But he was not yet dead, she could sense that, and thus it would be a violation of the laws.

The laws. Who gave a good damn about the laws anymore? She was seasoned enough to understand the simple rules of survival, but somehow it still bothered her. The powers had perverted it all, changing it from at least an honorable profession into a selling to the highest bidder and the entertaining of the mob. No longer was there any sense of *sessan*, the intricate set of codes and rules that had once bound those who could control the *mana*. The fighting for *sessan*, for the simple gaining of powers, honor, and face were gone. Increasingly it was for the kill and the lust of the kill.

For Varnel it was a means of fulfilling his increasingly perverted pleasures. And for the fighters of her House, few cared any longer about the intrinsic joy of the discipline required to control the *mana*, caring instead only for what it could give them in this plane.

That thought now disturbed her as well. For what did the Walker think of this? He was, after all, the most powerful of any in this plane, the one who had obtained so much *mana* that he could now jump between realms of existence. For him the struggles of this realm were most likely as trivial as the fighting of insects under the heel of a little boy who could crush them at any time.

And yet, should he not know and care? If this world had lost its honor, then what of the sense of *sessan* of the Walker himself? In less than two days Festival would start, and at the end of it the winner of all would then go with the Walker, to serve as his new acolyte into the deepest of mysteries.

If I win, what will I learn then? she wondered.

Somehow the thought suddenly disturbed her—for the first time.

A less than pleasant smell wafted around her. Startled, she opened her eyes and sat up.

"Ah, what I was really hoping to see."

Hammen was squatting by the edge of her pool like a frog sitting on a lily pad, his eyes bulging with unconcealed delight.

"What in the name of all the devils are you doing here?" she hissed, surprised not only by his stinking presence but also by the fact that she was embarrassed by her own nakedness. She reached out to a rack and fumbled for a towel to cover herself.

"You don't need a towel," Hammen moaned.

"Hammen!" someone said, and a hand came out of the shadows, slapping him across the back of the head so that he yelped softly.

Varena stepped out of the pool and snatched up her satchel at the sight of the stranger behind Garth's servant.

"A Benalish?"

The woman nodded.

"Both of you stink like a sewer."

"That's how we got in here," Hammen said, "and I must confess it was exciting to think that we were wading through water you might have bathed in." Norreen slapped him again.

"If you're found here, you're both dead," Varena whispered. "Get out now or I'll have to take care of you both."

Norreen's hand dropped to the hilt of her blade and Varena let her towel drop, freeing one hand while she slung her satchel over her shoulder in order to fight.

Hammen looked at her wide-eyed and grinned before finally tossing over the small bag that Garth had given him.

She grabbed it, still keeping a wary eye on Norreen.

"We thought you might enjoy the game we propose," Hammen said with a smile.

Racked with pain, Garth struggled to keep from screaming. There was almost a detached sense to the agony, as if he were watching himself from some place far away, floating above his body, while down on the rack he twisted and writhed.

He screamed, a wild, howling cry that was more rage than

anguish, for his training had long ago taught him how to divert pain into places where it would not darken his body and mind. And yet the man who did this to him knew of such places as well and his invisible fingers probed into Garth's soul, tearing at his thoughts, lashing him, cutting into his mind, and then attempting to reassemble the pieces.

There were no healing spells now, no blocks, no way of striking back, only the unrelenting assault to probe into the core of his existence. Finally there were but two paths left, to relent, to reveal, or to go down into the paths of darkness and the light which was beyond. Garth closed in upon himself and reached toward the second path.

There was remorse for all that he had dreamed and planned for; all that had moved him and kept him alive across the years was now for naught. All the years hidden away, training, secretly planning alone for what could and should be done were wasted now. The wonderful intricacy of it all would be lost forever. He would have to appear before the shadows to whom he had sworn so much, empty-handed. He could only hope that they would understand and forgive.

"No, not yet!"

The lashing of his soul stopped and instantly there was a soothing warmth that drew him back from the door that was already opening before him.

He wanted to go on through and yet could not. The very *mana* that all carried within, the power of life, refused to surrender while the cord was still intact.

Garth opened his eyes.

Zarel Ewine, Grand Master of the Arena, stood over him. There was almost a look of pity in his eyes, the sense of it so strong that Garth struggled not to give in to what he knew was simply another ploy.

Zarel reached out and touched him lightly on the forehead and the last of the pain went away.

"Wouldn't it be better to talk with me now?" His voice was soft and warm, like that of a caring mother whispering to a child sick with some strange and terrible fever.

Zarel nodded and unseen hands loosened the chains which had held Garth stretched out upon the rack. Hands helped him to sit up and a cooling draught was placed to his lips. He hesitated, wondering what seductive herbs and potions it might contain, and then drank it anyway. If they were going to try that, they could have forced it into him while he was stretched and semiconscious on the table of pain.

The drink cleared the rawness of his throat and he leaned over, coughing, fighting down the urge to vomit.

The drink was pressed to his lips again and he finished it, a cool lightness coursing through him, so that he felt as if he were somehow floating and all was now at peace. He turned inward with his thoughts again, concentrating what little power he still had to clear his mind.

"You can leave us now," he heard Zarel command, and behind him a door closed.

"This is really unfortunate, you know," Zarel said calmly.

Garth coughed and said nothing.

"Let me be frank with you," Zarel continued, and Garth heard a chair being dragged up by the side of the table.

He opened his eyes and saw the cold gleam in his tormentor's eyes. He could sense just how much this man was actually enjoying what was happening. There was no longer even a real rage in him. It was cold, detached—this torture and questioning was an entertainment, a challenge to be relished.

Garth looked at him warily.

"You are going to die. There is no sense in lying to someone of your skills. You have set out to make yourself my implacable foe. You have caused me humiliation, loss of property, and loss of face. That I cannot tolerate."

He sighed as if the whole thing was a terrible burden.

"That rabble, that stinking mob out there, can have their heroes, but they must be heroes I control." His voice rose slightly. "And you, One-eye, tried to set yourself up outside of my control.

"Oh, I will admit you are masterful, the way you triggered that fight between Kestha and Bolk, the way you flouted my laws. It's almost a waste." He shook his head as if truly saddened. "If you had but come to my door first and sought employment, I would gladly have given you rank."

Garth said nothing, for he knew Zarel was not really speaking to him at all, but rather to his own pride.

"A rank with power, gold, women, whatever it is you desire.

I think you have skill enough that you could even have been my second, for the one I have now is nothing but a lapdog."

Zarel paused, looking at him coldly.

"But no, you don't desire that, do you, One-eye?"

There was now a cold contempt in Zarel.

"You're of the old school and you hate me for it. Such a fool, such a fool . . ." And his voice trailed off as if he was looking into some far-distant place.

"Who are you?"

His voice was like a lash, startling Garth, who recoiled from the power of it. Again there was the flash of a struggle, the hope that he had been caught off guard, and the barrier was almost pierced.

Zarel smiled.

"You're growing weaker. You know I will have you before it's done."

"You can try," Garth whispered. "And then what? You'll know and I will be dead. It's the mystery that torments you, isn't it? The mystery and the fear."

Zarel stood up and turned away for a moment, his multi-hued cape shimmering in the torchlight.

Zarel finally turned back and, sighing, sat down.

"I will make this simple for you. The Walker is aware of you. The torment I give you would be just for the moment. Tell me and it is ended and you can drift into the long sleep. Don't tell me and he can make your suffering long and hard. And believe me, it can be for a very long time."

"So is that who he really is?" Garth asked. "Have you revealed the facade behind the mask of his power and his appeal to the mob?"

Zarel lowered his head for a moment as if caught in a blasphemy.

"You can control the *mana*," Zarel whispered. "You know the power of the red and the black, and he holds that power in abundance. Only a fool would think him otherwise. He is terrible in his power; for how else would he control such power? He answers to no one but the Eternal and even the Eternal is held at bay until *Ragalka*, the day of destruction and woe."

Zarel spoke as if almost talking to an equal about a truth that was disagreeable but had to be faced calmly and rationally.

"He will not let you escape into the lands of the dead, but will hold you in his hands as an amusement to be toyed with. It could be aeons before he grows bored with you and grants you release. That is what I offer you if you do not cooperate."

"And that is what he has done to those who have incurred his wrath," Garth said, his voice cold with rage.

Zarel stirred and looked at Garth with surprise.

"That is a concern of yours, isn't it?" And again there was the moment of probing.

Garth fell silent.

"That is a concern, isn't it? You have some design not only against me but against the Walker himself?" His words were like lashes that flayed Garth.

Garth stared straight at Zarel in cold defiance.

Zarel nodded slowly.

"Why did you come here, One-eye? Who sent you and why?"

"You will never know."

"Damn you!" And then he slapped Garth, the blow striking with such force that it blurred Garth's vision.

Garth looked at him coldly, spitting the blood out of his mouth into Zarel's face.

"You're afraid of me, aren't you?" Garth whispered. "Even when I am chained and in your hands, you're afraid of me and what I might be."

"I should kill you now!" Zarel said, raising his hand as if to deliver the blow.

"Go ahead. And then you'll never know for sure. You'll never know if there are more like me, plotting and waiting."

"You're from the House of Oor-tael, that's it."

Garth merely smiled.

"You will never know."

"I destroyed all of you. All of you. What's left are pitiful dogs that I hunt for sport."

"If that's true, then why do you fear me even now, chained in your dungeon?"

"I fear no man or woman."

"You say that for yourself, but it means nothing to me, for I can see the truth in you."

Zarel looked down at Garth and there was a flicker of fear in his eyes.

"You are driving toward the dark goal, the same as your Master did before you. And you are running a race. You must pay the tribute of *mana* each year to the Walker and yet you hold back more and more for yourself, to build the power so that one day you can be like him."

"How do you know that?"

"The entire world knows it," Garth whispered with a cold laugh. "Do you think the rest of us are such fools as not to see?"

Zarel stirred uneasily.

"And don't you think they fear you for it? They remember what you did to the House of Oor-tael in service to your Master. Now they see that you are doing it to them as well, slowly bleeding the Houses in the Festival. Yet you bribe the House Masters each year and they close their eyes, but only for the moment. It is all coming unraveled, the rage of the Masters, the rage of the mob, and soon the Walker will know."

"Is that what you desire, then?" Zarel asked. "To reach the Walker and tell him?"

Garth laughed.

"Perhaps."

Zarel looked around the room and chuckled.

"Do you know how many have tried to cast me down? All of them, all of them finish up here." He pointed to the chains on the wall, more than one of them holding rotting corpses and skeletons.

Garth smiled.

"I said before they feared you, but you don't see what that fear will produce. You think it will keep your enemies under control. But it can also drive them to acts of desperation. Soon there won't be enough chains in all the world to hold them. In the end either the mob or the Houses will tear you apart with their bare hands." Garth laughed, his rasping voice a chilling cackle.

"Who are you?"

Garth spit in his face.

Zarel, with a scream of rage, slapped him again and yet again, and all the time Garth continued to laugh. In his heart he silently prayed that he could provoke him into ending it now, to deliver the deathblow so that he could go into the shadows and at least leave Zarel tormented by the mystery.

The rain of blows stopped and he looked back up, the Grand Master standing over him, heaving for breath, his cloak splattered with blood.

"No. You'll not escape. You'll not escape."

Zarel turned away and started for the door and opened it. He paused and looked back.

"Do you know what the thousand cuts are?"

Garth felt a cold chill.

"Contemplate that, for in an hour it will be started on you. My man has skills, though, and by the time you are dragged before the Walker you will be but a remnant, blind, without fingers or toes, and without your manhood. I shall enjoy watching it.

"Drug him!"

And he stormed away, cursing.

Seconds later two of the torturers were at his side, grinning, one of them forcing his mouth open, the other pouring a draught down his throat so that he drifted into a fevered dream, unable to control his thoughts and thus will his heart to stop.

Swooning, Garth lay back, the two torturers laughing as they tightened his chains to stretch him back out on the table of pain.

Caught in his fear, the Grand Master walked down the dank corridor, ignoring the moans and cries of his other visitors in the basement of his palace. The hallway stank of them and of the open sewer drains set in the middle of the hallway, which served as a convenient place for the dropping of bodies and parts of bodies.

"Uriah!"

The dwarf turned, his features white with fear.

"What are you doing here?"

"You sent for me, Master."

He looked closely at the deformed fighter, wondering if the man had been eavesdropping on the conversation.

Zarel paused for a moment, struggling to control the turmoil within. One-eye had to be of Turquoise. But how? How could he have survived? He was too young, most likely barely a boy, and the Grand Master roamed through his thoughts, for there was a half-formed memory, one which he could not clearly recall, and that was even more troubling.

Uriah coughed nervously, bringing him back.

"Has his servant been found?"

"Not yet, Master."

"And Varnel, has he surrendered the satchel?"

"He says he can't."

"Damn!"

Zarel slapped Uriah with such force that the dwarf slammed against the wall and looked up at him, stunned and terrified.

"Tell Varnel I want that satchel and the hell with the price. He took three thousand just to bar the door; let him know that if he doesn't release the satchel, word of his betrayal might slip out.

"Offer him ten thousand if need be. I want that servant as well. He must know something and he doesn't have the mind of a fighter. He can't resist the way One-eye can."

Uriah held his cheek, which was red and swelling.

Zarel looked down at Uriah.

"Is there something else?" he asked, his voice suddenly gone cold.

Uriah shook his head, tears of pain and fear in his eyes.

"Damn you, get out of my sight."

Uriah scurried away and, cursing, Zarel continued on, suppressing a gag as the cloying stench of the dungeon wafted around him.

There was a momentary sensing that something wasn't quite right and he paused, senses alert, waiting. He heard the snuffling sobs of Uriah and the moaning diverted him. Angrily, he stalked out of the dungeon.

CHAPTER
9

"DAMN!"

The sound of the blow startled him and Hammen cringed against the side of the sewer, afraid to breathe. He looked over at Norreen, who stood calmly, blade out of its scabbard, staring toward the flickering circle of light straight ahead in the darkness.

He could hear Uriah whimpering.

"Tell Varnel I want that satchel and the hell with the price."

Hammen looked over at Varena, who smiled at the sound of Zarel's ravings.

"He took three thousand just to bar the door; let him know that if he doesn't release the satchel, word of his betrayal might slip out."

Varena stirred angrily, her features suddenly tight with rage.

"Offer him ten thousand if need be. I want that servant as well. He must know something and he doesn't have the mind of a fighter. He can't resist the way One-eye can."

Hammen wanted to snap out a curse, half-amused at the thought of a subterranean voice wafting up from the sewer telling Zarel to burn in torment.

"Is there something else?" Zarel shouted.

There was a pause.

"Damn you, get out of my sight."

Hammen waited and then, finally, started to slip forward. Varena's hand shot out, holding him, shaking her head in warning.

She seemed to be holding her breath, and Hammen could sense the ripple of power, as if she was struggling to block something out. The minutes passed and then, finally, she sighed, lowering her head as if exhausted. She looked over at Norreen and nodded. The Benalish woman slipped forward, moving with a catlike ease, not making a sound as she moved through the thigh-high sludge and filth. Hammen and Varena followed, stopping just short of the overhead grate.

She reached up and felt the side of the grate, then looked back at Hammen, nodding. He came forward and she hoisted him up, hissing a warning as he attempted to run his hands up the side of her body. He slipped a lockpick out of his sleeve and started to reach up.

"That'll keep the scum," said a voice overhead, and there was a hoarse laugh.

Hammen froze, Norreen remaining motionless.

A foot stepped straight on the grate, and Hammen closed his eyes, waiting.

"Where do you think the cutter will start?"

"Where else?" another voice replied, and there was a crude laugh.

"Nah. He saves that for later. Five coppers it's the hands first."

"Which one?"

There was a momentary pause.

"The right."

"Five coppers then." And again there was the hoarse laugh.

Seconds later Hammen felt something warm splashing on his face and he fought the temptation to take his dagger and drive it straight up through the grate.

"Ah, that's better, too much beer."

The two continued on.

Hammen reached up and slipped the pick into the lock that held the grate.

It was rusted. He tried to force it but it wouldn't give. He looked over at Varena.

"It's stuck," he whispered. "Use a spell."

"Might draw attention. Oil it."

He unslung a small tin tied around his neck, uncorked it with his teeth, and reached up, first oiling the hinges to the grate and then upending the rest into the lock. Oil dripped back down on his face, stinging his eyes.

He worked the pick again and still it wouldn't budge. Sweat started to bead down his face in spite of the cold damp of the sewer.

"What's going on?" Norreen whispered.

"I can get any leverage. It won't budge."

"Damn, keep working!"

"Hoist me up higher."

Norreen, grunting, pushed him up higher against the grate, and he grabbed it with one hand, sticking the other one through the grate to work the lock.

Hoarse laughter echoed in the distance, the only answer a moaning cry nearby.

"Shut up, damn you, or we'll cut the other hand off!" a voice echoed in the distance.

He heard footsteps drawing closer and again he froze, pulling his hand back down. Someone was going from cell to cell, opening peepholes into each cell to check on prisoners. The minutes passed, the guard drawing closer, stepping over the grate. He opened another peephole.

"Damn. Hey, Grimash, this bastard in here's hung himself."

"So what do you want me to do about it?" a voice echoed in the distance.

"Open the door so we can dump him."

Hammen looked over at Norreen.

"Leave it till morning."

"Come on, let's get it done."

"Oh, all right."

Hammen looked down wide-eyed at Norreen. She quietly lowered him and slipped back, away from the opening.

Footsteps echoed overhead and there was the sound of a door unbolting.

"Damn, he stinks. When did you last check him?"

"I don't know. I think they brought him in yesterday or the day before?"

"Damn you! Carry him then. What a stink."

The two guards cursed softly and there was the sound of

something being dragged. A shadow appeared overhead and there was the sound of a key snicking in a lock. The lock let go with a metallic pop and the grate was lifted up.

"Something wrong here."

"What do you mean?"

"The key. Look, it's covered in oil."

"So somebody oiled it."

"Who? I sure didn't."

"Just shut up and dump the stiff. He's enough to make a maggot gag."

The body plunged straight down, slapping into the muck, spraying the three in the sewer. It was stiff as a board, however, and rather than tilt over with the current of the sewer to be swept away, it lodged in place as if standing, its head banging up against the circle of stones directly beneath the grate. Hammen fought to suppress a gag. The corpse's face was invisible in the shadows except for a thin ray of light that revealed his blackened tongue protruding out of a face that was swollen like a balloon, the rope, made out of strips of rag, cutting into its gray-green neck.

The guards overhead looked down and one of them started to laugh.

"He likes it here. He doesn't want to leave."

"Well, get down there and push him."

"Nah, let's leave him. Actually it's kind of funny, him standing down there like that."

"Damn it, push him. It'll stink the place up."

"As if the customers are going to complain."

"Just move him."

A hand reached down through the grate and, grabbing hold of the corpse by the back of the head, pulled him back. The current started to swing the dead man's legs outward, and at that moment Hammen screamed.

Wide-eyed, Hammen found himself staring into the face of Petros, one of his brotherhood, a friend who only three days ago had shared the fleas and lice of their hovel.

Hammen's scream was answered by the two guards overhead, both of them jumping back in terror.

"Go! Go!"

Varena pushed past Hammen, knocking him over into the

muck so that he started to get swept away by the current, his dead friend bobbing beside him.

Looking up, she raised her hand and a blast of fire slammed upward, catching one of the guards and bowling him over. The other ran off in terror. Varena grabbed hold of the sides of the access hole and pulled herself up, Norreen starting to scramble up after her.

"I'm drowning!"

Norreen looked back at Hammen, hesitated, and then, cursing, waded after him, grabbing hold of him by his hair and pulling him back toward the opening. She pushed him, sputtering and choking, up through the grate.

Hammen flopped up onto the floor of the dungeon and rolled away from the guard, who was writhing back and forth, screaming hysterically, as he tried to beat out the flames that were engulfing him.

Norreen came out of the hole and her sword slashed down, cutting his cries short.

"Which one is his?" Norreen cried.

From down the corridor Varena came running back.

"He got away. We don't have much time!"

"Which one is his?"

She looked around, confused. Their plan of sneaking in and silently checking cells was now gone.

"He must be at this end!" She started to walk down the corridor, raising her hand as she passed each door, blasting locks off. Norreen followed, tearing the doors open.

Hammen lay on the floor watching them, still shaken by the memory of what was left of his friend.

"Hammen, watch the corridor!"

Cursing, he came to his feet and started down the hallway. All around him was bedlam, prisoners inside cells shrieking for release.

He turned back to the scorched remains of the dead guard and found the man's keys. As he worked his way up the corridor he started to unlock doors. Some of the victims within were beyond hope, chained to tables of pain or to walls, some of them looking up and weakly calling for rescue, food, water, or simply for an end to their torment. Tears clouded his eyes and he continued on. Behind several of the doors the prisoners were not chained and they staggered out.

"Get in the sewer and follow the current!" Hammen shouted, pushing them back. The men and women crawled away.

One of the them hobbled up to Hammen.

"Hammen," the voice was hoarse, croaking.

The man was familiar, his old handless friend from the hovel.

"Get out of here and tell the others, tell everyone," Hammen whispered. "Tell them it was One-eye who set you free. Go hide with Lothor's brotherhood, and I'll meet you there later."

The man grinned through a bloody face and scurried away to the sewer hole.

From down at the far end of the corridor he suddenly heard footsteps running, drawing closer.

"They're coming!"

"We've got him!"

Hammen looked over his shoulder. Norreen was coming out of a cell, Garth in her arms, Varena pushing past her and running toward him.

A crossbow bolt shot past, skidding off a wall, showering sparks. At the far end of the cellblock torches appeared.

"Move it!"

Hammen, needing no urging, ran back toward her and stopped at the sewer hole.

Varena raised her hand, and within seconds a great horde of rats appeared, shrieking and crying, running down the length of the corridor. Directly behind them a wall of fire rose up and moved after them, driving them toward the end of the corridor.

Norreen came up to the hole, carrying Garth.

"Hammen first!"

He looked down into the darkness, hesitating, and a foot caught him from behind. With a curse he fell in, going under and then coming back up, struggling to get his footing on the slimy bottom.

"Catch him!"

Norreen lowered Garth feetfirst and then she let go. He fell into the current and Hammen struggled to pull his head out of the water. Seconds later Norreen jumped in.

"Varena, let's go!"

The Orange fighter jumped down just behind her and overhead the brilliant glare of the fire winked out. But still there was the sound of the rats, squealing with delight as they fought for their meal, the guards shrieking and howling.

The two women pulled Garth up and started off, half walking, half swimming with the current. As they passed beneath another grate a spear was slammed down, nearly catching Hammen in the shoulder.

"The key, where's the damn key!" a voice raged overhead, and then they were past him. The sewer sloped downhill, the current picking up speed, following the gentle drop downward from the palace, which rested on the highest ground in the center of the Plaza.

They reached the mesh of steel bars set across the sewer, marking the edge of the palace. Grunting and cursing, they squeezed through the narrow opening that Hammen and Norreen had spent hours cutting out and then weaved past the snares and traps which had been cunningly set into the sewer wall, ignoring the skeletons from previous attempts at rescue which had failed, most likely years ago, and now hung impaled against the wall.

They passed an opening to their right and then a second, moving now in pitch-darkness. Far ahead they could hear the echoing voices of the prisoners Hammen had released.

"Why'd you let them go?" Varena asked sharply.

"It'll throw the chase off," he lied in response.

"Third on the right," Hammen announced. "Here it is."

He was almost swept past and hung desperately to the side of the opening until Norreen reached back to pull him in. Far up the corridor a thin flicker of light was visible, while from overhead, through a storm opening, could be heard the braying of trumpets. A thin shaft of daylight shone down through the opening and above the trumpets could be heard the shouting of the mob.

"One-eye! One-eye!"

Already word had spread.

Now fighting against the current, they continued up the sewer, passing two more openings as the level of sewage and muck dropped till it was down to ankle level.

Varena suddenly extended her hand. Ten fathoms straight

ahead came a rasping of metal on stone, and a lantern was
lowered.

Varena motioned for them to lie down. Hammen followed
her lead, his face in the muck, and watched as a head appeared,
upside down, looking first up the sewer and then back toward
them. A loud clamoring could be heard. The guard looked
straight at them and started to point, as if having seen them.
With a loud cry he suddenly plunged headfirst into the sewer,
smashing into the lamp, which went out in the filthy water.

"Come on!"

Varena got up and moved forward as they reached the unconscious guard. A wild melee was breaking out overhead, the mob
shouting and roaring, fighting with the Grand Master's warriors.

Just as Hammen stepped past the opening overhead, he
looked up and could see legs, people running, struggling.
Another warrior fell through the hole and landed feetfirst.
Cursing, he started to stand up, his cry of alarm cut short by
Norreen's blade.

They pressed on up the narrowing sewer, following
Hammen as he cut left, then right, then left again.

Finally Hammen stopped.

"This is it," he whispered.

They were at a juncture where four lines came in together,
illuminated by a thin narrow grate directly overhead. One of
the lines was dry and inside of it four oilskinned bundles were
stacked along with a dozen heavy skins of water.

Norreen and Varena gently laid Garth down.

Hammen crawled up by his side and looked down at his
face.

Garth tossed back and forth as if caught in a fevered dream,
mumbling softly.

"Father, no, Father . . . Father."

Varena crawled up beside him and, reaching into her
satchel, pulled out an amulet and laid it on Garth's brow. A
thin shimmer of light haloed his face and, ever so gradually,
the drawn lines of pain eased away. Hammen watched in
amazement as the swelling of Garth's battered face subsided,
the cuts from Zarel's ringed hand drew shut, and finally the
wound to his shoulder closed over. Garth sighed and then
almost seemed to fall in upon himself and, for a moment,

Hammen thought Garth was dead, his spirit having slipped away.

"Let him rest for now," Varena whispered. "Keep an eye on him."

She crawled back out into the junction of sewer lines and casually started to strip off her clothes, Norreen following her and doing the same.

She looked back and saw two eyes gleaming in the semi-darkness.

"Hammen, so help me," Norreen snapped, "this is the one thing I objected to in all of this." And taking her cape, she managed to drape it across the opening where he sat with Garth.

He started to move quietly forward to sneak a peek.

"Hammen, if I see your ugly face, you're a blind man," Varena said quietly.

"How about just one eye?"

"Take care of Garth! Wash him up."

Cursing softly, he struggled to pull off Garth's stinking wet clothes. Getting his trousers off, he started on the bloody tunic, finally taking a dagger to cut it away, while on the other side of the curtain he could hear the two women splashing water over themselves to wash off the filth.

"Damn! You think there'd be a little gratitude in this world," he hissed as he finally cut Garth's tunic free.

And then he froze. There was the thin tracing of a scar running down the length of Garth's right arm, and at the sight of it tears filled Hammen's eyes, coursing down his filthy cheeks.

The curtain was pulled back and, startled, he looked up to see Varena looking at him while toweling her hair.

"Come on, let me help you," she said quietly and he wiped his hand across his face to hide his tears.

She unstoppered another skin and poured it over Garth, using the towel to wipe the filth off. Norreen joined him and they soon had him cleaned. Hammen sat in silence, lost in thought.

"Well, you stink too. Now wash," Varena directed. "We'll dress him."

Hammen, surprised, pointed at himself.

"Me?"

"You think you can walk around up there smelling like you do? It's a dead giveaway! Now wash!"

"Go to the demons."

Varena calmly raised her hand and a snap of pain hit Hammen.

"Damn it, that hurts!"

"Next time it's twice as bad. Now wash!"

Cursing under his breath, he moved out into the junction and started to uncork a waterskin.

"Undress first."

Hammen looked at them, gape mouthed.

"You're kidding."

The pain hit again and, true to her word, it was twice as bad.

Mumbling imprecation after imprecation, he pulled off his tunic and trousers.

"Everything," Norreen said calmly.

He started to protest and Varena raised her hand.

"Well, give me some privacy at least!" he demanded as he struggled to raise the curtain back up.

Stripping the rest of the way, he started to wash, grimacing as the cold water splashed over him and the curtain fell.

Norreen and Varena looked at him and started to chuckle softly. Red-faced with rage and humiliation, Hammen turned around and they laughed even louder.

"Some ladies you turned out to be," he snapped angrily as he finished, and Varena finally handed him a towel to dry off.

He quickly grabbed his bundle of clothes and changed, feeling uncomfortable as clean cloth rubbed against his scrubbed skin.

The two women turned their attention back to Garth, and drying him off, they dressed him in fresh clothes.

"So are you interested in him?" Varena asked, looking up at Norreen.

"He's a good fighter. Though I didn't admit it at the time, he saved me from getting stabbed in the back. I owed him."

"That's not what I mean."

Norreen looked down at Garth.

'He's not of my clan."

"That wasn't the question."

"You certainly are interested," Hammen interrupted, looking straight at Varena.

"It meant nothing," she replied calmly, and Hammen chuckled.

"What a life. Two women dressing him together, one's already slept with him and the other wants to. What a life."

Norreen looked back coldly at Hammen.

"What he did with her doesn't mean a damn thing to me."

"Sure. Anything you say," he replied tauntingly.

Varena silently watched Norreen and her features started to turn red.

"Once we get him out of here my obligation's done," Norreen snapped. "He's yours if he means that much to you."

"I said I wasn't interested."

"Why don't you just bid on him?" Hammen sniffed.

"Shut up," both of them snarled simultaneously.

From the grate overhead a distant roaring cry broke out and was picked up, rolling closer. Footsteps could be heard, then more shouting, and finally the distinctive sound of crossbows snapping.

Suddenly there was a snuffling sound, a deep-throated breathing that echoed in the tunnels. A low, throaty growl erupted.

"Mastiffs," Norreen whispered.

"There's something down there," a voice cried.

"Pull the grate!"

Norreen reached for her blade.

"It's set into the stone and it's too narrow to get through."

"Well, damn it, find a way to get in; they're down there!"

Varena leaned over Garth, pressed her hands on either temple, and, leaning over, whispered softly into his ear.

He stirred, groaning softly. She whispered again.

With a cry he tried to sit up, and she clamped a hand over his mouth.

"They're down there, they're down there!"

Garth looked about wildly and Varena kept her hand firmly grasped over his mouth. Suddenly she leaned over, removed her hand, and kissed him lightly on the lips.

Hammen, in spite of his fear, fought to suppress a chuckle at the flash of anger on Norreen's face.

The terror in Garth's eyes subsided and Varena leaned back. Reaching over to one of the oilskinned bundles, she opened it up, drew out his satchel, and pulled it over his shoulder.

"Where am I?" He recoiled as more shouts echoed from above.

"We got you out of the dungeon," Norreen whispered, moving to kneel by him.

"How?"

"Hammen figured it out."

Garth looked over at Hammen, who was kneeling behind Norreen. The old man said nothing, his eyes filled with concern.

Garth reached out and touched him lightly on the shoulder and Hammen lowered his head.

Wordlessly he looked at Varena and Norreen and nodded a thanks.

"Well, now that this reunion's over, I'd suggest we get out of here," Hammen whispered, trying to suppress a sniffle.

He scurried past Garth, moving up the tunnel. Norreen helped Garth to his feet, ready to grab him if he started to collapse.

"I'm all right," Garth whispered as her hand shot out to steady him and, bending low, he followed Hammen.

They continued up the tunnel, scurrying quickly past a side channel that echoed with voices and the distant growling of a dog. Hammen turned down another line, then turned right again, and finally came to a stop.

"This is the turn," he whispered.

Varena paused, looking to where Hammen pointed.

"It comes out behind the street of the money changers. It's an empty courtyard. After the last fire swept the city, they changed the street so it's no longer used. Scale over the wall, head east, and you'll come up behind your House. You should get through in the confusion."

Without a word, Varena started up the tunnel and then paused and looked back.

"Garth."

"Yes."

"Get out of the city. Give it up. I don't know what it is you're after; I don't want to know. Just get out. If you stay and we have to fight, you know I won't hold back. My *sessan* will not allow it."

Garth smiled and said nothing.

"Benalish, he's yours now. Get him out."

"I don't take gifts from an Orange *hanin*," Norreen replied haughtily.

Varena laughed and disappeared up the tunnel.

From the direction they had just come, the baying of mastiffs echoed.

"Let's go," Hammen said, and, turning, he led them into a narrow tunnel opposite the direction Varena had taken. The tunnel was so low that they had to crawl on hands and knees until Hammen finally stopped and pointed up. Overhead was a grate at the top of a narrow shaft. Hammen turned and reached up. Grabbing hold of a slippery outcropping of rock, he pulled himself up, shouldering the grate aside.

He climbed out warily and, crouching, looked around. The ruined courtyard was a jumble of fire-blackened stones tangled with a dense overgrowth of vines. Just on the other side of a tottering wall could be heard a wild commotion and exuberant shouts.

"One-eye, One-eye!"

Hammen motioned for the two to follow him up. Garth came next and then Norreen. Just as she cleared the grate a loud barking erupted from directly below.

"They're out, they're out!"

Garth threw the grate back over the hole while Norreen pushed a heavy boulder on top of it.

"Damn it, clear that grate!"

Hammen pointed toward a narrow fissure in the wall, which led out into the alleyway. Garth and Norreen started for it and stopped when they heard Hammen laughing.

He stood over the grate, relieving himself and an angry cursing exploded from below.

"Payback time," Hammen announced savagely, and then, laughing, he followed his two friends out into the alleyway. As they reached the street Garth pulled his cape up around his head to cover his face and missing eye.

"The way out of the city is that way," Hammen announced, pointing down the street, trying to be heard above the tumult of the crowds pushing around them.

"I'm staying," Garth announced sharply.

"Damn it!" Norreen snarled.

He looked over at her and her protest fell silent.

"All right, we kind of figured that," Hammen said. "The Bolk House is just around the corner."

"How'd you know?" Garth asked.

"We just kind of assumed it."

The three shouldered their way through the crowd, which

was pushing and shoving, some of them moving toward the rioting in the Plaza, others moving to get away.

Reaching the side of Brown's House, they edged along the wall and finally reached the Great Plaza.

A mad chaos was sweeping the square, tens of thousands of people shouting and laughing, taunting, as a knot of warriors swept past. Wherever there was a storm drain hundreds, thousands were gathered around, shouting encouragement as if One-eye were directly beneath them. Back and forth in the Plaza could be heard laughing cries, "He's here, no he's over here, no here!" Warriors and fighters were trying to battle their way through the mobs, which pelted them with whatever was handy.

In some sections of the Plaza open fighting was breaking out, while around the Great Palace of the Grand Master a solid wall of warriors was slowly moving forward to drive the mob back.

Garth pushed his way through to the edge of the brown paving stones which marked Brown's half circle of territory in front of their House. A solid ring of fighters was drawn around the great semicircle to keep the crowd off their sacred land. But the mood was almost festive, the mob trading good-natured gibes with the fighters, the fighters obviously enjoying the humiliation the Grand Master was experiencing.

Garth edged up to the ring of fighters and looked around. Seeing what he wanted, he pushed his way through and came up directly in front of a towering bulky form.

"Naru," he said quietly.

Hammen, groaning with despair, started to back away.

"I saved you for this?" he moaned.

"Naru!" This time Garth's voice was more commanding.

The giant looked down at Garth and gradually recognition set in. His features turned from surprise to a stunned disbelief. Naru looked past him for a second as if wondering how he had thus appeared and then looked back again. This time his features were starting to contort with a murderous rage.

Garth, his hand in his satchel, pulled out a bundle and held it up.

"Fighter, this is your satchel. Some beggar stole it from you unfairly. I got it back and have been trying to return it. I even had to fight with the Grand Master to keep it safe."

Naru looked down at him, confused. He tentatively reached

out and took the bundle, opening it up. Hammen watched him, surprised by the almost-childlike look of joy that appeared in the giant's eyes.

Naru put the satchel on and Hammen waited, ready for the fight to begin. Naru, however, suddenly started to dance about, as if possessed.

"My spells, my spells!"

Garth stood in silence, watching him. Around him the crowd had been watching the exchange and recognition suddenly dawned.

"One-eye, he's here, he's here!"

A company of warriors not ten fathoms away was wading through the crowd. Hearing the cry, some of them started to turn but their commander, swearing at the mob, angrily pointed them in the opposite direction and they continued on.

Naru looked back at Garth and there was a look of genuine confusion in his eyes.

Garth smiled and extended his hands palms downward in a gesture of peace.

"May I join this House and fight at your side, Naru?"

Naru stood silent for a moment, obviously confused by the complexity of what he had to deal with. He looked back up toward the palace and then, finally, back at Garth.

"You play good joke, yes."

And reaching out, he pulled Garth onto the brown stones.

Stunned, Hammen watched as Naru slapped Garth heavily on the shoulders and beamed with pride as if he had somehow rescued him. The mob, seeing the display and moved by the sentimentality of the moment, howled with delight. Hammen looked over at Norreen.

"I guess I better go with him, the damn fool."

"Take care of him, Hammen."

"Come with us. Damn it, woman. They're always hiring warriors. It's too dangerous out there right now."

Norreen shook her head.

"Take care of him."

She turned and started to disappear into the mob.

"Norreen. He wants you, you know that."

"Tell that to Varena. She's easier," Norreen said with a sad smile, and, turning, she disappeared.

CHAPTER
10

TREMBLING WITH FEAR, URIAH LAY UPON THE floor of the audience chamber, cursing the fates that had made him such a creature of contempt. He well understood the role he was doomed to play. Though born with the ability of controlling the *mana*, he was born stunted as well. He had thought that as he learned to master the *mana* he could thus somehow gain respect, but it never came. There had been a time, an all-so-brief time, when it had been different. But the lure of power offered by Zarel had been too tempting to resist. To be captain of fighters rather than a lowly fighter whom the others never understood.

Others called him crafty, a sneak, a lickspittle of the Grand Master. He saw it simply as survival. He was captain of the fighters, to be sure, though there were some in his command who had more powers than he. Zarel had elevated him thus for one reason only—he could be controlled, and he cursed himself for knowing that cruelest of facts—he would tolerate any abuse that others would have long ago rebelled against . . . simply because his life had been one of abuse since the day he was born.

The room was deadly silent, the guard of warriors, secretaries, and court hangers-on frozen in place while Zarel struck Uriah yet again.

"You should have anticipated this, damn you! Didn't any of you think that they might try a rescue through the sewers?"

"My lord, the sewer gate had been barred shut years ago and set with traps. It was thought to be impossible."

"Well, it wasn't, damn it!"

The dwarf said nothing, emitting only a low grunt of pain when Zarel kicked him before turning back to his messenger, whom he had dispatched to the House of Bolk.

"Has Kirlen sent a reply?"

The armored warrior lowered her head and said nothing.

"Damn it all, what is it?"

Zarel looked as if he would raise his hand but the messenger looked up at him coldly. He stood, hesitant for a moment, and then savagely kicked Uriah once again.

"Did she say anything at all?"

"My lord, she told you to perform an action upon yourself which is physically impossible," the warrior replied slowly.

Zarel looked at the warrior, sensing that there was a certain defiance in the woman's tone.

"Go on."

"She declared that the one-eye is now officially a Bolk and that as such he is granted the right of the brotherhood to immunity from prosecution for crimes committed prior to his acceptance."

"Get out."

The warrior came to her feet, bowed low, and then strode out of the room. Zarel watched her go, realizing that he had suffered a tremendous loss of face. First off, the mob was now firmly on One-eye's side, they had a hero to worship who they felt was one of them. Worse, though, his own people were now suspect. The lock had been oiled and there was the chance that one of his own people had done it. He had killed the prison guards out of hand for their failure and now his warriors were upset over his fit of temper. His magic fighters were growing restless, angered at the humiliations hurled upon them by the mob. Even though several hundred of the crowd had been killed to quiet them down, he could sense that his own fighters were now upset, the lower ranks even fearful, for several of them had been killed during the day of rioting which had ensued.

And tomorrow Festival would start and half a million of

them would be brought together in one place. If something triggered them, the results could be disastrous. Some offering would have to be made to quell the mob and win them back. Though he hated to consider it, he knew he would have to dig into his treasures to buy them off.

"Send in the captain of my catapulters when you and I are done. I've thought of something that might be amusing for the Festival."

"Your catapult captain?"

"Just do as you are ordered."

Zarel turned away and for a moment Uriah thought he had been dismissed.

"Uriah, is there any chance we can get at One-eye between now and Festival."

The dwarf looked up and came to his knees.

"I don't think so, great lord."

"Why not?"

"Jimak, Varnel, and Tulan are all bribeable. Kirlen is not. There is only one thing she wants and that is your power and the path to being a Walker. Nothing you can offer her other than your own power would be sufficient and she sees in One-eye a means of causing embarrassment, perhaps even of throwing the mob against you."

Zarel looked down at Uriah.

"Sometimes, Uriah, I think you are too smart."

"Only in service to you, my lord."

"Why?"

Uriah hesitated.

"You are my lord."

"Not sufficient."

Uriah lowered his head.

"Because the others would never take me in."

Zarel laughed coldly.

"The traitor of Turquoise, the one who fed me all the information while wearing their colors and unbarred the gate for the Night of Fire."

Zarel smiled and looked down at Uriah, who squirmed uncomfortably.

"Who is this One-eye?" Zarel asked as if directing the question at himself.

Uriah looked up at him, saying nothing.

"You wore their colors for years, do you remember him?"

"No, Master," Uriah said quietly.

"Get out of here."

Uriah scurried away, barely avoiding the kick that was aimed in his direction.

As he closed the door he looked back at Zarel.

Who is he? the Grand Master had asked. Uriah smiled and limped away to nurse his bruises of the body and of the heart.

"You played good joke."

Garth smiled, forcing himself to stay awake as Naru poured another round of drinks. The giant looked over the side of the table at Hammen, who lay passed out on the floor of the feasting hall, and laughed.

"Old man weak and now he stink bad." Naru laughed.

Garth tried to nurse his drink along, his head swimming, wishing that he had control of one of the rare spells of curing drunkenness.

"Oh, but that bad trick you play on Naru." The giant looked down into his drink and shook his head.

"Sorry, but if you remember, we were fighting at the time."

Naru looked over at Garth and his eyes narrowed for a moment as if he was struggling to decide whether One-eye was a friend or not. His features finally relaxed.

"You beat Grand Master and return my spells. You still my friend."

Garth nodded, having gone through this discussion more than a score of times in the last several hours. Naru started to pour another drink, looking at Garth sadly when he realized that his new friend was not keeping up.

"Too bad I'll beat you at Festival."

"Of course."

"Naru hear people say Grand Master will declare final fights to be to death."

Garth stirred and looked over at the giant.

"Where did you hear that?"

"Oh, Naru have friends. Grand Master do this more and more to make mob happy."

"Why don't you and the others refuse?"

"Can't. Grand Master is Grand Master of Arena. When in arena can't say no."

"What about the House Masters?"

"Oh, they make good money from it, pay back of contracts, so they happy."

Naru chuckled.

"Besides, Naru like breaking bones. Get many spells and *mana* from fallen, even though Grand Master keep part."

The giant looked back at Garth and sighed.

"Too bad I must break your bones. I think I still like you."

Naru raised his goblet to drain it, the movement setting off an inertia that kept the giant moving backward so that he fell off the back of his stool. He crashed to the floor, emitted a single belch, and passed out.

"One-eye."

Startled, Garth turned to see Kirlen, the House Master of Bolk, standing in the doorway. The woman was bent over with age, hair long since gone from white to a sickly yellow, her wrinkled skin hanging loose on her face as if it had already lost hold upon the bones of her body. Her black robe clung to her slender frame as if she were a skeleton held up only by the staff she leaned against, holding it with both of her gnarled hands.

Garth slowly came to his feet and she motioned for him to follow her. Garth looked down at Hammen, who was sleeping alongside Naru, and realized that there was nothing he could do to rouse his friend. Moving carefully, so that he would not fall down, Garth stepped out into the corridor and walked behind Kirlen as she shuffled down the hallway and turned into her private quarters. The room was overly heated from a roaring fire and she went over to it, extending her hands and rubbing them. Garth looked around at the sparsely furnished quarters, which seemed almost like a monk's cell, with nothing more than a cot and a desk piled high with books and scrolls. The four walls, however, were lined with bookcases crammed to overflowing. The room smelled musty, ancient, and somehow dangerous.

"Naru can be tedious, especially when he is drinking," she said quietly.

"He's interesting enough."

"He's an idiot. One of those rare savants who can barely empty the proverbial boot of its contents but somehow able to control the *mana* with remarkable ease. Someday soon he'll get killed." She pronounced her prediction with casual indifference.

She looked back at him and smiled, revealing a row of blackened stumps.

"I disgust you, don't I?"

"No, my lady."

"And suppose I asked you to share my bed?" she inquired, pointing to the narrow cot and cackling softly.

Garth said nothing.

"No, the Benalish woman, or Varena of Fentesk, with her golden red hair, now that would be different."

She turned away for a moment and he almost felt a sense of pity for the flash of pain in her eyes.

"If you have the power I think you have, why don't you rejuvenate yourself?" Garth asked.

She laughed, her voice breaking into a sigh.

"Ah, then I would have you, wouldn't I?"

"That is not the question I asked," Garth replied.

"Do you know how old I am?"

"I've heard rumors, my lady."

"I lost count of the rejuvenations centuries ago. I lost count of the spells, the potions, the amulets that I burned upon dark altars. Each time I was made young again, but inside, inside one can be young but once. Youth is innocence on the inside as well as on the outside. No matter what spells I use, that innocence comes but once in a lifetime for all of us.

"Each time you turn back the hourglass you never quite gain back what you had, you lose a day, a week, a month. There are limits to the powers of this plane and I reached them long ago. Oh, I can live on for centuries yet to come, but only the Walker can grant me back my beauty and my passions."

She paused for a long moment, looking into the fire. "Or by being a Walker myself."

"And he will not grant it, and would most definitely block you from becoming one."

She looked back at him, her eyes filled with a cold rage.

"You know, there was a time, a time so long ago I can barely remember it, when Kuthuman the Walker and I were lovers. How he praised my beauty then, how he pledged eternal fidelity to me."

She cackled and then spit into the fire.

"And then he turned away as I grew older and could not reclaim my charms. He forgot such things and became consumed instead with other passions. To pierce the veil, that was all he desired."

"He promised to take you with him, didn't he?"

"How did you know that?"

"I've heard rumors."

She stirred angrily.

"Who? Who says these things?"

"The Grand Master has it whispered about by his agents," Garth replied softly.

"Damn him forever." She poked the fire with her staff so that a sparkling swirl of flames soared up the chimney.

"So he forgot you in his moment of triumph, didn't he?"

The old woman looked back at Garth as if he had spoken too much, bringing into words the humiliation of her heart.

"I helped him, you know, I helped him down through so many long years." She pointed to the bookcases and the piles of dusty scrolls. "It was I who learned the paths and the spells, and the incantations to bridge the planes."

"So why don't you go yourself?"

"The *mana*. It is the *mana* which gives one the power to control magic in this plane. It is the *mana* as well which has the power to open the doorway into other realms when one knows the hidden path. I knew the path, but it was he who controlled the *mana*.

"He tricked me. On the Night of Fire he betrayed me as well."

"The Night of Fire?"

"When Zarel stormed the House of Turquoise, murdering their Master and stealing their trove of *mana*. I was betrayed as well."

Garth said nothing, his features calm.

"That means something to you, doesn't it?"

"I heard the stories," Garth replied.

Kirlen smiled.

"Yes, I helped him. I agreed not to object, not to rally to the side of Turquoise in return for the door to be opened for me as well.

"The following morning he was gone and Zarel was the new Grand Master."

"Why did he betray you?"

Kirlen laughed coldly.

"Why not? The gateway to limitless worlds was now open. And with it the power to take anything he desired. Even now he strides the universe, conquering, stealing, pleasuring himself. What need had he of an old hag whom he had once loved when they were both young. He can have anyone now and love is nothing but a hindrance."

She looked back into the fire.

"I learned that long ago, One-eye." She turned and looked over at him and then hobbled across the floor, drawing closer so that her fetid breath washed over Garth.

"This is the final face of love," she hissed. "This is the final face of loyalty, of honor, of glory, of vengeance, of all that is living. It is this," she said, and, laughing, she pointed to her sagging folds of flesh, yellowed hair, and toothless mouth.

"So why the sudden loyalty to me?" Garth whispered in reply.

Kirlen drew back and laughed.

"You humiliated him. Even now Zarel trembles. Perhaps he fears for his power and his life. For that I thank you."

Garth bowed low, struggling to keep his balance and to keep his mind focused, for there was more. He could sense there was far more.

"You're of the House of Oor-tael, aren't you?"

He looked back up and could feel the power radiating around her, coiling outward, fingers of light probing toward him. He tried to force an inner calm as she reached into him.

He could feel her eyes probing into him and he was startled by the power of it, for she was almost as strong as the Grand Master. He felt a lash of rage as her probing slowed and then finally stopped, unable to reach into the very core.

"You're strong, One-eye."

Garth said nothing, not daring to lower his guard.

"I think you are strong enough that if I tried to challenge you to a fight, you could actually harm me."

Again he was silent. Her thoughts withdrew and he struggled not to sag down from exhaustion and drunkenness. He realized now that Naru's actions were at her behest, to keep him awake after all that had happened and break him down with drink and simple exhaustion.

He looked at her and smiled.

"I can be of use to you," he said softly.

"I should kill you now."

"You know the mob is behind me. The Grand Master might hold power as a holder of *mana* but not even that power can control half a million who will be sitting in the arena come tomorrow. I am of Brown as well and that power reflects upon you. That can be of use to you."

She smiled, her lips trembling.

"And suppose you are of Turquoise? You would have reason enough for vengeance upon me given what I just told you."

"If I wanted such vengeance, I could do it now." He flicked a finger toward the bookcases.

A startled cry escaped her and she started to bring her hand up.

"I would be a fool to burn them, for then we would fight here and now," Garth said, lowering his hand and looking back at her.

She looked back nervously at her books and then again at Garth.

"You have the knowledge hidden within your books. But your path now is through the Grand Master because it is he who has amassed the *mana* and I suspect will soon have enough to try himself to become a Walker. Kill him and you could succeed to his throne and take all that is hidden within his vaults.

"That is your next step. Do that and the Walker does not care who rules here, only that they are loyal to him and serve his needs."

"He would know what I desire."

"Don't you think he knows what Zarel desires as well, what all of us desire?"

She said nothing.

"Power, immortality, and eternal youth, which only being a Walker can bring. Kill Zarel at the end of Festival and you will have a year to prepare before the Walker returns once again. I dare say that within that year you could gather enough *mana* to do as you please."

"How?"

"Zarel did it for his Master."

Kirlen chuckled darkly.

"You're goading me not only into killing Zarel, but the other House Masters as well."

Garth smiled and said nothing.

"Why do you desire to help me?"

"Perhaps you could grant a one-eye immortality as well when the time came."

"Perhaps I would not need a scarred face when that time came."

"I'm willing to gamble on that. At the very least there would be room for advancement, perhaps as a House Master or Grand Master myself."

Kirlen chuckled.

"Revenge and power. I think I might like you after all, One-eye."

She turned and looked back at the fire.

"You've given me nothing all that new. I've thought it before. If that is all you have to offer, your usefulness is at an end."

"I can help you. I could trigger the mob to bring about the Grand Master's death."

Kirlen smiled.

"And suppose you win the tournament. You would be gone, to go as a servant to the Walker in other realms. Then what?"

"Do I really want to win?"

"All fighters do."

"Then why haven't you done so and thus gained the path in that manner?"

Kirlen laughed coldly.

"I prefer to go in my own right and not as a servant," she finally said softly.

"If I win, I win and will take the glory. But even in the process of doing that I can manipulate the mob to your favor and perhaps trigger the results you desire. Because that is the final part of the problem. The power of the *mana* is strong, but when half a million of the city turn against you, even a Grand Master might be overwhelmed. To have the mob on your side is worth the power of a hundred fighters. And if I don't win, I will still be here to serve you."

"Of course you will," Kirlen said with a smile.

"Master."

Garth opened his eyes with the greatest reluctance. It took several seconds to realize that the room was not actually spinning. The sight of Hammen looking down at him finished it, especially when the old man's breath washed over him. He half crawled out of bed and staggered to the privy room, ignoring Hammen's coarse laughter as he knelt over the hole to offer up his last meal to the god of excessive drink.

Cursing and spitting, he came back into the room.

"I've laid out a change of clothes, oh exalted Master," Hammen announced. "I'd suggest burning what you're wearing now."

"Shut up."

"Such gratitude."

Garth looked at him, bleary-eyed.

"How come you're not hung over?"

"More years' experience and, besides, I had the good sense to pass out before you. I must say old Naru is even more impressed with you now."

"How is he?"

"Down in the steam room soaking it out, where I'd suggest that you head now. Festival ceremonies start at noon and you want to be ready for it."

Garth stripped down and followed Hammen down to the lower level steam room and went into the swirling mist, finding a wooden bench in the corner. He looked around and, in the shadows, saw Naru stretched out on a bench, snoring loudly.

Hammen came in a minute later with a birch switch.

"Get out of here with that," Garth snarled.

"Shut up and take it like a man," Hammen replied as he set to his task with what Garth suspected was a little too much enthusiasm for his work.

"Naru's really not such a bad fellow," Hammen said, nodding to the giant, who stirred, groaned, and then rolled over. "We had a long talk this morning. If you could call it talking."

"And?"

"Kirlen wants you dead."

"Did he say that?"

"No, but you could read between the lines, as they say. Kirlen ordered him to drink you under the table."

"I sort of figured that out."

"She also told him to challenge you then."

"So why didn't he?"

"He passed out first. I think you're presenting old Naru with a real moral dilemma. He's forgotten about the kick; his brain can't hold more than one thought at a time. He just remembers the return of his satchel."

"So if he won't do it, there must be someone else."

"Naru's their best fighter and has been for years. I think she has it figured that you can take anyone else, and besides, she wants it done quietly and to make it look legitimate, a fair grudge match. But it won't happen until the last day of Festival."

Garth grunted a reply as Hammen struck him a bit too hard across the lower back with the birch switch.

"Once more like that and I'll take the damn switch to you."

"Got to beat the poison out," Hammen said cheerfully.

"What's the advantage of killing me then?"

"When, at the end of Festival? Trigger a riot, the Grand Master loses face in front of the Walker, and she eliminates him."

"You got all of that from Naru?"

Hammen smiled.

"It doesn't take much to figure it out. Actually, Master, I think it's time simply to get the devil out of here. You've had your fun, you've bearded the Grand Master, now take your winnings and move on."

Garth turned and looked over at Hammen and smiled.

"Not yet."

"Damn it, Garth, you don't stand a chance. All four Houses and the Grand Master want you for one thing or another. Give it up."

Garth smiled and said nothing.

"I found out where Norreen is hiding."

Garth stirred and looked back at him.

"Ah, that got your interest, didn't it?"

"Where is she?"

"I sneaked out this morning and talked to a couple of lodge brothers. If you want to know anything in a city, make friends with the thieves. They're up in arms anyhow since the Grand Master broke the code and murdered my friends. The ones who escaped with us yesterday are really spreading trouble. Anyhow, they found her hiding out at the edge of town and are keeping an eye on her. I could get you to her and we could be on our way."

Garth shook his head and stood up, grabbing hold of Hammen's hand before the old man could start lashing his chest.

"Enough. Let's get dressed."

"Anyhow, if you're so stupid as to stay, I also found a hiding place for you. It's right on the Great Plaza." Hammen paused and lowered his voice to a whisper. "Where the House of Turquoise used to be. It's the building to the left of the Drunken Dwarfs tavern. It's a knocking shop."

"A what?"

"A brothel. One of my innumerable cousins runs the place. He knows you on sight. Just get in there and he'll take you up to the top floor, which is ours to use."

"Alone, I trust."

"If you want it that way." Hammen sighed.

"Thanks. And make sure your friends keep an eye on Norreen."

"You're really taken with her, aren't you?"

Garth smiled.

"Sort of."

Hammen cackled and then pointed toward the back door of the steam room. Garth started toward it, smiling as he passed Naru, who was snoring away.

"This heat could kill him," Garth said and he leaned over to shake the giant awake, but Hammen pushed him on.

As they opened the door Garth stopped at the sight of the pool room.

"This isn't the way out." And he started to turn back.

Hammen shouldered into him and Garth, losing his balance, tumbled into the water.

"You've yet to get your ice water bath," Hammen announced calmly as the room echoed with Garth's roaring curses.

Still cursing under his breath, Garth One-eye formed up with the other fighters of his newly adopted order. Rank on rank they stood, the eighty-seven fighters of the House of Bolk, present for this, the Nine Hundredth and Ninety-Eighth Festival of the Western Realms.

The tension in the audience room was electric as the fighters, resplendent in their brown doeskin tunics, trousers, and leather capes stood in formal ranks of order, their tunic fronts glistening with battle honors won in Festivals past. Garth came into the room quietly, moving toward the back of the four-man-wide column.

"One-eye."

Garth turned and saw Naru at the front of the line, looking back at him and motioning for him to come up to his side.

"You good fighter, march as Naru's escort."

Garth looked over at the ranks and saw that this gesture on the part of the House's highest fighter had won him more than one additional enemy.

Naru looked back at the other fighters and chuckled.

"He is Naru's friend, isn't he?"

Several of the others laughed coldly as Garth moved past their ranks and came to the front of the column to stand to the left of Naru and directly behind the brown-and-gold-striped pennant of the House. Trumpets echoed in the audience room and Garth followed the lead of the others, bowing low as the doors into the private quarters of the Master of the House were flung open to the accompaniment of rolling drums, crashing cymbals, and shrieking pipes.

Garth looked up and could not conceal his amazement.

Fifty warriors, dressed in brown leather armor and helmets, were bearing a massive dais nearly two fathoms across. The platform was ringed with skulls cast from the finest crystal, and set into each of them were eyes of rubies and circlet crowns of spun gold. Atop the dais stood six more warriors and upon their shoulders rested a second, smaller golden platform and throne of silver. Kirlen, however, did not sit on the throne, but rather was hovering above it as if she was sitting upon an invisible cushion, legs crossed, spindly arms folded across her brown and golden surcoat, while above her floated a Kurdasian carpet to act as a sunshade. Resting at the foot of the throne was a golden lockbox that actually seemed to be radiating power. Within it was the yearly tribute of *mana* bundles from the House of Brown, which would go to the Walker.

Her bearers turned toward the main door and, with the trumpeters lining the corridor blowing a fanfare, the door was flung open. A roaring like an ocean torn by a hurricane thundered into the hallway as Kirlen was carried out into the Great Plaza. Behind her marched a company of Brown warriors, heavily armored, cocked and loaded crossbows at the ready. Next came the servants of the House, bearing flowers, pots of smoking incense, and urns of copper coins to throw to the crowd. Garth watched as Hammen moved in the middle of the procession, a look of disgust on his face as he lugged along a pot of money.

Naru growled out a command and the pennant bearer stepped out from the audience room and into the main corridor. The fighters of Bolk moved forward, already strutting in their pride and arrogance.

Garth marched behind Naru, struggling to hide his disdain for the whole rigmarole. They turned into the main corridor, which was now filled with the sweet smell of incense, and finally stepped out into the blazing light of the noonday sun. As they emerged from the House a thunderous tumult erupted and Garth felt his heart quicken.

The Plaza was packed from end to end with a flood of humanity. The entire city and the hundreds of thousands of visitors, who had traveled from the far corners of the Western Realms and even from beyond the Flowing Seas to witness the fight, were all jammed together. During the night, after the rioting of the day before had been quelled, thousands of laborers had constructed viewing stands lining the procession paths leading to the center of the Plaza and ringing the palace of the Grand Master.

Most of the places were rented to the nobles and well-heeled merchants, so that they could be above the shoving, roiling, stinking crowds. Even as Garth looked around in amazement, one of the viewing stands collapsed and the crowd let out a hearty roar of approval at the downfall of those who thought themselves to be the betters of the mob.

The screaming multitude of Brown supporters pressed in on all sides as the procession made its way into the Great Plaza. The mob around Garth was waving brown pennants or strips of dirty brown cloth, chanting, cursing, hollering, lost in a mad frenzy of joy. As the servants ahead of the fighters made their way through the narrow path held open by ranks of warriors of the Grand Master, the struggling masses pushed and shoved for the copper coins and free admission tickets to the Festival that were being tossed out by the servants. Garth saw an entire urn go tumbling through the air and laughed at Hammen's effort to be rid of the burden, most likely after filling his own pockets to overflowing first.

"One-eye!"

It was a lone voice but within seconds the cry was picked up and raced through the mob, the chanting rising, swelling, echoing above the hysterical roaring of the cheering mobs who were gathered about the processional paths being taken by the three other Houses.

"One-eye, One-eye, One-eye!"

Garth looked over at Naru, who turned and gazed back at him, and he could sense the fighter's sudden confusion. The mob had a new hero. The giant looked around and glowered, angered at the fickleness of the mob. Garth moved to stand directly behind Naru and, reaching out, he took hold of the ends of the giant's cloak, lifting it off the ground in a show of obeisance by playing the role of a servant. Naru, looking back over his shoulder, grinned and returned to strutting. Those closest to the procession, who could see Garth's actions, fell silent in confusion, but half a dozen ranks back his gesture was invisible and the crowd continued to roar for Garth.

The procession, moving slowly, made its way toward the palace and, as they passed, the mob fell in behind them, waving their pennants and cheering. At the edges of Bolk's procession crowds following the House of Fentesk to the left and the House of Kestha to the right brushed against the supporters of Bolk. Fights started to break out between the rival groups, the brawls adding to the general aura of celebration and excitement.

Each of the four processions came into the central part of the Plaza and now the Masters of each House started into their shows. Sparkles of light appeared above the processions, clouds formed fifty fathoms overhead and lightning bolts flashed across the Plaza. Dragons of light soared through the air and for a moment an Ingkara dragon wrestled with Fentesk's, the crowd screaming with delight when Fentesk's dragon exploded. This nearly triggered another brawl between the supporters of the two Houses until Ingkara, following the rules of the procession not to engage in any displays of conflict, caused its own dragon to disappear in a puff of smoke, thus ending any direct challenge of power.

Directly in front of the great pyramid-shaped palace of the Grand Master the four processions finally came together and marched before the front of the palace. Tulan of Kestha floated atop a gray cloud, flashes of lightning dancing around him, illuminating his presence with an unearthly light. Varnel of Fentesk appeared to be riding on a pillar of fire that flared around him, and Jimak of Ingkara rode astride a coiling funnel of wind, which howled and whistled, the pennants of his followers whipping over their heads, the miniature tornado catching up hats and flinging them high into the air to float back down.

Garth caught a glimpse of Varena at the head of the Orange column of fighters, moving with a cool, almost languid, ease, and for a brief instant she spared him a quick glance and then looked away. The turmoil of the hundreds of thousands jamming the Plaza was at near fever pitch, and for a moment Garth sensed that in fact all semblance of control was about to break down into a wild bacchanal of rioting.

And then, as if from high overhead, a clarion trumpet note sounded, cutting through the insane roaring. The note changed into a chorus of trumpets that echoed up and down, counterpointing each other in a wild, minor-keyed harmonic. Great drums rolled, booming with a deep, insistent rumbling,

joined in by the thundering chords of an organ, the sound
magnified and echoing back and forth across the Plaza. A hidden
doorway, halfway up the side of the pyramid, slid open,
and a golden shaft of light streamed out. The fountains about
the palace, which had been stilled until this moment, leaped
to life, soaring fifteen or more fathoms into the air, the geysers
directly in front of the palace catching the light coming from
the pyramid and breaking it into a rainbow stream of colors.
Puffs of smoke burst out around the top of the pyramid and
booming explosions erupted, caused by some frightful
alchemy, while yet more streams of smoke soared upward, detonating
into multihued bursts, followed by yet more thundering
explosions that caused the mob to scream with fear and a
wild ecstasy of abandon.

A cataclysmic volley of explosions wreathed the top of the
pyramid and then a great flag rose up out of the smoke, unfurling
to reveal the shimmering, rainbow-hued pennant of Zarel
Ewine, Grand Master of the Festival and Arena, Most High
and Exalted Ruler of the Western Realms, and Mortal Legate
of Kuthuman, He Who Walks in Unknown Places.

The crowd, which only the day before had fought against
the Grand Master, started to cheer, caught up in the abandon
of the moment, as if all were forgiven. A shadow darkened the
stream of light bursting out of the pyramid and then, as the
trumpet, organ, and drum fanfare reached a mad crescendo,
the Grand Master appeared, floating out of the opening in the
pyramid as if he was riding the beam of light, which haloed
and silhouetted him in a celestial fire.

As the last echo of the fanfare and thunderous explosions
died away the hundreds of thousands in the Great Plaza fell
silent. The Grand Master remained motionless and then, as he
slowly extended his arms outward, almost as if preparing to
offer ritual challenge, and even though the gesture was one of a
noble greeting, an uneasy murmur raced through the crowd.

Zarel remained motionless. Below him a balcony of gold slid
out from the side of the pyramid and he floated down, landing
lightly on his feet. As he did so the four House Masters did the
same, though Garth could detect a slight defiance in Kirlen,
who stopped just short of alighting and waited until Zarel was
standing like other mortals. She remained hovering for several

more seconds and then came to rest upon her dais. Her gesture was not unnoticed by Bolk's supporters and a ripple of applause raced through the crowd, counterpointed by catcalls from the rest of the mob and, surprisingly, some shouts of approval as well.

Zarel waited for a long moment, his gaze fixed upon Kirlen as if preparing to offer a rebuke. He finally turned slightly, as if to ignore her instead. Garth waited, sensing the subtle interplays, Kirlen defiant, with the slightest hint of support from the other three House Masters, which transcended, for the moment, their mutual hatreds.

Garth looked back up at Zarel and saw that the Grand Master was now staring straight at him and he could sense as well the barely suppressed rage, the man struggling with the temptation to order a massacre if need be in order to get at him.

Garth let the slightest of smiles crease his features and he bowed with a mock disdain. Again, the mob standing at the edge of the lines of fighters saw the interplay and, again, there was a smattering of applause.

Zarel remained silent, his features turning crimson. To those farther away the interchange was not visible and the long delay was becoming tiresome. A restless stirring swept the Plaza. Zarel looked away from Garth and back out across the Plaza and the crowds fell silent.

"Today is the first day of Festival!"

A numbing explosion of cheers erupted across the Plaza, so loud that Garth felt as if sound had almost taken physical form. Looking around him he saw the arrayed fighters were being swept up in the excitement, eyes wide, breath coming in short gasps, some of them raising their arms in an involuntary gesture as if already within the fighting circles.

Zarel rose up and floated off the high dais, lightning swirling around him, and again there was the trumpeting, the drums, the high minor chord shrieks of the organ. He came to a hover above a great platform sheathed in solid gold and resting on great wheels that stood as high as two men and which was drawn by half a dozen mammoths in harness. With a hundred trumpeters sounding a fanfare, the head of the procession started off while yet more explosions erupted overhead. A solid phalanx of warriors marched in formation around the Grand Master's juggernaut-like dais and the mob pushed and shoved to let it pass, with more than one unfortunate falling beneath the feet of the mammoths or the great grinding wheels of the platform.

Behind him came Ingkara, marching in the place of honor, since it was one of their own who had won the last Festival and thus gained the honor of being the chosen servant of the Walker. Behind them came Fentesk, for placing second, then Kestha, and finally Bolk. The great mob surged around them as the procession made its way across the Plaza. A stampede erupted as the spectators rushed down the side streets, streaming ahead of the procession to form up at the gates of the arena.

The procession skirted past the vacant spot where the House of Oor-tael once stood and Garth, sensing that he was being watched, looked up to see Kirlen turning and gazing back at him. He lowered his head in respect, half expecting yet another lashing probe, but there was none.

The procession reached the great thoroughfare that led from the Plaza and down a long, sloping road for a thousand fathoms to the gates of the city. Every rooftop was crammed with spectators, the colors of the mob now intermingling, the supporters of the four Houses cheering themselves hoarse with excitement as their favorites passed. And yet again a chant arose . . .

"One-eye, One-eye, One-eye!"

Garth lowered his head and yet still the cry echoed around him. For a brief moment he looked up and there was a flash of dark hair and stained leather armor on a rooftop, and then she disappeared.

The procession finally reached the gates of the city. The heat under the noonday sun was intense, even for this autumn day, the air thick with smoke, incense, dust, and the smell of unwashed bodies. Dozens were passing out now, falling, those around them robbing the sunstruck. Great barrels of wine and beer were opened at nearly every street corner, with mugs full of drink going for a copper, the cheap brews inflaming the mob to an even wilder hysteria.

Garth breathed a sigh of relief as the procession of Bolk

warriors finally passed under the gate and, for a brief instant, the noise and sun were blocked out. As the procession emerged out the other side, Garth finally saw the arena below and he felt his blood quicken.

The arena was built into a natural, bowl-shaped valley just outside the city gates, just to the south of the harbor, which was crammed with shipping. The fighting area measured over three hundred fathoms across, the entire circumference ringed with seats that rose up for over a hundred rows, providing seating for more than three hundred thousand spectators. On the sloping ground that stretched from the arena up to the city wall hundreds of thousands more who could not get tickets were gathered to watch the spectacle, though all they could hope to see was the struggle of antlike creatures far below. Already the sloping ground was jammed by the mob, while down below in the arena, those who could afford seats were already streaming in and filling the stands.

As the procession made its way down the hill the cheering within the arena rose up to greet them. The head of the procession finally turned and went beneath a high-arching gate and stepped out into the center of the arena and the multitude roared with an insane frenzy, so that Garth felt as if he was facing the attack of a demon howl. The arena was clearly divided into four areas, marked by the fluttering pennants waved by the spectators. The procession, still led by Zarel, moved across the center of the arena floor and then broke in four different directions, each group of fighters taking positions in front of the sections of the arena reserved for its supporters. The fifth section was on the western side of the arena, directly beneath the tote board, which would show the odds for each of the fights. Here would sit the nobles and well-heeled merchants, as well as the fighters and warriors of the Grand Master, where they could catch the afternoon breeze wafting in from the sea. Directly in front of this section, out on the edge of the arena floor, was the high throne reserved for the Grand Master of the Arena, Zarel Ewine.

As the Brown contingent of fighters reached its section Garth breathed a sigh of relief. The formation came to a halt and then broke ranks to take seats in a shaded viewing stand resting on the edge of the arena floor. The procession had done nothing to help his still-throbbing hangover. The howling of the mob echoed back and forth in the arena, intensified, it seemed, by the heat, swirling dust, the smell of unwashed bodies, and the thick, heavy scent of greasy food cooking in hundreds of stalls that lined the top ring of the stadium.

Again there was the fanfare of trumpets and, surprisingly, the mob settled down almost instantly, a silence for which Garth was immensely grateful.

Across the far side of the stadium Garth saw the antlike figure of the Grand Master step forward, while from out of a tunnel set into the side of the arena came a procession of hooded monks bearing a great smoking brazier. The mob sitting in the arena came to its feet and Garth looked around to see that his fellow fighters now stood with heads bowed.

The Grand Master approached the brazier, raised his hands, and the flames leaped heavenward, black smoke coiling straight up into the sky, spreading outward on the faint wisp of a breeze coming in from the sea.

"On the third day of Festival shall come the Great Walker of Realms Unknown to take his tribute and the fighter chosen on the arena floor."

Zarel's voice, enhanced by magical powers, projected to the farthest ends of the arena, washing over Garth like a wave.

"In three days' time let us find the fighter who shall be worthy to be known as servant of He Who Rules over All!"

"So be it!"

The reply was roared out by half a million voices, but Garth stood silent, except for the faintest of curses escaping his lips that was lost in the wild insanity of screams.

CHAPTER
11

ZAREL EWINE, GRAND MASTER OF THE ARENA, looked around at the howling mob which filled the arena.

"Sometimes I wish you all had but one neck," he snarled under his breath, dropping the power of far speaking so that his true thoughts could not be heard.

The circle of monks lifted up the brazier and carried it back into the tunnel, while a dozen monks, cowls covering their faces, remained behind, standing respectfully to the left side of Zarel's juggernaut. From the far corners of the arena the four House Masters now approached, this time on foot, for the only magics allowed in the great fighting circle were those of the fighters engaged in the contest and that of the Grand Master himself. Behind each of them were four warriors, bearing between them a heavy gold urn, which contained golden disks with the names of the fighters of the Houses engraved thereon.

He waited, disgusted by the wild howling of the mob and what he suspected was the deliberately slow pace of Kirlen, who hobbled along, resting heavily on her staff. The four stopped at the foot of the great juggernaut and Zarel finally stirred, stepping down from the throne to the fanfare of trumpets and drums.

At the foot of the throne was the ceremonial circle of choosing, a solid sheet of gold several fathoms across which was set into the sand-packed floor of the arena. To one side of the circle the monks stood silent, their cowls pulled up to cover their faces, and before them was placed a silver-inlaid table. Zarel stepped into the circle and the four House Masters followed while the servants carried the urns over and placed them on the table.

Zarel looked at the Four Masters, his cold gaze settling on Kirlen.

"Is his name in your urn?" he finally asked.

"Who?" Her voice was filled with a cold sarcasm.

"Damn you, you know of whom I speak."

"He is enlisted in my House by the right of my choosing and you may not interfere."

"He is a wanted felon."

"He was a wanted felon," Kirlen replied sharply, "or have you forgotten the rules? No fighter may be arrested during Festival or taken at any time from his House."

Kirlen looked around at the other three House Masters for support.

"He's dangerous," Jimak of Purple replied. "You should have killed him."

"You only say that because he's not wearing your color. Besides, you had him and would have more than happily betrayed him to Zarel for what I suspect was nothing more than another golden trinket."

"I did no such thing."

"He betrayed all of us," Tulan interjected.

"Of course he did," Kirlen chuckled coldly. "But I'm the one who has him now and he'll fight for me and he'll win. I think, Zarel, your rage comes from the fact that it will be the Walker who will finally have him and not you. Let him decide what to do with One-eye."

"You seduced him away from me," Varnel of Fentesk snapped, looking over angrily at Kirlen. "That was in violation of the rules."

"Well, that's too bad," Kirlen replied tauntingly. "Go over and ask him to come back like a good boy."

"Shut up, all of you," Zarel snarled.

"How dare you," Kirlen hissed. "You might be Master of the Arena, but together we have more power than you."

"Try it," Zarel replied heatedly. "Just try it. Without me and the arena you would be nothing."

"Rather it is the other way around," Kirlen replied. "You can't even control one lone *hanin*. You are a joke and unfit to rule."

Zarel fixed her with his gaze and then he noticed that the mob had fallen strangely quiet. There was an electric-like tension in the air, as if they somehow sensed that something was going wrong down in the golden circle.

"I'll remember that after this is over."

"I hope you do," Kirlen replied coldly.

Zarel, struggling to control his rage, turned away from the four Masters and beckoned for the monks, who had stood to one side, to be guided over. Assistants approached the monks, while others uncoiled a long hose of a curious black substance at the end of which was attached a bell-shaped funnel, the other end of the hose disappearing inside the access tunnel.

Four of the monks were led over to the urns. Their cowls were pulled back to reveal that the four men were blind and that their ears had been sewn shut. They were the Choosers of Combat, one of the most exalted positions to be held in the city. In payment for that honor their eyes had been taken from them and their ears closed over so that they could not see what they did, or hear a whisper of coaxing to reach to a certain spot in the urns which contained the names of the fighters.

A trumpet fanfare sounded and the arena settled down to an unearthly silence. The monks each reached into an urn and pulled out a golden disk, upon which was written the name of a fighter from one of the four Houses. In turn they deposited the disks into a black leather bag, which was placed at the end of the table. A fifth blind and deaf monk then reached into the bag, drew out two disks, and placed them to his left. Then he drew out the other two disks and placed them to his right.

Another monk, who had not surrendered his sight, now stepped forward and picked up the funnel attached to the hose which snaked back into the main tunnel. He looked down at the first two disks, while to his side stood two more monks, who acted as witnesses.

"Haglin of Fentesk," he announced, speaking into the funnel, "versus Erwina of Bolk, circle one."

His words were carried across a hundred fathoms up to the men and boys who manned a great display board mounted along the top of the west side of the arena. The crowd was silent, all heads turned to gaze at the board. Seconds later more than a dozen boys scurried up the framework of the tote board bearing letters and symbols which spelled out the names of the first two contestants, their personal symbols, House colors, and assigned circle for the fight.

"Lorrin of Kestha versus Naru of Bolk, circle two."

The gold disks were set aside and the blind and deaf monks were directed by their assistants to draw out four more disks, which in turn were divided by the final decider of matches.

"Alinar of Fentesk versus Ogla of Bolk, circle three."

Dozens of boys now swarmed over the tote board and the first match was finally spelled out. A wild, hysterical cheering erupted and it seemed as if the entire spectator stand was suddenly buried under a blizzard of paper as the howling mob pulled open their gambling sheets to check the records of the fighters and calculate odds. The mob then looked back at the board, waiting expectantly while the official master of the numbers decided upon the odds that would be offered. The numbers finally appeared, three to one in favor of Erwina of Bolk over Haglin of Fentesk.

The crowd reacted in its usual manner, hooting derisively at odds which were, as always, stacked in favor of the Grand Master. At the top of every stairway leading down into the arena the betting booths were now open for action and by the tens of thousands the spectators swarmed out of their seats to place their first bets, while in the stands tens of thousands more haggled out private wagers. Such betting was, of course, illegal in the arena; only bets placed with the Grand Master were allowed, and hundreds of his agents were hidden in the crowd, ready to arrest any who tried to run their own private operations. The laying out of the first twenty-five matches continued, odds going up on the boards, the crowd roaring its disapproval at some of the offered bets and then racing to wager their coppers, silvers, and golds on what they thought were sure wins. The first arrests were made as well, fights breaking out as the Master's agents tried to carry off illegal bettors so that warriors had to push their way down through the aisles and benches, their clubs rising and falling to clear a path.

The first set of twenty-five matches was finally decided and Zarel, without another word, turned away from the four Masters, dismissing them as if they were nothing more than servants. As Kirlen turned and stepped out of the circle she made a show of spitting on the ground, which caused a ripple of approving shouts to rise up, especially from the quarter of the arena dominated by Brown's followers.

The old woman stopped and looked around, cackling with delight at the shouts of approval. Ignoring the injunction against the use of magic other than for fighting, she snapped her fingers and a spinning circle of fire formed around her. She lifted into the air and drifted back over to her section. The other three House Masters, seeing her actions, did likewise, and the entire arena erupted with shouts of delight over this act of defiance.

As Kirlen reached the area where her fighters were sitting she lowered herself back to the ground and walked defiantly through their ranks, stepping up to her canopied throne. As she walked through her ranks she looked over at Garth.

"He wants your head," she said with a laugh.

Garth nodded, saying nothing, and then looked back at the tote board as the last of the twenty-five matches was posted.

"You're not in the first round, Master," Hammen announced.

"That's fine with me, my head's still splitting."

"I told you to stay in the cold bath till it was gone."

"Do that again and I'll kill you. I hate the cold."

Hammen reached into his tunic and pulled out a small flask.

"Since you won't be fighting for a while, perhaps a touch of the cruel will help cure you," he replied, and offered up the flask.

Garth took it, ignoring the disapproving stare of Naru, who was sitting beside him, and downed a long gulp. The fiery liquid coursed through him and he felt the pain start to leave.

There was another flourish of trumpets, signaling that the time for betting was drawing to a close, and Hammen looked around excitedly.

"That bastard gets cheaper with his odds every year. It's nearly impossible to get a good bet in on this game anymore. He's pushing his greed a little too far and you know damn well he wagers on the sure wins his people pick. Count in the ten percent betting fee on every wager and he cleans up every time."

Garth smiled and said nothing as the second trumpet sounded and the last frenzy of betting was played out, those at the end of the lines pushing and shoving to get up to the booths where the bookmakers furiously passed out precut wooden tokens marking a bet in return for the tons of coins being pushed over the transoms.

Each token was numbered to signify on which fighting circle the bet was being placed and notched to show if the bet was for or against the favorite. To prevent counterfeiting, the shape, size, and color of the tokens to be used in any given fight was a heavily guarded secret. Once used for a round the tokens were retired and might not be used again for years.

The trumpets sounded the third time and those chosen for the first round of fights stood up. Naru rose and stretched lazily.

"She is easy," he announced in a bored tone. "I be right back."

As he swaggered down the aisle and out onto the arena floor, joined by the other fighters from Brown, a loud hysterical cheering erupted. Hammen, unable to contain himself, stood up on his chair to get a better view.

"Damn, I liked it better up in the stands. You can see better," he complained, looking down at Garth as if he should somehow arrange for seats up with the mob. Naru walked over to his assigned fighting circle fifty fathoms away, the roaring of the crowd rising to a fevered pitch. Fighters from the other three Houses were now out on the arena floor moving to their circles, the crowd chanting and screaming. As they reached their circles they stepped into the neutral boxes, their servants taking their cloaks.

Some of the fighters went through a quick series of exercises, stretching and bending, others stood calmly, others knelt down and, with heads lowered, concentrated their thoughts. To each of the circles a fighter of the Grand Master's now came to serve as referee.

The trumpets sounded their strident calls, once more warning the fighters and the mob that the fights were about to begin and the roaring of the crowd died away. From atop his throne Zarel now stood up and held his arms out. Again his voice sounded high and clear.

"To the honor of the Walker."

The fighters in the circles turned and raised both their hands in salute.

"Spells must be contained within the limits of the circles. All fights of the first day to be for spell prize unless both fighters declare it is a grudge match to the death."

There was a moment of silence as the referees in each circle turned and queried the two fighters they were observing.

"Circle seven, Farnin of Bolk and Petrakov of Fentesk, to the death," Hammen predicted. "Last year Farnin's lover was killed by Petrakov. The mob's been hoping for this matchup."

On three of the poles which stood by each circle a red flag went up, and one of them was at the seventh circle. A wild, insane cheer went up.

"Petrakov is a dead man," Hammen announced gleefully.

Zarel raised his arms heavenward.

"Prepare!"

The fighters in the circles stepped out of their neutral boxes and into the arena.

A whistle sounded and an angry roar went up from the crowd.

Garth looked over at Hammen.

"Circle eleven. The Purple fighter started a spell before the call to fight. He's out."

Garth looked over toward the eleventh circle on the far side of the arena, amazed at how Hammen could see what was going on, let alone instantly know what had happened. From out of the circle the Ingkaran fighter was already submitting to having a spell taken from his satchel and presented to the winner of the match. As he started to walk back toward the Purple side of the arena, a loud, angry howl rose from the crowd, while from the Gray side a happy cheer erupted since Purple was the favorite to win.

Jimak rose from his throne with an angry curse and pointed his hand.

There was a flash of light and an instant later, where the disgraced fighter had stood, was only a smoldering heap of charred bones. A burst of applause erupted from the crowd and, turning, Jimak bowed to Ingkara's followers, who now felt that their honor had been restored.

"Hell, he was only a second-rank anyhow," Hammen sniffed approvingly. "His contract for the year wasn't worth a damn after such a disgrace."

The crowd finally settled down and all eyes were turned back toward Zarel.

He held his arms aloft until all was silent and then suddenly dropped them, his voice booming out across the arena.

"Fight!"

An instant later the arena erupted in an insane maelstrom of light, explosions, the roaring of animals, the shouts of demons, dwarfs, ogres, and other summoned creatures, and above all, the wild, gleeful screaming of half a million spectators.

Hammen, beside himself with joy, leaped up and down on his seat, howling with delight.

"Circle five, finished!"

Garth looked to where he pointed. The Fentesk fighter was already down, unconscious, the skeletons he had summoned ground to dust by berserkers and a firestorm, the referee bending over the fallen man to take a spell from his satchel and present it to the winner.

"Naru's done as well," Garth announced, pointing to where the giant had crushed his opponent's dwarfs with his own hands, then unleashed a demon howl which had bowled his opponent over, knocking her out of the circle.

The stands behind Garth erupted with wild shouts for one of their favorites. After claiming his prize, Naru swaggered back to the section where the Bolk fighters stood shouting their approval and swarming around the champion.

A loud groan went up from the crowd when, against all odds, Petrakov knocked Farnin, the sentimental favorite of the mob, off his feet. Petrakov flayed him with a psychic lashing so that the man writhed back and forth. Hammen, beside himself with emotion, screamed imprecations, and Garth shook his head with disgust. Petrakov was now simply torturing his opponent. He continued the lashing, even though he injured himself in the process. He finally stepped across the circle, drew his dagger, and started to slash Farnin across the face, while the crowd, except for Petrakov's loyal followers in the Orange sector, booed loudly. Finally he grabbed hold of his opponent by the hair, lifted him up, and hacked his throat open from ear to ear, a river of scarlet spilling out in the circle.

A loud cry erupted from the Brown fighters, several of them moving to rush into the arena and place a spell of healing on their comrade. A wall of light shimmered up, cast by a dozen fighters of the Grand Master who stood nearby each of the sideline stands of the fighting Houses, blocking Farnin's comrades from entering the arena.

Petrakov, with a disdainful gesture, tossed Farnin aside, the man's head lolling back obscenely. Farnin kicked feebly, hands clutching at his torn throat, blood squirting out between his fingers, and then was still. Without waiting for the circle master, Petrakov reached down and cut Farnin's satchel off and held it aloft triumphantly, spit on the corpse, and then walked away.

"In the old days that never would have been allowed except in the final matches," Hammen growled. "The Grand Master encourages it now because the mob loves the sight of blood. The next fight with Petrakov and the betting will be ten times as much, especially if he's pitted against another Bolk."

The last of the fights were played out, the victors returning with their spoils, a single spell for standard matches, or the full satchel for a death match, minus, of course, the one *mana* fee taken by the Grand Master when blood was spilled. One of the three death matches, however, ended with no one the winner. Both fighters had cast simultaneous spells which had killed their opponents. Those who had not bet on the match laughed with hysterical glee since in such cases the Grand Master kept all bets and claimed the satchels of both of the fallen as well, while those who had bet on one or the other howled with rage.

The Bolk fighters returned to the stands around Garth, the winners beaming with pride, the losers looking crestfallen, gazing nervously up at Kirlen, who ignored them with haughty disdain. Their contracts for the forthcoming year were now worth less and she would not let them forget it.

The last of the fights over, stretcher-bearers raced out into the arena to carry off the unconscious and the dead while from out of the access tunnels entertainers charged into the arena— dwarfs, jugglers, fire-eaters, and petty magicians. Several dozen wagons, drawn by zebras or tigers, bears, and even a mammoth, came galloping out. Mounted on the back of each wagon was a small catapult and, at the sight of them, the crowd came to its feet and pointed nervously, wondering why the Grand Master was bringing heavy weapons into the arena.

The dwarfs manning the catapults cranked them back, loading the firing arms with clay pots, and pointed their weapons toward the crowd.

An angry cry started to swell and wherever the weapons were pointed the mob struggled to back away. The dwarfs, laughing with insane delight, fired the weapons. A loud roar rose up and Hammen, curious, stood up to watch. The pots slammed into the stands and burst open. There were gasps of amazement from the mob and then a mad scurrying, for the pots contained prizes—sweetmeats, lottery tickets, and, most surprisingly of all, copper, silver, and gold coins.

A wild cheering erupted as the catapult teams moved around the edge of the arena, reloading their weapons with yet more pots and firing them into the crowd, which now rushed back and forth in a mad frenzy to catch the prizes.

Hammen, shaking his head, sat back down.

"Wish you were up there?" Garth asked.

"You're damn right I do, rather than having to sit down here and get nothing."

A catapult, drawn by mammoths, raced past, firing a clay pot nearly the size of a man up into the arena.

The mob howled with delight and a rippling of cheers honoring Zarel rose up.

"Masterful," Garth said, shaking his head.

"It doesn't take much to win a mob back, especially when the winning back is paid in gold."

"Do you know anyone on their catapult teams?"

"No. Why?"

"Just wondering."

Hammen looked over at Garth and smiled wickedly.

"Do you want to rob them? Is that it?"

"No. I was just wondering."

"I have a friend who could find out. He owns a little illegal business."

"What kind?"

"Potions and such. Get rid of a spouse that's become tiresome, seduce a girl who won't say yes, even get some courage when you need it, those kinds of things."

"And his customers?"

Hammen smiled wickedly.

"Some of the highest. Nobles, great merchants," and he lowered his voice, "and Uriah, the captain of Zarel's fighters. It'd be easy enough to find out through him. My cousin says he's shooting his mouth off all the time about how important he is and all the people in court that are beholden to him."

Garth turned away at the mention of the dwarf's name.

"Something wrong, Master?"

Garth smiled sadly and looked back.

"No, nothing. I want to talk with this friend of yours after the game. Could you arrange it?"

"A potion for a certain Benalish girl?"

"Damn you, no. Just arrange the meeting, will you?"

Hammen, laughing softly, nodded.

In front of Zarel's canopied throne the blind and deaf monks now started to draw out the names of the next round of contestants.

A great cheer erupted when two favorites, both of them ninth-rank fighters—one of them Varena—were pitted against each other. The other names were posted one after the other and the mob rushed to place its next round of bets in a wild frenzy of excitement.

Hammen looked back expectantly at the stands behind him where the mob sat.

"I'll be back in a minute," he suddenly announced, and, leaving Garth's side, he went up to the barrier where a bent-over man who looked somehow familiar to Garth stood waiting. There was a quick and furtive exchange, a handshake, and Hammen came back.

"I bet everything we had on Varena," he told Garth quietly.

Garth nodded and looked back to where the bent-over man stood.

"He looks familiar."

"He should. He was in prison just down the row from you. I got him out in the confusion."

"I take it he doesn't have much love now for the Grand Master."

Hammen chuckled as if Garth had just uttered a comment of incredible stupidity.

"Does he know as many people around here as you?"

"He should. He's head of one of the brotherhoods."

"Tell him to meet us tonight."

"Master, not again."

"Just do it when you go to get our winnings."

The trumpets sounded the warning and the entertainers cleared the arena area, followed by the wagons, which fired their last round of pots, one of them winging directly over the Bolk fighters to crack open at the edge of the stands. Dozens tried to leap over the wall to gather up the prize only to be met by the Grand Master's guards, who beat them back with clubs and the flats of their swords, those getting clubbed howling and cursing, those farther up in the stands roaring with delight at the entertainment.

The trumpet sounded the final time, the fighters marched out, and Garth stood, catching a glimpse of Varena as she went to a circle at the far side of the field. Again there were several red banners marking blood matches, one of them causing the crowd to gasp with amazement since it was a sixth-rank fighter against a second, a matching that was little short of suicide on the part of the weaker.

"Some of them do it because they're crazy, others on the long shot of winning a satchel of spells that would take them decades to earn in the older way of gathering *mana* and studying," Hammen declared with obvious disdain.

Zarel stood up and again made the ritual pronouncements, his arms raised heavenward. He dropped them.

"Fight!"

Again there was the wild explosion of spells, the flashes of light, creatures appearing to do battle, clouds of dust and cyclones of fire. In one of the circles a giant spider appeared, causing the caster of the spell to be disqualified when he lost control of the creature, which stampeded out of the fighting circle when it was set upon by a pack of wolves. The spider raced toward the edge of the fighting floor, heading for the grandstands, the crowd panicking, abandoning their seats and stampeding. Fighters of the Grand Master raced after it, striking it repeatedly with fire, turning it aside just as it reached the stands. Several of the spectators were caught by its spray of acidic poison, disintegrating into bubbling clouds of pulpy steam before the spider was finally destroyed. The fighter who had lost control of the spell walked away dejected, stripped of his spider spell as penalty, though the spectators gave him a warm round of applause for the exciting show, which would be talked about endlessly in the days to come.

One by one the fights ended. The sixth-rank versus second-rank death match dragged out longer than most had expected, ending when the second-rank fighter finally turned and tried to run away. He was chased for more than a hundred fathoms across the arena by his taunting opponent, until Zarel, disgusted, stood up and, raising his hands, blasted him into oblivion just before he ran through the circle where Varena and her opponent were fighting out a classic match of spell versus counterspell that had the mob on its feet.

Garth watched the fight intently, mentally noting the spells she was forced to reveal.

"Unless she's holding back, she'll have no secrets now in the later matches," Hammen noted calmly. "Too bad for her. But then again, Master, you'll have to face her sooner or later, so it's to your advantage."

All the other matches were finished but still the two fought on, the crowd falling silent when there was a lull, cheering or groaning in turn when one or the other seemed to be getting an upper hand. Twice Varena was knocked down, once by a charging berserker that crashed through her line of fire creatures, and again by several attacks from black knights. She finally turned the fight around when her opponent cast a black spell of life draining, for which she held a counterspell that gave her additional strength rather than weakened her, regaining what she had lost from the previous assaults. She pressed forward, relying heavily on fire spells mixed with swirling storms of ice, and her rival finally collapsed into unconsciousness, his power drained.

Varena, staggering with exhaustion, stood in the center of the circle while the circle master took a spell from her opponent's satchel and presented it to her. To the surprise of many she then made the gesture of laying hands on her opponent to revive him, an action that struck a chord with the mob, which cheered appreciatively as she turned and walked away. As she walked past Zarel's throne Garth could sense that somehow Zarel knew of Varena's part in his rescue as the Grand Master leaned forward and watched her closely.

"Doubled our money," Hammen hissed with delight as he settled back into his chair by Garth's side.

"You give your friend the message?"

"I don't know why, but I did," Hammen replied sulkily.

Garth settled back in his chair, ignoring the performers, who again flooded into the arena. The stands were nearly empty as the mob swarmed out of the arena, heading to the food stands and privy pits, except for the crowds that tried to maneuver to where the clay pots were going to rain down.

"This is your match," Hammen announced, and he looked over excitedly at Garth.

Garth, saying nothing, watched the tote board as the matches started to be listed.

"I bet that's us," Hammen said, pointing to the board as a boy scurried out on a catwalk and hung out a symbol before the first letter of the name had even been hung, the symbol a stylized rendering of an eye patch.

At the sight of Garth's symbol the crowd started to cheer. Garth sat back, watching, as his name, which on the board was simply "One-eye," was spelled out. His opponent, from Ingkara, was now listed, and confusion erupted among the crowd.

"Who is this bastard?" a Brown fighter asked, looking over at Garth as if he had the answer.

Garth turned and looked at Hammen, who sat in silence.

"He wasn't on the lists two days ago," Hammen announced. "Just a minute."

He got out of his seat and raced back toward the grandstands, whereupon several spectators broke out of the crowd and came down to meet him. They conferred quickly and Hammen came back.

"It's a setup," Hammen said angrily. "One of Zarel's men, at least eighth-rank or better. He was seen in the march down to the arena. Jimak must have taken a bribe to let him into Purple's ranks."

"So I'll fight him."

"He's an unknown, one of Zarel's lieutenants. It also means the choosing was fixed. One of the monks must have palmed the name disks to set it up."

"So it's fixed. What the hell did you expect?" Garth said quietly.

Garth, sensing that he was being watched, looked up and saw that Kirlen was gazing down at him.

She smiled and nodded her head.

The odds on the board went up, three to one against Garth. The confused murmuring in the crowd increased.

Hammen turned back to the grandstands and cupped his hands.

"It's a fix!"

Instantly his cry was picked up and echoed, a loud turmoil breaking out.

Hammen settled back in his seat, waited for a moment, and then stood up to head back to the wall.

"How are you betting?"

Hammen looked back at him with a hurt expression.

"Three to one against, we'll clean up. Besides, if you lose, I'm dead anyhow, so what the hell."

"Thanks for the confidence."

Chuckling, Hammen went up to the wall and returned a moment later as the first of the warning trumpets sounded.

"Naru bet on Garth."

Garth looked over at the grinning giant.

"I win either way," Naru announced as if he had figured out a monumental task of logic. "Make money or don't have to fight and kill you later." Naru roared at his own joke.

The third trumpet finally sounded and Garth stood up, Hammen by his side, and stepped out from under the awning into the late-afternoon sun. The arena erupted with wild cheering that spread from Brown to the other three-quarters of the stadium.

Garth, ignoring the cheers, walked toward his assigned circle and stepped into the neutral box, which was stained with blood from an earlier death match. Hammen took his cloak and watched warily as Garth's opponent came forward.

"I know that bastard," Hammen whispered. "He was captain of the guard down in Tantium. A killer. This doesn't look good."

Zarel Ewine leaned back in his throne and chuckled softly. The captain knew his job and what was expected. Later it would be a simple task to eliminate him rather than have to worry about the fact that the man might talk about the violations of age-old traditions, the fixing of the match, the bribing of the monk, who would have to have an accident as well, and, finally, the fact that the captain carried a spell given to him by the Grand Master for use in the arena.

Zarel took up his cup of wine and sipped at it contentedly, waiting for the fighters to get ready.

The captain from Tantium walked calmly over to his neutral box alone, without a servant, unclipped his cloak, and let it fall to the ground. Ignoring Garth, he bent over and stretched lazily, his bare arms rippling with muscles.

"He might try to take you physically," Hammen whispered. "Watch out for his blade. Look at his left boot; there's another dagger tucked in there for throwing. Poisoned most likely."

The final trumpet sounded and the circle master for Garth's fight stepped into the center and then looked over at Garth.

"How do you declare this fight?"

"Spell match," Garth said quietly.

The circle master looked back over at the captain.

"How do you declare this fight?"

"To the death."

The circle master turned and went over to the pole at the edge of the circle.

"Hey, what the hell are you doing?" Hammen shouted.

The circle master, ignoring Hammen, hoisted the red flag of a death match.

"This is a fix!" Hammen shouted, turning to look back at

the arena stands, his words drowned out by the eruption of screaming from half a million throats.

Hammen looked back at Garth.

"If I lose, get out of here quick," Garth said quietly, and then he lowered his head and closed his eyes.

"Fight!"

Garth opened his eyes and stepped into the circle. Concentrating, he started to pull upon the power of his *mana*, upon which would be built the power of his spells. Instantly he felt a block. The captain had already drawn upon his own *mana* and cast a blocking spell, draining Garth's power away. Garth felt a momentary flicker of fear. The man was powerful, extremely powerful, and skillful in his tactics.

Smoke swirled up in the center of the circle and half a dozen decaying corpses stepped out of the cloud, the stench of their corruption washing over Garth. He stepped back, still struggling to bring forth his *mana* as the first corpse staggered up, pale bone showing through the rotting phosphorescence of its face. Garth struggled to suppress a gag, his concentration broken as he had to dodge out of the dead man's grasp. Another one caught him on the shoulder, icy fingers digging into flesh and wrestling to draw away the spirit of life. Garth tore free and quickly moved away, feeling his strength draining away. In the center of the circle more forms appeared, plague rats, their green eyes glinting evilly. The rats charged. Garth danced about, crushing several under his boot but two managed to leap upon his legs, sinking their teeth in, their poison seeping into his blood. Staggering, he kicked them off.

At last Garth was able to raise his hand, the *mana* of the forest drawn into his control at last. A dark green fog swirled around him, blinding the undead. For a brief moment the attack was thrown off and he raised his hands, a cool stream of water cascading down from above, washing over his body, drawing out the poison.

His draw of *mana* continued to strengthen and yet he could sense that his opponent's was increasing as well. The fog started to disperse and Garth extended his hands outward and drew an image in the air. A second later there was a burst of light and a form coalesced, the mob roaring its approval at the appearance of a white knight mounted upon a rearing charger.

The knight, swinging a mace, trampled down the corpses that started to close in again on Garth and then turned to charge the captain. The knight's attack slowed and then came to a stop as if he were trapped in a dark web. The horse tried to rear up, neighing in pain, and then rolled over, crushing the knight beneath him. With his opponent, diverted by the attack of the knight, Garth was freed to counter the plague rats which still pursued him, by unleashing a swarm of stinging hornets that harried and tormented the rats, stinging with such viciousness that the rats, one after another, curled up and died.

Another strike lashed over Garth and he felt his *mana* withering away, his power draining down. His opponent, Garth realized, held powers equal to that of a House Master, or even a Grand Master, and as the thought raced through him, he looked at his opponent and saw the man's mocking gaze, as if his opponent were simply playing with him and held supreme confidence in the final outcome.

Garth waved his hands in a circle and managed to erect a circle of protection from his opponent's onslaughts. Then he doubled the circle. Though he was doing no damage to his foe, at least his attacker was no longer damaging him. More undead appeared, but were repulsed by the screen. There was another strike toward his *mana*, but it was stopped as well. The captain now turned his attention toward the hornets, which were swarming toward him, and in an instant they fell to the ground, their power to fly drained away. Writhing about, they curled up and died.

For a moment there was no attack from either side. Garth spared a quick look around and saw that nearly all the other combats were finished. The attention of the mob was entirely focused on the death struggle in the middle of the arena. In the center of the circle a darkness appeared and started to drift toward Garth, a frozen shade of terror. He felt his outer circle of protection fall beneath the attack. Garth raised his hands and an instant later a stand of trees appeared to encircle him. He stepped out of the circle of protection and then moved like a shadow himself, drifting silently. The frozen shade floated past him, looking, probing. Garth extended the line of trees so that they filled his half of the circle. He felt his power growing and, with a snap of his arm, he pointed behind the frozen shade. One of the trees came to life and grabbed hold of the shade with branchy arms, tearing it apart.

The mob, unable to see what was happening, cheered with a wild frenzy so that the sound of the struggle was drowned out. Moving stealthily, Garth darted to the edge of the forest he had created. His opponent was moving to the edge of the woods, hands raised. Bolts of lightning came down out of the sky, blasting the forest with blow after blow. Garth motioned toward the captain and the tree-walker crashed out of the woods. Reaching down, it snatched at the captain, lifting him up into the air. A wild frenzy of cheers erupted as the fight again became visible. The captain, writhing in pain, pointed both hands at the tree-creature's face; the creature staggered backward, fire burning its eyes. Howling with pain, the creature staggered around in a circle, the mob laughing at its antics.

Garth raised his hand and the creature disappeared, its torment ended. At the same instant he raced up to the captain, lashing out with his feet, kicking to break the man's knee. The captain dodged the blow, tripping Garth to the ground. Laughing sardonically he lashed out in turn, kicking Garth's side so that the sound of ribs cracking could be heard. Garth rolled away, raising his hands. Tiny forms appeared, looking almost comical, for they were nothing more than woodland fairies. They buzzed about on silver wings and then closed in. They lunged at the captain's eyes, with tiny spears causing him to howl with pain and back away. Behind Garth the forest he had created was in flames, thick coils of dark smoke soaring into the heavens, the fire crackling and hissing.

Garth, gasping for breath and unable to take the time to heal himself, conjured yet again, sending a bear into the melee. The bear was blocked by Ironclaw Orcs, who hacked at it with heavy scimitars, the bear in turn ripping them apart. From overhead a rain of stones started to fall, smashing into what was left of the forest. Garth could feel his power draining away.

He erected yet another circle of protection to buy time in order to replace the *mana* his opponent had rendered useless.

The captain stood on the other side of the circle, streams of blood coursing down his face and arms from the attack of the fairies, who now lay scattered about. He wiped the blood from his eyes, his features contorted with rage. Garth reached outward, probing into the man's thoughts in a bid to ascertain what he might attempt next. Garth smiled and, with a raised hand, sent another swarm of fairies in.

They were dead within seconds but again they had managed to stab his opponent, and the sight of the captain flailing at them sent the mob into hysterical laughter.

The captain turned his attention away from Garth for a second. His features contorted with anger as he hurled a curse back at the mob. Though his words could not be heard, his flash of temper set them to laughing even louder.

The captain turned back and angrily pointed at the ground. Dwarven warriors appeared. He moved his hand again, and yet again, summoning forth creature after creature so that dwarfs, orcs, goblins, skeletons, and even demonic creatures were arrayed. As he prepared his attack Garth in turn gathered his own *mana* in, building up his strength. He came back up to his feet and walked back to the middle of the circle. His act of defiance caused wild cheering to erupt as Garth stood alone, as if ready to battle the summoned creatures without benefit of magic other than the dagger he now flicked out.

The captain laughed with cold contempt, raised both hands heavenward, and then pointed them straight down. A fissure opened in the ground directly before him. An expectant hush fell over the arena.

A black cloud rushed upward, like steam hissing out from the gates of hell. The shadow swirled about, turning and coiling, and took form.

"A Lord of the Pit!"

Garth turned and looked over his shoulder at Hammen, who was stepping backward in fear.

"Pit Lord! Pit Lord!" The cry thundered from the mob, and those who had bet upon Garth groaned with despair even as they came to their feet to watch the finale of the show.

The demon loomed upward, great clawlike hands stretching out, black mouth gaping open, flame washing over its teeth, its fire red eyes glowing like hot coals in a furnace.

The captain lowered his hands, the demon looking back at him. The captain pointed at the dwarven warriors. The demon, laughing, turned and swept them up in his claws,

devouring them as they screamed and yelled. The other creatures summoned by the captain, now realizing that they were
called forth as a sacrificial offering to the dark power, tried to
move away, but the captain pointed at them in turn, freezing
them in place.

After finishing his repast the demon, with heavy, lumbering
steps, advanced on Garth. His mighty clawed hands reached
out. Garth, in turn, raised his hands and a river of ice seemed
to pour from the heavens, striking the monster on the arms,
the ice instantly turning to hot steam. The Lord of the Pit,
roaring with pain, staggered back.

The captain next pointed at the berserkers and the creature devoured them in turn. His strength redoubled by the
feast, the demon charged again, howling with mad fury.
Garth waved his hands in reply and instantly he was encased
in holy armor. The monster tried to sweep him up in his grasp
but each time his hands touched the armor there was a flash
of steam. For long minutes they struggled thus until the
demon's power slowly started to abate and the armor in turn
became translucent and then disappeared. The mob was now
at a fever pitch as the Lord turned away, its features contorted
with rage, and started back toward the captain.

Quickly the captain pointed next at the orcs he controlled.
The demon pounced upon them, devouring them as they
screamed and writhed. Garth did nothing, watching the captain's actions. He had conjured forth a creature that was
almost beyond his ability to control. He had to keep feeding it
in order to keep it under his command. The captain waved his
hand yet again, attempting to conjure up more replacements
for the creature's feast. But this time all he could bring forth
was half a score of plague rats before he lowered his head in
exhaustion.

The Lord of the Pit, satiated for the moment, turned back to
attack Garth once more. It started to advance and Garth
replayed again a power he had used before, quickly erecting a
wall of living trees and then stepping behind it. The Dark Lord
approached the woods, brimming with hatred for a creation of
such tranquility. Rearing up, it started to slash at the woods
with his mighty claws, as Garth reinforced his barrier of protection. The monster's hooting roars thundered around the arena,

drowning out even the wild, insane cheering of the mob which was beside itself with rapture over such a marvelous display. The demon finally tore into the line of trees, grabbing hold of the trunks. It howled with pain as if the silvery bark was made of nettles of pain. It tore the trees up, flinging them aside, crashing through to the other side.

And then, exhausted, it sank down for a moment. Turning, it started to lumber back toward its master's side of the circle, looking at the remaining feasts the captain had set out in order to maintain control.

Garth leaped forward, hands raised, and within seconds the demons, skeletons and rats that the captain had prepared for the demon were gone, vaporized by Garth's frenzied attack.

The captain hesitated, shocked by the suddenness of Garth's onslaught. The demon reared up, howling with rage that his meal had been denied. The captain quickly raised his hands but his own *mana* was drained in the act of creating the monster and the meals necessary to control it. He pointed, trying to bring forth another creature. There was a thin pop of light and the only thing that appeared was a lone tiny sprite which, at the sight of the Lord, took wing and flew straight up and away. The demon, its mouth lolling open, watched the sprite fly away, then it fixed its gaze on the captain.

With a loud cry it lunged forward. There was a brief flash, as if a circle of protection was being raised. Garth turned and looked toward the throne, where Zarel was standing, his arms raised. Hammen, jumping up and down, pointed toward Zarel in turn and a wild, hysterical cry rose from the mob at the blatant interference on the part of the Grand Master. Zarel, looking around, dropped his hands, and the circle of protection disappeared.

The captain, screaming in terror, was lifted up into the air. The Lord of the Pit, gloating over its prey, pulled in opposite directions, tearing the man in half and then devouring him in two quick gulps. As the life force of the captain disappeared the power which he controlled ended as well. With a flash of fire and smoke the demon disappeared.

Garth slowly walked across the circle, not waiting for the circle master to reach the prize first. Reaching down he picked up the blood-soaked satchel of his opponent and held it aloft.

The mob broke into an ecstasy of cheering. The Bolk section of the arena swarmed forward, leaping over the barriers, ignoring the blows of the warriors who tried to stop them. By the tens of thousands they swarmed onto the arena floor.

"One-eye, One-eye!"

The circle master came up and reached toward the satchel of the captain. Garth fixed the man with his gaze.

"It was you who made it to the death; the prize is mine."

"It belongs to the Grand Master," the fighter hissed.

"Then try and take it now."

The man looked at him, and then back toward the throne, where Zarel stood. The mob swirled in around Garth, swarming about him. Hammen pushed his way through to Garth's side.

"Thank the Eternal for this mob; I think Zarel was going to come down and fight you right now."

The referee backed away and then extended his hand.

"*Mana* payment for a death fight."

Garth reached into the satchel taken from his foe, drew out a small silken bundle of black *mana*, and tossed it into the outstretched hand of the referee, who quickly scurried away.

Putting his arm around Hammen's shoulder for support, Garth forced his way through the mob, sensing the rage that Zarel was now feeling at the humiliation he had endured and the loss of one of his most powerful spells.

"Master, how are you?" Hammen asked anxiously.

"I managed to heal the ribs but I'm still hung over," Garth replied. "Let's go find a drink, and then there's some things I need you to get for this evening."

"What things?"

Garth simply smiled.

CHAPTER

12

THE CITY WAS IN A STATE OF BEDLAM. DURING the games rival gangs, taking advantage of the fact that nearly anyone who could afford it had gone to the arena, had set to looting. Supporters of Ingkara had raided Fentesk sections of the city and a mob of Kesthans attempted to loot Purple, while Bolk had simply gone after everyone else. Fires had broken out in several quarters of the city and the glare of the flames filled the midnight sky.

"Ah, how I love Festival days," Hammen growled, pausing to look furtively around a corner and then turning to watch the flames engulf the home of a much-hated merchant down the street.

"It wasn't always this way," Garth said, more as a statement than a question.

Hammen spit on the ground.

"The old days are dead as are all old days." He paused for a moment and sighed.

"Maybe it wasn't as golden as some want to remember," Hammen finally said, "but at least the games were not for the entertainment of the mob. Back then they were tests of skill and practice, a time of truce before going out again to wander and study, or to serve a contract with a prince who treated his fighters with honor. Now it is for blood, contracts, and the delight of the mob."

Hammen shook his head and then chuckled sadly as some looters raced past, bearing a heavy barrel between them.

Hammen looked back up at Garth.

"All right, Garth, the game's over. We increased our money six times over today. Even minus my commission you've got enough to live like a prince for the next couple of years. Besides that, you've got a spell usually only a Master ever holds. Why don't you take it and get the hell out of this madhouse?"

Garth smiled and shook his head.

"I've still got some things to do."

"Damn it, son, today was a fix. The captain was a fix, the spell was obviously given to him by the Grand Master, and they set you up for a death match. Do you think he'll play any fairer tomorrow?"

"Actually, yes," Garth said quietly. "The mob knows, your people have passed the word around. He'll play it straight tomorrow, at least until the Walker comes to back him up."

Garth paused, turning to look back as the merchant's house collapsed, a shower of sparks soaring heavenward. A laughing, drunken crowd was gathered around outside, raising tankards of ale and wine in salute to the fire while the merchant cursed and swore, pulling out great tufts of his beard in anguish.

Hammen slowed, still troubled by their conversation on the way back from the arena at the end of the day's fights.

"I think what you asked my friend to do is insane."

"You said he hates the Grand Master for the death of his son last year. Remember it was you who first pointed out the connection."

"I was just musing, that's all. Talking about what the Grand Master has done."

"It's an obvious path to what I want done. You've been carrying that ruby of mine around and it's time we put it to good use."

"It's a terrible risk for my friend. He could be denounced and dead before the offer is barely out."

"It'll be amusing," Garth said. "And besides, the person we want to bribe is a customer of his for illegal potions. He has some leverage over him."

"Do you know how many bribes it'll take to arrange such a thing?"

"You already saw me take care of it."

"The man, or should I say creature, you're attempting to bribe will pocket your money and forget about it."

Garth smiled and shook his head.

"You don't know the nature of guilt and vengeance very well. Half a dozen wagonloads of pots are simply mixed in, that's all. No one will be able to trace it, and our friend comes out the richer for it."

Hammen looked around nervously.

"You're talking about bribing the captain of Zarel's fighters, Uriah the Groveler."

Garth smiled sadly.

"Yes, Uriah." His voice was distant and wistful.

"That was a ruby worth at least a hundred gold," Hammen groaned.

Garth looked back as if drawn from a distant land.

"When you bribe high you have to be willing to pay," he said quickly.

"And yet you appeared before me penniless and I actually trusted you."

"I had to keep my reserve."

"And is there any reserve left?"

"A little," Garth said with a smile. "Later, tomorrow after the games, I want you to go out through the gate of the city down where we first met. Walk exactly one thousand fifty paces."

"Your paces or mine?"

"Mine, damn it. How could I know what yours were?"

"I'll try to manage."

"Anyhow. Go exactly one thousand fifty paces. There is an ancient tomb on the right side of the road, about a hundred paces up the side of the hill. In the back of it the bricks are weak. Tucked in behind the bricks is an oilskin bundle. Bring it back to me and, for the sake of the Eternal, don't open it."

"So now I'm your errand boy too."

"I'd go myself, damn it, but a lot might happen tomorrow."

"Like your getting killed."

"Then the bundle is yours as a reminder of me. I think you'd find it interesting."

Garth continued to shoulder his way through the swirling crowds, thankful that a light rain was falling so that his drawn-up hood and drooping, wide-brimmed hat did not seem out of place.

Reaching the Great Plaza, he pushed his way into the crowds and moved forward with a purposeful stride.

"Damn it," Hammen hissed, but he kept close to Garth anyhow as his companion approached the perimeter around the palace. A line of guards was drawn up just inside the row of fountains, warily watching the crowds which streamed past. Since the riot of the day before the tension between the Grand Master's warriors and the city's inhabitants was at near-breaking point.

Without slowing down, Garth pushed through the edge of the crowd and broke into a run, charging straight at the nearest warrior. Before the man even had time to react Garth caught him full in the solar plexus, the blow doubling the man over in spite of his leather armor. The warrior to the man's right turned, startled by the sudden attack, and Garth, spinning around, slammed a balled fist into the man's neck just behind his ear. Pulling out his dagger he sliced the man's purse off his belt, cut it open, and then heaved it into the startled crowd. This started a mad scramble for the money, which jingled on the dark pavement. Three more warriors came running over, swords drawn. Garth stepped past the first one, knocking him over with a simple tripping of feet. The second came in warily, slicing low. Garth jumped over the blow and, as he did so, kicked the man in the face. The third slowed, came to a stop, and then, turning, started to run, blowing his whistle, sounding the alarm.

The mob, which had been stunned by the sudden onset, now swarmed forward to rob the downed warriors. Garth turned and quickly strode away into the darkness, while behind him came the trumpet call of the alarm. Within seconds a company of warriors came charging out of the palace and waded into the crowd.

The excitement started to draw spectators from across the Plaza and Garth dodged his way through the human tide which swept forward to watch. As the heaving, shouting crowd drew closer they were drawn into the spreading fight as the ill feelings between the Grand Master's guards and the mob exploded.

Garth continued across the Plaza, moving straight at the House of Kestha. Just before reaching the outer circle of paving stones that marked Kestha's territory he tore off his cloak, revealing an Orange uniform underneath, though his face was still concealed by his wide-brimmed hat. Garth pointed toward one of the guards standing at the entryway into the House.

"Who is it?"

Hammen squinted, peering through the gloom and mist.

"Josega. At least I think so. Fourth- or fifth-rank."

"Good enough. You know what to do."

Garth broke into a run, charging across the gray paving stones.

"Josega, you cowardly bastard!"

Josega, who had been lounging wearily against the wall of his House, stirred, looking up as the Orange robe raced toward him. Even as he started to raise his hands, Garth caught him with a bolt of fire from above that knocked the man head over heels, laying him out unconscious on the pavement. The other guard started forward to meet Garth, not seeing Hammen coming up from the other side. Hammen caught the other guard across the back of the head with a blow from his staff.

The two pulled out daggers and, even as the alarm was raised inside the House, they ran off, the satchels of the two fallen guards in their hands.

"Well, at least they won't get killed now in the arena," Hammen gasped as they disappeared back into the crowd, which had not even noticed the robbery, their attention drawn instead to the growing clamor of the riot.

"Do you always find a moral balm for your sins?" Garth asked.

"It helps."

Garth pushed his way across the square, which was now resounding with the angry shouts of the mob. Crowds raced past him, many of them carrying clubs, pikes, carving knives, and even the occasional crossbow. Over by the palace the fighting was now in full swing, warriors pushing their way outward with overlapping shields, the mob pelting them with offal, pieces of firewood, paving stones, and whatever else they could lay their hands on.

Garth edged his way around the riot and moved toward the House of Ingkara. He stopped and tore off the Orange tunic he had been wearing, to reveal a Brown robe underneath.

"Haven't you had enough?" Hammen asked.

"Not yet. Now the same as last time."

A minute later the two were running away, carrying two more satchels of spells, their pursuers cut off by the mob.

Garth slowed and then, at a casual pace, crossed back over into Bolk's territory. Half a dozen fighters were at the gate, watching the spreading riot.

"What's going on out there?" Garth asked, coming up to stand by Naru. The giant looked down at him curiously.

"All sorts of fighting tonight," the giant rumbled with amusement. "You not know?"

"No, I was out for a little pleasure around behind the House."

"What kind pleasure?"

"The female kind."

"Ah, you break training. Mistress not like that." Naru guffawed loudly and then looked up, his eyes narrowing at the sight of a dozen Ingkaran fighters storming onto the pavement belonging to Bolk.

"Get off our territory!" Naru shouted, stepping out from the main gate to face the approaching Purples, who slowed at the sight of the giant.

"Two of our men were robbed of their spells by one of yours!" a Purple shouted.

Naru said nothing, gazing down contemptuously at the fighter. The Purple seemed to hesitate and then he set eyes on Garth.

"It was him, One-eye."

Naru threw back his head and laughed.

"He good fellow, he out robbing women of their honor, not dogs of their offal. You Purple are the lapdogs of the Grand Master."

With a wild cry of anger one of the Ingkarans raised his hand. A twisting cyclone suddenly appeared, the wind racing out from it as frigid as an arctic night. Inside the cloud a form took shape and stepped out from the cloud. The ice giant moved slowly toward Naru as if its joints were still locked in blocks of frost but it came forward with a deadly purposefulness, raising its steel war hammer, a howling cry like the wind on a winter night thundering from its open mouth.

Naru, laughing, dodged the strike. With a balled-up fist he struck the frost giant with such a blow that the giant's head splintered into tinkling fragments. With that the fight was on. Cries for Purple and shouts for Brown echoed on the Plaza. Brown fighters and warriors came charging out of the House to aid their comrades. The crowd, which had been storming toward the riot around the palace, slowed, turning to watch the show. Bets were hurriedly placed. Partisans of Ingkara and Bolk shoved forward to watch the fight and within seconds were fighting with each other as well.

From the next section over could be heard the cries for Fentesk and Kestha, an explosion piercing the darkness, the crowd oohing and aahing as bolts of lightning shot overhead from the top of Fentesk's House.

Garth stayed in the shadows, ignoring Hammen's excited cries as the fight spilled out into the Plaza, the mob now joining in as well, the partisans of the different sides turning on each other with gleeful abandon. No warriors or fighters of the Grand Master intervened to stop the brawl since all were tied down holding back the mob around the palace.

Suddenly there was a great explosion of light around the palace and, from atop the Grand Master's palace, bolts of fire stormed down indiscriminately into the mob, knocking over hundreds.

"I think I'll go in and take a nap," Garth said calmly and, turning away from the spectacle, he walked through the door, stepping over the unconscious body of a Purple fighter whom Naru had tossed more than half a dozen fathoms. The giant, bellowing with delight, continued to wade into the battle, fists rising and falling.

Garth went through the door and paused. He looked down at Hammen.

"Why don't you go turn down my bed, Hammen."

Hammen, staring wide-eyed at Kirlen, who stood before them, nodded and slipped past the Master of Bolk.

"Masterful, One-eye, a masterful act of cunning."

"And what is that, my lady?"

"The riot out there. Don't you think I know how it started? Don't you think the Grand Master does too?"

"He has no proof. Perhaps he is just reaping the whirlwind of his misrule."

"And you are his moral judge? Hundreds will be killed out there."

Garth nodded.

"It would have come anyhow. No one out there is being forced to riot and murder. They're only imitating their betters."

Kirlen laughed coldly, leaning heavily on her staff.

"Our games match for the moment," Kirlen finally said, and, turning, she hobbled away.

"That bastard! I know it's him!"

Uriah looked up at Zarel.

"How do you know that, sire?"

His voice was filled with a wary caution.

"How dare you! I should take your head for your insolence."

To Zarel's shocked disbelief Uriah for once did not blanch.

"If you kill me now, Master, I fear a rebellion will sweep this palace. Right now our fighters are outside this very building holding back the mob. If their captain should die by your hands, what would they say?"

"Concerning you, not much," Zarel snarled.

"But of things in general," Uriah replied, amazed as the words poured out of him. "Eleven fighters have died in the rioting of the last several days, more than two hundred warriors as well. They are not happy, my lord, and though my death might mean nothing, then again it could mean an awful lot."

"What has come over you?"

Uriah swallowed hard, trying to control his fear.

"You violated the rules of the arena not once but four times today. You planted Silmar in the House of Ingkara, you gave him a spell, you had the circle master declare it a death match, and then you tried to intervene."

"How do you know that?"

"He told me this morning. He took the assignment but feared it would be his death. So he told me just before going over to stand with the House of Ingkara."

Zarel started to raise his hand.

"Go ahead. So far it's a secret. But kill me and the entire city will know what they only suspect right now. That will end all betting, for the mob will no longer trust you at all. Go ahead. You see, my lord, I left instructions with someone detailing all and if I die, it will be revealed."

Zarel hesitated, stunned by the sudden turn of his second.

"And I could reveal all about the role you played in the fall of Turquoise."

"You have held that over me for twenty long years, Master, and I groveled before you. But for this moment I want to be treated as a man."

Zarel laughed.

"You are nothing but a deformed animal."

"Then why do you make me your captain of fighters?"

Zarel smiled coldly.

"Because I could control you."

"You still can but the price has changed."

"What do you want?"

"Control of the House of Bolk," Uriah replied evenly.

"I have no control over who is selected as Master of a House."

"Then find a way. You will have to kill Kirlen before this is over or she will kill you. Isn't it obvious that she is behind this One-eye?"

"How can I trust you afterward?"

"You can't. For that matter how can I trust you? Perhaps that is the beginning of the only type of relationship that can last in this world."

Zarel nodded wearily and sat back down.

"Can you bring the mob under control?"

"Difficult, but yes, though I worry about tomorrow in the arena. A single spark will set them off."

Uriah hesitated.

"If that spark should come, then you will have to kill the mob by the thousands and drive them into the dirt. Nothing can be held back."

Uriah nodded in agreement.

"Master, will you bring him down tomorrow?"

"I plan to kill him during the procession to the arena. I have my assassins taking their positions even now. He will never make it out of the city."

"Suppose he eludes that trap?"

"Not in the arena. It is too risky." Zarel paused.

"Let the Walker have him as a servant and you'll be done with him. He is working toward some plan, not only against you, but against the Walker as well."

"How do you know this?"

"You asked me to find out all I could," Uriah replied. "He is dangerous beyond measure."

Zarel lowered his head.

"Get out."

"Do we have our agreement?"

"Yes, damn you. Now get out."

Uriah, head bowed low, turned and hobbled out of the room.

"And bring that damn mob under control!"

As the door slammed shut the dwarf sagged against the wall, suddenly unable to control the trembling of his limbs. He fought down the sudden urge to vomit. For years he had dreamed of standing up to Zarel, and always feared death would be the payment.

He felt as if he had been possessed by a demon. Was that it? His visit to the dealer of potions had been for the purpose of gaining powders so that he could have his way with one of the court women; it was the only way he ever could have one, by first drugging her. The offered drink had seemed innocent enough and then this sense of power and defiance had taken hold.

He was suddenly tempted to go back, find the man, and kill him.

But why? It had worked somehow, or was it even the drink at all? He stuck his hand into his pocket and felt the leather pouch and the weight of the ruby inside. The request was simple enough and the payment a bribe in and of itself sufficient for a dozen nights of pleasure without need of potions.

I've been promised the House of Bolk when Kirlen falls, Uriah thought with a grim smile. *My own House and freedom from Zarel's torments*. The dream washed over him and he could see himself being carried on a sedan chair of gold like Jimak's, and surrounded by concubines who would make Tulan drool with envy.

Uriah smiled at the thought.

But who did the bribe come from in the first place? he suddenly wondered. There was a suspicion and that alone sent a chill through him. For there was the memory of before, of long before, and how he had once been such a source of innocent amusement and had even been loved.

Uriah lowered his head and walked down the corridor into the darkness.

Zarel sat in silence. What had possessed Uriah? Was it a simple madness or did he somehow sense that the position of the Grand Master might be slipping? But there was the deeper fear now, the realization that somehow One-eye was something far different. Something that would not be solved by simply letting him win the final match and then be taken away forever.

Could One-eye know of my own plans and reveal them to the Walker, perhaps even bartering to save his own miserable life in the process? Could that be it? He had to accept the fact now that One-eye was out to destroy him, and perhaps Uriah was right, One-eye wanted something from the Walker as well.

Zarel sighed and leaned forward on his throne.

Could it be that One-eye even knew that the entire process of the Festival was a sham? Perhaps even now he understood that one of its many purposes was to select the best fighter each year so that the Walker could take him away . . . and then kill him so as to eliminate a potential threat, not only to the existing order of things but to the Walker as well? One-eye had proved his cunning. It would be the mark of a fool not to assume that this man had figured it out.

Zarel looked up again, almost ready to call Uriah back.

No. Not him and not now. That would be another game to play out in its own good time. There would have to be another way to destroy One-eye.

Suddenly Zarel sat back and started to laugh, for it was all so obvious, so wonderfully and simply obvious what had to be done, and in the process it might very well clear the way for a new Walker.

Stretching lazily, Garth watched as the names for the next match were registered on the tote board. The first match of the second round of eliminations had just finished and he waited to see against whom he would be pitted in the next round after having sat out the opening fight of the day. At last his symbol appeared and the mob roared its approval and then fell into contemptuous laughter when the name of a second-rank fighter from Kestha was posted as his rival.

Garth looked over at Hammen, who shrugged.

"Maybe he's backing off and deciding to play it straight; the mob is less than happy with the bastard today."

That dissatisfaction was evident throughout the city. Several hundred homes and businesses had burned in the rioting of the night before. Scores were dead and hundreds injured. The tension was even worse over the fights between Fentesk and Kestha, which had left half a dozen fighters dead, one of them the second highest ranking fighter in Kestha, and the fighting between Bolk and Ingkara, which had resulted in the deaths of eight more. Following Hammen's advice, Garth had slipped out of the House before dawn and hidden down by the arena, avoiding the grand march and the possibility of a trap on the part of Zarel, leaving a note for Kirlen not to have his name dropped from the day's lineup.

Hammen's advice was true to form, when on the march down to the arena a fight had broken out. Within seconds nearly half of Zarel's fighters had come pouring out of a side street and swarmed in among Brown's ranks. They looked about expectantly and Kirlen had laughed with cold, sardonic glee when it became evident that the fight was a cover for a move against Garth, who was not in the column of march.

The mob in the arena waited, wondering where its favorite was, fearful that he had left as mysteriously as he had arrived. The trumpet sounding the call for the fighters echoed and half a million were now on their feet, watching as the fighters for the second round of the second elimination stepped out onto the field.

"It'll be a setup. He won't let you off that field alive," Hammen said gloomily.

"You can always stay up here in the stands."

"Like hell. I've seen it through this far though only the Eternal knows why."

"Well, let's get on with it," Garth announced, and he stood up, casting aside the heavy cloak under which he had kept himself concealed. He pushed his way through the stands and down to the barrier that marked the edge of the fighting field and leaped over the wall, turning to help Hammen down. Instantly half a dozen warriors raced toward him, assuming he was an overeager fan. Garth turned to face them.

A wild cry of delight rose up from the audience, racing out from the point where he was standing.

"One-eye!"

The guards slowed, coming to a stop, looking at him with openmouthed surprise. Garth strode past them as if they were not there. The mob, taken by the fact that he had been sitting with them, broke into thunderous applause as Garth walked across the field to the circle assigned to him for the next match.

The circle was directly below Zarel's throne and Garth looked up at him, smiling, and saying nothing.

Zarel stood up, gazing down with open hatred, and Garth turned his back in an open display of contempt. The roaring of the mob redoubled.

"He could kill you like this," Hammen shouted, trying to be heard above the howling mob.

"He doesn't have the guts to do it now," Garth said quietly as he stepped into the neutral box. "If he touches me now, half a million will storm this field."

"Put not your trust in the mob."

"I don't, but I do trust their hatred of him."

His opponent, a young woman from Kestha, came forward and stepped into her box, looking over anxiously at Garth.

"How do you declare this fight?" the circle master asked, looking over at Garth.

"Spell match."

The circle master turned and looked back at the woman and she gave the same reply.

The fight was over in seconds. Even before she had drawn up sufficient *mana* to mount a defense, Garth's mammoth had her pinned to the ground, the woman looking up at the beast in wide-eyed terror. She raised her hand in token of submission and Garth called the great beast off and then conjured it out of existence. The circle master approached the woman to take her spell offered in wager and Garth extended his left hand, palm downward to indicate that he would not accept the wager, the crowd roaring their approval at his chivalrous act.

He walked back calmly to the stands where the Bolk fighters sat. Many of them looked at him with obvious suspicion, but Naru shouted with delight.

"Good, I can still fight you. I thought you run away."

Garth laughed, and went over to a table set with fresh fruits, cheese, and decanters of wine for the refreshment of the fighters, scooped up a handful of pomegranates and, taking a jug of wine, went over to an empty seat, motioning for Hammen to follow.

Kirlen, sitting upon her throne, looked down at him.

"You missed the morning procession."

"I thought it best for reasons of health."

Kirlen laughed coldly.

"It would have been amusing to see how you handled it."

"No sense in causing trouble."

"Like last night?"

Garth smiled and, saying nothing, settled down in his seat to watch the show.

The third elimination round started and he was called out immediately for the next round, returning back to his seat less than half an hour later, this time carrying a red spell of fireball taken from his unconscious opponent, the crowd now at a hysterical pitch of excitement, even though it now took the betting of a silver on One-eye to win back a copper.

With the end of the third elimination the noontime recess was called. In the stands the mob milled about, arguing loudly about the remaining forty fighters. Several favorites had fallen early, including Omar of Kestha, who had been rated as one of the favorites, and the legendary Mina of Ingkara, who had been taken off the field minus his feet, which had been bitten off by gnomes while he lay unconscious. The issue was made even more interesting because of the deaths of the fighters the night before, nine of whom had survived the first round of eliminations. Their deaths had upset the more elaborate forms of betting and tens of thousands were less than pleased when black markers were placed next to the names of the deceased.

Since the betting was not just on individual fights, but also on a wide variety of permutations, including combinations of fighters, win averages for Houses, and percentages of wins by Houses during each round, the crowd was in a decidedly less than happy mood. A number of bets placed at the end of the first day had been voided by the deaths, the losses going into Zarel's coffers, thus convincing many that the Grand Master had set up the previous night's riots to pad out his own pockets and gain revenge for the unruly behavior of his citizens.

Loud arguments raged in the stands between the partisans of one group or another, occasionally breaking down into brawls that swept back and forth through the crowd and at one point even spilled out onto the arena floor until a line of warriors drove the mob back.

As the noon hour progressed gangs of laborers erased the circles used for the first two series of matches. Only twenty pairs would fight in the next elimination in two sets of ten and new circles were drawn, each circle now twice as big as before, at just under fifty fathoms across. This meant that spells of greater power, which might have been difficult to contain inside the smaller twenty-five-fathom circles, could now be brought into play.

A high clarion call sounded, signaling the end of the noon hour. As the crowd poured back to its seats the catapult wagons came galloping out from the access tunnels and moved around the edge of the arena. The catapults fired more clay pots into the crowd and, as they burst open, wild cheering broke out.

Hammen turned in his seat to watch the show and cocked his head to hear the cries of the audience.

"The pots are filled with more gold," Hammen announced, his voice suddenly edged with longing, as if he wished to be back up in the stands.

Garth chuckled softly, saying nothing.

As the word of the prizes within the pots spread, the crowds came close to stampeding in their eagerness to position themselves near where the next pot might land. Fights broke out as people piled atop each other in their eagerness to snatch up a single coin, sufficient to keep them in ale or wine for half the winter. The dwarfs lashed their teams around the arena, firing their weapons, and then, pointing to where the pot landed, howled with delight at the antics of the mob.

From out of the access tunnel came scores of young women dressed in diaphanous gowns. As they danced around the edge of the arena they reached into oversize pouches that bounced against their naked hips and tossed handfuls of gold trinkets, and even gems, into the stands. This set off a near-insane frenzy of cheering, which became even wilder when, from out of the north, four dragons, each half a dozen fathoms in length, came soaring in. The crowd looked up, on the edge of panicking, fearing that the great beasts were out of control and intent upon attacking the audience. The dragons, however, flashed into puffs of smoke and from out of the spreading clouds came a heavy rain of silver necklaces, baubles, and yet more coins.

The clouds, after emptying out their rain, drifted down into the center of the arena and coiled in around the throne of the Grand Master. The clouds became one and swirled inward. There was a flash of light, an explosive roar, and there, standing upon his throne, returning from his midday meal, was Zarel Ewine, the Grand Master.

The mob broke into a wild, hysterical cheering and Zarel, turning to each corner of the arena, bowed low.

Hammen, shaking his head with disgust, spit on the ground.

"The mob," he said coldly. "Now all is forgiven."

"But not for long," Garth replied.

The last of the women and dwarf catapult teams left through the access tunnel and a groan of disappointment rose from the crowd.

"Don't worry, my friends." Zarel's voice boomed across the

arena through the power of his far speaking. "They will come back again at the end of the day's festivities with even more gold."

His words were greeted with cheers of anticipation.

Garth looked back over at Hammen and grinned.

"Is it taken care of?"

"I can't promise, but you sure did pay enough."

"Fine."

"The drawings have started," Hammen announced, and he pointed across the arena field to where a single monk was now reaching into a golden urn.

"It's no longer by Houses," Hammen said.

"You could be matched up against your own from now on."

As he spoke Naru looked over at Garth and grinned.

"Maybe we fight now and I take all your spells."

"Maybe."

"One-eye!" The cry rose from the mob. Garth looked up to see that he was being pitted against an Ingkaran fighter.

"Who is he?" Garth asked.

"Ulin. Tough, maybe an eighth-rank by now. He's incredibly fast gathering his *mana* in. I'd suggest going for him physically; otherwise, you might have a tough time of it right from the start."

Garth stood up and looked over at Naru.

"Not this round."

"Don't lose, One-eye. I still wish to fight you."

Naru's match appeared on the board and the giant stood up, laughing and stretching.

Together they went out onto the field, the mob coming to its feet and applauding two of its favorite champions. Garth turned and looked back up into the stands. Some of the spectators were now sporting eye patches, which were being hawked by souvenir salesmen, and he could only shake his head over this new style that had taken the fancy of the crowd.

Naru thumped Garth on the back so that Garth nearly lost his footing as the giant turned to go to his own circle.

The trumpet sounded again as Garth reached his circle and stepped into the neutral box. Across the fifty-fathom width his opponent stood ready, arms already extended.

Zarel stood up.

"By my decision there shall be a new rule for fights, starting with the fourth elimination."

The audience fell silent in anticipation.

"If either of the two fighters declares it to be a death match, then so it shall be. Payment on all bets of a death match shall not be charged my ten percent fee. All winnings are thus yours to keep. No spell of healing may be used on the fallen."

There was a moment of stunned silence and an instant later the arena erupted in wild cheering.

"The mob," Hammen sniffed angrily. "They're back in his pocket."

"Except for the private bookmakers. He just put them out of business unless they can offer better odds."

"Also, my friends. Any fighter who declares a death match and makes his kill shall receive from my hands, from my personal hoard, a spell which he may draw out of my personal satchel, or five hundred pieces of gold."

From the arena floor many of the fighters raised their clenched fists in gleeful salute.

"He's spending a fortune to buy them back," Hammen said.

"And the House Masters will lose all their best people," Garth said quietly. "Masterful."

Garth looked back toward where Kirlen sat and could sense her rage. If the House Masters dared to try and raise a protest over the slaughter, the mob would riot, but this time against them. Zarel had outmaneuvered them for the moment and in the process had weakened them as well.

The circle master for Garth's fight came to Garth's side and extended her hand. In it were a white chip and a black.

"Choose death or a single spell match," she said coldly.

"What about the public declaration?" Hammen asked.

"Tell your servant to shut up or I'll have his tongue ripped out," the woman snapped.

Garth looked at her coldly and then took the white chip.

"A spell match."

She looked at him with open sarcasm and, turning, started across the circle to Garth's opponent.

"Brilliant," Hammen snarled. "Most fighters will assume the other's going for a death match anyhow so they'll choose it as well in hopes of winning the Grand Master's prize. It's going to be a slaughter pit out here."

The woman stood before Ulin, extending her hands and Ulin took one of the proffered chips, signifying his choice of a death or single spell match. She went back across the circle and, pulling out a red flag, raised it. Red flags appeared all across the arena floor and the crowd went wild with bloodlust.

"Fight!"

Garth leaped into the arena, moving fast, charging straight at his opponent. Ulin stood with arms extended, rushing to draw in his *mana* and create the first spell. Garth continued his charge, drawing out his dagger. Ulin looked up at him and started to point even as Garth slammed into him, striking Ulin on the side of the head with the dagger's hilt. Ulin crumpled up, falling over backward.

Ulin, howling with rage, came up with his own dagger and lunged in low at Garth. Garth jumped aside.

"Just lie down, damn it, and act like I knocked you out!" Garth snapped.

Ulin, however, driven by a wild rage, came at him again, feinting low and then going for a throat slash while all the time turning to work around toward Garth's blind side.

Ulin's hand scraped across the arena floor and he tossed a handful of sand into Garth's face, blinding him. Garth staggered backward, the screams of the mob rising to such a hysterical pitch that he could not hear where his opponent might be approaching from.

Garth fell backward, as if guided by instinct, and felt Ulin go over him. Rolling on his shoulders, Garth somersaulted over, landing on his feet, trying to wipe the sand from his eye.

Ulin pressed in again, not even giving Garth time to raise a circle of protection. Garth rolled again, Ulin's blade slicing his shoulder open, and the sight of the blood caused the cheering to become even louder.

Barely able to see, Garth sensed another blow coming in hard and he raised his left arm to ward off the blow. The dagger sliced his wrist open, the icy pain of the hit stunning him.

Ulin pulled back and then dived in again. Garth ducked under the blow, coming in low and sweeping out with his legs. He caught Ulin just below the left knee and the fighter went over. Recovering, Ulin leaped upon Garth, struggling to pin him to the ground. The two rolled in the dust and Ulin moved to drive his dagger into Garth's eye. Garth jerked his head aside as the blow came down, the dagger slicing open his cheek.

Howling with delight, Ulin yanked his dagger free from the sand and raised it for a killing blow.

Just as the blow started to descend Garth managed to wrench his right hand free from Ulin's grasp and drove the blade upward. The dagger slipped in just below Ulin's chin, piercing through the roof of his mouth and up into his brain.

Ulin's downward strike faltered, going wide. Garth let go of his own blade as Ulin, with a near-supernatural strength, somehow staggered back to his feet, Garth's dagger driven up to the hilt into the bottom of his jaw.

A gasp of amazement went up from the mob at the sight of the man staggering about and then, ever so slowly, his legs crumpled and he collapsed to the ground. Garth, panting for breath, came up on his knees, the screaming of the mob thundering around him, deafening him so that he wanted to cover his ears and shut the sound out.

He felt hands grasping him around his shoulders.

"Heal yourself, heal yourself, you're bleeding to death!"

Wide-eyed, Garth looked over at Hammen and then back at Ulin.

"You don't have time for him, damn it, heal yourself now!"

Garth, gasping for breath, nodded and concentrated upon his *mana*. The power came slowly as he felt himself weakening. At last the power was there and Garth slowly extended his hands. The blood pouring out of his wrist, arm, and face stilled, the skin drawing back over upon itself even as he felt his strength return.

Yet still the thunder washed over him and, squinting from the glare of the hot afternoon sun, which reflected off the packed sand of the arena, he stood up, gasping for breath.

"Why didn't you just stab him with your first blow?"

"I thought I could knock him out."

"Cut the chivalry. This is death match and you better fight it that way," Hammen snapped.

Garth looked around the arena where half a dozen fights

were still going on. In a circle at the south end of the arena a great spider was scampering around, holding a fighter aloft, the man writhing in agony, the mob in that section jumping up and down in their seats with wild abandon. On the east side two small armies of undead and skeletons were busy slashing at each other, while in the ring to the north of Garth a fighter was strutting about, holding up the head of his slain foe.

Garth walked over to Ulin's body and looked down.

"Damn you," Garth sighed and, reaching down, pulled out his dagger, wiped it on the sand, and then cut the man's satchel off, tossing a *mana* bundle to the referee. The crowd broke into wild applause.

Garth turned to walk back to Brown's stands.

"Too bad you didn't declare it a death match, One-eye," the referee taunted. "You could have gotten a prize."

"I don't need any more spells and the hell with the blood money," Garth snapped in reply.

Still gasping for breath, Garth slowly walked across the arena floor, ignoring the wild howling of the mob, which stood to give him an ovation. Stepping under the awning, he went over to the food and wine, pouring himself a drink, while out in the arena the last fights were played out.

"What happened to Varena?" Garth asked, turning to look back out on the field.

Hammen pointed up to the tote board.

"She won."

Garth nodded, saying nothing.

Naru came back in, covered in blood and holding the satchel of a Fentesk fighter.

"Not this much slaughter in years," Naru announced gleefully. "Many good spells."

He shouldered up beside Garth and, taking up a decanter of wine, drained it off with loud, thirsty gulps followed by a rolling, self-satisfied belch.

"Ah, now better. Perhaps we fight, I take *your* satchel now."

Garth looked up at Naru.

"You know, it's hard to admit, but I've almost come to like you."

Naru chuckled, his voice edged with sadness.

"Me almost like you. Too bad."

"Fighter, make not friend of fighter."

Garth turned to see Kirlen standing behind him.

"This slaughter is because of you. You realize that, don't you? All the Houses will lose their best today and tomorrow."

"So stop him."

"We can't." Kirlen waved toward the mob, which was on its feet, howling with bloodlust as two fighters, their spells expended, staggered about the fighting circle, slashing at each other with daggers.

"He's killing more fighters out there today then we'd lose in a half dozen Festivals, just so he can get at you and win the mob back."

Garth sipped at his wine.

"And all of you will be the weaker for it. Like I said, the four of you should stop him."

Kirlen shook her head, saying nothing.

"Let me guess. He paid all of you off, didn't he? The potential loss of contracts made good over the next couple of years."

"The bastard," she said softly, her voice barely audible above the screams.

"And of course you took it."

"The others did too."

"But of course," Garth replied, his voice filled with contempt. "So why don't you try and kill me now and get the rest of the bribe?"

"In due time, in due time."

Garth, shaking his head, returned to his seat.

An explosion of sound swept over the arena as the last fight ended with a mutual kill, the two fighters stabbing each other, and neither one with a single heal spell left. They writhed about for what seemed like an eternity and then both were still. The spectators screamed hysterically, jumping up and down over the spectacular finish to the fourth round. Even though any who bet upon it had lost their money, still they cheered over an ending that would be argued about in the taverns and on street corners for years to come.

"They're certainly getting their money's worth today," Hammen said coldly, before downing a beaker of wine.

The urn containing the names of the survivors was now brought out again and the monk started to draw out the new fighting pairs. The first names started to go up and the entire arena came to its feet.

"You're fighting Naru," Hammen whispered.

"Damn."

Garth slowly stood up and looked over at the giant, who stood gaping at the board until his servant finally told him what the symbols meant. Naru turned and looked back at Garth and, with a huge beefy hand, motioned for Garth to walk out with him. As Naru started out from under the awning and into the bright light of the arena Kirlen hobbled up to his side, said something, and then turned her back as Garth walked by.

Garth came up to Naru's side.

"This will be to the death, One-eye."

"Too bad. Like I said, I was getting to like you, even though you are as dumb as an ox."

Naru threw his head back and laughed.

"All think that funny. How come Naru so dumb and yet control *mana* so well? Don't know."

"A freak of nature," Hammen sniffed.

"I like you too," Naru said, looking down at Hammen. "You be my servant after One-eye dead."

"Not likely."

"How much did Kirlen offer you?" Garth asked.

"Choice of her spells I kill you."

"Did you ever think why she wants me dead?"

"You cause trouble."

Naru looked back down at Garth and shook his head.

"Somehow this not seem right. Naru like good fighting, but too many friends die today. Too many. Naru have no one left to play with when this done."

As they reached their circle Garth looked around and saw Varena walking slowly toward her circle, a Purple fighter moving to take the other side.

"Who is that against her?" Garth asked.

"It's not good. That's Jimak's favorite. The way the fixing is going on, I wouldn't be surprised if he loaned some of his own spells. I hope she got the same offer from her Master."

"Damn fool wouldn't take it," Garth said. "Too much honor."

"Don't worry about her now," Hammen replied. "Remember,

you caught that big lummox by surprise last time. He won't let it happen again. Don't let him get close to you. If it turns to hand-to-hand he'll rip you apart and pick his teeth with your ribs. How are you feeling?"

"Still a little light-headed from the last fight."

"Just great," Hammen sighed.

The final trumpet sounded and the referee came over to Garth, showing him the two tokens. Again Garth took the white. The Master went over to Naru and a moment later she returned to her box and sent up a red flag, to the cheering of the mob.

"Good luck, Master."

"You never wished me luck before."

"Well, you never needed it before."

"Thanks for the confidence."

"It's not a question of confidence," Hammen replied. "It's a question of being a realist."

"Fight!"

Garth stepped into the circle and, concentrating his will, he immediately started to draw upon his *mana*. He delayed launching an attack, deciding instead to hold back, building up his strength as much as possible. Naru finally made the first move, sending a mammoth forward and Garth finally replied by again creating a wall of trees, fronted with an impenetrable growth of brambles against which the mammoth raged and trumpeted, especially when the brambles started to pierce the mammoth's feet. Garth was surprised when Naru, using *mana* he had not suspected the giant would employ, sent wolves into the attack. They slipped through the trees and Garth, in turn, created wolves to fight and block them. An explosion from another circle erupted, nearly knocking Garth over and he spared a quick glance back to see Varena and her opponent engaged in desperate struggle, the circle engulfed in flames.

Garth turned back to his own fight and was startled when he could not see Naru. The giant seemed to have disappeared!

There was a crashing of trees and to Garth's left, at the edge of the circle, the giant came crashing through, the trees around him withering and dying. Garth conjured one of the trees to life. Naru, laughing, turned on it, fighting it hand to hand, tearing limbs off the tree and tossing them aside so that the tree-creature simply fell over and collapsed.

Now came wave after wave of attack against Garth, orcs and goblins, enraged dwarfs swinging their battle-axes, and nameless creatures out of the darkness.

Garth countered by striking at Naru's *mana*, weakening the lands that supported his magic, setting up circles of protection for when Naru's minions came too close, counterattacking with winged creatures and Llanowar Elves that gleefully struck at the dwarfs, crushing them down.

His *mana* weakened, Naru was forced to withdraw to his own half of the circle, laying out a wall of fire. The two stood gasping for breath, Naru shaking his head and laughing, the laughter coming like the panting of a bull.

"You good fellow. Too bad must die now."

Naru waved his hands and a new onslaught began. Creatures in the air, on the sand, and rising up from underneath, coming one after the other. Garth gave ground slowly and the mob, wild with hysteria, sensing that the fight was coming to a climax, roared with delight.

Garth erected more trees, stepping back slowly, warding off the attacks that broke through but each time it seemed as if he had less power than before. Naru again reached the edge of the forest and waved his hand. Some of the trees ignited in flame and Garth instantly replaced them. Again there was the burst of fire and again they were replaced.

Naru stood back for a second, shaking his head with frustration. Garth stood at the far side of his circle and then, ever so slowly, he fell down on his knees as if his final power had been expended.

Naru, with a wild cry, raced into the trees, which towered up over him, the crowd roaring insanely, expecting him to crash through and deliver the coup with his bare hands.

Garth instantly came to his feet and pointed straight at the forest. Above the roaring of the crowd another sound now washed over the stadium, the miniature forest shaking and trembling. A loud, howling roar exploded and from out of the forest a green head appeared, its fangs glinting in the hot, late-afternoon sun. The head of the Craw Wurm weaved back and forth, like a serpent's, looking for its prey. The creature arced over, its long sinuous body weaving up out of the forest and then crashing back down.

A loud, bellowing roar of pain thundered out of the woods. Trees swayed back and forth, crashing over. For a brief instant a stone giant started to form at the edge of the forest. Garth waved his hands and the Craw Wurm's tail lashed out, toppling the giant. Continuing to control the Wurm, Garth now redirected its attack at Naru.

More trees toppled and then, from out of the forest, the Craw Wurm emerged. Wrapped in its scaly coils, Naru struggled to get free, bellowing with pain. The Craw Wurm threw another coil around the giant's kicking legs, crushing him under its weight.

The mob, driven to an ecstasy of excitement, howled insanely. Naru continued to fight, managing to bring forth another burst of flame from above. Garth countered by blocking the fire, and then increased the Craw Wurm's strength. The Wurm threw another coil over Naru, pinning his arms and squeezing.

The giant's face turned dark purple. A loud scream of anguish burst from him as if the cry had been crushed out of his body. Naru's head lolled back in unconsciousness.

The mob, screaming with insane frenzy, cheered wildly, even though it was one of their old favorites who had just been defeated.

The Craw Wurm raised its head, preparing to bite down and devour its meal.

The screaming of the mob thundered.

Garth One-eye raised his hand.

The Craw Wurm seemed to freeze and then, in a puff of smoke, it disappeared.

Naru, still unconscious, tumbled to the ground and was still. Garth walked over to the giant's side and pulled his dagger out.

A hush settled over the mob, confused by this action and then realization set in that Garth meant to deliver the death blow with his own hand. Some cheering broke out but many fell silent. This was no longer killing in the heat of combat and there was an uneasy stirring.

Garth held his dagger aloft and then with a dramatic flourish threw the blade out of the circle. A stunned gasp swept the arena.

"He was a worthy foe and my friend!" Garth shouted, the mob surprised that a mere fighter held the rare spell of far speaking. "I will not murder him for the pleasure of a Grand Master who has perverted the rules of the arena."

"Kill him. It is a blood challenge."

Garth turned and looked back at Zarel.

"I won the match, you cannot deny me that. But I will not commit murder for you."

Zarel, screaming with rage, started to point at Garth.

"Will you violate that rule as well?" Garth taunted.

"Let them live!"

It was a lone voice, that of a woman, and Garth looked across the arena to see someone standing, wearing the dark leather armor of a Benalish warrior. Her cry was instantly picked up by the mob.

"Let them live, let them live!"

Garth started to create a shield of protection while all the time staring at Zarel, waiting. Furious with rage, Zarel looked back out at the mob, which was on its feet, some of them already spilling over the wall, ready to storm onto the arena floor. Zarel, his features white with fury, sat back down.

Turning his back on Zarel, Garth reached down and touched Naru on the forehead. Naru stirred and opened his eyes.

"Funny. Is this afterworld?"

Garth smiled and shook his head. Extending his hand, he was nearly pulled over as Naru weakly got to his feet.

"You mean I lose and you still alive."

"Something like that."

"I am disgraced, One-eye."

"I called it a spell match so, damn it, give me a spell and we're even."

Naru fumbled weakly in his pouch. He hesitated for a moment and then pulled the amulet out.

"Juggernaut, most powerful I have," Naru said evenly.

Garth took the amulet, and then shook Naru's hand, the exchange causing the mob to erupt into a wild frenzy.

The two walked back to their corner, Naru resting his hand on Garth's shoulder for support.

Kirlen, leaning on her staff, ignored Naru as they came into the shade, the giant staggering over to the table of food, picking up a heavy amphora of wine, and inverting it over his open mouth, the wine cascading down his pale, drawn face like a river.

"Your sentimentality won you no friends here," Kirlen said.

"I brought back your best fighter alive."

"And you."

Garth smiled and said nothing.

A loud cheer went up and Garth looked over his shoulder and felt a momentary tightening in his chest. Varena was down on the ground. But her opponent was down as well and ever so slowly Varena came to her feet and held her fist up in triumph.

Garth turned back to face Kirlen.

She smiled coldly and turned away.

Garth went back to his seat. The arena thundered with noise in celebration of the end of the fifth round of eliminations.

"It's time for the winners to get their wreaths," Hammen announced, coming to Garth's side.

"Then I think it's time for me to go."

"I think he has something planned for you."

Garth smiled.

"Let's see how the timing works."

"Maybe you should just skip out now and be done with it."

Garth laughed and strode out onto the field. Greeted by a loud ovation, he walked slowly toward Zarel's throne. From out of the tunnels the dwarf catapult teams emerged and the roar of the mob resounded even louder. Watching honors for favorite winners was one thing, but the chance for free gold was far more important.

"He plans to divert the mob with bribes while you're taken," Hammen said.

"It will be an interesting surprise. Let's just hope it gets started quickly enough," Garth replied.

As he approached the throne the other surviving fighters lined up beside him. He looked over at Varena, her features pale and haggard, and nodded a greeting. A brief smile flashed for a second and then she turned away. Garth looked at the other fighters, who stared at him coldly. The new rules meant that all of them were now gazing at men and women who would either be their victims or killers come tomorrow.

Zarel stood up and floated down from the throne to alight on the sand of the arena floor. Four of his fighters came forward bearing a golden tray, upon which rested the laurels given to those who had reached the final day of eliminations. Garth could not help but notice, though, that a solid phalanx of warriors was pouring out of the access tunnels, followed by nearly all the Grand Master's fighters. They moved out onto the arena floor in order to surround the golden circle.

"All of you shall be my guests at the palace tonight," Zarel announced calmly.

"I've already been there once. I think I shall decline," Garth replied calmly.

Zarel turned to face Garth. In the background was the rattle of dozens of crossbows being raised.

In the distance the mob was still howling with delight, but not for what they assumed was a simple boring ceremony to end the day's fun. Nearly two score of wagon-carried catapults were now out, their dwarf crews loading up the first pots. The weapons fired, the mob howling with joy as the clay pots arced up into the audience.

"If you fight, I wonder if they would even notice," Zarel said. "They're getting stuffed on gold. I daresay as well that some of your opponents here would be more than happy to have you out of the way. In fact, if you were gone, we could dispense with the blood sport for tomorrow and return to the more traditional form."

Garth looked sidelong at his potential rivals. He saw only Varena giving him a nod of support. Garth stretched and simply smiled.

The first of the clay pots crashed down into the audience and the mob surged to where the golden treasures would land.

The dwarf crews were hurriedly reloading, firing again and yet again. But the tone of the mob was already changing. The wild exuberant shouts were replaced within seconds by mad cries of panic and pain.

Zarel hesitated and looked up from Garth. The pots continued to rain down on the audience . . . breaking open to disgorge stinging scorpions, hornets enraged by their disturbing trips, and hissing poisonous vipers.

For several seconds all seemed to be frozen, Zarel looking at the mob, not understanding, the guards surrounding Garth with weapons raised, and the angry howling of the mob growing ever louder.

More pots rained down, bursting open, the terrified spectators writhing about, screaming in panic and rage, the vipers coiling around whoever was nearest, swarms of hornets stinging whatever flesh they came in contact with.

In the section of the stand closest to Zarel's throne a Benalish woman leaped up onto the containing wall of the arena.

"Zarel! Zarel is killing us! Kill him!"

With drawn sword she leaped down from the wall. Like a dam bursting open, the mob started to flood down the stadium rows, gaining the wall and piling over it, the flood spreading out across the entire length of the arena.

The dwarf crews, still not comprehending what they were doing, continued to fire the pots into the audience. As the mob swirled around them they threw the rest out of their wagons, thinking the crowd was simply after loot. Their actions infuriated the mob even more and the wagons were swarmed under.

The warriors surrounding Zarel turned to face outward and stem the mad onrush. Panicked, they lowered their weapons and fired. Zarel turned back to face Garth, at last realizing what had happened and knowing that somehow One-eye was behind it.

He was greeted by a green cloud of smoke.

Ducking low, Garth darted around the throne, followed by Hammen, and was almost instantly lost in the crush of warriors struggling to form ranks and face the enraged mob that, by the hundreds of thousands, was now storming out onto the arena floor.

"Behind you!"

Garth turned even as Varena dropped a warrior who was about to bring his sword down on Garth's back. Garth leaped aside as the flame-scorched body tumbled over. The three pushed their way through the warriors, who were staggering backward as the onrushing wall of the mob slammed into them.

Garth raised his hands and the warriors to either side recoiled from him, a dark terror gripping their hearts. He pushed his way through the ranks, using terror to clear a path, Varena by his side. They broke through into the struggling mob and at the sight of him the mob parted, cheering wildly, and then pushed on again, shouting with rage.

Garth gained the edge of the arena and climbed over the wall. The stands were still half-full, except for wide circles of empty spaces now controlled by the creatures that had burst out of the pots. Garth ascended the steps, reaching the top of the arena.

The betting stands were in shambles, the mob looting them. Beneath each stand was a chute down which was dropped the money taken in betting to arrive in carts far underground by which, through hidden tunnels, the winnings would be taken back to the palace. Some of the mob were tearing at the holes with their bare hands, shouting curses down the holes. Still others vented their rage on the booths, tearing them apart board by board.

The arena floor was chaos. A dark knot of warriors held in the center. The Master's fighters were now in the fray, casting out walls of fire to drive the mob back.

"I'm going back to my House," Varena said.

Garth turned and looked at her, taking her by the arm.

"Maybe you should leave."

She pulled her arm free.

"I've studied all my life for the chance to be the servant of the Walker. I'll not stop now."

Hammen sniffed and said nothing.

"That means we'll have to fight tomorrow."

"I know."

"And if it comes to killing, then what? You know that bastard will require it tomorrow."

She looked at him, saying nothing.

"Leave, Varena, for the sake of the Eternal, leave."

"I'll see you tomorrow," she said quietly and, turning, she disappeared into the swirling mob.

"Same advice I've been giving to you," Hammen said.

"And I'm just as pigheaded. Now come on, we've got work to do."

CHAPTER
13

THE DOOR INTO THE ATTIC SWUNG OPEN AND
Garth turned expectantly.

"Were you able to find her?"

Hammen shook his head.

"Damn."

"Some people say she was killed at the start of the riot, others that the Grand Master's warriors took her prisoner. There's not a word of that Benalish woman at the moment."

Garth said nothing, turning back to peek through the narrow window. Out in the Plaza all was finally still. Carts moved back and forth through the shadows, hooded monks picking up the hundreds of dead who littered the area around the palace. Fires still flickered across the city and in the distance could be heard the roar of the mobs. From out of the main street that led down to the harbor, a solid column of warriors was marching, their shields and spears glinting in the glowing light. Down below even the normal flow of business had quieted down, something for which Garth was extremely grateful.

"Zarel's called in troops from Tantium. The ships are arriving even now. He's stripping the countryside bare," Hammen announced. "They say maybe a thousand or more people and several hundred warriors were killed down in the arena. The mob was still holding it when I left but I guess the troops are finally clearing it."

Garth nodded.

"And the package I hid outside the city gate?"

Hammen held up the oilskin bundle and dropped it on the floor.

Garth nodded his thanks and, bending down, picked it up as if it was a treasured and fragile object.

"Master?"

Garth looked back at Hammen.

"I think I'm quitting your service."

"Why?"

Hammen shook his head.

"Go on, out with it."

"In the beginning it was different. I thought you were out on a lark, have a little fun, tweak the nose of Zarel, and make a profit. Though you've never said anything, I always suspected who you were as well."

"But that's changed, hasn't it."

Hammen nodded sadly.

"I passed along the front of the harbor tonight. They're taking the carts down and dumping the dead in, letting the tide take them out. The sharks and empreys are having a feast; the water's churning with the feeding."

He fell silent for a moment.

"Don't you have any remorse, any feelings over this?"

Garth turned away from Hammen to look back out the window as a company of warriors raced past and then disappeared into the night.

"Yes."

"Then why? Thousands have died."

"You have sympathy with the mob, is that it?"

"I was the mob," Hammen replied.

"And what were you then? If you had not been with me, you would have been up in the stands howling for blood, trembling with ecstasy as a fighter hacked the guts out of an opponent. That was your life, wasn't it? What are the permutations of tomorrow's bet, can I get the right combination and win a thousand over the blood of someone else?"

Hammen lowered his head.

"I had to survive."

"You call that surviving. That bastard in the palace has perverted everything the *mana* was intended for. He's turned it into sport and money contracts and the Walker allowed it. That's all the mob now lives for."

"And Garth the liberator has come to change that? What right do you have anyhow? You've killed more in the last four days than Zarel does in a year. Are you any better than him now? Or is this all only for your own revenge?"

Garth shook his head and looked away.

"Damn you, don't look away from me!" Hammen snapped.

Startled, Garth looked back at the old man.

"Don't you feel anything about this?"

"I'm sick to death of it," Garth said quietly. "But there's no other way. I tried to think of another path but I couldn't find it. Yes, I want to bring the bastard down, bring him down and all the corruption he has created. He has given the people of this realm an opiate, the circuses, the Festival, and corrupted the guilds of fighters and everything around them. They've all been seduced by it and this is the only way I know to bring an end to it, to lance the corruption and let the pus run out of it until it's healed. It was better than hiding in the gutter like you."

Hammen stood up and angrily kicked over his chair.

"You have no idea how I survived. What it took. And who are you to judge? Who are you to come sauntering in here and calmly decide to destroy it all? Because of you I lost four of my closest friends and have watched my city descend into chaos. At least before you there was order and the mob was happy."

Garth reached down into his satchel, pulled out a small silken bundle and tossed it to Hammen. The old man caught it, and held it. Garth looked closely at him and smiled.

"You can control the *mana*, can't you? I can sense that."

Hammen lowered his head and let the bundle drop.

"You were once Hadin gar Kan, master fighter of the House of Oor-tael, weren't you?"

Hammen started to shake and he lowered his head.

"Damn you," Garth snarled. "You were the master fighter of Oor-tael, weren't you!"

Hammen, sighing, picked up the chair and sat down heavily.

"And this is what you've become. A pickpocket, a street thief, a comic actor. A nothing."

"Who are you to judge me now?" Hammen whispered. "I escaped the Night of Fire. I hid for weeks in the sewers and when I came out there was nothing left. I could never touch the *mana* again. I had betrayed my Master by fleeing. I would be tortured to death if found, and picking up my satchel again was the surest way to be found. So I threw it into the sea."

Hammen was racked by a shuddering sob.

"Just leave me alone. I had almost forgotten after all these years. Why did you have to come and drag up the moldering corpses of the past? The House was dead, the Master dead, and all my comrades dead. There was nothing left. Are you saying I should have charged the palace alone and killed the bastard?"

Hammen laughed sadly through his tears.

"For what? It was finished and he had won."

Hammen looked up at Garth, tears streaming down his gray cheeks.

"And who are you, Garth One-eye? I suspect, but who are you?"

"A memory, nothing more. Just a memory," Garth said quietly. "One that refused to die."

"Go away then. I don't need any memories or nightmares to awaken me. Tomorrow the Walker comes and nothing can stand before him. Zarel is just a puppet, a paper-thin mask behind which the true evil lurks. He will dust you away like chaff on the wind. The folly is over. Now go away."

"I think I'll stay and see what happens," Garth replied softly.

Hammen stood up wearily.

"I'm leaving. I'll have no more to do with this. You'll be dead tomorrow, Garth, and all the killing of the last days will be nothing but waste. I want no more of it. No more."

Hammen went to the door and opened it.

"Hadin."

The old man looked back.

"Hadin died twenty years ago."

"Hammen."

Hammen turned with a swiftness that caught Garth off guard. The blow of his staff caught Garth across the temple, knocking him over and sending him into oblivion.

Hammen stood over Garth, looking down sadly. Reaching into his pocket, he pulled out a length of cord and tied Garth's hands behind his back, binding him tightly. Then he reached into Garth's satchel, feeling the power of the *mana.*

Mere touching it sent a shiver down his spine, conjuring memories the way smelling the scent of a flower might rekindle a long-lost dream of first love. He took the satchel from Garth and stood upright. All the memories washed over him, filling him with a fierce joy mingled with infinite sadness for all that was done and all that was gone forever.

Again he was young and filled with strength and was the first of fighters for the House of Oor-tael. Again all was before him and the power of the memories forced tears to his eyes.

He looked down at the body stretched out on the floor before him and he felt a sharp pang in his heart, the clear sight of the *mana* showing all, so much that he had known but could not quite believe.

He tore his gaze away from Garth and, drawing on the *mana,* found the spell he desired. He placed it on Garth, the power of it pinning him to the floor so that even after he awoke he would be frozen in place for hours until the spell finally broke down.

He started for the door and then turned back, kneeling down by Garth's side.

"Galin."

The name was spoken as a whisper. The old man reached out with a loving hand and pushed the hair back from Garth's forehead, the way he had done so many years before when Galin was but a boy, the son of the House Master of Oor-tael, who would come to his father's favorite fighter and sit on his knee for a tale of adventure.

"The Eternal keep you, boy," Hammen whispered.

Standing up, he shouldered the satchel and walked out of the room. The door slipped shut behind him.

"It's almost dawn."

Zarel wearily looked up and nodded his head.

"And?"

Uriah looked around nervously.

"Go on."

"He deserted Bolk during the rioting. He has not reported to any of the other Houses."

"Will you stake your life on that report?"

Uriah remained silent.

"Damn you, will you stake your life on that?"

"Yes, Master."

"I want it made clear to the House Masters. If One-eye fights today in their uniform, I will turn my fighters loose on them, right there in the arena. I beat the mob today. They won't dare to intervene. Is that understood?"

"Yes, Master."

"Uriah."

"Yes, Master?"

"The pots, the clay pots. How?"

Uriah felt his blood run to ice.

"Someone added them into the shipment. The creatures were conjured, their power maintained by a small bundle of *mana* in each of the pots."

"And how did they get in?"

"I don't know, Master."

Zarel fixed Uriah with his gaze and a lash of probing washed over him. Uriah stood still, struggling to control his thoughts.

"You're afraid, Uriah."

"I'm always afraid before you, sire."

"I feel you're concealing something from me, some knowledge, something that you know and I don't."

"I wouldn't dare," Uriah whispered.

Zarel finally nodded and laughed with a hoarse whisper.

"No. You're too much of a coward to try and deceive me."

Zarel turned and looked away, satisfied that in his terror the dwarf was thus still loyal to him.

"You understand what's to be done. Once the Walker leaves at sundown we attack the House of Bolk and kill Kirlen. I want Kirlen's head placed in my lap before the night is over. Bolk is to be destroyed for their insolence."

"The Walker?"

"He'll be gone and it will be another year before his return. What can he do then?"

Uriah said nothing in reply.

I will also have that hag's books and her mana, Zarel thought. *Perhaps that will be enough to do it. If not, then the other Houses will go as well, their mana adding to the strength needed to pierce the veil. It has to be now. My support is slipping thanks to this damned One-eye. It has to be now.*

"And the mob? You'll have a quarter of the city, all the Brown supporters, looking for murder."

"Let them try," Zarel snapped. "Fentesk's followers have always hated Bolk more than the others. Make sure today that Fentesk's stands are showered with gifts. Tonight I want them satiated with blood and wine. They'll back me."

"And myself?"

"As I promised. You will be the new Master of Bolk."

Uriah smiled.

"The Walker is not to know of what happened here this week. If Kirlen tries to approach him, I want her dead. We can blame the troubles on her."

"And what if One-eye appears?"

Zarel hesitated. Perhaps it might just be as he surmised, that this One-eye was out for bigger game, that he had something planned against the Walker. *Perhaps, just perhaps it might work to my advantage. But then again, he might be out after me.*

"I think he's gone," Zarel said quietly. "He must be gone; there's no place left for him now."

And Uriah could sense that his master's words were meant as much to reassure himself as they were meant to try and convince someone else.

Uriah withdrew and finally let his thoughts relax. The memory of what he had seen in the arena still haunted him. In the other fights One-eye had been nothing but a distant figure. But he had come to stand before the throne and in that moment all was made so clear. He was Galin. The boy who so long ago had ridden on his hunched-over back, laughing with childish squeals of delight and then enfolding him with childlike hugs and kisses.

But now he is a man, Uriah thought, *a man who must be betrayed if I am to survive.*

* * *

Groaning, Garth One-eye stirred. He tried to stretch but could not move. His arms were pinned and he tried to move his wrists. He could feel the cord that bound his wrists but there was more holding him.

"Damn him!"

Garth tried to turn, somehow to move out of the circle of the spell, but he remained pinned to the floor, as helpless as a swaddled infant.

The second bell of morning sounded as the sun broke over the horizon, rising dark and ruddy through the pall of smoke that hung over the city, its light shining in horizontally through the shutters of the garret.

"Help me this day," he whispered. "Help me finally to set you to rest, both in my soul and in the lands you now walk. Help me now!"

He lay in silence for long minutes, concentrating, trying to break the spell through force of will. But it would not break. Beads of sweat rolled down his face, stinging his eyes, and still he prayed, turning his thoughts outward, and then he sensed the presence.

The door cracked open and a dark form stood before him.

He exhaled nervously.

"Last night I somehow sensed you were looking for me," she said softly. "I knew where you were hiding; I followed you from the arena last night. I had to come."

He heard her footsteps and she knelt down by his side.

"Hammen's doing?"

"Yes." His voice came as a hoarse whisper, the power of the spell still holding him.

She pulled her dagger out and he could just barely see her waving it about in a ritual manner. She moved around him, waving the dagger, cutting the air above him, then waving it again. As if a great weight had been pulled back, he felt the spell shatter. Gasping, he sat up and she cut his bindings.

"You called for me, didn't you?" she whispered.

Exhausted from the struggle, his head throbbing from the blow, he nodded.

"I saw Hammen leaving here with your satchel."

"So why didn't you come quicker? He's been gone for hours."

"I half agreed with him. But then I sensed your calling and"

—she fell silent for a moment—"damn you, Garth, I couldn't say no." She leaned over and kissed him lightly on the lips.

"Enough of that for now," he whispered. "Where the hell did that bastard go?"

"Toward the arena."

"The oilskin bundle in the corner, please bring it to me."

She went across the room and brought it back to him.

He brushed off the dirt that had clung to it from the hole where he had hidden it before first coming into the city. Untying the hemp rope wrapped around the bundle, he slowly opened it up and spread out the contents. Bowing low before it, he struggled to fight back the tears that clouded his eye.

Recovering his composure at last, Garth stood up and slowly started to undress. He hesitated, looking down at her.

"You might not remember but I helped to dress you once before"—she paused—"along with Varena."

"Could you help me one more time?" Garth asked quietly.

The procession weaved its way down the main boulevard that ran from the center of the city, out through the gate, and on to the arena. The crowds lining the street were sullen, barely raising a halfhearted cheer even when the remaining champions passed by.

Zarel looked around at the crowds. They wouldn't dare to try anything, not today, not with the Walker arriving. The crowd stared at him in silence, barely stirring when the girls flanking his sedan chair tossed out coins.

The procession reached the gate and for a moment he had a view of the harbor below. The water was dark with bobbing bodies and splashes of pink where the giant empreys and sharks continued their feeding frenzy. There was so much to eat that the harbor would not be cleaned by the time the Walker arrived. It would have to be explained. An outbreak of plague would be sufficient.

The procession continued on to the arena, which was already packed to overflowing, the hills above the arena black with people for this, the final day of Festival and the arrival of the Great Lord.

The parade passed on into the access tunnel and a moment

later emerged into the brilliant sunlight flooding the arena floor, the white sand reflecting the midmorning light with a glaring intensity. A thin cheer rose up from the crowd, more in anticipation of the events ahead than for the Grand Master.

"I wish all you bastards had but one neck," Zarel growled, mumbling his favorite sentiment when he contemplated the crowd.

The procession circled the arena floor, this time staying back far enough from the arena wall so that no objects hurled from the stands could reach Zarel. There was a scattering of catcalls and a light shower of wine bottles and beer tankards, the Grand Master's agents in the stands scrambling to chase down the culprits, the crowd stirring angrily. Finishing the circle, the mammoths were unhooked from Zarel's throne and driven back through the access tunnel. An expectant hush settled over the mob.

Zarel waited as the four Houses moved to take their positions at the four cardinal points around the golden circle, while the seven remaining champions took their positions in a line directly behind Zarel. Zarel stepped to the edge of the golden circle set in the arena floor and the four Masters moved to their positions around him.

He looked at each in turn, Kirlen of Bolk, Jimak of Ingkara, Tulan of Kestha, and Varnel of Fentesk.

"What you have allowed to happen is unconscionable," Zarel snapped angrily.

Kirlen cackled obscenely.

"Tell it to the Walker. Tell him how you can't control anything. Tell him what an incompetent fool you truly are that one lone *hanin* can plunge your realm into chaos."

"And where is he?"

Zarel fixed each of them in turn with his gaze and sensed that none now held the man.

"Your offerings of *mana?*"

The four stirred reluctantly and finally turned, looking back to the ranks of their fighters. From each of the four colors came two fighters bearing a strongbox. The four boxes were set down, the air around them shimmering, so powerful was the concentration of *mana*. The boxes were opened and the contents turned over, the bundles spilling out into the golden circle.

Zarel looked down at them and nodded.

"And yours?" Kirlen asked sarcastically.

Zarel laughed coldly and motioned for one of his fighters to bring forth an urn, which was inverted over the pile.

"One hundred more *mana*," Zarel stated.

"A fraction of what you extort. I think you're holding out for your attempt at being a Walker," Kirlen hissed.

"How dare you!"

"I dare because it is the truth," Kirlen said.

"And where did you hear this falsehood?"

Kirlen smiled.

"One-eye." And as she said the words she looked to the other three House Masters, all of whom nodded in support.

"That is why you grow stronger and we grow weaker. We pay the tax but you steal even more and turn over only a fraction," Jimak snarled.

"And you believe the word of a *hanin?*" Zarel asked coldly.

"Perhaps more than yours," Tulan interjected. "When you became Grand Master and the House of Oor-tael was destroyed, what deal did you make with the Walker? Was it to bleed the *mana* out of our lands in exchange for your power? All these years have you been holding back?"

"Don't you see who One-eye is?" Zarel snarled. "He's not after me; he is after all of us."

"The mask is off," Varnel said calmly. "That is now evident."

Zarel stared coldly at the four House Masters.

"Later, we will talk of this later." He motioned for them to step away from the circle.

The four drew back slowly, defiantly, as Zarel stepped into the center of the golden circle. Waving his hands over the *mana* which had been offered, he drew the power into himself. For a brief instant he felt as if he could almost pierce the veil himself, so great was the concentration of power. But the spells, the hidden incantations he still did not know and the door remained closed. Through the shimmer of light he could see Kirlen looking at him hungrily.

Old crone, I'll know after tomorrow, he thought with a cold smile.

The mob, which had been waiting in expectant silence, stirred, coming to its feet.

Zarel seemed to grow in stature, rising upward, a shimmering light swirling around him. The Grand Master raised his hands to the heavens, silently uttering the words that would drift through the planes, calling upon the Great Lord, the Walker, to come for the time of choosing and for the offering of the gift of power.

Long minutes passed and then at last there was a stirring, like the first faint breeze of morning drifting down from the high mountains. The pennants lining the stadium stirred, snapping lazily, dropping, twisting, rising again. There was a deathly hush, the air suddenly heavy, as if a storm were brewing far over the horizon. The sun seemed to grow pale in the morning sky, its light growing cold, dimming, the sky overhead darkening though there was no cloud above.

The darkness deepened. Then, overhead, it took form, a point of blackness in the zenith of the heavens, spreading out like a black stain upon clear, crystalline waters. The darkness spread across the heavens. An icy wind thundered down out of it, howling, shrieking, thundering with an unearthly roar.

The darkness twisted, turning in upon itself, a cyclone of inky black that pulled inward, flashes of light wreathing around it in a ghostly, unearthly, blue-green glow. The dark cloud raced down out of the heavens, drowning out the cries of fear. Excitement and terror sounded from half a million voices. The black cloud hovered above the arena, boiling, roiling, flashes of lightning wreathing it in fire.

The cloud continued to coil inward and as it did so it seemed to take form, a dark head peering downward, eyes of fire, beard of lightning, and brow of ghastly flame. The mob was now in an ecstasy of madness, screaming, pointing up at the darkness, mouths open, trembling hands pointing, a frenzy taking hold of them so that they roared with terror and a dark abandon.

The darkness swirled downward, touching the golden circle. Zarel, with head lowered, drew back and away. It was now a pillar of blackness, soaring a hundred fathoms in height, a circle of fire dancing around it, flashing and thundering. The head reared back, its mouth open. A cold sardonic laugh echoed like thunder against the hills. Eyes of fire gazed down hungrily at those who worshiped it and those who feared it and those who, with averted eyes, loathed it.

The pillar swirled down as if drawing in upon itself. There was a thunderclap roar and a blinding flash of light that dazzled the vision so that all turned away, covering their eyes, crying with pain.

In the center of the circle of gold stood the Planes Walker in human form, a tall, sinuous figure that seemed somehow to be not quite real, tall and wavery in his black robes. He appeared to be present, to be real, and yet not to be, as if he were nothing but a wisp of smoke that would disappear. He looked slowly around, a smile creasing his bloodless lips. At one instant it appeared to be almost a friendly smile, filled with warm amusement, and then in the same instant it was a smile of cunning, of power, of contempt for all who could never comprehend all that he truly was in his darkness and majesty.

He looked down at the pile of *mana* that rested by his feet and nodded his approval. The bundles would grant him access to the psychic power which controlled the land.

"The offering is good." His voice seemed to be a whisper and yet, to the farthest ends of the stadium, all could hear it. At the sound of his voice, deep and rich with power, the mob broke into a wild hysterical roar, as if the terror had been washed away.

The Walker leaned back, a wild laughing cry of delight escaping him. For again he was in human form and the pleasure of it was upon him. The shadowy nature of his existence dropped away and he was now solid in flesh. At the sight of him, looking like a young golden god of power and fierce vitality, the mob went wild.

The Walker stepped clear of the circle and from out of the ranks of warriors came bearers carrying yet more urns, which they dumped over his shoulders, the gold cascading out. He laughed with delight as he picked up the coins, feeling them, his eyes afire. Jimak stared in silence, his breath coming heavy at the sight of the riches. The Walker flung his hands upward and the coins, as if caught on the wind, swirled out in a golden rain, fluttering down into the stadium, the mob cheering. More bearers came forward, bringing the finest of wines, and he drank hungrily, throwing the goblets, and Tulan licked his lips at the scent of the wine. And then from behind the ranks of warriors there came women in the sheerest of robes that were as translucent as the web of a spider. Some were tall and pale of skin with golden hair; others tawny-skinned with tresses of curly black; and still others exotics from distant lands that were but fabled realms. Varnel stood silent, trembling at the sight of them. They were of every shape and form, slender and boyish of body, full and voluptuous, tall and dusky, and he reached out to them eagerly, fondling, grasping, laughing, and the mob cheered lustily.

As he did so he looked over at Kirlen and the old woman was silent, her eyes filled with hatred. Laughing, he turned away.

"It is time for the games!" the Walker announced, and his voice was filled with bloodlust and the mob howled with delight.

The Walker extended his arms in salute, the heavy coils of muscles rippling, and he stretched with the pleasure of the sensation, pulling in the chosen woman of the moment with one hand, fondling her with open abandon while scooping up a goblet of wine with the other, forcing her to drink some, then holding the goblet aloft in salutation to the howling masses.

He ascended the throne, which Zarel now relinquished to him. He leaned back, looking up at the blue sky that spanned overhead and for a moment was silent, his features strange and distant. And then he stirred, his dark laughter drowning out the voice of the mob so that the stadium echoed with the thunderous peals.

Gaining the throne, he kissed the woman with a wild, passionate lust, groping at her like an animal in heat, tearing her robe off. Then, as quickly, he released her, pushing her aside, waving for yet more wine and food. He scooped up the delicacies and devoured them like one who had awakened from a fevered dream and now sought sustenance.

He then tossed aside the goblet, upended the tray of food set before him, and looked out across the arena.

"Let the first match be chosen!"

At the base of the throne Zarel motioned for the blind and deaf monk to make the first choice.

"Azema of Kestha versus Jolina of Ingkara."

The mob cheered with bloodlust and swarmed toward the betting booths to place their wagers. The entire arena floor was now available for the final round of fights and minutes later, at the far end of the arena, Jolina stepped out, while at the north end Azema of Kestha stepped into the neutral box to prepare.

The Walker stood up, grinning, surveying the arena, waiting for the mob to finish its betting.

"How is this match today?" he asked, looking down at Zarel.

"In your honor, Great Lord, all matches today are to the death."

The Walker stared at Zarel, probing inward.

"Why?" his voice whispered so that only Zarel could hear.

"I can explain later, my lord."

"It will create bad blood in the Houses."

"The bad blood is already there, my lord. It is time for a cleansing."

"And the one you told me about?"

"Win or lose, my lord, he is yours. The Houses were getting too strong again; they needed to be leeched of some of their strength. This way they cannot stand against my power, or yours."

"You had best be right, Zarel, or this is your last day as Grand Master."

"I am right, my lord, and it is in service to you that I do this."

The Walker nodded and looked up again.

"To the death then!"

Hammen, who was once known as Hadin gar Kan, slipped down through the rows of the arena, occasionally catching glimpses of the fight. His view was obscured by the jam-packed mob which was standing on the benches, leaping up and down in an ecstasy of abandon. Explosions thundered across the stadium, the two contestants below locked in violent conflict, the arena, across its three hundred fathoms of width, filled with fire, dueling creatures, demons, smoke, flying beasts, and unearthly clouds of darkness. In the open space of the fighting floor all powers could now be brought to bear, no longer constrained by the tight space of the circles used in the elimination matches of the previous days.

As the crowd pushed and shoved, swaying back and forth, Hammen found small openings and slipped through, moving ever closer to the arena floor. He moved stealthily, avoiding the gaze of warriors stationed in clusters throughout the arena, and watched for the agents of Zarel, who were positioned to take any who might make trouble this day. He moved like a shadow, something he could still do though it had been twenty long years since he had last touched *mana* with the intent of drawing upon it. And all the time the memory of what he had once been haunted him.

Why had Garth ever come into his life? Why did he have to conjure back all that was, a time when the House of Oortael still lived and stood for what the world of fighters had once been? He felt now like a dream moving through a dark world of abandon, a dream that was crushed and at any moment would die forever.

It had died. He had been telling himself that for twenty years. It had died on the night the Walker had gathered the power no longer to be simply a mortal of this world, no longer to be simply a Grand Master, but instead to have the power of a demigod and walk between worlds and fight in unknown realms. All that stood in his path was the House of Oor-tael and the refusal of the House Master, Garth's father, to relinquish part of the *mana* he controlled to make the circle of power complete. For without more of the colors of *mana* controlled by the House of Oor-tael, the circle could not be drawn.

And thus had the House of Oor-tael been stormed on the final night of Festival twenty years ago, the other Houses conspiring to throw down their rival and in the process grant the Walker his desire. And so he had moved beyond the world, leaving his lieutenant to rule in his stead, and to twist and pervert all that was.

The nightmare of the Night of Fire washed over Hammen, who had once been the master fighter of Oor-tael, for he had fled when the House was stormed. Fled because at that moment he believed there was nothing more to fight for.

I should have died then, he thought. *I should have stood by my Master and his family and died. But I fled into the bowels of the earth to hide, to come out as Hammen the thief, the pickpocket, the master of a brotherhood of the low. I should have died.*

I should have died.

He edged his way down to the wall, just as the fight on the

arena floor reached its climax. Varena of Fentesk cast down the last protective barrier of her opponent from Kestha. The man crumpled. She hesitated, looking for a moment back at the throne.

"Finish him!"

The crowd picked up the thunderous words of the Walker.

"Finish him! Finish him!"

Varena raised her hand and the Gray fighter simply disappeared in a scarlet cloud.

She walked over to where the body had been and picked up her opponent's satchel. With head lowered, she strode off the field, ignoring the ovation that greeted her victory.

"Thus ends the sixth round," Zarel announced, "Igun of Ingkara winning the fourth match by default. Now begins the seventh round."

Hammen pushed his way up to the stadium wall, stood upon it, and leaped down onto the sand. Several fighters moved toward him and he raised his hand, knocking them over.

"I stand as witness to One-eye, who has earned the right to combat!" Hammen shouted, drawing upon the *mana* which was now in a satchel resting on his right hip. His voice echoed across the arena and the mob, stunned by the intrusion, fell silent.

"He is *hanin*, without color," Zarel screamed. "He cannot fight."

The Walker stood up and looked down at Hammen.

"I am Hadin gar Kan, first fighting master of the House of Oor-tael, body servant of Garth One-eye, and I stand as witness to him."

"Hadin." The Walker's voice was a dark whisper as if a memory was but half-formed.

Hammen walked out into the center of the arena.

"He won the right of combat."

"So where is he?" the Walker whispered, his voice echoing across the arena.

"Gone."

The Walker chuckled.

"And what do you want, beggar?"

"As his servant I can claim the right to fight in his stead.

Those are the ancient rules which existed even before you first darkened this world."

The Walker leaned back and laughed coldly.

"Fine. It will be fun to watch you die."

But even as he spoke there was an eruption of cheering from the south side of the arena, starting at the top of the stands. For a moment the Walker thought it was for him and, smiling, he looked over his shoulder.

The cheering spread, even as a path opened up down the side of the stadium, the crowd surging, pushing back.

Garth One-eye reached the arena wall and leaped down onto the arena floor, followed by the woman of Benalia.

"One-eye!"

The cry was picked up and turned in an instant into a tidal wave of noise. Garth strode across the arena floor, coming up to stand in front of Hammen.

"Just what the hell are you doing?" Garth whispered.

"I was trying to save your damn stupid life," Hammen replied wearily.

"This way?"

"If I was killed, your satchel was gone, and you would be powerless. You would have left."

He hesitated.

"I failed to save you once; I thought I could now," the old man said as he lowered his head.

"You never failed me," Garth whispered, "and you never failed my father before me. You fled when there was nothing left to fight for. When my father was already dead."

Hammen looked up and smiled sadly.

"At last you say it, and again there is nothing I can do."

"You can start by giving me back my satchel."

Hammen took the satchel off and held it out to Garth.

Garth stepped back from Hammen and tore off the cloak in which he was wrapped to reveal the fighting uniform of the House of Oor-tael. A stunned gasp of amazement rose from the stands at the sight of the forbidden colors. Garth slung the satchel over his shoulder.

"I claim the right of combat! I am known as Garth One-eye. I am the son of Cullinarn, Master of the House of Oor-tael."

Zarel stepped forward, motioning for his fighters to gather

around him, but he was stopped as if by an invisible hand.

The Walker's sardonic laugh echoed over the arena.

"Most amusing. I love an amusing joke. You may fight."

Garth, without an acknowledgment to the Walker, turned and started to walk toward the far end of the arena.

"Damn it, Garth, either you'll leave here feetfirst or go with that bastard."

"I know."

"What the hell for?"

Garth looked over at Hammen and smiled.

"Didn't I tell you from the beginning to stick around and you'd find out why?"

Hammen looked over angrily at Norreen.

"Thanks a lot."

"You should have told me to stay out of it."

"Would that have changed what you did?"

"No."

"You're both mad," Hammen snapped, even as he struggled to keep up with Garth.

Garth laughed, shaking his head.

"You still have our money?"

"Yes."

"Then go wager it on a win. You'll need the cash when this is done."

"Like hell. I'm staying down here with you."

Garth looked over at Norreen.

She shook her head. "I'm staying."

"All right then, but once this is done and I'm gone, they'll kill you."

"Good of you to worry about us now," Hammen growled.

As they approached the neutral box at the far end of the arena they walked past the viewing stand of Bolk. Out in front stood Naru, who raised a clenched fist to Garth in salute, the giant gazing at him with a worried look.

"Too bad you die or he takes you," Naru said.

"Then next year you're the champion," Garth replied, and the giant grinned.

Garth stepped into the neutral box, the mob in the stands swarming up to the betting booths to place their bets, but the Walker gave them no time.

"Fight!"

The combat was over in minutes, the mob watching in awed silence as Garth stepped into an immediate attack, blocking the dark spells of his opponent with a casual ease, shattering the power of his *mana*, and then closing in for the kill with yet another attack of a Craw Wurm. He paused before the final coup but his opponent, screaming with rage, countered at the moment of hesitation with a demonic attack and Garth lowered his head as the Craw Wurm lunged, devouring the fighter.

Garth stood in the center of the arena, ignoring the ovation that greeted his victory as he picked up his fallen opponent's satchel and then walked to a place in the arena between the stands of Ingkara and Kestha, a place where long ago had been the corner of the fighting field reserved for the House of Oor-tael .

Zarel looked up at the Walker.

"He is dangerous."

"Of course he is dangerous; otherwise, he would not have survived in hiding for twenty years. You told me he was dead."

Zarel looked away and the voice lashed through his mind.

"You told me he was dead."

"Yes."

"But you did not see the body."

Zarel hesitated.

"Well?"

"He was only a five-year-old boy. He could not survive that fire."

Zarel struggled to seal off his thoughts, his memories of that night. Of the boy dragged before him, how he had gouged the boy's eye out to torment his father, and of the boy, in spite of the agony he was in, staring at him coldly with but half his vision. His father, fighting desperately, was still in the House, which was engulfed in flames.

And he could remember the wail of agony when the father had seen the boy and begged to trade lives. At that moment the boy had torn loose from the grasp of the guard and raced into the burning building.

He was dead; he was supposed to be dead.

How could I have not seen clearly that it was he? Zarel wondered. But then again he was only a meaningless boy, a nothing, a pawn for a moment of bargaining.

"Fool! He is still out there now."

"And he leaves the arena dead or with you," Zarel replied hastily.

"He knows that," the Walker replied, and Zarel sensed the nervousness.

He's afraid, Zarel realized.

"He knows that. He knows he can't escape. Therefore, he must have something planned. After all these years he would not come here just to commit suicide."

"Are you afraid, my Master?" Zarel asked silently, looking back up at the throne, and he felt an instant lash of rage.

"I will kill him as I kill all who win the tournament," the Walker snarled in reply. "As I think I might kill you for not controlling this world better."

As Zarel struggled to control the surge of fear, sensing the cold laugh of his master, he turned and looked back at Uriah and the realization came. The dwarf had somehow known from the beginning. Fool. He had hidden his knowledge out of some perverse form of loyalty and sentimentality.

Uriah looked toward him and Zarel smiled as if all was as it should be. There would be time enough later for a special torment.

"Arrange the next fight for my amusement," the Walker snapped angrily.

Garth watched the tote board and breathed a sigh of relief when he saw that he would not yet have to face Varena. She would fight someone from her own House this time. As he exhaled noisily and turned away, he saw Norreen staring at him.

"She's a friend. I don't relish what I have to do."

"You should have thought of that earlier," Hammen said.

"Whichever way it turns out, whoever steps into the arena today is dead; I just don't want to do it myself."

He looked back over at Norreen, who was still looking at him.

"Are you jealous? Is that it?" Hammen taunted.

"A Benalish woman doesn't need anyone outside her clan."
Hammen laughed crudely and spit on the ground.

"You'll both be dead anyhow in a little while, so the question is moot."

Garth smiled and said nothing.

Out on the arena floor the next battle was joined and
Varena was instantly on the defensive, her opponent, also
from Fentesk, launching into a savage attack of liquid fire. She
erected a wall to block him and he responded with an earthquake that shook the entire arena and tumbled the barrier
down. Varena countered with aerial attacks by stinging
insects, and even an outlandish balloon filled with goblin warriors. The balloon went down under the counterstrike of
elvish archers, their arrows turning to flames which set the
balloon on fire.

Twice Varena was knocked down by her opponent and the
mob came howling to its feet, believing that the fight was
over. And twice she recovered—the second time gathering
enough *mana* to leap forward with a violent series of counter-
strikes that her opponent parried with less and less strength.
She moved closer to her foe, striking down his defenses. Then,
with a final blast, she destroyed him, with a combination of
fire striking from above and a psychic blast that drained her
own strength but finished him.

She walked slowly from the arena field, her assistant rushing over to the body of the fallen to retrieve his satchel.

"It means I'll have to face her," Garth said quietly.

"If you live through this one."

"Gilganorin of Ingkara versus Garth of Oor-tael." The voice
of the Walker was filled with amused sarcasm.

Garth stepped out of his corner and walked over to the neutral box, the crowd cheering lustily, bouquets of flowers raining down around him. He stepped into the neutral box and
started to concentrate in preparation.

"Fight!"

Startled, he looked up. The Walker was laughing at the
joke of having started the fight without warning.

Garth, bent over low, ran to one side of the arena as a black
cloud snapped across the arena floor and came to a stop over

his head, a rain of acid cascading down where he had just been standing. Next a fissure opened in the ground and he leaped back as stone giants emerged from the hole, their heavy granite war clubs crashing down, smashing the ground to either side of him. He struggled to erect a wall and they burst through it, their voices sounding like dark echoes from a ghostly cave.

He concentrated his thoughts and sent out attacks on his opponent's *mana*, the force draining out of Gilganorin's lands. The stone giants tumbled down into heaps of rocks. With a running bound Garth leaped over the fissure and laid out a line of living brambles and trees to form a barrier. Again he drew on the Craw Wurm but these were countered in turn by attacks of fire, which ignited the woods. The Craw Wurm, in turn, was destroyed by a dark elemental, which Garth then destroyed by an elemental that he conjured in response.

Gilganorin slowly started to move forward as well, diverting Garth with minor attacks of insects, rats, wolves, and undead. Garth countered each, and played out the same offensive, using creatures that required little *mana* to create while storing his power up for a killing strike. He sensed that he was gaining the advantage, Gilganorin being unable to store up *mana* as well, driven instead to the defensive, the countering of attacks, and resorting finally to protective wards to block attacks which could damage him.

And then, suddenly, to Garth's amazement, Gilganorin simply stopped fighting and extended his hands outward, palms facing down to the ground in the signal of submission and surrender. Garth, nodding in acknowledgment, held his next attack back, sending the berserkers back into the oblivion from which they were conjured. He extended his left hand, palm downward, as a sign that he accepted the surrender while still holding his right hand high as a gesture of victory.

A gasp of amazement arose from the mob. There was a time when such an act was usually the end of a fight, when an opponent knew that he was beaten and it was senseless to continue. But this was supposed to be a death match.

"I asked not for a death match," Garth shouted. "I accept your surrender. You may keep your spells."

Gilganorin bowed low in reply and turned to walk back to

his corner . . . and then he simply ceased to exist. A cylinder of blackness appeared to wrap around him, there was a shower of blood spraying out, and the cylinder of night was gone. All that was left was a smear of blood soaking into the sand.

"When I say it is to the death, it is to the death," the Walker snapped peevishly, and then he turned his attention back to the woman he had been amusing himself with while the fight had been going on.

A gasp rose from the crowd and Garth sensed that even many in the mob had been offended, for Gilganorin was an old favorite, who for several decades had always survived into the final rounds and was noted for squandering his prize money on free drinks for his fans for weeks after a Festival.

Annoyed at the protest over the death of a favorite, the Walker turned away from his amusement and waved his hand. A cloud formed over the arena and the mob fell silent, not sure what he was about to do. He was, after all, the Walker, and though he might not have the power to take on half a million at once, he could certainly do damage to quite a few tens of thousands before being forced to flee. The cloud turned dark and from it a rain of silver trinkets began to fall. The mob struggled to pick them up, but even then there was no gratitude—it was simply money to be taken and nothing more.

The Walker leaned back on his throne, watching the mob.

"What is wrong with these bastards?" he asked silently, looking down at Zarel.

"You killed one of their favorites."

"So what; he disobeyed me."

"They might not see it that way."

"Suppose I burn the city in reply?"

"That would damage you in return, my lord. For without the peasants and the mob, the *mana*, the power of the lands, forms more slowly. Next year's tribute would not be as great."

"Damn them," the Walker hissed. He looked back at the woman, who waited for him and, with an angry curse, he pointed at her. In an instant her young, rounded body shriveled up, turning into limp folds of hanging leprous flesh, her face distorting into an obscene visage of running sores. She looked down at her body and started to scream hysterically.

Laughing, he pushed her off the throne, so that she tumbled down the steps onto the arena floor. She continued to scream, until finally, annoyed at her whining, he pointed at her again. She melted down into a boiling mass of flesh. The mob, which had been watching the show, was silent, and the Walker looked at them, annoyed that they did not see the humor in what he had done.

He pointed to another girl and motioned for her to join him. Trembling, she ascended the stairs.

"Let's have the final match. That ought to please them," the Walker announced.

"It's time for the noonday meal."

"Fight, then eat."

Garth, who had been lying under the shade of the arena wall, stirred and looked up. He sat up, squinting at the bright midday sun. There was a strange silence in the arena as the tote board announced the pairing of Garth against Varena. In the stands he could hear the spectators discussing the fact that there was a rumor that the two were lovers.

He looked over at Norreen, who was sitting against the wall, calmly sharpening her sword on a whetstone.

"Look, like I said before," Garth sighed, "it really meant nothing."

"Where I come from we mate until castes change and our chosen one is higher or lower than us. To wander outside of that rule is to invite vendetta by the other and the other's family."

"We never mated permanently, as you so calmly put it, so there's no laws broken."

"You desired to do so with me, didn't you?"

"Desire and completion are two different things."

"One leads to other."

"And did you desire me?"

She savagely drew her blade across the stone and looked up at him.

"It's too late now, One-eye."

"You should have left him tied up back there," Hammen interjected, "and had your way with him."

"And you'd be dead now," Garth replied.

"Maybe not. I was the master fighter of Oor-tael."

"Twenty years ago. I think, Hammen, you're a bit rusty now."

"Thanks for the vote of confidence."

A trumpet sounded and the crowd, which had been sitting in silence sullenly watching the Walker, stirred.

Hammen turned and looked toward the tote board.

"They're placing the announcement."

"Final match." The Walker's voice drifted across the arena. "Garth of Oor-tael, Varena of Fentesk. Come forward to the throne."

Garth stood up and adjusted his satchel, which bulged with the prizes he had won. He looked down at Norreen.

"I think it best that you stay behind. Ritual allows only the fighter and his servant. If you draw his attention, it might be unpleasant for you."

Norreen nodded slowly.

"Somehow I'd like to think you have a plan for all of this and there might be a chance we'd one day see each other again."

Garth laughed softly.

"Finally, an admission of affection."

She stood up, letting her sword drop, and, reaching out, grabbed him fiercely, kissing him with a mad passion. The crowd, which had been leaning over the wall watching and eavesdropping, broke into a lusty cheer.

Norreen stepped back.

"Damn you. Now look what you made me do. I've broken caste rules." She struggled to keep her voice from breaking.

"Stay close to Hammen once this is over and make sure the old geezer gets out of here alive. I'm asking you to be his shield bearer."

"Damn! That's for royalty," Hammen sniffed.

Garth smiled and turned away, stepping out into the arena. As he walked across the sand-packed fighting floor, Hammen by his side, the mob came to its feet and broke into applause. He waved casually, stepping around the fissure from the previous fight, where a score of mammoths were hauling great carts of earth to be dumped to close the rift.

From the other side of the arena he saw Varena approaching and, turning away from the throne, he walked up to meet her.

She looked at him and smiled.

"You know I will fight to win. I have to."

"Do you have any idea anymore what it is that you're really fighting for?" Garth asked, moving to walk alongside her.

"Because this is what I trained for, this moment."

"And afterward?"

"To be the servant of the Walker in other worlds, to have the mysteries revealed, to leap by his side between worlds like a god."

Garth shook his head sadly.

"And for that you would kill me?"

She looked over at him and smiled.

"Isn't that your intent as well? You saw what happened to Gilganorin. There is no backing away now, Garth. Only one of us may go. I'm just sorry it is you that I have to do this to."

"Fighter, make no friend of fighter," Garth said calmly.

Varena smiled sadly and nodded.

Approaching the high throne they fell silent, their servants stopping at the outer edge of the golden circle.

The Walker, chewing on a leg of roasted pork, looked down at them and smiled.

"So who is it going to be?" he asked.

Neither answered.

"You know, Garth, this is all rather amusing. I think you have something for this woman and she you. And yet both of you would sacrifice that in order to serve me and learn the final mysteries."

"Would you care to share the mystery now and spare us the trouble of a fight?" Garth said.

The Walker smiled, laughing softly.

"To the death," he finally whispered, "and for the winner, the answer to all."

He waved a hand of dismissal and as Garth turned he saw a cold look of satisfaction in Zarel's eyes.

"Either way you lose," Zarel whispered.

"Maybe it's the other way around," Garth snapped in reply.

Garth looked back at Varena and smiled.

"I'm sorry." Turning, he started back across the field to the neutral box.

The mob was on its feet, standing in silence as the climax of Festival drew nigh.

Reaching the neutral box, Garth looked over at Hammen.

"There won't be much time afterward. I think he'll leave at once. I could sense something there; he's under some sort of pressure."

Hammen nodded.

"Something isn't right with him," Hammen said. "Usually he acts more like a gross buffoon, eating, wenching, gambling. There's something not right with him now."

"If possible, I think you know what I want you to do." Reaching into his satchel, he pulled out a small bundle and tossed it to Hammen.

Hammen stepped into the box and, reaching out, he placed his hands on Garth's shoulders.

"Galin. All these years I thought you dead." His voice choked. "I remember the day your father came out of the birthing room carrying you proudly. I remember the day he called us in so that we could see you take your first step. And the day we laughed when you first used *mana* and burned your little fingers, cried, and then tried again."

"Stop going sentimental on me now," Garth said.

"If I had known you were still alive in that fire, I would have come back for you."

"You wouldn't have found me," Garth said softly. "Even as my father died he used the last of his power to send my mother and me far away. You would not have found me until I wanted you to and that was not until she died and I was free to do what she had forbidden."

He paused.

"To get revenge."

His features were set as if cast in ice. He withdrew Hammen's hands from his shoulders.

"Take care, Hadin gar Kan."

"The Eternal be with you, Galin."

The trumpet sounded and Garth turned away, calming his inner self so that he felt as if he were drifting in another world.

"Fight!"

The words came like a whisper on the wind, the cries of the mob like a haunting whisper drifting across a frozen sea.

He stepped out of the neutral box, reaching into his powers, the power of the *mana* drifting up to him—the power of distant lands now locked in the silken bundles, the power of the mountains, the islands across the Flowing Seas, the plains, forests, swamps, and deserts.

He waited, not letting too much of the power come at once, waiting for her first move. He could sense that she, too, was building her strength, drawing on her *mana* in turn and then, with a wave of his hand, he cast the spell of destruction, of Armageddon, which destroyed all the *mana* that had been drawn by both. He could sense her startled response, the brief instant of surprise. He quickly re-formed his own powers, letting them rush upward, the strength surging through him, and he launched an attack. He struck with a disrupting scepter, which forced Varena to lose yet another point of power. He then drew on a rare artifact which granted him the ability to control even more power than a fighter could normally hold. Then he projected his power outward so that for a moment he was able to read her thoughts and know what she knew and what she planned to do.

Thus even before her first attack—a wall of flashing swords which swept across the field—he was prepared to block it, the swords falling to the ground and melting away. She countered with a rain of fire, which he extinguished with a flood of ocean which moved like a wall across the arena floor. On the tops of the waves rode great beasts of the deep, their open jaws gnashing, their rows of razor-sharp teeth glinting in the sunlight.

The ocean, in turn, cascaded down into a fissure that Varena opened across the width of the arena floor. In response Garth sent creatures flying over the fissure. From out of the depths came unearthly forms, hydras of many heads that snatched at Garth's attackers, striking them down as fast as they appeared. Garth sent a wall of swords back to decapitate the hydra. The blades struck, and seconds later the beast had twice as many heads. It crawled out of the pit and moved toward Garth with ponderous motion.

The mob cheered at the sight of such a rarity.

Garth watched it approaching and then lowered his head and averted his eyes.

Before him there appeared the bent-over form of a woman covered from head to foot in a long cape. Bemused laughter erupted from the mob at such a strange defense. With eyes still averted Garth reached out and tore the cape away from the old woman.

The Medusa stood up with a triumphal scream, the vipers that were her hair writhing and hissing. The hydra's long serpentine heads rose up, a chorus of bellows erupting from it as the creature turned to stone.

The Medusa, laughing coldly, turned toward Garth who, with eyes still averted, grabbed hold of her cape and tossed it over her head. Reaching into his pocket he pulled out a small disk of a mirror and held it up as she tore the cape off, ready to attack him. But at the sight of herself she screamed in anguish and turned to stone as well.

The mob, which had been watching this unusual counterattack outside the range of the Medusa's awful powers, broke into appreciative applause for the artistic defense that Garth had offered and the manner in which he controlled a spell that was as dangerous to the wielder as it was to the intended target.

Controlling the hydra had drained Varena of much of her power and Garth suddenly raced forward, leaping over the fissure to land on her side of the fighting field.

Garth now drew upon defensive spells to ward off the series of weak attacks Varena cast in an attempt to slow him while he was building his own power. Then, to his surprise, she used a spell of destruction as well, shattering both her *mana* and his at the same time. She then struck him with a psychic blast which, though it did damage to herself, hurt him far more. He staggered backward from the blow, almost falling into the fissure. He erected a circle of protection to block her strikes and then moved quickly to heal the damage she had inflicted.

She struck again, but this time he was prepared, reversing the spell, which struck back at her so that she fell to her knees.

Garth moved closer, ringing her in with a wall of twisted brambles. She struck them down with fire but behind the brambles he had tree-creatures waiting, which moved toward her with ponderous steps. She dodged back and forth, trying to avoid their blows, until one of them snagged her by the leg and lifted her into the air.

A giant appeared by her side and, with raised axe, hewed down the tree that held her. Then it turned to struggle with the others, the tree-creatures sending out shoots and roots, wrapping them around the giant's legs and arms. The giant howled with a berserk fury, cutting and slashing with its man-size axe, felling trees which Garth replaced with yet more.

The mob, taken by this amusing spectacle, roared with delight, cheering on the giant and then the trees as they battled amidst a growing mountain of broken limbs, wood chips, and splinters.

Varena, recovering slowly, moved back from the struggle, calling down bolts of lightning to ignite the trees, which hooted with a wild fury as their branches burned, the arena filling with smoke from the conflagration.

Garth called down a swirling storm of ice and rain to extinguish the fires and then brought forth a giant of his own, so that the two struggled and cut at each other in the steam and smoke.

Garth suddenly felt a stinging blow at the back of his neck and, turning, he saw a great swarm of wasps, each one as big as his thumb, swirling around him. The insects went for his eye, stinging him on the cheeks, the nose, the forehead, the pain of the stings causing him to curse wildly, his face instantly swelling up from the venom.

Caught off guard, he lost his concentration for a moment, the venom coursing into his blood, causing him to feel light-headed and weak. He went down on his knees, covering his face, the stings so savage that his hands filled with blood. At last concentrating his waning strength, he conjured up the smallest of sprites who, with lances drawn, did battle with the wasps. He rolled out from under the cloud and came back up to his knees and uncovered his face.

He was blind, his eyelid swollen to the point that he could not see. He could sense that Varena was rushing toward him with dagger raised for the kill. Drawing in his remaining power, he erected a wall of stone, which he knew would block her for the moment. Staggering, he got to his feet and then drew upon the one spell he had been holding in reserve.

Instantly, all the powers she controlled came into his hands and she was drained of all that she could control at that moment. The shock of this blow staggered her so that he could hear her scream of frustration.

It was time to finish it and he called upon the power he had taken from Naru the day before. A dark cloud swirled before Garth and a towering form emerged. It rode upon great wheels that towered to twice the height of a man, the wheels rimmed with black iron as thick as a man's hand. The juggernaut rolled forward slowly, crashing through the wall he had erected and then through another wall she struggled to erect with what little power remained to her. She focused that power upon the juggernaut, draining herself of all she had to stop it in its course. The great structure tottered and then exploded with a thunderclap roar of fire and red smoke.

And it was at that moment that he threw all that he had against her, staggering her with repeated psionic blasts which, though they weakened him, did damage to her that was far more devastating. The third blow lifted Varena up off her feet, slamming her to the ground, where she lay still.

Garth slowly walked up to her, stepping aside as the juggernaut came crashing down with an explosive roar which all but drowned out the howling of the mob.

He looked down at her, her features pale, drawn, and drained of all but the slimmest flicker of life.

"Finish her!"

He looked up at the Walker.

"Finish her or die!"

Garth raised his hand and pointed at Varena. A psionic blast slammed into her body, a convulsive shudder ran through her, driving the last of her soul from her mortal remains.

Garth lowered his head, turned away, and then looked up at the Walker with a cold defiance.

"I am your chosen servant, my lord."

CHAPTER
14

THE WALKER LOOKED DOWN AT GARTH, GRINNED, then turned his attention back to Zarel.

"I am leaving now," his voice whispered.

Surprised, and barely able to conceal his relief, Zarel looked up at the Walker, who stood upon the throne.

"My lord, will you not come back to the throne and continue your enjoyments?"

"I might come back later, after I take care of him," he said, and nodded toward Garth. "I will also come back to see that you have regained control here, and when I do, all had better be in order."

The Walker looked back over at the woman, who reclined naked upon the silk divan. He could see the terror in her eyes. He raised his hand and, though she tried to look up at him seductively, her features paled. He snapped his fingers and a cut diamond, the size of a small walnut, appeared between his thumb and forefinger. He tossed it between her breasts and, laughing, turned away. Scooping up a decanter of wine, he strode down the steps of the throne platform and approached Garth. Draining off the decanter, he tossed it aside.

"So, One-eye, you've won."

Garth said nothing, staring straight at the Walker.

"So now you are my chosen servant of the year. Come and I will show you all that you desire and deserve to know."

The Walker turned away and looked out across the arena.

"I proclaim Garth, whom you call One-eye, the winner of this Festival."

There was a ripple of a cheer, but most stood silent, and the Walker frowned, looking back at Garth.

"I think they are not happy with the victory."

"It might be other things, my lord," Garth said quietly.

The Walker looked over at Varena, who was slowly being dragged away by her servant and Hammen.

"You should claim her satchel, as is your right."

"Where I am going, I suspect there is no need of it."

The Walker, chuckling softly, nodded.

He looked down at two monks who knelt at the edge of the circle, holding a great silken bag which contained the *mana* tribute, the bag pulsing with a radiant light. Kuthuman greedily reached over, took the bag, and looked back at Zarel.

"I suspect there is not as much in here as I expected."

Zarel lowered his head, saying nothing.

"If that is true, you know I'll be back sooner rather than later."

"Why not check now?" Garth said quietly.

Kuthuman looked over at Garth, his features troubled.

"Later." And he said the words coldly, looking back at Zarel, who gazed at Garth with unconcealed hatred.

"It is time to go," the Walker announced, and he fixed Garth with an icy stare.

"This will be amusing."

He raised his hands high.

Garth felt as if an opaque screen had been drawn around him, the world beyond drifting off into a hazy, fog-covered shadow. Sound distorted as if the mob were shouting from down the end of a long underground cavern. The world darkened. He looked up and the sun, which had been blazing with such a hot intensity, was now a dull red, darkening into night.

And then he began to fall. His stomach tightened and he suppressed the urge to cry out with fear, wondering for an instant if he were already dead. The ground was no longer beneath his feet, yet he felt no rushing of wind, no sense of flying. The opaque shadow drew in tighter, all going dark. Again he looked up at the sun. It was gone. Overhead there was a narrow cone of light, of brilliant purple, and out of it streaks of light snapped past. Yet it was almost as if he did not see the light, but merely sensed it. He wanted to reach out and touch the lights yet knew that somehow they were impossibly far away. He looked down at his feet. A small disk of dark red was drawing in upon itself, shrinking into a pinpoint, becoming nothing, the lights streaking past him shifting in an instant from purple to red, then disappearing.

Garth felt a surging of power, a sudden delight coursing through him, as if the infinite universe had been reduced to a toy that now rested in the palm of his hand. He reveled in the power, allowing it to course through his soul. Time lost all meaning, all sense, and he was not sure if a second had transpired or aeons.

"Now you know the power of the infinite," a voice whispered to him.

For the first time Garth was aware that there was a presence with him. It was dark, foreboding, and yet for this instant he could sense an almost benign amusement, as if the Walker was an indulgent old man, showing new wonders to a child.

"The power you wielded is but nothing compared to what I am."

The light ahead shifted, drifting out of purple into blues, greens—an infinite variety of a million hues. He felt as if he were soaring into the heart of a sun that was exploding into rainbows of fire.

Garth felt as if he could reach out and, with the flick of a finger, set suns spinning on their courses, that with the palms of his hands he could mold and shape worlds, and with his breath set the firmament swirling. He felt as if he had become a god and the power of it was all-consuming, reaching into his soul with its seductive strength.

He laughed, his voice echoing through the night.

The sensation of falling stopped and he felt a pressure on the soles of his feet. All was dark and then, ever so slowly, a hazy light formed, out of focus, as if he looked up into the sunlight from the depths of the sea. The light swirled, sparkled, and then took form.

He was standing in a shady grove, the trees around him reaching up into a crystalline blue sky flecked with high, drifting clouds. The air was rich with a heady scent of springtime flowers. Tropical birds of red, green, yellow, and dazzling white darted past, their songs echoing like a heavenly choir.

Garth turned, smiling, watching them pass.

"It is like paradise," Garth whispered, and he was surprised that his voice was knotted, a tear blinding him.

And then the memory came. It was warm, soft, laden with the gentle light of childhood. It was the garden of his father's winter palace, far in the southlands. He looked around closely. There on the green grass was a favorite toy, a wooden rocking horse upon which he would ride and dream of glorious charges. Next to it was a stuffed mammoth, the right tusk gone, the fur knotted from his tiny fingers busily twisting and tying the wool.

It's a dream.

But it was not. He knelt down on the grass and, reaching out, he touched the horse, which rocked slowly back and forth.

He heard a soft laughter, rich and warm with love.

"Papa."

He stood up, expectant. A shadow moved behind high bushes that were heavy with orange-and-yellow blossoms.

For an instant he felt as if all the years had been stripped away.

I can see. I can see with both eyes!

He moved as if in a dream, running on short legs, laughing, his voice high and filled with shrieks of delight.

Again there was the laugh.

"Come, Galin. Mama's waiting."

The shadow stepped out from behind the grove of trees. He was tall, red-haired, beard and mustache cropped short, a circlet of turquoise stones resting upon his brow, his long flowing robes of a simple cut, embroidered with edging of richest blue.

"Papa!"

He moved around the edge of a fountain, which danced and splashed. A gentle breeze took the water, spraying him with a fine mist, and he laughed at the coolness of it, the rainbow of light.

He reached up to his face to wipe the spray from his eyes.

His hand touched the patch over his left eye.

Stunned, he pulled his hand away and at that instant all faded. The garden melting, shifting, falling away. For the briefest of instants he thought that he did indeed see his father, standing before him with his sad, gentle eyes, reaching out. The image drifted as if falling away into a long dark tunnel and he wanted to reach out to it.

"Papa?"

The image held for a moment, the sad eyes gazing at him, a hand outstretched, beckoning, and he started to step forward toward it.

No! He's dead. Murdered.

The image faded and Garth turned away, tears coursing down his face. He looked up again.

He was standing on a darkened field that stretched away into an eternity. No sun lit the sky, the world illuminated as if by an unseen and unholy light. Dark green clouds, moving impossibly fast, roiled overhead, racing by. The wind was damp, cold, and filled with a pungent acrid smoke that held with it the stench of corruption. Before him was a darkness that was shadowy, not fully formed, wavery, as if nothing more than mist. The form moved, its black robes fluttering in the breeze, and for a brief instant he caught a glimpse of a skull-like visage. He felt his blood go cold.

The shadowy form drew closer.

"I wanted to make it easy for you," a voice whispered. "You would have died believing that it was your father you embraced."

"And so this is the reward for winning," Garth said quietly.

"You knew that from the beginning, didn't you?"

Garth nodded.

The Walker chuckled softly.

"You interest me, Garth, or is it Galin?"

"Garth. The other died long ago."

"It was too bad. I remember you well. You were eager, smart, able to use *mana* almost from the day you were born. You came of good blood."

"My father and you were once friends. He saved your life once."

The shadow nodded.

"Back when all was young," Kuthuman whispered. "And that is why I wanted to give you the gift of a gentle death, at least a small token back to a friendship from another age."

Kuthuman sighed, and in his voice was an infinite weariness.

"But unfortunately you were too strong—you saw through the mirage."

Garth said nothing, still so shocked by the power of the mirage that he found it difficult to control the tears. Nor would he admit that for a moment he had been taken in entirely.

"You kill all who win the Festival, don't you."

"Are you hoping for an exemption?"

"No. I know better than that. Besides, there is too much between us."

The shadow sighed and to Garth's surprise actually sat down.

"Let us not finish this yet. Sit down, you must be weary."

Garth hesitated.

"No tricks this time. Now that you know, I owe you that as well, as the son of a friend. Besides, it would be a passing pleasure to talk as I once did, without pretenses, without groveling fear. When the end comes for you I will grant you release as a man, standing with weapon in hand as is your right."

Garth sat down on the chilled ground.

The shadow sighed.

"I always kill the winner of Festival."

"You don't want any future competition."

"Of course not. You think the poor fools who so eagerly compete would have figured that out by now. As in your world, in the world that was once my sole realm, the *mana* is scarce. It is drawn slowly out of the lands, created by the life force of every creature who lives, and then tamed and controlled by those few born with the power to see it, to concentrate its power and use it. It took much of that *mana* for me to break down the barriers between worlds and to walk as a demigod between them. It takes the tribute of many such worlds for my power to be sustained and to grow.

"Now, do you think I would share such power with others? The power to walk between worlds, to be a Walker, rests upon that. If I allowed others to gain that power, they would be a threat as they grew."

"So you strangle them in the cradle. You let us choose who

might be the next threat and then you take them and kill them."

The shadow nodded.

"Unfortunate, isn't it," he whispered as if troubled by the dark necessity of reality. "If I did not, there might be a day when someone could gather enough *mana* unto themselves so that they too could then pierce the veil of worlds and walk as I now do. And if they did, then what would there be, yet another to struggle against in a universe of struggle."

"You know that Zarel even now hoards the *mana*, your *mana*, so that he might pierce the veil."

"Carrying tales, are we?"

Garth smiled.

"It serves a purpose."

"To turn me against my servant?"

"Perhaps."

The shadow laughed.

"He is ambitious; I knew that from the beginning. So ambitious that he would help me kill your father, not out of any loyalty to me but simply to get me out of the way so that he could then prepare for the final step as well. You tell me nothing that I don't already suspect."

"And?"

The shadow paused and seemed to diminish in form. Garth watched him intently, feeling the power drain away from Kuthuman until he almost disappeared. Long minutes passed, neither of the two moving, and then the strength returned.

"A struggle elsewhere?"

The shadow nodded.

"So it is the same out here, then?" Garth asked quietly, an almost-sympathetic tone in his voice.

"The same. I thought, somehow, when I crossed through the barrier that I was free."

Garth felt as if he could almost see a wistful smile on the shadow's face.

"Ah, those first moments. They were a delight beyond imagining. It was a childlike joy for all was new, fresh, innocent to my eyes as if it were the first day of creation. I soared like an eagle, piercing through the veil of tears, of time, of eternity. Death would never now touch me, I believed. I would be eternally young, striding the corridor of time, and control all that I surveyed."

He paused for a moment.

"And then I met the others."

"Who were Walkers like you."

The shadow nodded.

"You should have assumed that," Garth said. "Our own legends spoke of the younger days when there were demigods who struggled for control of our world and how they disappeared and we were alone. You should have assumed that you would meet such."

"I was intoxicated with the power. I thought the legends were just that, mere legends. Or at worst there were others who had slain each other and the universe was now empty except for the power of the Eternal."

"You discovered differently."

"It is a universe of strife. Even now as I sit and talk with you I struggle to hold what little I have. Even now I walk in other realms, fighting, using *mana*, taking *mana* in conquest and losing it as well. It is an infinite struggle for power and I am but one of many. There are powers beyond mine that are terrible to behold, those who would drain me of my strength as if they were drawing blood out of my veins. And if they triumph over me, I shall be a dried husk, blown on the winds of eternity, doomed never to live and doomed as well never to die."

"And you have done such in turn."

The shadow chuckled, its voice cold as night.

"Ah, how I have driven my enemies before me and laughed to hear their lamentations. I have broken into their worlds, taking unto myself what is rightfully mine. That which I cannot hold I have laid waste to so that it is useless to them and the *mana* is drawn out of their lands and into my hands. I control much now, numbers beyond imagining."

"But it will never be enough. There will never be rest, will there?"

The shadow stirred.

"You are, perhaps, too wise, Garth. For once here there is no choice. It is either to grow or to be driven into the void, stripped of all powers with all eternity before you or until the

Eternal stirs and draws the circle closed. So there is no choice, no choosing. The struggle goes on without rest."

"You are, even now, strained almost beyond your ability to hold what you have."

"How do you know that?"

"If it was not so, you would have stayed longer after the Festival. You would have lain with women, drunk deeply of wine, and amused yourself with the adoration of the mob. Yet you came to take your tribute of strength, and tarried but for a moment before fleeing back here"—and Garth waved his hand toward the timeless dark plains—"this dead world of darkness."

The shadow nodded.

"Why here? This is hell itself. I would have thought you leaping through the infinite or tarrying in palaces of gold in worlds of unsurpassing delight. Why this nightmare world?"

"This is the heart of my realm. It is from here I can reach out to all other places, to erect the walls that keep the others out. When I walk within a realm and assume mortal form I am blind and know not what my enemies plot. Even in the brief instant I was away, returning to the place I had been born to take my tribute, a plane of existence was blocked to me and now I must war to win it back as I do now, even as we talk."

The shadow's voice was dark and filled with weariness, so that Garth almost felt a moment of pity, if one could pity the being that had taken all that he had once loved.

Garth started to laugh, the sound of it strange upon the dark and barren plains. He stood up and, turning, looked around.

"I have hated you my entire life," Garth said. "You were once Grand Master, and had been for well nigh unto a millennium. And then you came to fear death and you desired the power of the infinite. You perverted all that the Houses had once been and the purpose of the *mana*. You used its strength to pierce the curtain between worlds so that you could walk as a demigod and thus be immortal. And now this is your realm!"

Laughing, he pointed out at the murky darkness.

The shadow stood up.

"I found it amusing to spare you for a moment. Your father was once my friend and thus I granted a boon to you. I am no longer amused."

"Think on that. There was once a time when my father, a

mere mortal, thought so much of you that he nearly died to save you from an assassin. He carried the marks of that poisoned dagger until the day he died. You know, there was once a time when such as my father loved you and called you friend. When a woman loved you with such aching intensity that her heart was shattered, and now she is nothing but bitterness and hate. You gave all that up, all of it. For this." And he pointed out across the dark plain.

Garth's voice tightened with emotion.

"My father trusted and believed in you until he burned to death, the last of his power stripped by your groveling servant, Zarel, to be used in your unholy quest. You betrayed him and now this is your reward. You are so terrified of losing what you now control that you exile yourself to this dark world, unable to enjoy even the pleasures of a beggar—the sun in one's face, the laughter of children, the taste of wine or even of simple bread."

"You know nothing," the shadow hissed. "Your father could have been the Grand Master after I was gone and after him it could have been you. It was his arrogance that destroyed him and cursed you to half blindness."

"He chose death in preference to slavery."

"Enough of this," the shadow whispered. "Your value as a diversion is at an end. I was half thinking of actually sparing you. A sentimental gesture for a universe that is pitiless. I don't think that will happen now."

"Then go ahead," Garth said quietly.

The shadow started to rear up and extended its arms.

Garth smiled and slowly raised his arms as well.

The shadow hesitated and then laughed.

"You never did answer what I first wanted to know. You undoubtedly had figured it out that I killed the winners of the Festival so that they would not one day be a threat. So why did you come forward and win?"

"Because," Garth said evenly, "I think I can beat you as well."

The shadow laughed.

"So you will be like me. You certainly had good training. You left your servant to die, and you murdered a woman who loved you for the chance."

"You would have killed her in turn," Garth said coldly. "I would like to think that I saved her."

"You sound like a philosopher with that logic. You still killed her."

With an angry cry Garth raised his hand to strike.

The shadow, laughing easily, dodged the fireball.

"If that is all you can start with, this will be boring. Bid my greetings to your father."

Garth felt a rushing of wind, and the air around him raced inward. He tried to breathe and, doubling over, gasped and started to choke in a green cloud of sulfurous smoke.

Hammen, his arms around Varena's shoulders, struggled to remove her body while Zarel and all the others were diverted by the presence of the Walker. Varena's body servant moved feebly, shaking with tears.

"Shut up, girl, and help me," Hammen snapped.

"Keep your filthy hands off of her," the girl replied. "Let her rest."

"Damn it all, girl, I'm trying to save her before the cord of her spirit is severed, now help me."

The girl looked over at him wide-eyed, unable to move.

"Damn all women," Hammen whispered under his breath, tempted to simply let the body drop and beat a hasty retreat before it was too late.

He continued, however, to struggle with the body, slowly dragging it away. Though he did not want to, he finally looked up and saw the Walker moving up to stand before Garth.

Damn it, no.

He lowered Varena to the ground and started to stand up. The Walker started to raise his hands.

Torn between loyalties, he finally decided. Taking the amulet and *mana* that Garth had given him, he placed the amulet upon Varena's brow. Drawing on the *mana* he called to her spirit, sensing that none but the slenderest of threads still linked it to her body. The spirit, to his surprise, struggled against him, attempting to break free and break the cord to its mortal form, holding him to his task so that he had to reach outward with all his strength to seize hold of her and pull her, struggling, back into her body.

Varena's servant gasped with astonishment when a groan

escaped from her mistress. A dark cloud suddenly blocked out the sun and Hammen looked up at the swirling storm rising heavenward. He looked over fiercely at the girl.

"Keep the amulet on her forehead!"

Reaching down with a dagger, he cut Varena's satchel free and stood up, sensing the powers she controlled.

He looked over his shoulder and saw a knot of Orange fighters approaching and motioned for them to take the body.

He stood up and pointed.

"Zarel, you bastard!"

His voice carried across the arena and the mob, which had been watching the ascension of the Walker, stirred and fell silent at Hammen's challenging cry.

Zarel looked over at Hammen and started to raise his hands.

"You bastard. The games are a hoax! You know, and the House Masters know, that the winner is not taken to be a servant of the Walker. The winner is taken to be murdered by him. And you are his accomplice!"

Screaming with rage, Zarel pointed at Hammen, who with a sneer of contempt drew on Varena's *mana* and easily diverted the fire. He raised his hand in turn, knocking Zarel over with a blast of answering fire.

The arena erupted in chaos. From the corner where Garth had stood before the final match Norreen, sword raised high, came charging forward, turning to look back at the mob, urging them on. They came swarming out of the stands like a dark wave. Hammen, cloaking himself in a cloud of green smoke, fell back toward Varena, even as Zarel's fighters and warriors came swarming out to protect their lord.

Hammen reached Varena's side and screamed in rage as the Fentesk fighters who had been coming to her aid slowed at the approach of Zarel's fighters and, turning, fell back. But the mob surged forward and, within seconds, Hammen found himself in the center of a swirling melee. He struggled to hold Varena up so that she would not be trampled under the crush. Someone shouldered him aside and heavy, beefy hands reached out to take the woman. He looked up at Naru, who was grinning.

"I take woman where you want."

Norreen came through the crush to join them and together they fell back toward one of the access tunnels. As they reached the tunnel, however, Hammen slowed and then looked back.

"Someone's got to lead these poor bastards," he said quietly.

"I think, old man, you should think about saving your own hide at the moment," Norreen said.

Hammen shook his head.

"I did that once before; I've lived with it ever since. I guess I'm tired of living."

He looked back up at the sky.

"Especially now."

"You crazy man," Naru said. "I thought you make good servant for me now One-eye gone. But you crazy man." And the giant laughed.

"Norreen, show this hulk where to take her. I don't think she'd be safe back at her House anymore."

"Like hell. I'm fighting and, besides, I can't stand her."

"Damn it, Benalian. Just do it. It's what Garth would have wanted."

She lowered her head.

"Thanks a lot."

Hammen smiled.

"Now get out of here."

The old man turned and waded back into the crowd, his voice rising above the tumult, shouting for members of his old brotherhood to rally to his side.

"Let's go," Naru announced, looking down at Norreen and grinning. "Naru lucky. He have two women now."

Norreen's sword flicked out, cutting him lightly across the leg so that the giant yelped and stepped back.

"Come on, you ox, let's find a place for this woman and get back into the fight."

CHAPTER

15

GARTH STAGGERED THROUGH THE DARK CLOUD, nearly blind, choking on the poisonous air. He again erected a circle of protection, which filtered the poison out, letting thin wisps of breathable air flow into his starving lungs.

Another blow hit him and the circle collapsed.

Cursing, Garth waved his hands over his head, drawing out yet another circle, and again the barrier was erected. He waited, but there was no attack. He probed outward, searching with his senses.

The Walker was there, and yet not. He was struggling, but it was against something else, something dark and powerful. There was time now, and Garth took advantage of it while his foe was diverted by another struggle with something far more dangerous and insidious.

Garth gathered in his strength, and then drew on spells that caused the strength to double and yet double again. He raised his hand, forming a circle before his eye with forefinger and thumb, and the power to look into the spells of his opponent was created.

He was stunned by all that he saw, hundreds of spells, many of them undreamed of, obviously taken in realms and planes of existence unknown to mortals. And yet there was a weakness as well.

The *mana*, the precious *mana* that fueled the power of the spells, was weak, spread out and diverted by a myriad of struggles. So it was as he suspected.

All that he had learned in the years of growing and planning was true after all. The fading books, hidden in the place of refuge his father had sent him to, the place where he had studied and learned, had spoken of this. What his father had suspected and written down was true, that the hold the Walkers had upon their powers had a weakness after all.

Garth smiled inwardly and continued to let his strength build.

The struggle between the Walker and the other foe came to an end and again the Walker's power became focused. He turned back to face Garth.

"I'm sorry for the interruption," the Planes Walker said, his voice a haunting whisper. "One of my enemies thought it was a convenient time to try and take back what I had seized from him. Of course you'll understand that such a concern was more important than my sport with you."

"Of course."

"Ah, I see you've used the time well. Your power is stronger now. Good, good, the challenge is more amusing. Usually, when I bring a winner here they tend to grovel and whine at their fate. You have your father's blood in you. I like that.

"Shall we begin?"

Garth extended his hands.

The Walker extended his hands as well and the dark plain upon which they stood was suddenly illuminated with a shimmering light, the green clouds rolling back to reveal a dark red sun overhead that filled half the sky. A golden circle outlined a flat, open field that stretched to the far horizon, which seemed impossibly far away.

"An arena field for our amusement," the Walker announced.

A red shimmering lit the field and an instant later a demonic horde was deployed, scimitars, tridents, and skull standards raised high. With a keening howl they raced forward.

Garth extended his hands and a living wall was erected before him, momentarily blocking the attack. Move followed countermove. A Lord of the Pit under the Walker's control emerged out of the ground and Garth, in turn, hurled it back upon the demonic hordes, destroying them, the monster roaring with delight as it rent the creatures and devoured them. A dark force of nature was next brought forth to tear the demon apart. Dragons fought in the sky overhead, doppelgängers stalked each other, hydras battled atop the wall, which came crashing down, and djinn struggled on the ground between the two fighters.

"You are more amusing than most," the Walker announced. "If I did not have an engagement elsewhere I think I would actually let this play out longer."

"Then finish it," Garth taunted. "Or don't you have the strength? Do it and be damned."

The Walker raised his hands with an angry curse and stepped forward. Garth staggered backward, pushed by an invisible power that lashed into his soul. He drew forth a rank of bodyguards to take the punishment but within minutes they had collapsed, writhing in agony and dying.

More blows slammed into Garth, draining his strength, and he started to crumple, going down on his knees.

The Walker drew closer and looked down at Garth, who was leaning over, panting for breath.

"Too bad, One-eye. I've enjoyed our visit. I sense that your life force is nearly spent."

Garth looked up at him, his face drawn and pale.

"Go to hell, you bastard."

The Walker sighed.

"I think I am already there."

He raised his hand and pointed downward with the final blow.

Garth raised his hand, drawing on the one spell that he had kept hidden until this moment.

The blow of his opponent struck and, for a brief instant, Garth thought that his conjuring had failed and he was falling into the lands of the dead. And then it took hold. All the damage that he had sustained was drawn out of him and he was again whole. At that same moment all that he had suffered slammed into his opponent. With a loud cry the Walker staggered backward, his shadowy form hissing, coiling upon itself and writhing on the ground. Its howls of agony caused Garth to cover his eye lest it be shattered.

Garth was on his feet, racing up to the Walker's side. The shadow was changing, taking a near-human form. And again Garth used his power to look inward, to sense all that his opponent had.

He found it and, reaching out, snatched the one form of power he had come for and, with it, the *mana* of his world that controlled it and gave it strength.

The Walker howled in impotent rage, struggling to heal himself even as he slipped away.

With an invisible hand Garth grasped the spell that opened the portal of worlds, that changed reality, twisted the flow of time, and made all things possible. He struggled against the Walker to take as well the *mana* that bound and controlled the spell.

The Walker started to recover, screaming in rage as that which gave him access to the world of his origin was pulled away from his grasp. Garth struggled and swayed, ignoring the explosive pain to his hands, trying not to feel, not to notice that fire was curling his fingers black.

He felt his hold on the Walker's spell starting to slip as his foe regained his strength. Reaching inward Garth drew on what little he had left and in that moment his own power and *mana* were doubled. He wrenched the control of the planes gate away from his opponent and fell backward. The Walker came back up and, howling with a mad demonic rage, raised his hands and pointed.

Damn, now that I've got it, how do I use it? Garth wondered, even as the blow hit him.

He felt fire racing over him, a heat as intense as the sun engulfing him. Garth One-eye pulled his strength inward and focused it on the power of the gate. The Walker, screaming hysterically, attacked yet again and Garth felt himself falling away.

"Massacre them all," Zarel growled, looking down angrily at Uriah. "Any who do not stand with me now are against me."

"All the Houses?"

"All of them. If we give them time to organize, they might ally with the mob against me. I want this finished. You heard the Walker as well. He said he'll be back."

"And what will he say of this massacre?"

Zarel looked coldly at the dwarf.

I won't be here so it won't matter, he thought with a grin of satisfaction. *With the mana taken and the capture of Kirlen's books, the path will be open.*

"Have our fighters and warriors prepare to sally forth at the midnight bell."

"Against all four Houses, sire? They still have, even after the desertions and deaths in the arena, well over two hundred and fifty fighters to our two hundred."

Zarel cursed and looked down at the gold inlay in his floor. Kirlen could not be bribed except with power and, besides, she was the first and most important target. Tulan and Varnel—their hatred evident—could not be swayed. But Jimak, Jimak could always be swayed for the moment and then eliminated later.

"Empty the coffers of gold as a bribe. Send it over to Jimak at once in return for his pledge to stand by my side."

"And what will you tell the Walker if you destroy them?"

"Tell him, I'll pile *mana* taken from the dead around his feet. That will buy him off. When it is finished you can rebuild a new House of your own."

Uriah nodded and slowly withdrew.

Zarel watched him leave.

"And your turn will come as well," he whispered.

Zarel turned away from the door, his heart racing.

How much time do I have? he wondered. *And still, what is One-eye's game in all of this? Can it be that all along he was out after Kuthuman and that even now he is struggling to throw him down? If so, then so much the better. Kuthuman will be delayed in his return and I'll be gone. If it is the other way around, that Kuthuman has been vanquished, then One-eye will be weak and easy to overthrow as well. The first step, however, is to make sure Kirlen is finished and her precious scrolls and books taken.*

Kirlen of Bolk sat hunched over upon her throne.

"Have you found Naru?"

The messenger shook his head.

"He's deserted, along with eleven other fighters."

She cursed angrily and spit on the throne-room floor.

"Send messengers to the other three Houses. Zarel has subdued the mob for the moment. It is obvious he now plans to move against us as well. We can either stand united at this moment or we will all die separately. I plan to attack at the midnight bell. Tell them to do the same and we can defeat him. Get their assurances that they will do so, and ask them to strike straight for the palace. Now go!"

The messenger ran out of the room.

Kirlen smiled softly.

One-eye had played his part well. The mob had attacked Zarel and he had slaughtered them without mercy so that they were forced to break and flee. But he did not follow up, he could not, for he had to conserve his remaining strength to use against the Houses. Only a fool would think that the Houses would not strike now to cast him down and take his *mana* for themselves. She knew him well enough to know that he now feared the Houses as a possible counter to him, or worse yet, the Houses would ally with the rabble to bring him down. The balance was broken and could not be restored—too much hatred now brewed on all sides.

Now was the time to strike at Zarel, and by leading the way she would be the next Grand Master, presenting the Walker with fait accompli upon his return.

Or perhaps, even better, she thought, *I can challenge him beyond the veil and gain the vengeance I deserve.*

She thought of Garth, who so unknowingly had created this opportunity for her. He had done his service well. All the hatreds of all sides, which had been contained for so long, had finally boiled to the surface thanks to him. Let all the corruption boil out now, she thought with a cold glee.

But why would he go so willingly into the Walker's grasp? she suddenly wondered. He could only have done so if there was a plan. It was obvious, she realized. He had from the beginning planned to challenge the Walker, somehow defeat him, and become one in his own right. If that was the case, he would be weak after the struggle and the chance of breaking through was even more possible now.

The opportunity was now and she stood up, calling for her fighters to prepare.

*   *   *

Tulan of Kestha and Varnel of Fentesk stood in the shadows, looking out anxiously across the Plaza.

"That old crone does have a point," Tulan said eagerly. "He plans to finish us now. This balance of power game has gone on too long. Either we kill him or he kills us."

"Perhaps we can win in either case," Varnel said calmly. "She will attack. This is not a trick to lure us out with her holding back. Her passion for power has consumed her. And besides, she is right, you know. Our best fighters died in the arena these last three days. If ever there is a moment when he can defeat us all, it is now."

"And yet," Tulan said silkily.

"And yet, suppose they are equally balanced in the struggle? All we need do is let them wear each other down. Perhaps if we attacked, and at least demonstrated our intent, she would press onward. But we hold back and let them bleed themselves against each other. Then, when the moment is right, we slaughter all of them together."

"And what of Jimak?"

"And what of him? We know he covets the gold that Zarel holds in his coffers. He will attack with a passion and bleed himself dry in the process. Let him."

Varnel smiled.

"And as for what we might want," Tulan sighed. "The women of Zarel will be yours, all of them in their multitude of colors, shapes, scents, and perverse practices."

Varnel licked his lips eagerly.

"And when we are done we can also hunt down those of our fighters who betrayed us and went over to the mob," Varnel said coldly.

Jimak of Ingkara sat alone in his counting room, gazing down at the mountain of gold spread before his throne. The strong-boxes had been carted over to him but moments ago, in payment for his pledge to fight by Zarel's side. He chuckled at the thought. Certainly he would fight, and when the other Houses were done and looted, then it would be Zarel's turn as well.

*   *   *

Hammen peeked out from behind the broken shutter. The midnight bell tolled with its deep, melancholy tone. The Plaza was silent, illuminated with flickering fires that still smoldered from the battles with the mob that had raged throughout the afternoon and into the early evening.

He looked back at a deserter from Kestha, who had come over to the side of the mob with the information that the Houses were planning to assault the palace at midnight.

"Nothing."

Even as he said the word a brilliant flash arced up into the sky. Flickering and hissing, it detonated over the Plaza, illuminating it with a harsh white light. Trumpets blared from the pyramid-shaped palace and from the five great doors an armed host came charging out, warriors at the fore with crossbows ready, followed by mobile catapults mounted on wagons, and finally the fighters.

They charged across the Plaza and from out of the gates of the Houses of the four colors fighters emerged as well. Hammen, chortling with glee, pulled the shutter wide open and leaned out to watch, joined by Naru, Norreen, and the lieutenants of his brotherhood, who had struggled to gain some semblance of fighting control over the mob.

Within seconds the Plaza was a churning sea of combat as nearly every spell known in the Western Lands was brought into play by the over four hundred fighters struggling in the Plaza. The concentration of *mana* was so intense that the Plaza pulsed with an unearthly light that glowed and flickered like heat lightning on a summer horizon.

The fighters of Bolk charged with violent attacks, reaching the very gates of the palace, while the fighters of Fentesk and Kestha held fast in the middle of the Plaza.

Naru, watching the charge of his old comrades, roared with delight and pounded the side of the windowsill so that the boards cracked.

"Purple is changing sides," Hammen gasped, and he pointed to the far side of the Plaza, where the ranks of Ingkara turned on the flank of Fentesk, caving it in.

Brown fighters, in turn, enraged by the betrayal, broke from their attack on the palace and charged toward the flank of Purple. For a brief instant Hammen saw Kirlen sitting atop her sedan chair, white hair fluttering in the wind, pointing toward the House of Ingkara. Liquid fire drenched the walls of the House and sheets of flame raced up its side.

Hammen, shaking his head, turned away.

"Madness," he sighed. "Nothing but madness."

Zarel, roaring with glee, turned his attention away from the onslaught of Bolk's fighters, who were now diverted by an even deeper hatred fueled by Ingkara's betrayal. Kirlen, raging and screaming, tried to turn their attention back on Zarel's palace, even though it was she who had lost her temper and focused her strength elsewhere just when the strength of her attack was at its peak.

It was evident that Kestha and Fentesk were holding back and would crush whatever was left.

Zarel turned to his reserves of fighters and warriors and directed them to attack Fentesk and Kestha while the fighters of Ingkara and Bolk struggled. The warriors surged forward with raised crossbows. Flashes of fire rained down on them and the fighters behind them threw up curtains of protection. A fissure raced across the Plaza, opening with a shattering roar. The buildings around the Plaza swayed. Prepared for such a defense, more warriors raced forward and threw light wooden bridges across the chasm. As the attackers raced across, dark creatures surged up out of the rift, pulling warriors down, the creatures at times fighting with each other for tidbits that kicked and screamed as they were torn asunder.

Zarel concentrated his fury against Varnel, sending down waves of attack from above—dragons and other winged beasts, bolts of lightning, sheets of fire, and rains of stones. Fentesk's fighters conjured spells of fire in response.

Zarel leaped the fissure, striking down a demon that rose up to tear him apart. His fury caused the fighters arrayed against him to blanch, turn, and run. The warriors who had managed to cross the fissure saw their chance and fired at the backs of the fighters, sending them sprawling to the ground. Many of the fallen tried to generate spells of healing to save themselves but the warriors of Zarel fell upon them with glee. Drawing swords, they cut off the heads of the wounded, holding them aloft in triumph before tossing them into the fissure.

Specially assigned warriors raced from body to body, cutting off the satchels of the fallen of all sides so that their spells and *mana* would become the personal trophies of Zarel. And the harvest was good as the fighters of Kestha and Fentesk fell back before the onslaught.

A personal duel arose between Zarel and Varnel before the gates of the House of Fentesk. Zarel, his powers fat with the booty he was taking in, soon drove Varnel to his knees. The House Master, looking up at Zarel with stunned disbelief, cried out in anguish as his opponent cast the final spell, causing Varnel to age a hundred years in the span of a dozen seconds. The man who had placed so much store in sensual pleasure wept bitterly as he slowly curled up into a whimpering ball of yellowed skin and sickly white hair.

The doors of the House of Fentesk were cast down and, even as the warriors and fighters of Zarel charged in, those who were hiding inside attempted to flee outward. Zarel pointed at one of them and the young woman froze and then, as if walking in her sleep, came over to stand before Zarel.

Smiling cruelly, Zarel reached out and grabbed hold of her, stirring her from her sleep. He forced her to look down at Varnel.

"There is your Master now," Zarel laughed. "Would you care to pleasure him?"

Varnel, with trembling hands, reached up.

"Malina." His voice was a hissing croak, his breath sick with corruption.

The girl recoiled and then broke into a contemptuous laugh, reaching over to put her arm around Zarel.

"Curse your fates and die," Zarel laughed, and he pointed down at Varnel, creating the same spell yet again.

Varnel, moaning in anguish, continued to age. As he did so his flesh fell away into dust until all that was left was a skeletal form wrapped in silken robes and a skull whose mouth was open in a final cry of pain.

Zarel pushed the girl aside and turned to go back into the fight.

Across the Plaza a thunderclap roar erupted and Zarel turned to look back. The House of Ingkara was bathed in flames; atop its battlements fighters writhed back and forth, dashing madly about, their cloaks on fire. Several hurled themselves off the high wall and fluttered down, trailing smoke and fire.

"Uriah!"

Zarel turned, looking, and saw his captain of fighters come through the press.

"Continue to push Tulan. If you take his House, his personal satchel is yours for the keeping. I'm going back to finish Kirlen."

The dwarf grinned sardonically and, turning, gave a fierce rallying cry and thrust himself into the fray.

Zarel watched him go, grinning coldly. He had promised him the satchel, but he had said nothing about how long he could keep it.

Motioning for his bodyguard to follow, Zarel raced back across the Plaza and was horrified to discover that the north end of his palace was bathed in flames from Bolk's renewed attack.

Zarel saw his foe and threw back his head, howling with rage. "Kirlen!"

Hammen stood transfixed by the madness playing out on the Plaza below.

"We should attack him now."

He looked over his shoulder. Varena stood behind him, her features pale and drawn.

"I gave you a sleep potion, woman, now take advantage of it. You're still weak."

"Give me back my satchel." She extended her hand.

"For what? So you can go out there and commit suicide after all I've done to save you? You're as weak as a newborn kitten. Now go lie down."

"Zarel has gone insane with bloodlust. He won't stop with the four Houses; next he'll turn his attention back on the mob. You have tens of thousands willing to fight. Throw them in before he wins."

"Young lady, while you were conveniently asleep we tried

just that. The streets from the arena all the way back to the Plaza are choked with the dead. We fell back because we could not stand with clubs and knives against spells and cross-bows. Let it play out. Perhaps they will weaken each other to the point that we can sweep him up at the end."

Varena sighed and reached over to the windowsill to brace herself. As she looked out she saw the front of her House collapsing in ruin, engulfed in flame.

She turned away with tears clouding her eyes.

"You should have let my spirit go in peace rather than bring me back to this ending."

She staggered away from the window and collapsed upon the floor.

Again Hammen looked out the window. The House of Kestha was now under siege, the building under attack from a score of stone giants and hill giants, who hammered at the wall with their massive clubs, while a juggernaut rolled slowly forward with relentless energy, crashing through the gates of the House. Warriors struggled in the confusion and fighters traded blows at short range. From atop the battlement Tulan appeared, and from his hands came a rain of fire, wind, storms, and lightning, which smashed most of the giants. And then a dark force appeared, rushing straight at the Master of Kestha. Screaming in rage, Tulan struggled as the darkness closed in, sapping the strength from his body so that his corpulent form started to shrivel, leaving his silken robes hanging as if draped over a skeleton.

Tulan staggered back and forth on the battlement, while in the Plaza below his agony drew harsh and mocking laughter from Zarel's fighters. With a mad curse, Tulan tore off his satchel and threw it up into the air. He raised his hands and pointed. The satchel disappeared in a puff of smoke.

Uriah, screaming with rage, pointed his hands at Tulan even as Tulan staggered to the edge of the battlement and, with a final curse, threw himself off the wall. His body, exploding in flames from Uriah's final spell, smashed on the hard pavement and split asunder.

Sickened, Hammen turned away.

"Of the four, he was perhaps the least harmful," the old man said.

A stream of warriors now poured into the House of Kestha to finish the slaughter. Out in the Plaza Uriah stormed back and forth, shouting with rage and then finally directing his fighters to turn and head back toward the fighting against Bolk.

"The Houses are dead," Norreen said, standing by Hammen's side and watching the slaughter. "Zarel will win and then there will be nothing to balance and offset him. If we have any chance left, it is now."

"We? I thought you were planning to get out of this madhouse."

"I kind of got involved, if only for the memory of Garth."

Hammen turned and looked back at his vagabond assortment of lieutenants.

"Juka, rally the mob on the street of sword makers, Valmar, the street of tanners, Pultark, the street of silk merchants, and Seduna, the street of butchers. It's impossible to try and coordinate it properly. Just get them to charge. Perhaps we can swarm them under while they're still out in the Plaza. If that bastard brings down the others and regains his palace, it is finished. Now move!"

The four men nodded grimly and left the room.

He looked back at Naru, who sat hunched up on the floor. "Don't worry, you oversize cretin, we'll still get one more fight in."

Naru grinned with pleasure.

"Kirlen!"

Zarel, drunk with slaughter and triumph, moved toward his most hated of rivals. The old woman watched him come, silhouetted by the conflagrations consuming the other Houses, and she knew her dream of overthrowing his power was finished. From atop the flame-scorched battlements of Ingkara she saw Jimak looking down and could sense his glee at her downfall.

She turned to face Zarel, barely noticing that most of her fighters had turned and fled, stripping off their uniforms as they ran. She stood upon her throne and, in her moment of defeat, knew all that was now lost. Her agony pierced to her very soul.

Turning, she fled back into her House. As she hobbled through the doors she heard the harsh laughter of her foes.

The door slammed shut behind her and she looked back at the two trembling guards.

"Hold it as long as you can," she screamed and continued along the darkened corridor, not even noticing the two young fighters as they turned and fled down another hallway in a desperate bid to escape the final destruction.

She reached her room and stopped.

Her books, her precious books, manuscripts, all the arcane knowledge in her search surrounded her.

She heard the battering on the door outside, the bursting of the hinges, and the harsh taunting cries of her foes.

She extended her hands, waving them in tight circles, pulling them in close around her withered body.

Zarel stood before the House of Bolk, watching, as the building started to cave in upon itself. A fighter emerged from the door, raced up to Zarel's side, and lowered his head.

"Well?"

"She's gone. The room was covered in ice."

"What!"

Zarel pushed his way through the door and raced along the corridor. He could feel the building drawing in upon itself, collapsing into ruin. He reached the end of the corridor and turned into her private quarters.

He could almost sense the ripple of laughter, the final taunt from the flicker of light in the center of the room. She had somehow fled. She was still trapped in this plane but she had escaped. A few bits of paper still swirled around the room and then fluttered into the light and disappeared.

The room was dark, and as cold as the grave.

Part of the ceiling overhead collapsed and Zarel leaped back with a wild curse. Turning, he fled back down the corridor and out into the Plaza. Behind him the walls of the House of Bolk crashed inward into rubble and ruin.

A mad rage consumed him. She had escaped. But she had to be somewhere within this plane and thus could be found again. With enough *mana* he should be able to conjure the spells that would find her before it was too late.

All that was left now was Jimak of Ingkara and as he turned to face the House he saw Jimak emerge. The old man walked slowly, looking around nervously at the carnage that covered the square.

The Plaza was aglow with a ghastly light, not only from the tremendous concentration of *mana* but also from the pyres of the three other Houses. Fighting still raged as the last survivors were tracked down, cornered, and destroyed.

"So you got what you wanted?"

Zarel looked over at Jimak, a sneer of contempt lighting his features.

"You betrayed your own for a handful of gold."

"I figured you would win."

Zarel said nothing, relishing the moment.

"We should have united against you the moment you declared that the fights were to the death. But we were all so intent on One-eye. We all wanted him and yet all hated him since we other three could not control him. If our best had not been slain in the arena, we could have held against you. That we should have seen more clearly."

The old man started to sway back and forth and Zarel suddenly realized that his satchel was open and was filled not with spells, amulets, and *mana* but rather with gold.

Jimak smiled.

"I cast my *mana* to the four winds. You shall not have it; your victory is hollow. I'd like to think that Kirlen, with all her hatred of you, has somehow escaped as well."

The old man fell over, gasping.

He looked up at Zarel.

"I thought the poison would be painless. I was wrong. But it will be over shortly. I'll see you in hell."

Zarel looked down at Jimak as he rolled over, his breath coming in labored, rattling gasps.

Screaming with rage, he kicked Jimak in the side and then turned away.

"Destroy Ingkara's House," he shouted. "Leave not one block upon another. And the same for the other Houses. Now gather before me the *mana* that has been taken from the fallen. Any who hold back I will kill with my own hands."

Uriah, who had been standing and watching the exchange between Zarel and Jimak, stepped forward angrily.

"You promised a House to me and the power that was in

Tulan's satchel. He destroyed them before dying. I claim what is taken from the other Kestha fighters as mine."

Zarel turned and, with a single blow, knocked Uriah over, sending the dwarf sprawling to the ground. Uriah struggled to regain his footing and Zarel knocked him down once again with a psionic blow that slammed the dwarf into unconsciousness.

Turning, Zarel glared at the other fighters.

"Do it!" But even as he spoke there was a new eruption of fighting on the far side of the Plaza.

"Damn it, now what?" he snarled angrily.

A warrior came through the press of fighters who had witnessed the downfall of their captain.

"The mob, sire," the warrior shouted. "They're attacking again."

Zarel turned and looked back at his fighters.

"Leave none of them alive this time. If this city is to be turned into a pyre, do it."

The fighters stood silent, not moving.

"You have a choice," Zarel hissed. "Either serve me now or die. You can all try to take me but with the power I have, I guarantee few of you will live to see the triumph. And those of you that do survive will be torn apart by the mob. Now go stop them."

Several of the fighters turned away and wearily headed toward the sound of the fighting. The rest, watching them go, finally turned and followed.

Zarel stormed after them, gathering in the *mana* that his still-loyal warriors now brought him in the dozens of satchels taken from the fallen of both sides. And he felt a surge of energy from the *mana* as he gathered it in, so that even the burden of its weight bothered him not.

He drew upon the renewed strength and, with a howl of delight, he sent a blast of fire across the Plaza—fire which struck into the mob with such force that a hundred or more were bowled over by the flame, their incandescent forms twisting and writhing in agony.

The mob, which had been angrily advancing from out of the thoroughfare of the silk merchants, turned in panic and started to flee. From the other boulevards that led into the Plaza came yet more and Zarel, laughing with sardonic delight, called down torments upon them as well, slaying hundreds with a power that was near to that of a demigod. And he sang with a fierce joy even as he drained his power in the killing.

And all turned and fled before his dark visage.

"It's lost, damn it, it's lost!"

Hammen, staggered by the terrifying power of Zarel, could only lean against the side of a shattered building, watching with numbed comprehension the slaughter taking place in the Plaza. He knew the attack had been a forlorn hope and it was evident now that it was doomed. The mob, which had taken far too much of a beating in the arena in the last two days of rioting, was spent, fleeing in every direction.

But the counterattack did not stop. Zarel, drunk with a mad glee, staggered about the Plaza, burning everything in sight. His warriors, and now many of his fighters as well, had given themselves over to riot, and rushed about as maniacs, killing the wounded, burning anything that would stand, spreading out into the side streets destroying as they went.

"Madness, it's all madness," Hammen whispered. He felt hands on his shoulders turning him away. He looked up at Naru and then over at Norreen.

"The world is his now," Hammen moaned. "At least before, at least before Garth came, there was a balance. Now it is gone. Damn, it's all gone and we are in the hands of a madman."

"Old man must leave," Naru said, and his voice was actually filled with a sad melancholy. "Zarel kill you, kill Orange woman and other woman if they found. Leave."

Shaking with fatigue, Hammen allowed himself to be turned away from the square.

A blast of fire slammed into the building he had just been leaning against. Naru, howling with pain, staggered out into the middle of the street, his great beard and mane of hair on fire. He swirled about, trying to put out the flames. Hoarse laughter came from out of the shadows and, stunned, Hammen looked up to see Zarel stalking toward them, moving with an unearthly speed. He struck Naru another blow and the giant crumpled.

Hammen turned to Norreen.

"Flee! At least find Varena and get her out."

"We're all finished," Norreen snarled. "Let me die as I choose." And, unsheathing her sword, she leaped forward to stand over Naru, who rolled about weakly on the ground.

Hammen, sighing, stepped forward to join her.

Zarel, now seeing whom he was facing, slowed, a grin of cold delight twisting his features.

With raised hands he slowly walked toward them, moving in for the kill.

Long he fell, so that he was not sure if he had slipped into eternity or if perhaps time itself had ceased to exist. He could sense as well the pursuit, though it was distant. He had slammed the door shut into the world from which he had come, but he knew that somehow he had not bolted it with sufficient *mana* to keep it thus barred forever.

Gradually his strength returned and he found a sudden joy, a realization that he had indeed crossed through the final barrier, that he was now a Planes Walker. The universe, with all its multiplicity of realities, awaited him if he dared. And yet he sensed as well the barriers that hemmed him in on all sides, the realms guarded so jealously by the others, and there were indeed others. He could sense them, some locked within their realms like demented misers, who kept the doors into their miserable realms locked out of fear that someone would want the squalor they had created. Others fought with a mad—insane—glee, struggling simply for the joy of it. There were triumphs and defeats, exaltation and despair. And all too rarely there was tranquility behind walls erected so high and so strong that no one could pierce into the gardens thus created. And he sensed as well the truth of how they had achieved that.

He felt temptation take hold of him, offering him all the powers of a demigod, for indeed in this brief moment that is truly what he had become, a Walker who could stride across the universe and do battle with forces dark or light as he might choose.

He hovered thus, torn between desires, and then he turned, sensing something else. And he knew. He looked back whence he had come and sensed that the barrier would fail and that his foe might again emerge. But with all the universe to race through it mattered not to him. And yet he sensed something else as well. He felt a lingering sadness, like a child called from play in a dangerous field to return to a task he wished would somehow go away, yet it would not.

He knew what he still must do, and there was an urgency to it that drew him back and downward.

Hammen did not even bother to raise his hands, knowing that it was useless even to try. Norreen would die as a Benalian, fighting with sword in hand, and thus bring honor to her caste. But as for himself, he realized that he was tired, that he was old, and, most of all, he was simply weary of the inequity of this world and wished to be quit of it forever.

"Do it, you bastard, and be done," Hammen snarled.

And even as Zarel raised his hand to strike, laughing with demonic fury, a shadow seemed to form. Zarel hesitated, looking up.

The shadow swirled in tight, spiraling downward, and Zarel stepped back.

It took form and Hammen, stunned, sat down heavily beside Naru.

Garth One-eye stood in the middle of the street.

Zarel stood silent, mouth opened in astonishment.

"I think we have something to settle," Garth said, his face set with a look of cold disdain.

Zarel said nothing, looking around nervously.

"Do you remember the night my father died?" Garth said sharply. "Do you remember me standing before you, a child half-blinded by your own hand? You were going to use me as a trade, yet both of us knew that you would not have honored it. You would have killed him and then me in turn. Do you remember my tearing away from your grasp and running back into the flames? You laughed when you heard my childish screams."

Garth stood silent for a moment.

"Do you remember!" His voice was a lash.

Zarel raised his hand and a fire elemental seemed to leap out from him, the flame washing over Garth. He disappeared in the maelstrom of heat and Zarel laughed coldly, stepping forward.

A gust of icy wind swept the Plaza, dispelling the elemental, and Garth still stood there. The fighting in the streets fell away. Zarel's warriors and fighters slowed in their frenzy, looking back fearfully. At the sight of the one whom their Master was confronting, they looked around in terror. The mob, which had been running in panic, slowed as well. Those who remained edged back toward the two foes.

Zarel backed out into the Plaza, Garth following. Blow and counterblow were struck, the two locked in a dark struggle that was filled with hatred and revenge. All the powers that both controlled were thrown into the fight so that their struggle seemed to exceed even the pitched battle that had been fought earlier between the different Houses.

Flames soared into the smoke-filled skies, dragons and flying beasts wheeled overhead, giants struggled, and dark creatures came up from the underworld below.

And Zarel slowly gave way. And as he did so all could see the growing terror in his eyes. His fear sapped the resolve of his fighters and warriors and strengthened that of the mob, so that it edged in closer.

The warriors of Zarel started to break, first one, then another and another, so that there was soon a stampede of them, swarming back toward the supposed safety of the palace. Fighters as well turned and fled in blind panic. A mighty roar arose and the mob surged after them, pulling them down, stabbing, beating, and killing without remorse those who had tormented them for so long. Here and there in the crowd Hammen's lieutenants managed to stem the fury of the mob, allowing fighters to strip themselves of their satchels, or warriors of their weapons, sending them off into the darkness shorn of their powers, to flee into the night.

Zarel, staggered by the blows of his opponent, fell back toward his palace, from which columns of smoke were now pouring as the mob stormed into the building, looting and pillaging.

Zarel turned one final blast of flame on Garth and though Garth was stopped by it, a circle of protection diverted the blaze, which quickly died.

Zarel stood alone, panting for breath, his *mana* diminished to the merest flicker of power as if he was but a first-rank fighter.

Garth stepped toward him and as he did so he reached for his dagger and unsheathed it.

Zarel looked at him, wide-eyed, and drew his dagger in turn. He leaped forward with a mad cry and Garth parried the blow. Their blades locked again, and yet again, Garth drawing back, blood coursing down his cheek, which was laid open to the bone.

"I'll cut your other eye out now," Zarel roared.

Garth moved to parry the blow and then Zarel extended his hand. A light flashed before Garth's face with a white-hot intensity. Garth staggered backward, momentarily blinded.

Laughing, Zarel came forward to drive his blade into Garth's throat. And then his hand froze and, with a cry of pain, he staggered away. Fumbling, he wrenched a small dagger out of his back and threw it aside, wasting precious seconds on a healing spell to stop the pain.

Garth, dispelling the fire before his eye, looked down and saw Uriah, lying on the ground next to Zarel.

Uriah looked at him and smiled, and for a brief instant Garth felt as if time was stripped away and again it was the dwarf who had been his friend so many years before.

"I'm sorry," the dwarf whispered, even as Zarel, with a scream of rage, turned and drove his dagger into the dwarf's heart.

With a mad cry of remorse and years of pain, Garth leaped forward.

Zarel, wrenching his dagger free from the dwarf's heart, turned and tried to duck under the blow. With a wild scream, Garth drove his dagger in.

Stunned, Zarel staggered backward, looking down at the hilt of Garth's blade, which was buried in his chest. He fumbled at it, a sob of astonishment escaping him. He waved his hand feebly to conjure a healing spell. Garth looked at him coldly, hesitated, and then raised his own hand to block it.

"I should have cut your throat that night, rather than simply gouged your eye out," Zarel hissed.

"Your mistake," Garth said softly.

Zarel collapsed onto the pavement.

"What do you have now?" Zarel whispered. "You lived for this moment. Now what will you have when all your enemies are gone?"

"I don't know," Garth replied sadly, even as Zarel closed his eyes and fell away into the darkness.

Hammen stood silently and watched as the last of the drama was played out. Garth turned slowly and looked at him. He seemed to Hammen to be again the small boy, confused and lost.

Once more Garth looked at Zarel, shook his head, and then turned to walk toward Hammen, a sad, distant smile lighting his features. Norreen, breaking through the crush of the mob, rushed forward and leaped into Garth's arms.

And then, as if the two were nothing more than an illusion, they disappeared, a darkness swirling around them. There was a momentary look of astonishment on Garth's face followed by understanding. His other foe had come back to claim him from other realms.

And even as he and Norreen were drawn away by their foe Garth smiled, the words forming, coming as a whisper.

"You're free."

He was gone.

The Plaza was silent, except for the crackling of the flames and the low, pitiful cries of the wounded and dying.

Hammen looked at the mob, which stood as if coming out of a dark dream.

"What now?" someone asked softly.

"I don't know," Hammen sighed. "I don't think he ever had a plan for afterward."

Hammen looked at the city, which was in flames around him.

"I don't know, and at the moment I simply don't care." And sitting down in the ashes, the old man silently wept.

CHAPTER

16

THE ROAD BEFORE HIM WAS A BRIGHT MOON-
light ribbon that traced over the hills of darkness. At the crest
of the hill ahead he could see the tavern, an old favorite
haunt, and he stretched in the saddle, glad that the day's ride
was nearly ended.

He looked over his shoulder at the young acolytes who rode
behind him. Though tired, they chatted eagerly, for tomorrow
they would reach the city. He half listened to their prattle and
boasts of what they would accomplish at the Festival, what
spells they hoped to win and the laurels of victory that they
would wear upon their brows when they next rode this way at
the ending of Festival time.

The old man listened, smiling to himself, able to do so
since they could not see him. He was, after all, the Master,
and they had never seen him smile, nor would they, at least
until they had won.

They rode into the courtyard of the tavern and the old man
dismounted, his joints creaking, cursing mildly at one of the
young men for not being quick enough to help him down.

He walked into the tavern and looked around cautiously. It
was late at night, but some travelers were still up, sitting by
the fire, chatting. They looked over their shoulders at him and
grins lit their faces.

One of them, tankard in hand, walked toward him. He knew the type and waited.

"So what are the chances this year?"

The old man looked him up and down.

"We'll win," he snapped, and his tone made it clear that he was not in the mood to talk odds and fighting records, or who would be the final winner.

The man backed away and returned sullenly to his friends.

The old man looked over at the innkeeper.

"See that my youngsters are fed and bedded down." Reaching into a purse which was tied to the strap of his satchel, he pulled out a gold coin and tossed it to the keeper.

Turning, he went back to the door.

"Master?"

The old man looked over his shoulder at the young woman who cautiously came up to his side.

"What is it?"

"Where are you going?"

"For a walk, some fresh air."

"You shouldn't go alone."

The old man laughed.

"I think I can take care of myself. Now get something to eat and go to bed—it's a long ride tomorrow to the city."

She hesitated.

"We think there's something out there tonight," she whispered.

"Go on, child, I'll be all right."

Reluctantly she turned away and rejoined her friends.

Opening the door, he stepped out into the moonlight and walked out onto the road.

The girl was right. There was something following them, he could sense that. He had felt its presence all evening, drawing closer. It felt familiar somehow and yet he could not be sure. If it boded ill, he wanted his young acolytes out of the way. They were nothing more than first- and second-rank fighters and would be slaughtered if it was a fight. But then again there were precious few fighters aboard now who were anything beyond first or second. Nearly all the rest had died in the Time of Troubles.

Slowly he walked back up the road down which he had ridden, finally reaching the crest of the hill.

And then he saw them. Two riders, moving at a casual pace, as if they had all the time in the world and there was nothing in it to fear.

The old man drew back into the shadow of the trees and watched them approach. One of the riders slowed and the old man heard the snick of steel being drawn and then there was a cool, distant laugh.

"Old man, if you mean to fight, at least come out of the shadows and stop skulking about."

He stepped into the road and looked up at the two riders, the moon behind him drifting behind a cloud so that the land was plunged into darkness.

"Who are you?" one of the two asked, her voice cool and aloof.

"Rather should I ask who are you? You've been following me for several hours now."

"It's a free road. Now who are you?"

The old man slowly extended his hands, ready to do battle.

"Hadin gar Kan, Master of the House of Oor-tael."

The woman laughed softly and there was the sound of a blade returning to its scabbard.

"Going to Festival?" she asked.

"That was my intention."

"Will you win?"

Her tone was one of simple interest and Hammen relaxed slightly.

"We plan to. The game should be interesting, mostly new fighters now. Ever since the Time of Troubles, that's about all we have."

"I heard about that," the woman said. "What happened?"

"You don't know?"

"We've been away."

"The old Grand Master and the four Houses were destroyed. New Houses have formed. The fights aren't the same anymore. They're like the old days again. Tests of skill with loss of a single spell and no more. The mob can bet if it wants but that's up to them. The final winner simply goes home after it is over. I am Master of Oor-tael. Another old fighter controls Bolk."

"And who is that?"

"Some dumb ox named Naru."

For the first time the other rider made a sound, a deep rich chuckle, and Hammen felt a cold shiver go down his spine. Even as he drew closer the woman spoke again.

"And who is Grand Master?"

"Varena, formerly of Fentesk."

"That bitch?"

"Damn it all!" Hammen shouted. "You two bastards, where the hell have you been?"

Norreen swung down from her saddle and, laughing, she approached and embraced Hammen. Hammen, however, barely noticed her and he continued to look up at the other rider.

"Garth?"

"It's me, old friend."

Garth slowly dismounted and then rushed forward, eagerly embracing Hammen.

"I thought you were dead, both of you," Hammen gasped, suddenly feeling weak and giddy.

"We thought so too," Norreen replied.

"So what happened?"

"We struggled," Garth finally said, his voice sounding distant, as if coming from the realms in which he had fought. "I thought it was finished but then his power was checked by an attack from other quarters. I used what *mana* I had left to finally seal the gate."

He hesitated for a moment.

"Funny. It almost felt at the end as if he simply gave up, as if he no longer really cared."

"You were Walkers then," Hammen said. "You were on the other side and all the universe was open to you."

Garth chuckled softly.

"One place is as good as another, and believe me, this place is better than most.

"Besides," Garth continued, his voice distant, "it was eternal struggle out there. After all that had happened I simply wanted some peace and here was as good as any."

"But you gave up immortality."

"We'll have our years. And in the face of eternity, what is immortality? I'll leave that to the Eternal. I think the way He set things up is good enough for us. I saw what it did to the others out there and I knew if we stayed, we'd become like them in the end. There were a few I sensed who finally understood that and returned to a world of their choosing to live as mortals. It seemed a sensible choice.

"Anyhow," he whispered, as if what he had seen and done was best left forgotten, "the gate to this realm is closed tight again. The *mana* here is strong, we don't have to worry about others coming through for a long time, as long as we prevent those still here from trying to reopen it."

Hammen shook his head.

"Damn you, I've mourned you for three years. At least you could have let me know you were safe."

"We just have," Norreen replied.

"Thanks for the quick notice," Hammen sniffed.

"So are you coming to Festival?"

Norreen looked over sharply at Garth, who cleared his throat nervously.

"I think it best that I skip it for now."

"So where are you heading, then?"

"There's a garden and an old house in the Southlands," Garth said, a wistful tone in his voice. "A good place to raise the family."

"A family?" Hammen chuckled.

Norreen, blushing, turned away.

"And what caste will he be?" Hammen asked, looking at Norreen.

"Tarmula of Benalia if he's born under the sign we planned for."

Hammen stood before the two, eyes brimming with tears, unable to speak.

"I always hated long farewells. Someday you must visit, but I know how affairs of this world run," Garth said, his voice suddenly husky and near to breaking.

He quickly embraced Hammen and then got back in his saddle. Norreen reached over and hugged him as well and laughed softly when Hammen patted her stomach.

"We'll call him Hadin," she said.

"Just Hammen, please."

She kissed him lightly on the cheek and, to his surprise, swung easily back up on her horse.

"Won't you stay with me for the night?" Hammen asked.

"A long ride ahead. We've been following you and your youngsters and wasted hours doing it."

Hammen, sighing, moved to stand by Garth's stirrup and, reaching up, he took his hand.

The moon drifted out from behind the clouds and Hammen gasped in astonishment.

"Your eye, Master, it's healed. You have two eyes."

Garth laughed.

"A little side benefit of being a Walker, even if it was but for a day."

Hammen reluctantly let go and Garth looked down at his old friend.

"You know I planned it from the start. Finding you as I did on the street was all part of the plan."

"I sort of figured that out."

"And if I should wander into your life again, it will be part of another plan as well. Take care, my friend, and bet my money well."

Garth spurred his mount and together the two rode off, the moon once more drifting behind the clouds so that they disappeared from view.

Hammen, shaking his head, slowly walked back to the tavern, thinking about the next Festival and the odds on wagers to come.

FREE

UNIQUE CARD OFFER

To celebrate the launch of America's hottest new gaming fiction series, Wizards of the Coast, Inc. and HarperPrism are making available, for a limited time only, two Magic: The Gathering,™ cards not for sale in any store.

Send a stamped self-addressed envelope and proof of purchase (cash register receipt attached to this coupon) to HarperPrism, Dept. JS, 10 East 53rd Street, New York, NY 10022.

Offer good in U.S. and Canada only. Please allow 4-6 weeks delivery.